I0576754

William H. L. Smith

The Practice in Proceedings in the Probate Courts

including the probate of wills - appointment of administrators, guardians, and

trustees - allowances - sale of real and personal estate - settlement of accounts -

distribution of estates

William H. L. Smith

The Practice in Proceedings in the Probate Courts
including the probate of wills - appointment of administrators, guardians, and trustees -
allowances - sale of real and personal estate - settlement of accounts - distribution of estates

ISBN/EAN: 9783337367817

Printed in Europe, USA, Canada, Australia, Japan

Cover: Foto ©Andreas Hilbeck / pixelio.de

More available books at **www.hansebooks.com**

THE

PRACTICE IN PROCEEDINGS

IN THE

PROBATE COURTS;

INCLUDING THE

PROBATE OF WILLS; APPOINTMENT OF ADMINISTRATORS, GUARDIANS, AND
. TRUSTEES; ALLOWANCES; SALE OF REAL AND PERSONAL ESTATE;
SETTLEMENT OF ACCOUNTS; DISTRIBUTION OF ESTATES;
ASSIGNMENT OF DOWER, WITH TABLE SHOWING
THE PRESENT VALUE OF ESTATES IN
DOWER; PARTITION OF LANDS,
&c., &c., &c.

WITH AN

APPENDIX OF PRACTICAL FORMS,

DESIGNED FOR THE USE OF EXECUTORS AND OTHERS
HAVING BUSINESS IN THE PROBATE
COURTS.

BY WILLIAM L. SMITH,

COUNSELLOR AT LAW.

THIRD EDITION.

BOSTON:

LITTLE, BROWN, AND COMPANY.

1876.

Entered according to Act of Congress in the year 1863, by
LITTLE, BROWN, AND COMPANY,
In the Clerk's Office of the District Court of the District of Massachusetts.

Entered according to Act of Congress in the year 1876, by
LITTLE, BROWN, AND COMPANY,
In the Office of the Librarian of Congress, at Washington.

CAMBRIDGE :
PRESS OF JOHN WILSON AND SON.

PREFACE.

THE design of this work is to present, in a concise form, the law and rules of practice regulating the proceedings in the Probate Courts.

The leading cases in which questions of probate law have been considered and determined, have been carefully collected and cited. And the instructions as to the formal proceedings have been prepared with the view of practically aiding the correct and safe discharge of the responsible trusts to which they relate.

The work is submitted to persons interested in the business of the Probate Courts, in the hope that it will, to some extent at least, supply a want that has been a subject of frequent remark.

W. L. S.

SPRINGFIELD, MASS., September, 1863.

SINCE the publication of the previous editions of this work, many changes have been made in Probate Law by legislative enactment, and the general principles which govern proceedings in the Probate Courts have been considered in cases decided in the appellate courts of this and other states. In preparing this (the third) edition, the changes made in the statutes, and the recent judicial decisions, have been cited, and every care has been taken to make the work complete.

W. L. S.

SPRINGFIELD, MASS., June, 1876.

CONTENTS.

CHAPTER XV.

CHAPTER XVI.

CHAPTER XVII.

CHAPTER XVIII.

CHAPTER XIX.

CHAPTER XX.

CHAPTER XXI.

APPENDIX.

INDEX TO CASES CITED.

[THE FIGURES REFER TO THE PAGES.]

THE PROBATE COURTS.

THE PROBATE COURTS.

CHAPTER I.

THE PROBATE COURTS — THEIR ORIGIN AND GENERAL JURISDICTION.

THE colony charter, under which the English settlers of Massachusetts emigrated and organized, contained no particular provisions for the establishment of courts. It was framed for the regulation of a commercial and land corporation, rather than with a view to the establishment of a civil and political government. The colonists were strongly attached to the spirit of the English law, and adopted its leading maxims, and its forms and modes of proceeding, so far as they were applicable and necessary to their peculiar condition and wants. The English probate jurisdiction, with which they were familiar, was confided to the ecclesiastical courts, whose jurisdiction was exclusive and entirely separate from the temporal courts. But there could be no ecclesiastical courts in the colony. There was no church establishment by means of which they could be organized on the English model, nor was such a system consistent with the religious sentiments and purposes of the people. Some new provision was therefore necessary for the exercise in the colony of the important powers given to the ecclesiastical courts in England. And as at that time there was no apparent necessity for the erection of a distinct probate court,

the power of admitting wills to probate and of granting administration was given to the county courts, which
were established under the general authority given by
the charter to the governor and assistants to govern the
company and their settlements. The county courts had
jurisdiction in common law, probate and equity, with an
ultimate appeal to the governor and assistants. The
earlier records exhibit probate decrees in the same pages
with judgments in civil actions and sentences in criminal
prosecutions. This provision, in the existing condition
of the colony, was practically sufficient. Orders were
passed from time to time, as experience suggested,
to promote the convenient and prompt settlement of
estates, but the probate jurisdiction remained with the
county courts until the dissolution of the colony charter.

Under the province charter of William and Mary,
granted in 1691, the courts were newly organized.
The superior court of judicature, the court of common pleas, courts of general sessions, and of justices
of the peace, were established. But the charter which
gave to the General Court authority to erect courts
with civil and criminal jurisdiction, ordained that the
governor and council should "do, execute, and perform all that is necessary for the probate of wills, and
granting administrations for, touching and concerning
any interests or estate which any person or persons shall
have within our said province or territory." Thus the
probate jurisdiction was taken from the common-law
courts, and in fact made independent of the legislative
power. The provincial legislature passed an act erecting county courts of probate, but it was negatived by
the king.[1] But under the authority vested in the governor and council by the charter, probate officers were

[1] Parsons, C. J., in Wales v. Willard, 2 Mass. 120.

appointed in the several counties, who were in effect surrogates, exercising a delegated authority, from whose decrees appeals were taken to the governor and council, who remained the supreme ordinary or court of probate. This was the beginning of the probate courts as distinct tribunals.

The courts, thus constituted, continued to exercise probate jurisdiction until the formal establishment of the county probate courts under the State constitution. Statutes were enacted by the provincial legislature recognizing their jurisdiction, extending their powers and duties, and to some extent regulating their proceedings. The constitution of 1780 provided for the regulation of times and places of holding probate courts, and for appeals from the judges of probate to the governor and council until the legislature should make further provision. This system continued in actual operation until the passage of the act of 1784, by which the probate courts were first formally established. That statute provided for the holding of a court of probate within the several counties of the commonwealth, and for the appointment of judges and registers of probate, and transferred the appellate jurisdiction from the governor and council to the supreme judicial court, which was constituted the supreme court of probate. The same statute authorized the courts of probate to allow wills, and grant administrations; to appoint guardians for minors and insane persons; to examine and allow the accounts of executors, administrators, and guardians, and to act in such other matters and things as they should have cognizance and jurisdiction of by the laws of the commonwealth.

The courts thus organized continued to exercise probate jurisdiction until the statute of 1858, c. 93, which abolished the office of judge of probate, and provided for the appointment in each county of a suitable person to be judge of probate and judge of the court of insolvency, and to be called the judge of probate and insolvency. The same statute provided for the election of registers of probate [1] and insolvency, to hold office for the term of five years, and transferred all the jurisdiction and authority then exercised by the judges of probate to the judges of probate and insolvency. The General Statutes of 1860 provided that judges of probate and insolvency should continue to hold their offices according to the tenor of their commissions, and that the judge and register of probate and insolvency in each county should continue to be judge and register of the probate court in such county. [2]

The peculiar and appropriate jurisdiction of the probate court, embracing the probate of wills and granting administrations, and their incidents, is the same as that of the English ecclesiastical courts. Such was the jurisdiction first exercised by the governor and council, and their surrogates under the province charter. But the powers of the probate court have been gradually increased by a series of state and provincial statutes, reaching back to the time of their separation from the common-law courts. Jurisdiction has been given to them of matters formerly within the exclusive cognizance of the courts of common law, and not analogous to any proceeding of the probate court as a court of ecclesiastical jurisdiction. These various statutes, based

[1] Registers of probate had been previously elected under stat. of 1856, c. 173. The General Statutes provide that a register of probate shall be elected in each county in 1863, and every fifth year thereafter. Gen. Sts. c. 10, § 4.

[2] Gen. Sts. c. 117, § 1; c. 119, § 1. By stat. of 1862, chap. 68, probate courts are made courts of record.

upon the suggestions of practical experience, and passed with a view of promoting the prompt and economical disposition of the matters to which they relate, have resulted in establishing the large jurisdiction now exercised by the probate courts.

This jurisdiction is separate and exclusive. By the separation of the probate and common-law jurisdictions under the provisions of the province charter, the separation between them became as well settled in this country as in England, and the same distinction has been substantially maintained. The decrees of the probate court, upon subjects within its jurisdiction, are conclusive and final, unless appealed from. They cannot be called in question in the common-law courts upon collateral proceedings. A writ of error will not lie to a judgment of the probate court; nor will *certiorari* lie from the supreme court to the probate court.[1] None of the processes devised to re-examine the decisions of the common-law courts are applicable to the probate courts.

And as the proceedings of the probate courts are not according to the course of the common law and cannot be revised in a common-law court, by a common-law process, its decrees, when the court exceeds its jurisdiction, are necessarily void. Other erroneous and irregular judicial proceedings, which can be revised by a superior common-law court, are voidable only, and are good and valid until reversed. But the irregular decree of the probate court is a nullity, and may be set aside in any collateral proceeding by plea and proof.[2] The sure and convenient remedy, however, of any party

---

[1] Peters v. Peters, 8 Cush. 542.

[2] Where original administration was granted after twenty years, contrary to the statute, it was held void in a collateral suit. Wales v. Willard, 2 Mass. 120, and see Hunt v. Hapgood, 4 Mass. 117; Smith v. Rice, 11 Mass. 507; Chase v. Hathaway, 14 Mass. 227.

aggrieved by a decree of the probate court, is by appeal to the supreme court of probate in the manner provided by statute.[1]

The supreme judicial court is constituted the supreme court of probate. This appellate jurisdiction is vested in the same court with that from the common-law courts, and that for a very wise reason, that there might not be conflicting decisions between two supreme courts administering the same laws; but in another and distinct capacity as if it were a distinct court.[2] It has a superintending and revisory power to re-examine and affirm or reverse all orders and decisions in probate, but as an appellate probate court.

GENERAL STATUTE JURISDICTION.

The jurisdiction of the probate courts is incidentally considered in the following chapters in connection with the various subjects of which they have cognizance. Their general jurisdiction is thus defined by statute:[3]

" The probate court for each county shall have jurisdiction of the probate of wills, granting administration of the estates of persons who at the time of their decease were inhabitants of or residents in the county, and of persons who die without the State leaving estate to be administered within such county;[4] of the appointment

---

[1] *Post*, chap. xx.

[2] Peters *v.* Peters, 8 Cush. 542. In the opinion in this case the subject of the jurisdiction of the probate courts is examined at length by Shaw, C. J.

[3] Gen. Sts. c. 117, § 2.

[4] *Post*, chap. v. — Where letters of administration have been granted in any county on the estate of a person dying without the commonwealth, parol evidence is admissible to show that the deceased left estate within such county, and so the grant of administration was valid, notwithstanding that no such esta e was included in the inventory exhibited to the judge of probate. Harrington *v.* Brown, 5 Pick. 519.

of guardians to minors and others, and of all matters relating to the estates of such deceased persons and wards; and of petitions for the adoption of children and the change of names.

When a case is within the jurisdiction of the probate court in two or more counties, the court which first takes cognizance thereof by the commencement of proceedings, shall retain the same; and administration or guardianship first granted shall extend to all the estate of the deceased or ward in this State, and exclude the jurisdiction of the probate court of every other county.

The jurisdiction assumed in any case by the court, so far as it depends on the place of residence of a person, shall not be contested in any suit or proceeding, except in an appeal, in the original case, or when the want of jurisdiction appears on the same record."

The probate courts, concurrently with the supreme judicial court, may hear and determine in equity all matters in relation to trusts created by will,[1] and have jurisdiction over all matters relating to the sale of trust estates;[2] and may hear and determine all matters arising under wills.[3]

MISCELLANEOUS PROVISIONS RELATING TO PROBATE COURTS.

[General Statutes, Chap. 117.]

SECT. 19. The several judges shall from time to time make rules for regulating the practice and conducting the business in their courts in all cases not expressly provided for by law; and shall return a statement of their rules and course of proceedings to the supreme judicial court, as soon as conveniently may be after

---

[1] Gen. Sts. c. 100, § 22.   [2] Stat. 1869, c. 331.
[3] Stat. 1873, c. 221.

making the same. The supreme judicial court may alter and amend the same, and make other and further rules from time to time for regulating the proceeding in the probate courts as it deems necessary, in order to secure regularity and uniformity in the proceedings.

SECT. 20. The judge shall make and issue all warrants and processes necessary or proper to carry into effect the powers granted to him; and when no form for a warrant or process is prescribed by statute or the rules of the court, he shall frame one in conformity with the principles of law, and the usual course of proceedings in this State.

SECT. 21. All his decrees and orders shall be made in writing, and the register shall record, in books to be kept for the purpose, all decrees and orders, wills proved in the court, with the probate thereof, letters testamentary and of administration, warrants, returns, reports, accounts, and bonds; and all other acts and proceedings required to be recorded by the rules of the court or a special order of the judge.

SECT. 22. When the validity of a decree is drawn in question in another suit or proceeding, every thing necessary to have been done or proved in order to render the decree valid, which might have been proved by parol evidence at the time of making the decree, and was not required to be recorded, shall after twenty years from such time be presumed to have been done or proved, unless the contrary appears on the same record.

SECT. 23. Orders of notice and other official acts which are passed as matters of course and do not require a previous notice to an adverse party, may be made and done in vacation as well as in court. [Registers of probate may issue orders of notice and citations at any time. Stat. 1863, c. 156. In any proceeding, notice may be dispensed with when all the parties entitled thereto assent to such proceeding, or waive notice in writing. Stat. 1874, c. 346.]

SECT. 24. Any warrant or commission for the appraisement of an estate, for examining the claims on insolvent estates, for the partition of real estate, or for the assignment, dower, or other interests in real estate, may be revoked by the judge for sufficient cause; and he may thereupon issue a new commission, or proceed otherwise as the circumstances of the case shall require.[1]

SECT. 25. In cases contested either before the probate court or supreme court of probate, costs in the discretion of the court may be awarded to either party, to be paid by the other, or to either or both parties to be paid out of the estate which is the subject of the controversy, as justice and equity shall require.[2]

SECT. 26. When costs are awarded to be paid by one party to the other, said courts may issue execution therefor in like manner as is practised in the courts of common law.

[Oaths required in proceedings in probate courts may be administered by the judge or register in or out

---

[1] As to the general power of a probate court to correct errors arising out of fraud or mistake in its own decrees, see Waters *v.* Stickney, 12 Allen, 1.

[2] *General rule as to costs.* Under the general rule, no costs are allowed in contested cases, in the probate court, or supreme court of probate. When the contest is made upon frivolous pretences, or for reasons which the appellant knew or ought to have known were unfounded, costs are allowed. But when the case presents questions of law, upon which the parties may not unreasonably differ and upon which either may properly claim the instructions of the court, no costs are allowed. Osgood *v.* Breed, 12 Mass. 536. See Nickerson *v.* Buck, 12 Cush. 332; Woodbury *v.* Obear, 7 Gray, 472; Abbott *v.* Bradstreet, 3 Allen, 587; Waters *v.* Stickney, 12 Allen, 17; Wilcox *v.* Wilcox, 13 Allen, 256; Bowditch *v.* Soltyk, 99 Mass. 141; Hebron *v.* Werner, 112 Mass. 269.

of court, or by a justice of the peace, and when administered out of court a certificate thereof shall be returned and filed or recorded with the proceedings ; provided that the judge may require any such oath to be taken before him in open court.   Stat. 1871, c. 122.]

SECT. 29.   Persons having business in the court may select such newspapers as they may prefer for the publication of legal notices ordered upon their applications ; but if the judge deems the newspaper thus selected insufficient to give due publicity, he may order the publication in one other newspaper.

SECT. 30.   The register shall make, without charge, one copy of all wills proved, inventories returned, and accounts settled; of all partitions of real estate and assignments of dower ; and of all orders and decrees of the court ; and shall deliver the same when demanded to the executor, administrator, guardian, widow, heir, or other party principally interested.   For additional copies of such documents, and copies of other papers, he shall be paid by the person demanding the same at the rate of twelve cents a page.

SECT. 31.   Each county shall provide all books necessary for keeping the records, and all printed blanks and stationery, used in probate proceedings.

SECT. 32.   No clerk or other person employed in the office of a probate court shall be commissioner of insolvency or appraiser or divider of an estate, in any case within the jurisdiction of the court, unless his appointment is requested by all parties in interest.

JUDGES OF THE PROBATE COURT.
[General Statutes, Chap. 119.]

SECT. 1.   The judges of probate and insolvency shall continue to hold their offices according to the tenor of their commissions ; and as vacancies occur they shall be filled in the manner provided by the constitution, so that there shall be one judge in each county.

SECT. 2. Each judge, before entering upon the duties of his office, in addition to the oaths prescribed by the constitution, shall take and subscribe an oath that he will faithfully discharge said duties, and that he will not during his continuance in office, directly or indirectly, be interested in or benefited by the fees or emoluments arising from any suit or matter pending in either of the courts of which he is judge ; which oath shall be filed in the probate office.

SECT. 3. The judges may interchange services or perform each other's duties when they find it necessary or convenient.

SECT. 4. If a judge is a party, or interested to the amount claimed of one hundred dollars exclusive of interest, in any case arising in his county, or is absent or unable to perform his duties, and no judge acts for him, under the provisions of the preceding section, or if there is a vacancy in the office in any county, the duties shall be performed in the same county by the judge of any other county designated by the register, from time to time, as necessity or convenience may require.[1] [No

---

[1] Coffin v. Cottle, 9 Pick. 287.

A judge of probate has no jurisdiction over a will containing a devise of more than one hundred dollars in value to a person of whose will he has been appointed executor. Bacon, Appellant, 7 Gray, 391.

Where the judge was a debtor to the estate, though the debt was wholly secured by mortgage, it was held that he had no jurisdiction and that the probate of the will before him was void. Gay v. Minot, 3 Cush. 352.

A bequest of money to trustees, to be devoted to the use and benefit of indigent persons in certain towns, does not make a judge of probate who is an inhabitant of one of those towns interested in the probate of

judge of probate and insolvency shall be disqualified from acting in any case by reason of interest, unless such interest is direct, and to the amount of one hundred dollars of principal claimed by or against him, nor until the same appears of record in the case. Stat. 1860, c. 145.]

SECT. 5. The register shall certify on his records the times during which, or the cases in which the judge of another county acts. Bonds required to be given to the judge shall be given to the judge appointed for the county, or, in case of vacancy, to the acting judge, and his successors in office, and all business shall be done in his name, or the name of the probate court, or the court of insolvency for the same county, as the case may be; but bonds may be approved, and other acts required

the will which contains the bequest. Northampton v. Smith, 11 Met. 390.

Where the judge had a valid claim against the estate of a deceased person, but had determined in his own mind not to enforce his claim, and exercised jurisdiction over the estate by granting letters of administration, it was held, that he was nevertheless interested as a creditor of the estate, and that the grant of administration was therefore void for want of jurisdiction. Sigourney v. Sibley, 21 Pick. 101; and such void administration is not rendered valid by the circumstance that exception was not taken to his jurisdiction. Ibid.

The appointment of a special administrator on the estate in which the judge is interested is void. Sigourney v. Sibley, 22 Pick. 507.

The fact that the judge had acted as the agent or attorney of a creditor, heir, or other person interested in an estate, although such action was illegal, does not make him interested so as to oust him of his jurisdiction. Cottle, Appellant, 5 Pick. 483.

A judge cannot act in any matter in which a near relative or connection is one of the parties; and a brother-in-law or father-in-law is such a connection. But he is not disqualified by the remote and contingent interest of a relative who is not a party to the proceeding. Hall v. Thayer, 105 Mass. 219; Aldrich, Appellant, 110 Mass. 189.

A judge who has written a will is disqualified to sit upon the probate of it; but, on appeal, it may be proved in the court above. Moses v. Julian, 45 N. H. 52.

to be done or certified by the judge may be approved, done, or certified, by the acting judge.

SECT. 6. No judge shall be retained or employed as counsel or attorney, either in or out of court, in any suit or matter which may depend on or in any way relate to a sentence, decision, warrant, order, or decree, made or passed by him ; nor for or against an executor, administrator, or guardian, appointed within his jurisdiction, in a suit brought by or against the executor, administrator, or guardian, as such ; nor in a suit relating to the official conduct of such party; nor for or against a debtor, creditor, or assignee, in a cause or matter arising out of or connected with any proceedings before him ; nor in an appeal in such cause or matter.

Stat. 1870, c. 275. Judges of the probate courts may transact business out of court at any time and place, when all parties entitled to notice therein assent thereto in writing, or voluntarily appear ; entering their decrees in such cases as of such sessions of the court as the convenience of the parties requires.

REGISTERS OF THE PROBATE COURT.

SECT. 7. Every register of probate and insolvency, before entering upon the duties of his office, in addition to the oaths prescribed by the constitution, shall take and subscribe an oath that he will faithfully discharge said duties, and that he will not, during his continuance in office, directly or indirectly be interested in or benefited by the fees or emoluments arising from any suit or matter pending in either of the courts of which he is register; which oath shall be filed in the probate office.

SECT. 8. He shall give bond, with condition that he

will faithfully discharge the duties of his office, to the treasurer of the Commonwealth, in a sum not less than one thousand, and not exceeding ten thousand dollars, as ordered by the judge, with one or more sureties approved by him.

SECT. 9. No register shall be of counsel or attorney either in or out of court, in any suit or matter pending in either of the courts of which he is register; nor in an appeal therefrom ; nor shall he be executor, administrator, guardian,[1] commissioner, appraiser, divider, or assignee, of or upon an estate within the jurisdiction of either of the courts of which he is register; nor be interested in the fees or emoluments arising from either of said trusts.

SECT. 10. The register shall have the care and custody of all books, documents, and papers appertaining to the courts of which he is register, or deposited with the records of insolvency, or filed in the probate office ; and shall carefully preserve the same, to be delivered to his successor. He shall perform such other duties appertaining to his office as may be required by law or prescribed by the judge.

SECT. 11. The judges for the counties of Suffolk, Middlesex, Worcester, Essex, and Norfolk, may each appoint an assistant register of probate and insolvency for his county, who shall hold his office for three years unless sooner removed by the judge. Before entering upon the discharge of his duties, the assistant register shall take the oaths prescribed by the constitution, and shall give bond, with condition for the faithful performance of the duties of his office, to the treasurer of the Commonwealth, in a sum not less than five hundred nor

---

[1] A judge or register of probate may be appointed guardian of his minor child. Stat. 1870, c. 263.

more than five thousand dollars, as ordered by the judge, with one or more sureties approved by him.

SECT. 12. The assistant register shall perform his duties under the direction of the register, and shall pay over to him all fees and sums received as his assistant, to be accounted for as required by law. He may authenticate papers, and perform such other duties as are not performed by the register. In case of the absence, neglect, removal, resignation, or death, of the register, the assistant may complete and attest any records remaining unfinished, and act as register until a new register is qualified or until the disability is removed.

SECT. 13. If a vacancy occurs in the office of register, the governor, with the advice and consent of the council, may appoint some person to fill the office, until another is elected, as provided in chapter ten.

SECT. 14. Upon the death, resignation, removal, or absence, of the register, if there is no assistant register, or if he is also absent, the judge shall appoint a suitable person to act as temporary register until a register is appointed or elected and qualified, or until the disability is removed.

SECT. 15. Such temporary register shall be sworn before the judge, and a certificate thereof, with his appointment, shall be recorded with the proceedings of each court in which he acts.

Stat. 1864, c. 93. All papers or instruments discharging any claim, or purporting to acknowledge the performance of any duty or the payment of any money, for which any executor, administrator, guardian, or trustee is chargeable or accountable in a court of probate, shall, upon the request of a party interested, be recorded in the registry of said court; and the registers of probate,

in their respective counties, shall enter, record, index,
and certify the original paper or instrument offered as
aforesaid, and shall receive for the service the like compensation as registers of deeds would be entitled to demand for like service, to be paid by the person leaving
such paper or instrument for record, at the time of leaving the same.

CHAPTER II.

THE probate of a will is necessary to establish its due execution. All questions as to the personal capacity of the testator, the signing of the will by him, and the attestation of the witnesses, must be determined by the probate court, or, on appeal, by the supreme court of probate. Such questions cannot be determined in the courts of common law,[1] and the decree of the probate court allowing or disallowing a will is conclusive, unless appealed from; it cannot be examined collaterally in any other court, except on a question of jurisdiction. But, until the will is admitted to probate, it is legally inoperative. Neither real nor personal estate will pass by it, for it cannot be used as evidence of title.[2]

THE FACTS TO BE PROVED IN SUPPORT OF THE WILL.

The party seeking the probate of the will must prove affirmatively:

That the will was signed by the testator, or by some person in his presence and by his express direction.

That the will was attested and subscribed in the presence of the testator by three or more competent witnesses; and

[1] Dublin v. Chadbourne, 16 Mass. 433; Parker v. Parker, 11 Cush. 519.

[2] Gen. Sts. c. 92, § 38. Shumway v. Holbrook, 1 Pick. 114.

2

That the testator, at the time when the will was executed, was of full age [1] and sound mind.

All these facts must be proved. Proof of any one or more of them is not sufficient unless all are established.

SECTION I.

AS TO THE SIGNING BY THE TESTATOR.

The statute provides that no wills shall be effectual to pass or in any way to affect any estate, real or personal, " unless it is in writing and *signed by the testator, or by some person in his presence and by his express direction,* and attested and subscribed in his presence by three or more competent witnesses." [2]

Questions as to the signing by the testator, and as to the attestation of the witnesses, have been frequently considered and determined by the courts.

It is not necessary that the testator's name be signed at the end of the will, though such is the common and advisable practice. Where a will commenced in the common form, " I, A. B., do make," &c., the whole will being in the testator's handwriting, it was held to be sufficiently signed, though there was no formal signature.[3] The signature, whatever may be its local

---

[1] Full age is reached on the day next preceding the anniversary of the person's birth. Thus, if he was born on the second day of January, 1840, he became of age on the first day of January, 1861; and as fractions of a day are not recognized by law, his full age was reached on the first instant of the latter day.

[2] Gen. Sts. c. 92, § 6. To this rule exceptions are made by statute in the following cases : Wills made in conformity with the law existing at the time of their execution; wills made out of the State which might be proved under the laws of the state or country in which they were made ; and the nuncupative wills of soldiers and mariners. Ibid. §§ 7, 8, 9.

[3] Grayson *v.* Atkinson, 2 Ves. 454; Coles *v.* Trecothick, 9 Ves. 249; Adams *v.* Field, 21 Vt. 256.

position, must have been made with the intention of authenticating the entire instrument. One signature is sufficient, though the will be contained in several pages or sheets, and even when the testimonium clause referred to the preceding sheets as severally signed, and the will was in fact signed at the end only, the signing was held sufficient, it being evidently the testator's intention that his signature should apply to the whole.[1]

The testator may sign his will by making his " mark ; " [2] and the fact that he was not able to write his name is not required to be proved.[3]

The testator's name may be written by some other person, but it must be done in his presence and by his express direction; and the fact that the will was signed in that manner should be stated in the attestation clause. Where the testator's signature was made by another person guiding his hand, with his consent, and he afterwards acknowledged it, the signing was held to be the act of the testator, and sufficient.[4]

It is not essential that the very act of signing by the testator should be seen by the witnesses. The statute does not require him to sign in their presence. His acknowledgment that the name signed to the instrument

---

[1] Winsor v. Pratt, 5 Moore, 484 ; Ela v. Edwards, 16 Gray, 91.

[2] Nickerson v. Buck, 12 Cush. 332. Under the English statute (1 Vict. c. 26, § 9), which requires the will to be signed by the testator or by some person in his presence, and by his direction, and the signature to be made or acknowledged by the testator in the presence of witnesses, it was held, that a will signed by a mark, without the testator's name appearing, was sufficiently signed, the will being identified aliunde. In re Bryce, 2 Curteis, 325. Where the maiden name of the testatrix was written against her mark instead of her real name, by which she was described in the will, it being a clerical error, the will was admitted to probate. In the Goods of Clarkes, 1 Swa. & Tr. 22.

[3] Baker v. Dening, 8 Adol. & Ell. 91.

[4] Stevens v. Van Cleve, 4 Wash. C. C. 262.

is his, accompanied with a request that the person to whom the acknowledgment is made should attest it as a witness, is sufficient. The acknowledgment of his signature need not be in express words. His declaration that the instrument is his, his name being then signed to the paper, is enough ; any form of expression implying that the will has been signed by him is sufficient.[1] In the case of White v. The British Museum,[2] where the will was entirely in the testator's handwriting, the testator merely requested the witnesses to attest it ; neither of them saw his signature, and only one of them knew what the instrument was ; and the execution was held to be sufficient. Tindal, C. J., said: " When we find the testator knew this instrument to be his will ; that he produced it to the three persons, and asked them to sign the same ; that he intended them to sign it as witnesses ; that they subscribed their names in his presence, and returned the same identical instrument to him ; we think the testator did acknowledge in fact, though not in words, to the three witnesses, that the will was his." This acknowledgment need not be made to all the witnesses at the same time, but is sufficient if made separately to each witness at different times and places.[3]

No formal *publication* of the will by the testator is necessary. In a large majority of cases, the testator declares in the presence of the subscribing witnesses that the instrument executed by him is his will, and the fact that such a declaration was made is recited in the attestation clause and proved in the probate court. But

---

[1] Tilden v. Tilden, 13 Gray, 110 ; Nickerson v. Buck, 12 Cush. 332 ; Hogan v. Grosvenor, 10 Met. 54 ; Dewey v. Dewey, 1 Met. 349 ; Hall v. Hall, 17 Pick. 373.

[2] 6 Bing. 310 ; and see Wright v. Wright, 7 Bing. 457.

[3] Hogan v. Grosvenor, 10 Met. 54 ; Dewey v. Dewey, 1 Met. 349.

such declaration is not necessary. There may exist very excellent reasons why the testator should not wish to disclose, and why the law should not require him to disclose, the fact that he has made a will at all;[1] either, as Swinburne says, "because the testator is afraid to offend such persons as do gape for greater bequests than either they have deserved, or the testator is willing to bestow upon them; (lest they, peradventure, understanding thereof would not suffer him to live in quiet:) or else he should overmuch encourage others, to whom he meant to be more beneficial than they expected; (and so give them occasion to be more negligent husbands or stewards about their own affairs than otherwise they would have been if they had not expected such a benefit at the testator's hands (or for some other considerations)."[2]

It must of course appear that the testator knew at the time he executed the instrument that it was his will. Such knowledge, however, need not ordinarily be proved by direct evidence; it may be inferred from the testator's observance of the formalities of execution required by the statute. It will generally be presumed on proof of the execution that he knew the contents of the instrument. But if the testator was incapable of reading from blindness, physical weakness, ignorance, or other cause, it is incumbent on the party offering the will for probate to meet such facts by evidence that the will was read to the testator previous to its execution, or that the contents were otherwise known to him.[3]

[1] Osborne v. Cook, 11 Cush. 532.

[2] Swinburne, Pt. 1, § 11. In Trimmer v. Jackson (4 Burn's Eccl. Law, 9th ed. 102), the witnesses were deceived by the execution, being led to believe that the instrument was a deed, not a will; and it was adjudged a sufficient execution.

[3] Sweet v. Boardman, 1 Mass. 262; Pettes v. Brigham, 10 N. H. 514; 2 Greenl. Ev. § 675. See Gerrish v. Nason, 22 Maine, 438.

A will may be properly executed without a *seal*, none being required by statute.

The statute prohibiting the transaction of business on Sunday does not apply to the execution of wills, and a will executed on that day is valid.[1]

SECTION II.

AS TO THE ATTESTATION BY THE WITNESSES.

The subscribing witnesses must subscribe the will in the presence of the testator.[2] The object of the rule is to enable him to have ocular evidence of the identity of the instrument which they attest. The mere corporal presence of the testator is not enough. He must be conscious of their act, and in a position where he can see it. If, therefore, after he has signed the will and before the witnesses have subscribed it, he falls into a state of insensibility, their attestation is not sufficient.[3] Nor will it be sufficient if they subscribe in a secret and clandestine manner, although in the same apartment.[4] It is not essential that the testator actually see the signing; it is enough if the situation of the respective parties be such that he may see it, and this is enough, even if the witnesses subscribe in another room. Where the testator lay in bed, and the witnesses went with the will through a short passage into another room, and subscribed their names on a table in the middle of that room, both doors being open, so that the testator might have seen them subscribe if he would, though there was no proof that he did see their act, the attestation was held

---

[1] Bennett *v.* Brooks, 9 Allen, 118.
[2] See Chase *v.* Kittredge, 11 Allen, 49.
[3] Right *v.* Price, 1 Doug. 241.
[4] Longford *v.* Eyre, 1 P. Wms. 740.

sufficient.[1] A blind man executing his will should be sensible of the presence of the witnesses through his remaining senses.[2]

On the other hand, though the witnesses are in the same room with the testator, it is not enough, if his view of the proceedings is necessarily obstructed. Where the testator was in bed in a room from one part of which he might, by inclining his head into the passage, have seen the witnesses subscribe the will, but could not see them in the position in which he actually was, the attestation was held not to be good.[3] The cause of the absence of the witnesses is not material; the effect is the same, even if the absence was with the consent or request of the testator.[4] If the witness subscribes in the testator's absence it is not sufficient, even if he afterwards acknowledges his signature in the presence of the testator.[5] An attestation made in the testator's room is presumed to have been made in his presence until the contrary is shown; if not made in the same room it is presumed not to have been made in his presence until it is shown to have been otherwise.[6] And it will be presumed in the absence of evidence to the contrary, that the witnesses subscribed in the most convenient part of the room, and the posi-

[1] Davy v. Smith, 3 Salk. 395. In Casson v. Dade (1 Bro. C. C. 99), the testatrix, being an invalid, executed the will when sitting in her carriage at the door of her attorney's office, the witnesses attending her; after having seen the execution they took the will into the office to subscribe their names, and the carriage was put back to the window, through which, it was sworn by a person in the carriage, the testatrix might have seen what passed. Lord Thurlow was of opinion that the will was well executed.

[2] Reynolds v. Reynolds, 1 Speers, S. C. 256.

[3] Doe v. Manifold, 1 M. & S. 294; Boldry v. Parris, 2 Cush. 433.

[4] Broderick v. Broderick, 1 P. Wms. 239.

[5] Chase v. Kittredge, 11 Allen, 19.

[6] 2 Greenl. Ev. § 678.

tion of a table, probable to have been used, would be considered.[1]

It is not necessary to the due execution of the will that the attesting witnesses should subscribe in the presence of each other. A will attested by three witnesses, who separately and at different places subscribe their names, at the request of the testator, and in his presence, is well attested.[2]

An attesting witness may subscribe by making his " mark," but such manner of subscribing is never advisable and seldom necessary.[3]

No particular form of words is necessary in the attestation clause which the witnesses subscribe, nor need it state the fact that the witnesses subscribed it in the testator's presence, though the fact that they did so is required to be clearly proved.[4]

SECTION III.

AS TO THE COMPETENCY OF THE ATTESTING WITNESSES.

The object of the statute in requiring every will to be attested and subscribed in the testator's presence by three or more *competent* witnesses, is to surround the testator, at the time he executes his will, with disinterested persons, who may protect him from frauds that might otherwise be practised upon his infirmity or debility, and to ascertain and judge of his sanity.

[1] Winchelsea v. Wanchope, 3 Russ. 444.

[2] Hogan v. Grosvenor, 10 Met. 51; Dewey v. Dewey, 1 Met. 349.

[3] Jackson v. Van Densen, 5 Johns. 144; Doe v. Caperton, 9 Carr. & P. 59. B. a witness, being unable to write, A. another witness, at his request, guided his hand. Held, that B.'s subscription was sufficient. In the Goods of Frith, 1 Swa. & Trist. 8.

[4] Eliot v. Eliot, 10 Allen, 357; Ela v. Edwards, 16 Gray, 91.

Competent witnesses are persons who are not dis-qualified by reason of interest, crime, or deficiency of understanding. The recent statutes which provide that no person shall be excluded by reason of crime or inter-est from giving evidence as a witness, do not apply to attesting witnesses to wills. They are expressly ex-cepted, and their competency must therefore be deter-mined by the rules previously in force.

It was formerly held, that an attesting witness who took a beneficial devise or legacy under the will which he attested was not a competent witness to prove its execution, but as it was found that to allow a will to be wholly defeated on account of the existence of such an interest on the part of a witness was productive of inconvenience and injustice, a statute[1] was passed which restored the competency of such a witness by destroy-ing his interest. The devise or legacy to the witness was made void, and he was admitted to testify. The same rule is established in this State, by the statute which provides that "all beneficial devises, legacies, and gifts, made or given in any will to a subscribing witness thereto, shall be wholly void unless there are three other competent subscribing witnesses to the same."[2]

A mere charge on the lands of the devisor for the payment of debts will not prevent his creditors from being competent witnesses to his will,[3] and a member of a corporation to which property is given by will, in trust for charitable uses, is a competent attesting wit-ness.[4] The executor named in a will is a competent subscribing witness.[5] An heir at law who is disinherited

---

[1] 25 Geo. II. c. 6. [2] Gen. Sts. c. 92, § 10. [3] Ibid.
[4] Loring v. Park, 7 Gray, 42.
[5] Wyman v. Symmes, 10 Allen, 153.

is a competent witness in support of a will.[1] A wife is not a competent witness to her husband's will,[2] or to a will which contains a devise to him.[3]

A person who has been convicted of an infamous crime is not a competent witness, such a person being considered as having no regard for the obligations of an oath. Certain crimes have been held to be infamous, and certain other offences have been held not to have a disqualifying effect. The precise rule does not clearly appear from the adjudicated cases. " It is probably the true test to inquire whether the crime shows in the perpetrator such a depravity of character or disposition to pervert the public justice dispensed in the courts, as creates a violent presumption against the truthfulness of his testimony; the difficulty being in the application of this test." [4] It has been adjudged " that persons are rendered infamous, and therefore incompetent to testify, by having been convicted of forgery, perjury, subornation of perjury, suppression of testimony by bribery, conspiracy to procure the absence of a witness, or other conspiracy to accuse one of a crime, barratry," [5] larceny,[6] and the receiving of stolen goods knowing them to have been stolen.[7] But convictions for adultery,[8] for " deceit in the quality of provisions, deceits by false weights and measures, conspiracy to defraud by spreading false news," [9] " the attempt, not amounting to a conspiracy, to procure the absence of a witness," the keeping of gaming and bawdy houses, it seems, do not disqualify.[10]

---

[1] Wyman v. Symmes, 10 Allen, 155.   [2] Pease v. Allis, 110 Mass. 157.
[3] Sullivan v. Sullivan, 106 Mass. 474.   [4] 1 Bishop, Crim. Law, § 645.
[5] 1 Greenl. Ev. § 373.   [6] Commonwealth v. Keith, 8 Met. 531.
[7] Commonwealth v. Rogers, 7 Met. 500.
[8] Little v. Gibson, 2 Chandler (N. H.), 505.   [9] 1 Greenl. Ev. § 373.
[10] 1 Bishop, Crim. Law, § 645.

The full pardon of one convicted of an infamous crime restores his competency as a witness; but the mere remission of his sentence does not.[1]

The statute provision that the will shall be attested by competent witnesses, refers to their competency at the time they subscribe. If, after the execution of the will, and before it is admitted to probate, either of the witnesses become infamous, insane, or otherwise disqualified, the will may be sustained by proof of the handwriting of those who are thus rendered incompetent to testify. If the witnesses are competent at the time they attest, their subsequent incompetency, from whatever cause it arises, will not prevent the probate and allowance of the will, if it is otherwise satisfactorily proved.[2] It has been held, that a person under the age of fourteen years is presumed to be incompetent, from defect of understanding, to attest the execution of a will, but this presumption may be rebutted.[3]

SECTION IV.

EXECUTION OF CODICILS.

A codicil is an addition or supplement to a will. By our statutes the term "will" is construed to include codicils.[4]

The formalities to be observed in the execution of codicils are the same as are required by statute in the execution of wills. The codicil must be in writing, signed by the testator or by some person in his presence and by his express direction, and attested and subscribed

---

[1] Perkins v. Stevens, 24 Pick. 277.

[2] Gen. Sts. c. 92, § 6.   [3] Carlton v. Carlton, 3 Chandler (N. H.), 14.

[4] Gen. Sts. c. 3, § 7, cl. 19.

in his presence by at least three competent witnesses.
The attesting witnesses may be the same persons who
subscribed the original will, or other competent witnesses. A will may have several codicils, and each
must be separately executed.

A codicil duly attested may communicate the efficacy
of its attestation to an unattested will or previous codicil
so as to render effectual any devise contained in such
prior unattested paper, when the several instruments
are written on the same paper. This may be the effect
when the codicil does not refer in terms to the unattested instrument; and even when written on a separate
paper if it expressly refers to the original instrument.[1]

The effect of a codicil ratifying, confirming, and republishing a will is to give the same force to the will as
if it had been written, executed, and published at the
date of the codicil.[2]

A codicil may have the effect of impliedly revoking
the later in date of two wills by expressly referring to
and recognizing the prior one as the actual will of the
testator.[3] A codicil will refer to the latest of several
wills if no express date is named.[4] A will revoked by
implication, as by a change in the testator's circumstances, may be republished by a codicil duly attested.[5]
So a will made by a person not of full age, or of unsound
mind, or otherwise incapacitated, may be made effectual
by a codicil republishing the same and duly executed
after the disability is removed. And a will executed
by a person under undue influence may be made valid

[1] 1 Jarm. on Wills (4th Am. ed.), 129.

[2] Brimmer v. Sohier, 1 Cush. 118; Miles v. Boyden, 3 Pick. 216;
Haven v. Forster, 14 Pick. 543; Pratt v. Rice, 7 Cush. 212.

[3] Crosbie v. Macdonald, 4 Ves. 610.   [4] Ibid.

[5] See 1 Jarm. on Wills (4th Am. ed.), 207; notes by Perkins, and cases
there cited.

by being confirmed and republished by a codicil subsequently executed, when the testator is free from such influence.[1] A codicil, by republishing a will, may give effect to a devise which would otherwise have been void on account of the devisee being a witness to the original will.[2]

SECTION V.

AS TO THE TESTATOR'S SOUNDNESS OF MIND.

The right of disposing of property by will is limited by the statute to persons of sound mind, and the question raised by this restriction is the one presented for determination in a majority of the contested cases.

To establish the testator's mental capacity it must appear that he possessed mind and memory sufficient to enable him to understand the nature and consequences of his testamentary act.

Mere ability to answer usual and familiar questions is not enough. The testator must have memory. "A man in whom this faculty is wholly extinguished cannot be said to possess an understanding to any degree whatever, or for any purpose. But his memory may be very imperfect; it may be greatly impaired by age or disease; he may not be able at all times to recollect the names, the persons, or the families of those with whom he had been intimately acquainted; he may at times ask idle questions, and repeat those which had before been asked and answered, and yet his understanding be sufficiently sound for many of the ordinary transactions of life. He may not have sufficient strength of memory and vigor of intellect to make and digest all the parts of a contract,

---

[1] Ibid. 1 Williams Ex. (5th Am. ed.) 185.

[2] Moores v. White, 6 Johns. Ch. 375.

and yet be competent to direct the disposition of his property by will. This is a subject which he may possibly have often thought of: and there is probably no person who has not arranged such a disposition in his mind before he committed it to writing. The question is not so much what was the degree of memory possessed by the testator as this: Had he a disposing memory? Was he capable of recollecting the property he was about to bequeath, the manner of distributing it, and the objects of his bounty? To sum up the whole in its most simple and intelligible form, were his mind and memory sufficiently sound to enable him to know and understand the business in which he was engaged at the time when he executed his will?"[1]

It is not necessary that the testator should be possessed of a mind naturally strong, to enable him to make a valid will. Mere weakness of understanding is not an objection, for courts cannot measure the size of people's understandings and capacities. "If a man," says Swinburne, "be of a mean understanding (neither of the wise sort or the foolish), but indifferent, as it were betwixt a wise man and a fool, yea, though he rather incline to the foolish sort, so that for his dull capacity he might worthily be termed *grossum caput*, a dull pate, or a dunce, such a one is not prohibited from making his testament."[2]

In a large proportion of the cases in which the sanity of testators is made a question, the alleged want of capacity is in the decay of the faculties resulting from old age, or the effect of disease, or both combined.

---

[1] Washington, J., in Stevens v. Vancleve, 4 Wash. C. C. 262; and see Hathorne v. King, 8 Mass. 371; Converse v. Converse, 21 Vt. 168; Kinne v. Kinne, 9 Conn. 105; Stewart v. Lispenard, 26 Wend. 253.

[2] Swinburne on Wills, Pt. 2, § 4.

But neither extreme old age, nor debility of body, will affect the capacity to make a will, provided the testator possesses the sound mind necessary to the disposition of his property. The law looks only to the competency of his understanding.[1]

EVIDENCE ON QUESTIONS OF THE TESTATOR'S SANITY.

The legal presumption in the absence of evidence to the contrary is in favor of the testator's sanity.[2] It was formerly held that, the testator's sanity having been testified to by the attesting witnesses, the burden shifted and was upon the party opposing the probate to show that the testator was not of sound mind; but the more recently decided cases hold that the burden of proving the sanity of the testator is upon him who offers the will for probate, and does not shift upon evidence of his sanity being given by the subscribing witnesses.[3]

The subscribing witnesses are regarded in law as persons placed near the testator at the time he executes his will, in order that no fraud may be practised upon him and to judge of his capacity. They are supposed to have satisfied themselves as to the testator's mental condition,

[1] In Van Alst v. Hunter (5 Johns. Ch. 148), the testator was more than ninety years old when he made his will. Chancellor Kent said, " It is one of the painful consequences of extreme old age that it ceases to excite interest, and is apt to be left solitary and neglected. The control which the law still gives to a man over the disposal of his property is one of the most efficient means which he has in protracted life to command the attentions due to his infirmities." In Reed's Will (2 B. Monr. 79), the testator was eighty years old and physically helpless from palsy, and his will was sustained. In Jennings v. Pendergas (10 Md. 346), a will made by a testatrix at the age of ninety-six was sustained.

[2] Baxter v. Abbott, 7 Gray, 71, Thomas, J., dissenting.

[3] Crowninshield v. Crowninshield, 2 Gray, 524; Williams v. Robinson, 42 Vt. 658; Gerrish v. Nason, 22 Maine, 438; Delafield v. Parish, 25 N. Y. 9; Barry v. Butlin, 1 Curt. Eccl. 638.

and are therefore permitted to give their opinions upon that point. They may be inquired of as to the grounds of their opinions on cross-examination, and other evidence is admissible to support or contradict them. Any person may testify as to the appearance of the testator, and to facts from which the state of his mind may be inferred, and medical experts may then be inquired of, as to the conclusions they draw from the circumstances and symptoms proved to have existed.[1] The mere opinions of witnesses who are not experts have been held inadmissible;[2] but in Baxter v. Abbott,[3] it was held that a physician who had practised many years in the testator's neighborhood, and had at times been his medical adviser, and who saw and conversed with him a short time before the making of the will, was competent to state his opinion of the testator's sanity, though he was not an expert on the particular subject of insanity.

Evidence of insanity both before and after the time of making the will is admissible.[4] The fact that the testator committed suicide soon after making his will may be proved, but is not conclusive evidence of insanity, for it is said his power of reasoning on other subjects may have been wholly unimpaired.[5] The fact that he

---

[1] Upon the trial of an issue of the testator's sanity, an expert, although he has heard all the evidence, is not to be asked, "Suppose all the facts stated by the witness to be true, was the testator laboring under an insane delusion, or was he of unsound mind? But the facts upon which his opinion is asked, should be put to him hypothetically." Woodbury v. Obear, 7 Gray, 467.

[2] Poole v. Richardson, 3 Mass. 330; Needham v. Ide, 5 Pick. 510; Commonwealth v. Fairbanks, 2 Allen, 511.

[3] 7 Gray, 71, and see Hastings v. Rider, 99 Mass. 622; Lewis v. Mason, 109 Mass. 169.

[4] Dickinson v. Barber, 9 Mass. 225.

[5] Brooks v. Barrett, 7 Pick. 97. A testator committed suicide on the day next after that on which he made his will, and the will was established. Chambers v. Queen's Proctor, 2 Curteis, 415.

was under guardianship as an insane person is *primâ facie* evidence of incapacity, but may be explained by other evidence.[1] The testator's declarations so near the time of making the will as to be a part of the *res gestœ* are admissible,[2] and the fact of his silence when the subject of his incapacity was talked of in his hearing has been allowed to be proved.[3] The fact that the will was written by the testator himself and is sensible in its provisions, is the best evidence of his capacity,[4] but a will is not to be invalidated merely because its provisions are imprudent and unaccountable. General facts upon the subject of insanity, though contained in books of established reputation, are not admissible.[5] The attestation of a will is not evidence that the witness believed the testator to be sane.[6]

Evidence is admissible to show that the testator's family, either on his father's or mother's side, were subject to insanity, or that his parents or other near relatives were insane.[7] The fact is well established that a predisposition to insanity is frequently transmitted from parent to child through many generations. Accord-

[1] Breed v. Pratt, 18 Pick. 115; Stone v. Damon, 12 Mass. 488; Hamilton v. Hamilton, 10 R. I. 538.

[2] 1 Greenl. Ev. § 108; Robinson v. Hutchinson, 26 Vt. 38.

[3] Irish v. Smith, 8 Serg. & R. 573.

[4] Overton v. Overton, 7 B. Monr. 61. See Davis v. Calvert, 5 Gill & Johns. 269.

[5] Commonwealth v. Wilson, 1 Gray, 337; Ware v. Ware, 8 Greenl. 42; Collier v. Simpson, 5 Carr. & P. 74.

[6] Baxter v. Abbott, 7 Gray, 71. On the trial of an appeal from the decree of the probate court allowing a will, it cannot be given in evidence against the will that one of the attesting witnesses who testified in the probate court to the testator's sanity, and has since deceased, declared, after the probate, that he wished to live to unsay what he had said, and that the testator was insane. Ibid.

[7] Baxter v. Abbott, 7 Gray, 81.

ing to Esquirol, this hereditary taint is the most common of all the causes to which insanity can be referred, and other authorities assert that no other cause can be assigned for the disease in a majority of all the cases. The disease may not appear in a child who goes through life without being exposed to any exciting cause, but with such predisposition, insanity supervenes from very slight causes. Hereditary insanity is induced by the same exciting cause in the offspring as in the parent, and often appears about the same age and under the same form.[1]

Evidence of merely eccentric habits, together with the fact that the will contains directions that appear absurd, will not establish the fact of insanity;[2] and it has been

[1] "As we might suppose, children that are born before insanity manifests itself in the parents, are less subject to the disorder than those which are born afterwards. When one parent only is insane, there is less tendency for the predisposition to be transmitted than when both are affected; but according to Esquirol, this predisposition is much more readily transmitted through the female, than through the male parent. Its transmission is also more strikingly remarked when it has been observed to exist in several generations of lineal ancestors: and, like other hereditary maladies, it appears to be subject to atavism; i. e. it may disappear in one generation and reappear in the next. Further, the children of drunken parents, and of those who have been married late in life, are said to be more subject to insanity than those born under other circumstances." Taylor's Med. Jur. 628. And see 1 Beck's Med. Jur. 725; Ray's Med. Jur. § 72.

[2] A will was opposed because it bore intrinsic evidence of the testator's insanity. After making certain bequests, the testator directed his executors to cause some part of his bowels to be converted into fiddle strings, that other parts should be sublimed into smelling salts, and that the remainder of his body should be vitrified into lenses for optical purposes. He afterwards said, "the world may think this to be done in a spirit of singularity or whim." He had expressed a wish to have his body converted to purposes useful to mankind, and had consulted a physician in regard to chemical experiments to be made upon it. It appeared that he conducted his affairs with shrewdness and ability, and that he was treated by those with whom he dealt as a person of indisputable capacity.

held that the life, opinions, and habits of a testator may be reviewed for the purpose of testing the allegations of insanity.[1] " Monomania is very liable to be confounded with eccentricity; but there is this difference between them : in monomania, there is obviously a change of character, — the individual is different to what he was; in eccentricity, such a difference is not marked; he is, and always has been, singular in his ideas and actions. An eccentric man may be convinced that what he is doing is absurd, and contrary to the general rules of society, but he professes to set these at defiance. A true monomaniac cannot be convinced of his error, and he thinks, that his acts are consistent with reason and the general conduct of mankind. In eccentricity, there is a will to do or not to do; in real monomania, the controlling power of the will is lost. Eccentric habits suddenly acquired are, however, presumptive of insanity."[2]

When the alleged want of capacity is in the weakness

Sir Herbert Jenner, in giving judgment, held that insanity was not proved, that the facts merely amounted to eccentricity, and on this ground he pronounced for the validity of the will.

[1] J. W. G. made his will in England a few weeks before his death, in which he gave several legacies, and directed the remainder to be paid over to the Turkish ambassador for the poor of Constantinople, and also for the erection of a cenotaph in that city, inscribed with his name, and bearing a light perpetually burning therein. It appeared that he had lived long in the East, had studied the Koran a great deal, and was an avowed believer in Mahommedanism. The prerogative court, on the ground of this extraordinary bequest, which sounded to folly, and on parol evidence of the testator's wild and extravagant language, pronounced him of unsound mind; but it was held, reversing that decision, that as the insanity attributed to the deceased was not monomania but general mental derangement, and as the proper mode of testing the allegation was to review the life, habits, and opinions of the testator, on such a review there was nothing absurd or irrational in the bequest, or any thing in his conduct, at the date of the will, indicating derangement; and therefore the will was admitted to probate. 29 Eng. Law & Eq. 38.

[2] Taylor's Med. Jur. 626.

and prostration of physical disease, an inquiry into the character of the testator's malady will sometimes aid in determining the question of his soundness of mind. It is well established that different diseases, though equally fatal, exercise very unlike influences upon the mental faculties. "Among the diseases which incapacitate an individual from making a valid will, or at least render his rationality doubtful, may be enumerated the following : lethargic and comatose affections. These suspend the action of the intellectual faculties ; so also does an attack of apoplexy ; and even if patients recover from its first effects, an imbecility of mind is often left which unfits an individual from the duty in question. Phrenitis, delirium tremens, and those inflammations which are accompanied with delirium, also impair the mind. Finally, in typhoid fevers, the low state which usually precedes death, is one that may be considered as incapacitating the individual. On the other hand, there are many fatal diseases, in which the patient preserves his mind to the last, and all dispositions of property made by him are of course valid. Of these, none is more striking than the clearness of intellect which sometimes attends the last stages of phthisis pulmonalis." [1]

Long-continued habits of intemperance may gradually impair the memory and other faculties, and produce a species of insanity, which will render the person incapable of making a will. A person, however, who is habitually addicted to the use of intoxicating liquors, and at times violently excited, may make a valid will when he is free from the excitement of liquor. It has been held that if the testator's habits of intoxication are not such as to render him habitually incompetent for the transaction of business, it is necessary for the party

[1] Beck's Med. Jur. 821.

objecting to his capacity on the ground of casual intoxication to prove its existence at the time the will was
executed.[1] The question in these, as in all cases where
unsoundness of mind is alleged, is whether the testator
knew and understood the business in which he was
engaged at the time he executed his will.

The testator's declarations to the effect that he was
induced to sign his will when he was under the influence
of intoxicating liquors, are not admissible evidence of
the fact that he was so incapacitated.[2]

Lucid Intervals. The party supporting the will may
show that the testator, although insane at some period
of his life, had recovered his reason, or that the will was
made during a temporary cessation of the insanity.
Lunatics occasionally recover for a time and are conscious of their acts. The lucid interval may be a few
hours or minutes in duration, or it may continue for
weeks, months, and even years. Evidence of a lucid
interval is to be examined with great caution, especially
in cases where the alleged interval was of brief duration.
A mere diminution in the violence of the disorder does
not constitute a lucid interval. It need not, of course,
appear that the predisposition to the disease had been
extirpated, or that the testator had regained the same
degree of intellectual ability that he possessed previous
to his insanity ; but it must appear that he was conscious
of his acts, and able to understand their nature and
consequences.[3] The fact that the will is a rational one
and made in a rational manner, though not conclusive,
is strong evidence that it was made in a lucid interval.[4]

[1] Andrees v. Weller, 2 Green, Ch. 604.
[2] Gibson v. Gibson, 3 Jones (Missouri), 227.
[3] Gombault v. Pub. Admr., 4 Bradf. (N. Y.) 226; Bannatyne v. Bannatyne, 14 Eng. Law and Eq. 581 ; 1 Jarm. on Wills (4th Am. ed.) 67.
[4] Nicholes v. Binns, 1 Swa. & Tr. 239.

In establishing the fact of a lucid interval, evidence has been admitted to show that the disposition of the testator's property made by his will was consistent with his intentions declared previous to his insanity.[1]

The rule that insanity proved to have existed at a particular time is presumed to continue, does not apply to temporary delirium connected with a violent disease.[2]

Partial Insanity — Monomania. The objection has been raised in some cases, that the testator, though of apparently sound mind upon general subjects, labored under an insane delusion in regard to particular matters, and that such delusions. operating upon his mind at the time he made his will, deprived him of his disposing capacity. Such delusions are said to be more commonly manifested in the testator's unaccountable antipathy to his children and near relatives, and unfounded suspicions of attempts by them on his life. But to defeat a will by evidence of an insane delusion merely, it has been held that the will must be traced to, and shown to be the offspring of, such insane delusion.[3] The declarations of

---

[1] Coughlen's case, referred to in Booth *v.* Blundell, 19 Ves. 508.

[2] Hix *v.* Whittemore, 4 Met. 545.

[3] In Greenwood's case, the testator being sick and delirious, took some medicine from the hands of his brother and imagined it was poison intended to kill him. He recovered and returned to his profession, — that of a barrister, but was never afterwards free from the morbid delusion. He disinherited his brother, who was his only next of kin. Two trials were had on the question of sustaining the will with conflicting verdicts, and the result was a compromise. Stated by Lord Eldon in White and Wilson, 13 Ves. 89.

A testator who, twenty-four years before his death, had a dangerous fever, during which he contracted a strong antipathy towards his brothers, which continued through his life, made his will shortly before his death, and disinherited them. There was no apparent cause for his antipathy. The will was set aside on the ground that his peculiar defect of intellect influenced his disposition of his estate. Johnson *v.* Moore's Heirs, 1 Little (Ky.), 371, and see Dew *v.* Clark, 3 Addams, 79; Thompson *v.* Thompson, 21 Barb. (N. Y.) 107.

the testator proceeding from partial insanity, are not admissible as evidence of the truth of his statements, but may properly be considered in connection with other facts in determining the general question as to his soundness of mind.[1]

SECTION VI.

WILLS INVALIDATED BY FRAUD AND UNDUE INFLUENCE.

The testator, in order to make a valid will, must enjoy full liberty in the disposition of his estate. A will obtained by fraud is of course void,[2] and the effect is the same where the testator is constrained by fear, or where undue influence is used to control the disposition of his estate. An instrument executed under such circumstances is not the will of the testator, but is the dictation of another person. Any condition of things that restrains the testator from the free exercise of his own judgment, incapacitates him as a testator.

Objections of this class more frequently arise in cases where the testator was either of weak mind naturally, or was enfeebled by age or disease, and therefore liable to be controlled by influences which would not affect a person of strong mind and good health. A person may be of sound mind and competent, if left to himself, to make a valid will, but he may be induced by the harassing importunities of those about him, and by the hope of quiet, to dispose of his property in a manner that his own healthy and unbiased judgment would not approve.

[1] Woodbury v. Obear, 7 Gray, 467.

[2] 1 Jarm. on Wills (4th Am. ed.) 41; 1 Williams (5th Am. ed.), 40; Davis v. Calvert, 5 Gill & Johns. 269; Dietrick v. Dietrick, 5 Serg. & R. 207.

A will made under such circumstances is regarded as a result of coercion, and cannot be sustained.

The degree of undue influence which will invalidate a will must vary with the circumstances of each case. The importunity or threatening successfully employed to coerce one person will have no effect on another. The mental and physical condition of the testator, his natural strength or feebleness of mind, the power and disposition of the person who seeks to control the testator, and the character of the influences brought to bear upon him, are to be considered. Honest suggestions and moderate persuasion do not amount to undue influence. To invalidate the will it must appear that the ill-treatment, threats, violence, or persistent importunity was such as to destroy the free agency of the testator.[1] In these cases, as in all others, the party offering the will for probate must prove the sanity of the testator, but if that fact is established, the burden of proving undue influence is upon the party alleging it.

It has been held, that the harmony of the will with the testator's disposition and affections, and his declarations in regard to it when in health, are facts to be considered in determining the question of undue influence.[2]

---

[1] Jarm. on Wills (4th Am. ed.), 37 ; 1 Williams Ex. (5th Am. ed.) 40.

Any one has a right by fair argument or persuasion, or by virtuous influence, to induce another to make a will in his favor. Miller v. Miller, 5 Serg. & R. 267. "Neither advice, nor argument, nor persuasion would vitiate a will made freely and from conviction, though such will might not have been made but for such advice or persuasion." Clayton, C. J., in Chandler v. Ferris, 1 Harr. 454.

[2] Evidence having been introduced that the will was procured to be made by the undue influence of the residuary legatee, it was held that evidence was admissible, on the other side, that a large part of the property of the testatrix was inherited by her from her minor son, who died many years previous, and who was greatly attached to the residuary

If it appears that the will was written or procured to be written by a person largely benefited by its provisions, the circumstance under which it was made will be more strictly inquired into.[1] Evidence that the testator was of feeble mind, and believed in ghosts and supernatural influences, has some tendency to show that weakness of mind which would be easily imposed upon by the exertion of undue influence.[2] Subsequent declarations of the testator, to the effect that he had been forced to sign his will, are not competent evidence of the fact that force was used.[3]

SECTION VII.

REVOCATION OF WILLS.

A will, executed in accordance with the requirements of the statute, is presumed to have existed until the death of the testator; but this presumption may be rebutted by proof of its revocation. The testator may

legatee, and had frequently expressed his intention, if he should attain the age of twenty-one years, to leave the bulk of his property to him, and that such intention was known to the testatrix. Glover *v.* Hayden, 4 Cush. 580. See Allen *v.* Pub. Admr. 1 Bradf. (N. Y.) 378; Waterman *v.* Whitney, 1 Kernan, 157; Shailer *v.* Bumstead, 99 Mass. 112.

[1] Clark *v.* Fisher, 1 Paige, 171; Darley *v.* Darley, 3 Bradf. (N. Y.) 481; Brydges *v.* King, 1 Hagg. 250; Dodge *v.* March, 1 Hagg. 612.

[2] Woodbury *v.* Obear, 7 Gray, 467. Evidence having been given that a devisee who was accused of having made use of undue influence, had represented to the testator that the wife of one of his sons was an extravagant woman, who would waste any thing that might be given to her husband, the opposers of the will were allowed to prove that her general behavior and character were good. Dietrick *v.* Dietrick, 5 Serg. & R. 207; and see Nussear *v.* Arnold, 13 Serg. & R. 323.

When a subscribing witness, who is accused of having been an accomplice in a fraud upon the testator, is dead, evidence may be given of his general good character. Provis *v.* Reed, 5 Bing. 435; but not if he is living. Doe *v.* Harris, 7 Carr. & P. 330.

[3] Ibid.; Jackson *v.* Kniffen, 2 Johns. 31; Smith *v.* Fenner, 1 Gall. (R. I.) 174; Moritz *v.* Brough, 16 Serg. & R. 405.

revoke his will at his pleasure. The manner of revocation is pointed out by statute : —

" No will shall be revoked, unless by burning, tearing, cancelling, or obliterating the same, with the intention of revoking it, by the testator himself, or by some person in his presence and by his direction ; or by some other will, codicil, or writing, signed, attested, and subscribed, in the manner provided for making a will ; but nothing contained in this section shall prevent the revocation implied by law from subsequent changes in the condition or circumstances of the testator." [1]

The revocation of a will, therefore, may be either *express* or *implied*. It is expressly revoked by some act of destruction done upon it with the intention of revoking it ; or by a new will or codicil intended as a substitute for it, or other writing, formally executed with the express intention of revocation.

EXPRESS REVOCATIONS.

The mere physical act of burning, tearing, cancelling, or obliterating a will, is not of itself sufficient to constitute a revocation. The act must be done *with the intention of revoking*. If the testator inadvertently obliterates his will, it will remain in force, notwithstanding such obliteration.[2] So, if he destroys it during a fit of insanity, or if it is destroyed by his consent, given after he has become *non compos ;*[3] or if it is destroyed

---

[1] Gen. Sts. c. 92, § 11.

[2] A will was burnt by the testator on the supposition that he had substituted another for it, but which was not duly executed. Probate of a copy of the first will granted. Scott *v.* Scott, 1 Swa. & Trist. 258.

[3] Idley *v.* Bowen, 11 Wend. 227 ; Ford *v.* Ford, 7 Humph. 92 ; Scrubly *v.* Fordham, 1 Add. 74. The testator, to revoke a will, must be at the same time competent to make a will, or the act of revocation will be a nullity. Smith *v.* Wait, 4 Barb. Sup. Ct. (N. Y.) 28. *In re* Downer, 26

by another person without his knowledge, it is not revoked.[1]

Burning. tearing, &c., in a slight degree, with a declared intent to revoke, is a sufficient revocation. Where the testator gave his will "a rip" with his hands, "so as almost to tear a bit off," and then threw it on the fire, it was held to be a revocation, though the will fell from the fire and was preserved, slightly singed, by another person, without the testator's knowledge.[2] If the seal be torn from his will by the testator under the mistaken impression that it is an essential part of the execution of the instrument, the intention to revoke being clear, it would be a sufficient revocation.[3]

A mere declaration of an intention to revoke a will, not accompanied nor followed by any act in fulfilment of that intention. is of course insufficient.[4] And there may be a change of purpose that will prevent a revocation. even when the act of destruction is partly accomplished. A testator, under the impulse of passion against his devisee. tore his will twice through, when his arms

Eng. Law & Eq. 600. The burden of proving that the will was mutilated by the testator when of sound mind, is upon the party alleging the revocation. Harris *v.* Berrall, 1 Swa. & Trist. 153.

[1] Onions *v.* Tyrer, 1 P. Wms. 345 ; Bennett *v.* Sherrod, 3 Ired. 303 ; Middleton *v.* Middleton, 19 Eng. Law & Eq. 310. The fact that a testator, who discovers such loss of his will neglects to make another, has been held to furnish a presumption of his intention to revoke. Steele *v.* Price, 5 B. Monr. 68.

[2] Bibb *v.* Thomas, 2 W. Bl. 1043 ; Doe *v.* Harris, 6 Ad. & El. 209.

[3] Avery *v.* Pixley, 4 Mass. 460. A testator, being ill in bed, called for his will, and one of the legatees named in the will deceived him by handing him an old letter in its stead. Held that if, from the rest of the testimony the jury believed that the testator destroyed that letter, thinking it to be his will, such circumstances would amount to a revocation. Pryor *v.* Coggin, 17 Geo. 444.

[4] The mere direction to another by the testator to destroy his will is not sufficient, unless some act of destruction is thereupon done. Giles *v.* Giles, 1 Coll. & Nor. 174 ; Ford *v.* Ford, 7 Humph. 92.

were seized by a by-stander, and he became pacified by the concessions of the devisee; he then fitted the pieces of the torn will together and remarked, "it's a good job it is no worse." This was held to be no revocation.[1] The declarations of the testator, accompanying the act of revocation, are admissible in evidence to explain his intentions.[2]

It is to be observed that the statute requires the burning, tearing, cancelling, or obliterating to be by the testator himself, or by some person in his presence and by his direction. If, therefore, the testator requests a person who has the custody of his will to destroy it, and it is accordingly destroyed, such destruction, if not effected in the testator's presence, would not be a compliance with the terms of the statute.

If the will is found obliterated in the testator's possession, the presumption is that it was obliterated by him, and the burden of proving the contrary is on the party offering it for probate; but if it has been in the possession of one adversely interested the presumption does not arise.[3] If the will is proved to have been in the testator's possession and cannot be found, it will be presumed that he destroyed it with the intention of revoking it,[4] but if it is traced out of his custody, the party asserting the revocation must show that it came again into such custody.

If the testator executes his will in duplicate, retaining one part and committing the other to the custody of

[1] Doe v. Perks, 5 B. & Ald. 489; Elms v. Elms, 1 Swa. & Trist. 155.

[2] 1 Greenl. Ev. § 273; Dan v. Brown, 4 Cowen, 490. As to partial revocations by obliteration, see 1 Jarm. on Wills, 158, and cases there cited.

[3] Baptist Church v. Roberts, 2 Barr, 10; Bennett v. Sherrod, 3 Ired. 303; Jones & Murphy, 8 Watts & Serg. 275.

[4] Davis v. Sigourney, 8 Met. 488.

another person, and then destroys one part, the inference generally is that he intended to revoke the will, but the strength of the presumption depends much on the circumstances. Thus, if he destroys the only copy in his possession, his intent to revoke is very strongly to be presumed; if he was possessed of both copies and destroys but one, it is weaker; and if he alters one and then destroys it, retaining the other entire, the presumption has been said still to hold, but weaker still; but the contrary also has been asserted.[1]

Cases have occurred where a will has been revoked and a codicil left entire, and the question has thereby been raised as to whether the revocation of the will has a revoking effect upon the codicil also. If, from its contents, the codicil appears inseparably connected with the will, it will be held to be revoked; otherwise, if it is independent of and unconnected with the will.[2]

A will is also expressly revoked by a new will or codicil, inconsistent in its provisions with the original will, or plainly intended as a substitute for it,[3] or by a writing which expressly declares an intention to revoke. A subsequent will which makes a new disposition of the whole estate is a revocation of the first, without any words of revocation; but if the subsequent will contains no clause of revocation and makes no disposition of the estate inconsistent with the former will, it does not operate as a revocation, but both instruments remain in force.[4] Where it appeared that the testator

---

[1] 2 Greenl. Ev. § 682.

[2] 2 Greenl. Ev. § 682. 1 Jarm. on Wills (4th Am. ed.), 169.

[3] When the intention of the testator to revoke his will appears clearly from a subsequent will, it is a sufficient revocation, although such subsequent will is inoperative on account of the incapacity of the devisee to take under it. Laughton v. Atkins, 1 Pick. 545.

[4] Brant v. Wilson, 8 Cowen, 56; Nelson v. McGiffert, 3 Barb. Ch. 158.

made a second will, *the contents of which were unknown*, it was held not to be a revocation of the first, because it did not appear either that it contained a revocatory clause or made a different disposition of the estate. And where it was found that the testator made a second will different from the first, *but it was not found in what the difference consisted*, it was held to be no revocation.[1] The burden is on the party offering the second will to show that it expressly revokes the former will or has different contents ; the mere words " this is the last will of me," &c., are not sufficient for that purpose.[2]

If the subsequent instrument, whether it be a will or codicil, disposes of a part of the estate only, although it professes an intent to dispose of the whole, it is only a revocation *pro tanto*, unless it contains words expressing the intention to revoke.[3]

A revocatory writing, intended for the express purpose of revoking a will, must be signed by the testator, or by some person in his presence and by his express direction, and attested and subscribed in his presence by three or more competent witnesses. The manner of execution is the same prescribed by statute for the execution of wills. If such writing is made in another State or country, it may be executed in the manner prescribed for the execution of wills in such other State or country.[4] If the writing declares merely an intention to do some future

---

[1] 6 Cruise's Digest (Greenleaf), tit. 38, c. 6, §§ 11, 14, and cases there cited. This rule is applied, even if it is found that the second will was stolen from the testator or destroyed by fraud. Ibid. note. But when the second will is missing parol evidence of its contents may be offered. 2 Greenl. Ev. § 688. But such evidence must be strong and conclusive. Cutto *v.* Gilbert, 29 Eng. Law & Eq. 61.

[2] Cutto *v.* Gilbert, 29 Eng. Law & Eq. 64.

[3] Brant *v.* Wilson, 8 Cowen, 56 ; Harwood *v.* Goodright, Cowp. 87.

[4] Bayley *v.* Bailey, 5 Cush. 245.

act of revocation, it will not amount to a revocation; it must be a *present actual revocation.*[1]

IMPLIED REVOCATIONS.

Another class of revocations are those implied by law from changes occurring in the condition and circumstances of the testator subsequent to the execution of his will. Such revocations are founded on the reasonable presumption that his will would have been differently made under such different circumstances. The marriage of a man will not revoke his will; nor will his will made after marriage be revoked by the birth of a child; but the rule is established that the concurrence of marriage and the birth of a child, after the execution of the will, works an entire revocation;[2] and the rule applies to posthumous children.[3] It has been decided that parol evidence of the intention of the testator, that his will should stand unrevoked, is inadmissible to control the presumption resulting from marriage and the birth of children.[4] The rule does not apply to cases where it appears that the changes in the testator's circumstances and obligations were anticipated and provided for by the will, as when the will makes provision

[1] Brown v. Thorndike, 15 Pick. 388. Where the revocations proceed from mistake, or from a false impression originating from deceit practised on the testator, it will be void; but where the testator merely expresses a doubt as to a fact, and upon that doubt revokes, the revocation would seem to be good. 6 Cruise's Digest (Greenl. ed.), tit. 38, c. 6, § 26.

[2] Warner v. Beach, 4 Gray, 163; Brush v. Wilkins, 4 Johns. Ch. 506; Havens v. Vandenburg, 1 Denio, 27.

[3] Doe v. Lancashire, 5 T. R. 49. It is the same if the testator died without knowledge of the fact that his wife was pregnant. Christopher v. Christopher, 4 Burrow, 2182; or if the child died in the testator's lifetime. Wright v. Netherwood, 2 Salk. 593.

[4] Marston v. Roe, 8 Add. & El. 14; Doe v. Lancashire, *supra.*

for the future wife and issue,[1] but provision for the wife only has been held insufficient.[2] The marriage of a feme sole has been held to be an absolute revocation of her will, even though her testamentary capacity was subsequently restored by the event of her surviving her husband;[3] but on this point doubts have been expressed, it being questioned whether her marriage worked a revocation or merely a suspension.

An alteration in the estate of lands devised by the act of the devisor may operate as an implied revocation of his will. A conveyance of the estate devised is a revocation of the devise; under such circumstances there is nothing left upon which the devise can operate. But the conveyance, to effect an entire revocation, must be of the whole estate devised. If it is of but part of the estate it is a revocation only to the extent of the conveyance.[4] The partition of an estate between tenants in common does not operate as a revocation of a prior devise made by one of the tenants of his share.

Entire revocations by implication of law are limited to a very small number of cases. The statute does not intimate what changes in the condition and circumstances of the testator are intended to work a revocation, but leaves them to be decided by the general rules of law; and the reported cases furnish but little information as to the effect of changes in the testator's condition except as regards marriage and the birth of children, and alteration in the estate devised. It has

---

[1] Kennebel v. Scrafton, 2 East, 530.

[2] Marston v. Roe, *supra*.

[3] 1 Jarm. on Wills (4th Am. ed.), 150; 1 Wms. Ex. (5th Am. ed.) 164.

[4] Hawes v. Humphrey, 9 Pick. 350; Ballard v. Carter, 5 Pick. 112.

For the rules as to revocation by alteration of estate, see 6 Cruise's Digest (Greenleaf's ed.), tit. 38, c. 6, § 58 and *seq.*

been held that revocation cannot be implied from the
long-continued insanity of the testator from soon after
the making of his will until his death;[1] nor from the
large increase in value of his property subsequent to the
making of his will, although such increase altogether
changes the proportion between the specific legacies and
the shares of the residuary legatees.[2]

The effect of a *partial* revocation by obliteration, or
by an alteration of the 'estate devised, is not a material
question in proceedings in the probate court. The
probate of a will settles all questions as to the formalities
of its execution and the capacity of the testator, but
does not affect the validity or invalidity of any particular
clause, or settle any question of construction. A revocation therefore, which does not wholly defeat the
will presents no question for the probate court to determine, and is no bar to its admission to probate.[3] All
questions as to the construction of the will must be
settled by subsequent proceedings in the common-law
courts.

SECTION VIII.

PROBATE OF WILLS — FORMAL PROCEEDINGS.

The will to be proved should be filed in the probate
office of the county of which the deceased was an inhab-

---

[1] Warner *v.* Beach, 4 Gray, 162.

[2] Ibid. "Though the testament be made in time of sickness and peril
of death, when the testator doth not hope for life, and afterwards he recover his health, yet is not the testament revoked by such recovery, or
albeit the testator make his testament by reason of some great journey,
yet it is not revoked by his return." Swinburne, Pt. 7, § 15.

For a general review of the decided cases upon the subject of implied
revocations, see 1 Saunders (Williams), 278, note.

[3] Hawes *v.* Humphrey, 9 Pick. 350.

itant, or in which he was resident at the time of his death.[1] With the will there must be filed a petition,[2] signed by the executor or other person who offers the will for probate, and addressed to the judge of the probate court, setting forth the place where the testator last dwelt, the date of his death, the fact that he left a will, and praying that the will be allowed. The full name of the widow of the deceased, if any, and the names, residences, and relationship of his heirs-at-law and next of kin should also be stated in the petition. If the next of kin are minors, the fact should be stated, and if they are under guardianship, the name and residence of the guardian should be given.

If the executor named in the will declines the trust, his renunciation in writing should be filed with the will.[3]

NOTICE TO PERSONS INTERESTED.

Upon such petition, a citation is issued by the register of probate to the heirs-at-law of the deceased, and all persons interested in his estate, to appear at a day named

---

[1] A person *non compos*, born in the county of Suffolk, removed, upon the death of her father, into the county of Middlesex, where she lived as part of her brother's family many years and until her death, being for the last years of her life under a guardian who provided for her support, whose residence was in Suffolk. Held that her domicile at the time of her death was in Middlesex, and that letters of administration on her estate granted by the judge of probate in Suffolk, were void for want of jurisdiction. Holyoke *v.* Haskins, 5 Pick. 20.

Where a citizen, having lived many years at W. in the county of M., purchased and furnished a house at B. in the county of S., and afterwards with his family spent his summers at his house in W., where he continued to pay his taxes, and his winters in B., where he died, it was held that probate of his will might be taken in the county of M. Whether probate in the county of S. would not have been valid likewise, *quære*. Harvard College v. Gore, 5 Pick. 370.

[2] See Appendix, forms No. 1-3.

[3] See Appendix, form No. 4.

and show cause, if any they have, why the will should not be allowed. The statute provides no form of serving the citation, nor does it provide in terms that any notice shall be given. The usual practice is to order notice to be given by publishing an attested copy of the citation in some newspaper printed in the county. The person presenting the will may designate the paper in which the citation shall be published, but if the judge deems the paper so designated insufficient to give due publicity, he may order the publication in one other newspaper.[1] The will is not required to be filed on a day when the probate court is held, but it may be filed and the citation issued on any day. The party offering the will for probate must serve the citation in accordance with its terms, and must make his return of the fact of service under oath, on or before the day fixed for the hearing.

Formal notice is dispensed with when the heirs-at-law and all persons interested in the estate of the deceased acknowledge or waive notice of the pendency of the petition, and the judge is satisfied that no person interested intends to object to the probate of the will. Such acknowledgment or waiver must be in writing and signed by all the heirs-at-law, and should be annexed to the petition.[2]

THE HEARING — EVIDENCE OF THE SUBSCRIBING WITNESSES.

When it appears to the court, by the consent in writing of the heirs-at-law or other satisfactory evidence, that no person interested in the estate intends to object

---

[1] The same rule applies to the publication of other notices and citations issued by the probate courts. Gen. Sts. c. 117, § 29.

[2] See Appendix, form No. 2.

to the probate of the will, the court may grant probate thereof upon the testimony of one only of the subscribing witnesses.[1] But if it does not so appear, all the subscribing witnesses, if they are within the State, must be produced at the time and place named in the citation. If there is a codicil to be proved, the witnesses who attested it must also be present. The subscribing witnesses, being considered in law as placed near the testator to ascertain and judge of his capacity, the party objecting to the probate of the will has a right to insist upon the testimony of all of them, if they can be produced.[2] Every clerk of a court of record, and every justice of the peace may issue summonses to procure the attendance of the witnesses.[3]

If it appears that a subscribing witness is dead, evidence is admissible to prove his handwriting.[4] If, having been competent at the time of his attestation, a witness has since become insane, or disqualified by reason of conviction of an infamous crime, or otherwise, his handwriting may be proved as if he were dead; but the fact of his incompetency must first be shown. If the witness cannot be found or resides out of the State, his handwriting may be proved, but it must first appear that a diligent search, satisfactory to the court under the circumstances, has been made for him. An indifferent inquiry, that leaves the matter in doubt, is not sufficient to let in secondary evidence of his attestation. In accounting for the absence of such a witness, answers to inquiries made of persons supposed to be able to give

---

[1] Gen. Sts. c. 92, § 19.   [2] Chase v. Lincoln, 3 Mass. 326.

[3] See Appendix, form No. 5.

[4] Nickerson v. Buck, 12 Cush. 332; Dean v. Dean's Heirs, 1 Williams (Vt.), 746; Jackson v. Luquere, 5 Cowen, 221; Jackson v. Le Grange, 19 Johns. 386.

information of him may be given in evidence.[1] If an attesting witness who made his mark is dead, his mark must be proved to be his, and for this purpose evidence is admissible to show that the witness lived near the testator, that he could not write, and that no other person of the same name lived in the same neighborhood, and this evidence has been held sufficient to prove the attestation.[2] Proof of the handwriting of a deceased attesting witness is *primâ facie* evidence that he duly and properly attested the will;[3] but the fact that he attested the will is not evidence that he believed the testator to be sane.[4] Where all the witnesses were dead, and no proof of their handwriting could be found, proof of the testator's handwriting was received as sufficient.[5]

It sometimes occurs, particularly where the will has been made many years before it is offered for probate, that an attesting witness does not retain a clear recollection of the circumstances attending the execution of the instrument, and in such cases less strictness of proof is sometimes required. In Dewey v. Dewey,[6] one of the witnesses testified that his name, which was upon the will, appeared to be his signature, but that he recollected

[1] Greenl. Ev. § 574.

[2] Doe *v.* Capeterton, 9 Carr. & P. 59. In this case the will was attested by the signature of V. and the marks of Charles and Mary Drinkwater, and all were dead. V.'s handwriting was proved, and Mary Drinkwater testified: " I am the daughter of Charles and Mary Drinkwater; they are both dead; they lived near the testator; my mother could not write, and my father wrote his name only; no other Charles Drinkwater and no other Mary Drinkwater lived anywhere in that neighborhood." The evidence was held sufficient. In Jackson *v.* Van Dusen, the witness made his initials, which were proved. 5 Johns. 144.

[3] Nickerson *v.* Buck, 12 Cush. 332.   [4] Baxter *v.* Abbott, 7 Gray, 71.

[5] Duncan *v.* Beard, 2 Nott & McCord, 400. Experts may testify to their opinion of the genuineness of the testator's signature, and may give their reasons for such opinion. Demerritt *v.* Randall, 116 Mass. 331.

[6] 1 Met. 349.

nothing about it. One of the other witnesses testified that the first witness did subscribe in the testator's presence, and this was held sufficient. Dewey, J., said: " The question is not, whether this witness now recollects the circumstance of the attestation, and can state it as a matter within his memory. If this were requisite, the validity of a will would depend, not upon the fact whether it was duly executed, but whether the testator had been fortunate in securing witnesses of retentive memories. The real question is, whether the witness did in fact properly attest it." [1] In the absence of evidence to the contrary, it has been presumed from the fact of attestation that the requisites of the statute have been complied with.[2]

If a subscribing witness should deny the execution of the will, he may be contradicted as to that fact by another subscribing witness; and even if they should all swear that the will was not duly executed, the party offering the will would be allowed to go into circumstantial evidence to prove its due execution. But where the attesting witnesses so deny their attestation, the evidence, to give effect to the will, must be very clear.[3] And where a witness has sworn that the testator was not of sound mind, his testimony has been successfully met by the evidence of other persons; and wills have been established notwithstanding the adverse testimony of all the subscribing witnesses.[4]

---

[1] Two of the three witnesses of a will nearly thirty years old, were dead, and their signatures were proved; the third recognized his signature, but had no recollection of the transaction. The will was allowed. Verdier r. Verdier, 8 Rich. (S. C.) 135.

[2] Clark r. Dunnevant, 10 Leigh, 13.

[3] See Jackson r. Christman, 4 Wend. 282; Handy r. The State, 7 Harr. & John. 42.

[4] 1 Jarm. on Wills (4th Am. ed.), 77; Kinliside r. Harrison, 2 Phill. 449; Le Breton v. Fletcher, 2 Hagg. 568; Landon v. Howard's Will, 2

The due execution of the instrument and the testamentary capacity of the testator having been established by the party offering the will for probate, the burden is upon the persons opposing the probate to sustain their objections. The rules observed as to the usual defences of fraud, undue influence, and revocation have been considered in previous sections of this chapter.

No particular form of words is necessary to constitute a valid will. It may be admitted to probate, however inartificial it may be in expression, provided it bears the character and is executed according to the requisites of a will. A valid testamentary paper may be in the form of a deed or a letter.[1]

A codicil written on a separate paper, not known to the parties to be in existence at the time of the probate of the will, may be subsequently admitted to probate. So may a codicil written on the back of the same leaf on which the will was written, if such codicil escaped attention at the time of the original probate.[2]

Upon the allowance of the will, if no appeal is taken, and if there is an executor named in the will who is competent and willing to accept the trust, letters testamentary will issue to him upon his giving a sufficient bond for the faithful discharge of his trust. If there is no executor named in the will, or if the executor therein named declines the trust, or is incompetent, some suitable person will be appointed administrator with the will annexed.[3]

Addams, 215; Peebles v. Case, 2 Bradf. (N. Y.) 226; Howard's Will, 5 Monr. 199.

[1] Bayley v. Bailey, 5 Cush. 260.

[2] Waters v. Stickney, 12 Allen, 1.

[3] As to granting administration, see chap. v.

Section IX.

PROOF OF WILLS MADE OUT OF THE STATE.

A will made out of this State, which might be proved and allowed according to the laws of the State or country in which it was made, may be proved, allowed, and recorded in this State, and will thereupon have the same effect as if it had been executed according to the laws of this Commonwealth.[1] This provision includes nuncupative wills.[2]

In such cases the same certainty of proof is required as when the will is made in this State, but the particular facts to be proved in support of the will must depend upon the requirements of the local laws of the State or country in which the will may have been executed.[3] It must be proved that all the formalities of execution made necessary by the local law, whatever they may be, were duly observed. The rules as to the testator's soundness of mind and the "presence" of the testator are of general application, and the formal proceedings in probate court are the same as in cases of wills made in this State.

Section X.

PROOF OF LOST WILLS.

A will, proved to have been duly executed, which cannot be found after the testator's death, is presumed to have been destroyed by him with the intention of revoking it, but this presumption may be rebutted by

---

[1] Gen. Sts. c. 92, § 8.   [2] Slocomb v. Slocomb, 13 Allen, 38.

[3] Bayley v. Bailey, 5 Cush. 215.

evidence.[1] It may be that the will was destroyed by
the testator in a fit of insanity, or that it was lost, or
accidentally or fraudulently destroyed. Such accidental
or fraudulent destruction will not deprive parties of
their rights under its provisions, if they can produce the
evidence necessary to establish the will.

The fact that the will was made by the testator must
be proved, and it must be shown that in its execution
the provisions of the statute were complied with. If
the fact of its destruction is not clearly proved, it must
be shown, to the satisfaction of the court, that it has
been lost. It must appear that an honest and diligent
search has been unsuccessfully made for it in the place
or places where it was most likely to be found, and
then evidence may be admitted to prove its contents.[2]
If the contents are proved, it can be admitted to probate.
But, in order to establish a will under such circumstances, the whole contents must be proved, and the
evidence must be strong, positive, and free from all
doubt.[3]

The party applying for the probate of a lost will,
should set forth in his petition all the material facts of
the case, and should file with his petition a paper containing the contents of the will.[4]

---

[1] Davis v. Sigourney, 8 Met. 487; Clark v. Wright, 3 Pick. 67; Idley
v. Bowen, 11 Wend. 227. "The presumption may be repelled, nor does
it require evidence amounting to positive certainty, but only such as
reasonably produces moral conviction." Sir John Nicholl, in Davis v.
Davis, 2 Add. 226. The presumption may be rebutted by probable circumstances, among which declarations of unchanged affection and intention have much weight. Patten v. Poulton, 1 Swa. & Trist. 55.

[2] Jackson v. Betts, 9 Cowen, 208; Dan v. Brown, 4 Cowen, 483;
Featherly v. Waggoner, 11 Wend. 599.

[3] Davis v. Sigourney, 8 Met. 487; Durfee v. Durfee, ibid. 490, note;
Johnson's Will, 40 Conn. 587.

[4] See Appendix, forms Nos. 6 and 7.

Section XI.

ALLOWANCE OF WILLS PROVED OUT OF THE STATE.

The executor or other person interested in a will proved and allowed in any other of the United States, or in a foreign country, may produce a copy of the will and of the probate thereof duly authenticated, to the probate court in any county in which there is any estate, real or personal, on which the will may operate.[1] With the authenticated copy of the will should be presented a petition in writing, signed by the person presenting the will, setting forth the place of the testator's last residence, the facts that his will has been duly proved and allowed in such other State or country by the court having jurisdiction of the case, that there is estate, real or personal, in the county in which the petition is presented, upon which the will may operate, and praying that it may be filed and recorded.

Upon such petition, the statute requires the court to assign a time and place for hearing the same, and to order notice to all persons interested to be given in some newspaper three weeks successively, the first publication to be thirty days at least before the time assigned.

Such notice having been given, if it appears upon the hearing at the time assigned, that the instrument ought to be allowed in this State as the last will and testament of the deceased, the court orders the copy to be filed and recorded, and the will then has the same effect as if it had been originally proved and allowed in this State.[2] After the will is so allowed and ordered to be recorded, the court grants letters testamentary, or of administration with the will annexed, as the circumstances of the

---

[1] Gen. Sts. c. 92, § 21.   [2] Parker v. Parker, 11 Cush. 519.

case may require, and proceeds to the settlement of the estate that may be found in this State.[1]

In cases of this kind no evidence of the execution of the will or of the sanity of the testator is required to be produced. The copy of the will, and of the decree of the court in which the will was originally proved, if properly authenticated, is conclusive, in the absence of any allegations of fraud, as to all the facts necessary to the establishment of the will, and as to the regularity of the proceedings and their conformity to the law of the State or country in which the will was originally proved.[2] The usual questions to be determined are, whether the record presented is duly authenticated, whether the court in which the will purports to have been proved had jurisdiction, and whether there is any real or personal estate in the county on which the will may operate.

SECTION XII.

PROOF OF NUNCUPATIVE WILLS.

A nuncupative will is a verbal disposition of the testator's *personal* estate, to take effect after his death. The statute provides that "a soldier in actual military service, or a mariner at sea, may dispose of his wages and other personal estate by a nuncupative will, as he might heretofore have done." The same provision was contained in the revised statutes (1836), and is the only provision relating to nuncupative wills in the statutes of this State.

Previous to the revised statutes any person, being in his last sickness, might dispose of his personal estate by a nuncupative will, and the manner of making and estab-

---

[1] Gen. Sts. c. 92, § 23.   [2] Crippen v. Dexter, 13 Gray, 330.

lishing such a will was prescribed at length by statute
(1783, c. 24). That statute, however, did not apply the
term "nuncupative" to the testamentary dispositions of
soldiers and mariners, but provided that they might dispose of their personal estate as they might have done
before the passage of that act. The same exception was
made in the provincial act, 4 W. & M. c. 3; and the
statute of frauds (29 Car. II. c. 3), which particularly
prescribed the manner of making and proving nuncupative wills, provided that soldiers and sailors might dispose of their personal property as they had previously
done. The distinction between nuncupative wills, and
the unwritten wills of soldiers and sailors, was recognized
at a very remote period. The unwritten wills of soldiers were denominated military wills, and other verbal
testaments nuncupative wills.[1] The revised statutes of
this State applied the term nuncupative to the wills of
soldiers and mariners, but expressly reserved their previously existing rights as to their testamentary dispositions. It has been held accordingly in this State, and
in other States where a similar provision of statute exists, that the rule governing the only unwritten wills
now recognized, is the common law as it stood before
the passage of the statute of frauds.[2] The wills of seamen have been held to come within the reason and the
rule of military testaments.[3]

---

[1] Swinburne, Pt. 1, §§ 12, 14.

[2] In the Goods of Arthur White, 22 Law Rep. 110; Hubbard v. Hubbard, 4 Selden, 196.

[3] It has been held that the purser of a man-of-war is within this description, and that it includes the whole service, applying equally to superior officers up to the commander-in-chief as to a common seaman, being
at sea. In re Hays, 2 Curt. 338. And it has been held to apply to merchant seamen. Euston v. Seymour, cited 2 Curt. 339. A cook on board
a merchant ship is a mariner. Ex parte Thompson, 4 Bradf. (N. Y.) 160.

Although no form of words is needed to constitute a good nuncupative will, it is very necessary that the testator's declarations should plainly express his intentions. Swinburne says: " As for any precise form of words, none is required, neither is it material whether the testator do speak properly, or unproperly, so that his meaning do appear." " And although in written testaments it be also required that the words and sentences be such as thereby the testator's meaning may appear; yet more specially is it required in a nuncupative testament, for more supply may be made in written testaments than can be made in nuncupative testaments, concerning the testator's meaning." [1] Nuncupative wills may be made not only by the proper motions of the testator, but also in answer to the interrogation of other persons.[2]

To prove a nuncupative will, it must appear that the testator was either a soldier in actual military service, or a mariner at sea, at the time when he made his testamentary declarations. The English courts have held that the privilege does not extend to soldiers quartered in barracks, either at home or abroad, but that the sol-

[1] Part 4, § 29.

[2] Swinburne, Pt. 1, § 12. While in his last sickness, and about an hour before he died, being of sound mind, on being asked as to the disposition of his property, the testator said in the presence of several witnesses, that he " wished his wife to have all his personal property." Beckwith, the mate of the vessel, then asked him, if he wished her to have all his real property, and he replied, " yes, all." He was then asked if he had no will, and he replied that he had had one, but it was destroyed. He was then asked by B, what he should tell his wife, and he replied, " tell her I loved her till the end." He was subsequently asked by B. who he wanted to settle his affairs, and he answered, " I want you to do it." He did not ask any one to bear witness that what he stated was his will. These conversations were proved by four witnesses. It was held that they constituted a good nuncupative will, and that the evidence was sufficient to show that the testator intended to make B. his executor. Hubbard v. Hubbard, 4 Selden, 196.

dier must be engaged on an expedition at the time.[1]   In behalf of seamen, however, the rule has been carried to the extreme limit of construction.[2]   The substance of the testator's requests or instructions must be established, and it must be proved to the satisfaction of the court that the testator intended by his declarations to make a testamentary disposition of his property.   It must appear, of course, that the testator was of sound mind.

No particular number of witnesses is required to establish a nuncupative will, but every fact necessary to support it should be proved by the most positive evidence. The great danger of mistake, particularly in cases where the testator's declarations were not reduced to writing soon after they were made, and the obvious facilities for the fraudulent setting up of such wills, render it necessary that the evidence should be subjected to the closest scrutiny.   Unless it is made morally certain that the declarations proved contain the true substance and import, at least, of the alleged nuncupation, and embody the testator's real testamentary intentions, the will cannot safely be allowed.[3]

The person applying for the probate of a nuncupative will, should set forth in his petition the material facts of

[1] Drummond v. Parish, 3 Curteis, 522; White v. Ripton, ibid. 818.

[2] A sailor, while the ship was in a foreign harbor, obtained leave to go on shore, where he was so injured by an accident, that he did not return to the ship, but died of his injuries in a few days after the accident.   His nuncupative will was held to be the will of a seaman "at sea," though he was not on board the vessel at the time.   In the Goods of Lay, 2 Curteis, 375.

[3] In the probate court of Suffolk county, a nuncupative will was admitted to probate on the testimony of one witness, who was also a legatee under the will; the court held that he was not an "attesting witness," and therefore not disqualified by reason of interest.   In the Goods of Arthur White, 22 Law Reporter, 110.

the case, and the substance of the testamentary declarations of the testator.[1] The usual notice must be given before any hearing upon the question of proving the will can be had. At the hearing, the will is reduced to writing in the form in which it may be established by the evidence, and is then admitted to probate.[2]

A nuncupative will executed in another State, according to the law of that State, which would not have been valid if made here, may be proved in this State, and have the same effect as if it had been executed according to the laws of this State.[3]

[1] See Appendix, forms Nos. 8 and 9.

[2] The use is to prove it by witnesses and then to write it. Swinburne, Pt. 1, § 12. "Being after his death proved by witnesses and put in writing by the ordinary." Bac. Abr. Wills, D.

[3] Slocomb v. Slocomb, 13 Allen, 38.

CHAPTER III.

DEPOSIT, CUSTODY, AND PROCEEDINGS IN CASE OF CONCEALMENT OF WILLS.

A WILL, when executed, if the testator sees fit, may be deposited in the Registry of Probate in the county where he lives, for safe-keeping, and the register, upon being paid the fee of one dollar, is required to receive and keep it, and give a certificate of the deposit thereof. The will so deposited must be enclosed in a sealed wrapper, indorsed with the name of the testator, his place of residence, the day when, and the person by whom it is delivered, and may have indorsed thereon the name of the person to whom it is to be delivered after the testator's death.[1]

Such will, during the lifetime of the testator, can be delivered only to himself, or to some person authorized by him, by an order in writing duly proved by the oath of a subscribing witness; after his death it will be delivered to the person named in the indorsement on the wrapper, if there is a person so named who demands it. In the mean time it cannot be opened or read. If not so demanded it will be publicly opened at the first probate court held after notice of the testator's death. It will then be retained in the registry until it is offered for probate; or if the jurisdiction of the case belongs to another court, it will be delivered to the executors or

[1] Gen. Sts. c. 92, §§ 12, 13.

other persons entitled to its custody to be presented for probate in such other court.[1]

The statute requires every person, other than the register of the probate court having the custody of a will, within thirty days after notice of the death of the testator, to deliver it into the probate court which has jurisdiction of the case, or to the executors named in the will; and if without reasonable cause he neglects to do so after being duly cited for that purpose, he may be committed to the jail by warrant of the court, there to be kept in close custody until he so delivers the will; and he will be further liable to any party aggrieved for the damage sustained by such neglect.[2] In order that such a citation may issue, a petition setting forth the facts should be presented to the court. Any person interested may petition.[3]

Upon complaint under oath made to the probate court by a person claiming to be interested in the estate of a person deceased, against any one suspected of retaining, concealing, or conspiring with others to retain or conceal any will or testamentary instrument of the deceased, the judge may cite the suspected person to appear before him and be examined on oath upon the matter of the complaint.[4] The citation may be served by an officer qualified to serve civil process, or by a private person. If by a private person, the fact that service was made as ordered must be proved by his affidavit. The affidavit may be conveniently indorsed on the citation.[5]

---

[1] Gen. Sts. c. 92, §§ 14, 15.

[2] Ibid. c. 92, § 16; Stebbins *v.* Lathrop, 4 Pick. 33; Hill *v.* Davis, 4 Mass. 137. This section applies to executors having custody of a will as to other persons. Com. Rep. 1831, c. 63, note; Stat. 1875, c. 210.

[3] See Appendix, form No. 10.

[4] Ibid. Nos. 11, 12.   [5] Ibid. No. 13.

If the person cited refuses to appear and submit to examination, or to answer such interrogatories as are lawfully propounded to him, or to obey any lawful order, the judge may commit him to the jail, there to remain in close custody until he submits to the order of the court.[1] All such interrogatories and answers must be in writing, and signed by the party examined, and filed in the probate court ; but the person examined cannot be required to criminate himself.

On such complaint the judge in his discretion may award costs to be paid by either party, and may issue execution therefor.[2]

The will, after being admitted to probate, remains on the files of the probate office, except that, after the expiration of thirty days from the probate decree, upon the petition of the executor, or of any person interested in the estate of the testator, after such notice thereof as the court shall require and hearing had thereon, the court may permit the original will to be taken from the files of such court, if it shall appear that such original will is necessary to be used in any foreign country for the purpose of establishing the right or title of such executor, legatee, or person to the estate of the testator therein, and to use the will for that purpose.[3]

[1] See Appendix, form No. 14.   [2] Gen. Sts. c. 92, §§ 17, 18.
[3] Stat. 1876, c. 165.

CHAPTER IV.

AN executor is the person to whom the testator has confided the trust of administering his estate, according to his last will and testament. He can derive his office only from a testamentary appointment confirmed by a decree of the probate court. The appointment is generally made by express words contained in the will, but it may be made constructively by other than express words. The form of petition for the probate of a will in common use, made by the executor named in the will, prays that administration be granted to him; and when the will has been proved and allowed, letters testamentary are issued to him, provided that he is legally competent for the office and gives bond for the discharge of the trust as required by law.

WHO MAY BE EXECUTORS.

Any person may be nominated as executor, but all persons are not legally competent to act in that office. A minor or an infant *ventre sa mere* may be nominated in the will; but if at the time of proving the will the executor named therein is not of full age, administration with the will annexed is granted to some other person during his minority, unless there is another executor nominated in the will who accepts the trust, in which case such other executor administers until the minor arrives at full age : he can then by giving bond be admitted as joint executor.[1] If the executor named in the will is physically or mentally incapacitated, administration is granted to some other person. Any objection that would cause the removal of an executor is sufficient to prevent the confirmation of his appointment by the court.[2]

A married woman may be an executrix, administratrix, guardian, or trustee, and bind herself and the estate she represents, without her husband joining in any conveyance or instrument whatever, and be bound in the same manner and with the same effect in all respects as if she was sole.[3]

EXECUTORS TO GIVE BOND.

General Bond. The executor, before letters testamentary are issued to him, is required to give bond with sufficient surety or sureties, in such sum as the judge of the probate court shall order, payable to the judge and his successor, with condition to return to the probate court, within three months, a true inventory of the estate of the deceased ; to administer according to law and the will of the testator, all the personal estate and the proceeds of all real estate sold for the payment of debts and legacies ;[4] and to render upon oath a just and true account of his administration within one year, and at any other time when required by the court. When two or more persons are appointed executors, none can intermeddle or act as such but those who give bond.[5]

[1] Gen. Sts. c. 93, § 7.

[2] As to removals, see *post*, chap. viii.　　　[3] Stat. 1874, c. 184.

[4] But he may be exempted by the court from giving bond for the proceeds of sales of real estate, except when authorized to sell it. Gen. Sts. c. 101, § 13.

[5] Gen Sts. c. 93, § 2. As to bonds, generally, see *post*, chap. xix.

Bond when the Executor is Residuary Legatee. If it appears to the judge that the bond above described is not necessary for the protection of any person interested in the estate, he may permit an executor, *who is residuary legatee,* instead of giving such bond, to give a bond with condition to pay all debts and legacies of the testator, and such sums as may be allowed by the probate court for necessaries to the widow or minor children; and in such case he is not required to return an inventory.[1]

An executor therefore, who is residuary legatee, may give a bond in the common form, which requires him to return an inventory of the estate; or he may be excused the labor and expense of making an inventory by giving bond to pay debts, legacies, and allowances. It is at his own option to give one or the other. The reason of this indulgence is, that as he is residuary legatee, no person can have an interest in procuring evidence of the assets except the creditors, legatees, and family of the deceased; and if he binds himself to pay all their claims, the amount of the assets is of no concern to any person except himself. But if he chooses to bind himself to pay the debts and legacies, he must abide by the consequences of his election. He must fulfil the condition of his bond, whether the assets are sufficient for the purpose or not. The condition of the bond is not to pay if there are assets, but to pay at all events. By giving such a bond he conclusively admits assets, and the admission will bind him and his sureties, even if the estate proves insolvent.[2] If, on the other hand, he gives a

---

[1] Gen. Sts. c. 93, § 3.

[2] Colwell *v.* Alger, 5 Gray, 67. In a suit to recover a legacy, the plaintiff need not give any proof, except such bond, that the executor has assets in his hands. Jones *v.* Richardson, 5 Met. 247.

A bond to pay debts and legacies, given by an executor who is

bond in the common form and returns an inventory, he
will be responsible for the assets, but no further. When
the executor knows that the estate is sufficient to meet
all the claims against it, with the charges of administration and the allowances made to the widow and children
of the testator, he may safely give a bond to pay the
debts and legacies; but where there is any doubt whatever of the sufficiency of assets, he should give bond in
the common form and return an inventory.[1]

An administrator with the will annexed gives a bond
in like manner and with like condition as is required of
an executor. If such administrator is residuary legatee, the court may permit him to give a bond to pay
debts and legacies, with like effect, as though he was
nominated executor in the will.[2]

When no Sureties are required. Executors are exempted from giving a surety or sureties in their bonds,
when the testator has ordered or requested such exemption, or that no bond should be taken, or when all the
persons interested in the estate who are of full age and
legal capacity, other than creditors, certify to the court
their consent thereto; but not until all creditors of the
estate, and the guardian of any minor interested therein,
have been notified, and had opportunity to show cause
against the same.[3] The judge, however, may, at or be-

---

residuary legatee, who has thus been excused from returning an inventory within three months, cannot, after the expiration of a year and a
half, be cancelled or surrendered by the probate court, or supreme court.
Alger *v.* Colwell, 2 Gray, 404.

[1] The giving of the bond to pay debts and legacies does not discharge
the lien on the real estate of the testator for the payment of his debts,
except on such part as shall have been sold by the executor to a purchaser
in good faith and for a valuable consideration; all estate not so sold may
be taken on execution by any creditor not otherwise satisfied, in like manner as if a bond had been given in the other form. Gen. Sts. c. 93, § 4.

[2] Stat. 1870, c. 285.

[3] Notice by publication in a newspaper is sufficient. Wells *v.* Child, 12

fore the granting of letters testamentary, require bond with sufficient surety or sureties, if he is of opinion that the same is required by a change in the situation or circumstances of the executor, or for other sufficient cause.[1]

Whenever an appointment of an executor, administrator, guardian, or trustee, shall be vacated or declared void by reason of any irregularity, or want of jurisdiction or authority of the court making the same, the person so appointed such executor, administrator, guardian, or trustee, shall be held to account for all money, property, or assets, which shall have come to his hands as executor, administrator, guardian, or trustee, or by reason of such appointment, in the same manner as if the appointment had been regular and valid; and any bond given in pursuance of such appointment shall be held to be valid and binding, both on the principals and sureties, for that purpose.

Payments made to or by such person as executor, administrator, guardian, or trustee, if in other respects properly made, may, with the approval of the probate court, be ratified and confirmed by the executor, administrator, guardian, or trustee, who may be afterwards legally appointed.[2]

" Whenever the authority or validity of any act or proceeding of a person acting as executor, administrator, guardian, or trustee, shall be called in question by reason of any alleged irregularity, defective notice, or want of authority in such person, any party interested in or affected by the same may apply to the probate court having jurisdiction of the subject-matter in respect to

---

Allen, 330. A bond without surety approved by the probate court, without notice to creditors, is not such a bond as the statute requires; and the statute of limitations against executors will not begin to run from the filing of such a bond. Abercrombie v. Sheldon, 8 Allen, 532.

[1] Gen. Sts. c. 93, § 5.   [2] Stat. 1873, c. 253.

which the act or proceeding in question has been had; and the court, after notice to all parties interested, may hear and determine the matter, and confirm the act or proceeding in whole or in part, and authorize and empower the executor, administrator, guardian, or trustee, aforesaid, or any successor or other person who may be legally appointed to act in the same capacity, to ratify and confirm the same, and to execute and deliver such deeds, releases, conveyances, or other instruments, as may be found necessary for that purpose, provided that no act or proceeding which the court might not have authorized in the first instance, upon proper application, duly made, shall be so confirmed under any construction or authority of this act." [1]

If a person appointed executor refuses to accept the trust, or, after being duly cited for that purpose, neglects to appear and accept the same, or neglects for twenty days after probate of the will to give bond, letters testamentary are granted to the other executors, if there are any capable and willing to accept the trust; and if there are none, or if the executors are dead, or none are named in the will, administration of the estate with the will annexed is granted to such persons as would have been entitled thereto if the deceased had died intestate; but after the expiration of the twenty days, and before letters testamentary or of administration are granted, the court may grant letters testamentary to any person appointed executor who gives the bond prescribed by law. [2]

[1] Stat. 1874, c. 346.   [2] Gen. Sts. c. 93, § 6.

CHAPTER V.

WHEN a person dies, not having disposed of his property by will, he is said to die *intestate*, and the law prescribes the manner in which his estate may be settled, and the rights of all persons interested secured.

IN WHAT CASES ADMINISTRATION IS GRANTED.

Administration may be granted by the probate court for each county of the estates of persons who at the time of their decease were inhabitants of or resident in such county.[1]

Administration de bonis non. If a sole administrator dies before he completes the trust committed to him, or is removed by the court, or resigns, administration *de bonis non* (of the estate not administered) will be granted, provided there is personal estate left unadministered to the amount of twenty dollars, or debts to that amount are remaining due from the estate.[2]

Administration with the will annexed. In certain cases administration is granted of testate estates; where the testator omits to name an executor in his will, or when the only executor named in the will is dead, or refuses to accept the trust, or after being cited for that

---

[1] Gen. Sts. c. 117, § 2.   [2] Ibid. c. 101, § 1.

purpose does not appear,[1] or fails to give bond for twenty days after probate of the will,[2] or is a minor,[3] or otherwise legally incompetent. In such cases administration with the will annexed is granted.

Administration de bonis non with the will annexed. When a sole executor or administrator with the will annexed dies after entering upon the duties of his trust and before it is discharged; or is removed by the court; or resigns, administration *de bonis non* with the will annexed is granted, provided there is personal estate not administered to the amount of twenty dollars, or debts to that amount are remaining due from the estate, or that there is any thing remaining to be performed in execution of the will.[4]

Special Administration. At any time and place, the judge of a probate court, having jurisdiction of the matter, may, in his discretion, appoint a special administrator to collect and preserve the effects and estate of a deceased person, and deliver the same to whoever shall be appointed administrator, or other person entitled thereto.[5]

Ancillary Administration. When a citizen of another State or country dies leaving estate to be administered in this State, administration of such estate may be granted here.[6] In such case, the administration granted

---

[1] Gen. Sts. c. 93, § 6.   [2] Ibid.   [3] Ibid. § 7.
[4] Ibid. c. 101, § 1.   [5] Stat. 1876, c. 200.

[6] A debt due the deceased from an inhabitant of this State is estate that may be administered here. Piquet, appellant, 5 Pick. 65; Emery v. Hildreth, 2 Gray, 231. So are articles of furniture and plate, though of small value; any thing corresponding to *bona notabilia* in England would be sufficient for that purpose. Harrington v. Brown, 5 Pick. 521. When a debtor takes up his residence in this State, after the death of the creditor in another State, administration on the creditor's estate will be granted in this State; and so when goods are brought into this State.

here is treated as merely ancillary or auxiliary to the principal administration granted in the jurisdiction where the deceased dwelt.   The appointment, however, of an administrator in the State where the deceased had his domicile is not a necessary prerequisite to the granting of such ancillary administration ; but administration of the estate in this State may be granted, although no administrator has been appointed in the foreign State; and even if the deceased left a will, which has never been offered for probate in the place of his domicile.[1]

WITHIN WHAT TIME ADMINISTRATION MUST BE APPLIED FOR.

Administration is not *originally* granted after the expiration of twenty years from the death of the intestate, except when property accrues to the estate, or belonging to the estate first comes to the knowledge of any person interested therein after that time, in which case original administration may be granted on such property at any time within five years next after it so accrues or becomes known ; but such administration can affect no other property.[2]

But if administration has once been granted, and left unfinished by the death, removal, or resignation of the

Dawes *v.* Boylston, 9 Mass. 337 ; Wheelock *v.* Pierce, 6 Cush. 288 ; Pinney *v.* McGregory, 102 Mass. 186. *Prima facie* evidence that a deceased non-resident had conveyed real estate in this State, in fraud of his creditors, is sufficient to warrant the grant of administration here. Bowdoin *v.* Holland, 10 Cush. 17.   See Crosby *v.* Leavitt, 4 Allen, 410.

[1] Bowdoin *v.* Holland, 10 Cush. 17.

[2] Gen. Sts. c. 94, §§ 3, 4.   If a creditor who has failed to receive his dividend from an insolvent estate has deceased, an administrator may be appointed to receive and administer said dividend, although more than twenty years have elapsed since the creditor's death.   Ibid. c. 99, § 28.

executor or administrator, administration *de bonis non* may be granted after the expiration of twenty years. There is no statute limiting the time of granting administration of estates left unadministered by a former executor or administrator.[1]

IN WHAT COUNTY ADMINISTRATION MUST BE APPLIED FOR.

The petition for administration must be presented to the probate court of the county of which the deceased was an inhabitant or in which he was resident at the time of his death.[2]

If the deceased person died without the State, application must be made to the probate court of the county in which he left estate to be administered.[3]

TO WHOM ORIGINAL ADMINISTRATION IS GRANTED.

The statute [4] provides that —

" Administration of the estate of an intestate shall be granted to some one or more of the persons hereinafter mentioned; and they shall be entitled thereto as follows: —

" First. His widow, or next of kin, or both, as the probate court shall deem fit; and if they do not either take or renounce the administration, they shall, if resident within the county, be cited by the court for that purpose."

---

[1] Bancroft *v.* Andrews, 6 Cush. 493.

[2] Gen. Sts. c. 117, § 2. As to jurisdiction of the probate courts depending on the question of residence, see *ante*, page 50, notes.

[3] Pinney *v.* McGregory, 102 Mass. 186.

[4] Gen. Sts. c. 94, § 1.

"Second.   If the persons so entitled are incompetent, or evidently unsuitable for the discharge of the trust, or if they neglect without sufficient cause for thirty days after the death of the intestate to take administration of his estate, the probate court shall commit administration to one or more of the principal creditors, if there is any competent and willing to undertake the trust."

The policy of granting administration to those most directly interested in the estate of the deceased has been long established.   The statute 31 Edw. III. c. 11, which first took from the clergy their exclusive right to administer, provided that "the ordinaries shall depute of the next and most lawful friends of the dead person intestate to administer his goods;" and the statute 21 Henry VIII. c. 5, provided that administration should be granted "to the widow of the deceased, or to the next of his kin, or to both, as by discretion of the same ordinary shall be thought good."   This language of the statute Henry VIII. was followed in our statute of 1783 (c. 36), and still stands without material change.

Who are next of Kin.   In this State, the degrees of kindred are computed according to the rules of the civil law, which makes the deceased person the point from whence the degrees are numbered.   Thus, a man's parents are related to him in the first degree, and so are his children.   Both are equally near, but in granting administration the children, if competent, are preferred, they having a more direct interest in the estate.   A grandson is in the same degree of kindred to the intestate as the intestate's brother, but is preferred for the same reason.

Kindred are lineal or collateral.   Lineal consanguinity is that subsisting between persons who are all in a direct line of descent, one from the other, as between

son, father, and grandfather; or father, son, and grandson, reckoning either upwards or downwards. Collateral kinsmen are those who are descended from one
common ancestor, but not one from the other. A man
and his cousins are collateral relations; they both descend from the same grandfather, but not lineally.

The next lineal kindred of an intestate are easily ascertained by counting either directly upwards or directly
downwards to his nearest living relative. His father
and son are both in the first degree; his grandfather
and grandson both in the second. The nearness of a
collateral kinsman to the intestate is ascertained by
counting upwards to the common ancestor of both, and
then following the branch downwards until the collateral kinsman is reached, reckoning one degree for each
person. Thus, the intestate's brother is in the second
degree; this is seen by counting upwards to their father,
their common ancestor, one degree, and then downwards, collaterally, one degree, to the brother. The
intestate's uncle is in the third degree, and so is his
nephew. His cousin is in the fourth.

Following this computation of kindred, and observing
the preferences arising from interest, administration of
the estate of an intestate will be granted to his next of
kin in the following order: first, to children; second, if
there are no children. to parents; third, if there are no
children nor parents, to brothers and sisters, either of
the whole or half blood; fourth. to grandparents; fifth,
to nephews, nieces, uncles, aunts; sixth, to cousins.
No distinction is made between kindred on the father's
or mother's side. They are all in equal degree of kindred, and hence it may happen that there are persons
equally related to the intestate and equally entitled to the
administration, who are not related at all to each other.

As to the Right of the Widow and next of Kin to administer. The statute does not give the widow an *exclusive* right to administer her husband's estate if there are next of kin who also claim the right, and are suitable persons. The right is first in the widow *and* next of kin, either or both, as the court may deem fit ; and the personal suitableness of the widow and next of kin is to be considered in making the appointment. If the widow is evidently unsuitable, the next of kin, if competent, is entitled to the sole administration. If the next of kin is unsuitable, she, if competent, may take administration alone. If both are suitable, the court may grant administration to either, or jointly to both ; and if both are unsuitable, the application of both will be refused.

And where there are several persons equally entitled to take administration as next of kin, and equally suitable, the probate court has power to appoint one or more of them.

If the widow and next of kin, as is often the case, renounce the administration, their renunciation does not give them a *right* to nominate a substitute.[1] There may be creditors whose right to administer under the statute is prior to that of any such substitute. But where there are no creditors who are suitable, or if the creditors refuse, after being cited, to take the administration, any suitable person will generally be appointed on the recommendation of the widow and next of kin.

Nor will the renunciation of the next of kin, or the fact of their incompetency, give to other relatives of the intestate any *right* to administer. The preference made by the statute is of the *next* of kin, and if they decline, or are unsuitable, creditors are preferred to other kindred.

---

[1] Cobb *v.* Newcomb, 19 Pick. 337.

As to the suitableness of the Widow or next of Kin.
The question of suitableness must depend, in some
measure, upon the facts of each case.[1] A person may
be entirely suitable to administer when little more than
some formal proceeding is necessary for the settlement
of the estate, and may be unsuitable when the duties to
be discharged are of a different character. The object
of administration is to dispose of the estate of the intestate so as to secure the rights of creditors and make the
best provision possible, under the circumstances, for the
kin of the deceased. A person of unsound mind is of
course unsuitable for such a trust, and so is a person
whose relation to the estate is such as to create the presumption that he would not administer with a due regard to the rights of those interested in the estate. The
fact that one of several next of kin is also a creditor of
the estate, is rather adverse to, than in favor of, his being
preferred. So, if he owes the estate, especially when
the balance due has not been definitely ascertained. A
man who is accustomed to business details is more suitable for the office of administrator than one who is not.
Unsuitableness may be occasioned by physical debility,
want of memory, or any infirmity which would prevent
the efficient discharge of the duties required. In deter-

---

[1] It has been held that the widow may be set aside, if she has barred
herself of all interest in her husband's personal estate, by her marriage
settlement, or has eloped from her husband, or lived separate from him.
If she has been divorced, *a mensa et thoro*, she forfeits, it should seem, her
right to administer. 1 Wms. Ex. (5th Am. ed.) 363.

Where, upon the application of the widow, it appeared that she was
under the influence of a person who was indebted to the estate in a large
amount, and who was charged with combining with the intestate in his
lifetime to defraud his creditors, and that such application was made at
the request of such debtor and not to protect or subserve the interests of
the widow, it was held that she was an unsuitable person to administer.
Stearns *v.* Fisk, 18 Pick. 24.

mining the question of suitableness, the relations of the
applicant to the estate and to the other parties interested,
the character of the duties which the condition of the
estate will be likely to require of the administrator, and
his personal fitness for those duties, are to be considered.
A minor cannot administer.[1] A citizen of another State
or country, if otherwise suitable, may be appointed to
administer in this State.

The fact that one who is personally unsuitable is ready
to give bond with sufficient sureties for the faithful discharge of his trust, does not make him suitable. The
remedy of parties damaged by his official misconduct, by
action on his bond, may subject them to expense of liti-
gation for which they can have no legal adequate remedy; and besides, an administrator, if so disposed, may
prejudice the interests of parties concerned without being exposed to any action.[2]

As to the Right of Creditors to administer. If the
widow and next of kin are incompetent, or evidently
unsuitable, or if they neglect for thirty days after the
intestate's death to take administration of his estate, the
court grants administration to one or more of the principal creditors. This right is given to the creditor under
such circumstances, in order that the collection of his
claim may not be defeated for want of an administrator.
The creditor applying must satisfy the court that he is
a creditor, and this he may do by exhibiting his books
of account or other evidences of debt. The amount of
his claim seems not to be material,[3] but the claim must
be one which by law survives.[4] The creditor cannot be

---

[1] McGooch *v.* McGooch, 4 Mass. 348. [2] Stearns *v.* Fisk, 18 Pick. 27.
[3] Arnold *v.* Sabin, 1 Cush. 525. In this case the claim of the creditor
who was appointed was for *fifty-eight cents.*
[4] Smith *v.* Sherman, 4 Cush. 408; Stebbins *v.* Palmer, 1 Pick. 71.

appointed, however, until after the widow and next of kin have been cited, and had opportunity either to take or renounce the administration. The same considerations as to personal suitableness apply to a creditor who petitions for a grant of administration as to one next of kin. If the deceased left no widow, husband, or next of kin in this State, administration is granted to a public administrator in preference to creditors.

As to the Right of other Persons to administer. The statute regulating the granting of administration further provides : —

" 3d. If there is no such creditor, administration shall be granted to such other person as the court shall deem fit ; provided, —

" 4th. That if the deceased was a married woman, administration of her estate shall in all cases be granted to her husband, if competent and willing to undertake the trust,[1] unless by force of a marriage settlement or otherwise she has made some testamentary disposition of her separate estate, or some other provision, which renders it necessary or proper to appoint some other person to administer her estate ; and

" 5th. If the deceased leaves no widow, husband, or next of kin, in this State, administration shall be granted to a public administrator in preference to creditors."

When Administration is granted to a Public Administrator. The statute provides for the appointment in each county of one or more public administrators, and makes it the duty of such administrator to administer

---

[1] If the marriage was voidable, the husband will be entitled to administration, unless sentence of nullity was pronounced before her death. If it was void from the beginning, he is not entitled to administer. 1 Wms. Ex. (5th Am. ed.) 357.

upon the estate of any person who dies intestate within his county, or dies elsewhere, leaving property in such county to be administered, and not leaving a known husband, widow, or heir in this State. But the administration will not be granted to the public administrator when the husband, widow, or any heir of the deceased claims in writing the right of administering, or requests the appointment of some other suitable person, if such husband, widow, heir, or other person accepts the trust and gives bond; and such husband, widow, heir, or other person may be appointed after letters of administration have been granted to a public administrator, and before the final settlement of the estate. Upon such appointment of a successor the power of the public administrator over the estate ceases.[1]

TO WHOM OTHER THAN ORIGINAL ADMINISTRATION IS GRANTED.

Neither the widow nor next of kin have a *right to claim* the grant of administration *de bonis non*.[2] The priority of right to administer is regulated entirely by statute, and a distinction in this particular is made between original and other administration. It is provided, in case of the death or resignation of the original executor or administrator, without having fully administered the estate, that administration *de bonis non* may be granted "to some suitable person;"[3] and in case of the removal of the executor or administrator, "to such person as shall be deemed fit."[4]

These provisions, while they do not exclude any person from the administration, give the probate court

---

[1] Gen. Sts. c. 95, §§ 1–4.
[2] Russell v. Hoar, 3 Met. 190.
[3] Gen. Sts. c. 101, §§ 1, 5.
[4] Ibid. § 2.

full discretion in the selection of the new administrator. In some cases where administration with the will annexed is granted, the next of kin may have no interest in the estate. They may take nothing under the provisions of the will, or their legacies may have been paid to them by the original executor. In such cases, the residuary legatee, or other person interested under the will, is entitled to administer, the general policy of the law in granting administration being to give the management of the property to the person who has the beneficial interest in it.

PROCEEDINGS IN PROBATE COURT. — PRACTICE.

The Petition. The person claiming administration must apply by petition in writing to the probate court having jurisdiction of the case.[1] The petition should set forth the fact of the death of the person whose estate is to be administered, the time of his death, the county of which he was last an inhabitant, or in which he was resident, and the grounds on which the petitioner claims the right to administer. The petition should also state the name and residence of the widow, if any, of the deceased, and the names, residences, and degree of kindred of his next of kin. If the next of kin are minors, the fact should be stated. If the petition is by a creditor, the fact that the widow and next of kin have neglected for thirty days since the intestate's death to take administration should be stated.

If the petition is for the appointment of a special administrator, the reasons for which letters testamentary or of administration are delayed, whether in consequence

---

[1] As to jurisdiction, see *ante*, pages 60, 76.

of a suit concerning the proof of a will, or other cause, should be stated in the petition.

If the petitioner is a stranger to the estate, the reasons upon which he bases his application should be fully stated.

When a public administrator petitions, the fact that the deceased left no husband, widow, or heir in this State should be set forth.

If the petition is for other than original administration it should set forth the fact of the death, resignation, or removal of the executor or original administrator; and it should also appear from the petition that there is personal estate of the deceased remaining to be administered to the amount of twenty dollars, or that there are debts to that amount remaining due from the estate, or that something remains to be performed in execution of the will.[1]

Notice to Persons interested. The next step in the proceedings is the notification of all persons interested of the pendency of the petition. This is absolutely necessary when the petitioner is a creditor or other person than the husband, widow, or next of kin of the deceased, unless all persons having an equal or prior right to administer assent to the appointment of the petitioner, or renounce their right. The neglect of the widow and next of kin for thirty days after the intestate's death to take administration does not render their citation the less necessary, although a literal construction of the statute would seem to indicate otherwise.[2] The citation need not be personally served upon the widow and next of kin. It may be difficult in many cases to ascertain who are the next of kin, and if per-

[1] As to petitions for administration, see Appendix, forms Nos. 15–25.
[2] Arnold v. Sabin, 1 Cush. 525.

sonal service was required the proceedings would necessarily be attended with uncertainty and delay. The statute does not define the manner in which the citation shall be served, but leaves it to the discretion of the court. Ordinarily, publication of a general notice to all parties interested will be a sufficient citation. Any person interested in the estate may appear and show cause for or against the appointment of the person named in the petition.

If the person or persons whose right to administer is prior or equal to the petitioners renounce administration in writing, the delay and expense of a citation may be avoided. But if the person having such prior claim comes into court and verbally declines to take administration, it is not enough. The renunciation, to be effectual, must be recorded, and should therefore be made in writing in all cases.[1]

As to Proof of the Death. The questions usually raised in cases where the petitioner's appointment is contested relate to his suitableness for the trust, or to the priority of his right. It is not often that any doubt exists of the death of the person whose estate is the subject of the petition, but such cases occur where the long-continued absence of the person, without being heard of, renders his death probable, though the fact cannot be proved. After the lapse of seven years, without intelligence concerning him, the law presumes that he is dead, and administration is granted accordingly.[2] It must appear, however, that he has not been heard from by persons who would have been likely to hear from him, if living, or that ineffectual search has been made

---

[1] Arnold v. Sabin, 1 Cush. 525 ; and see Stebbins v. Lathrop, 4 Pick. 44.

[2] See Jochumsen v. Suffolk Savings-Bank, 3 Allen, 87.

for such a person. But though the presumption of death does not attach to the mere lapse of time, short of seven years, the fact of death may be found from a shorter period, when other circumstances concur; as, if the party sailed on a voyage which should long since have been accomplished, and the vessel has not been heard from ; under such circumstances administration has been granted after the lapse of one year.[1]

Administrator's Bonds. The appointment of the administrator or administrators is made complete by the approval of the bond required of them by statute. The bond must be with sufficient sureties, in such sum as the judge of the probate court orders, payable to the judge and his successors, and with condition, in the case of an original administrator, to return into the probate court within three months a true inventory of all the estate of the deceased ; to administer according to law all the personal estate and the proceeds of all real estate sold for the payment of debts ; to render upon oath an account of his administration within one year, and at any other times when required by the probate court ; to pay any balance remaining in his hands upon the settlement of his accounts to such persons as the court shall direct ; and to deliver his letters of administration into the probate court in case any will of the deceased is thereafter proved and allowed. The condition of the bond required of an administrator *de bonis non* is the same as that of an administrator originally appointed.

Administrators with the will annexed, and adminis-

---

[1] Administration was granted in January, 1858, on the estate of A., who sailed from Liverpool in January, 1857, for Valparaiso ; the voyage should have been made in ten weeks ; nothing had been heard of the ship. *Held,* that payment by the underwriters of the amount for which the ship was insured was very strong evidence in support of the petition for administration. In the Goods of Main, 1 Swabey & Tris. 11.

trators *de bonis non* with the will annexed, are required
to give bond with condition to return an inventory of
the estate within three months ; to administer according
to law and the will of the deceased all the personal
estate, and the proceeds of all real estate sold for the
payment of debts and legacies ; and to render an account
upon oath within one year, and at any other times when
required by the court.[1]

The bond of a special administrator is conditioned to
return an inventory within such time as the judge shall
order : to account on oath for all the goods, chattels,
debts, and effects of the deceased that shall be received
by him as such special administrator, whenever required
by the probate court ; and to deliver the same to whoever shall be appointed executor or administrator of the
deceased, or to such other person as shall be lawfully
entitled to receive the same.[2]

A public administrator may give a separate bond for
every estate which he is called upon to administer, or he
may give a general bond for the faithful administration
of all estates on which administration is granted to him
as public administrator. His separate bond is the same
as that required of other original administrators, with
the further condition, that if an executor or administrator is appointed as his successor in any case, to surrender
his letters of administration into the probate court, with
an account of his doings therein, and to pay over to his
successor all property of the deceased not administered.[3]
His general bond is conditioned to return into the probate court, within three months from the time letters of
administration are granted to him on the estate of any

---

[1] An administrator with the will annexed who is residuary legatee
may give bond to pay debts and legacies. Stat. 1870, c. 285.

[2] Stat. 1876, c. 200.   [3] Ibid. c. 95, § 6.

person deceased, a true inventory of the estate of such
person; to administer according to law the personal
estate of such person, and the proceeds of all real estate
sold for payment of debts; to render an account of his
administration of every such estate within one year from
the date of his letters of administration thereon, and at
least once in each year until the trust is fulfilled, and at
any other times when required by the probate court; to
pay the balance of every such estate remaining in his
hands upon the settlement of his accounts to such persons as the probate court shall direct, and when such
estate is fully administered to deposit the whole amount
remaining in his hands with the treasurer of the Commonwealth; to deliver the letters of administration on
the estate of any person into the probate court, in case
a will of such person is thereafter proved and allowed,
and upon the appointment of a successor as administrator of any estate, to surrender his letters of administration,
with an account on oath of his doings, and upon a just
settlement of his accounts to pay over to his successor
all property of the deceased not administered.[1]

But any administrator may be exempted from giving
bond for the proceeds of sales of real estate, except
when authorized to make such sales.[2]

Upon the approval of the bond by the judge of the
probate court, letters of administration issue to the person appointed, who may forthwith proceed in the execution of his trust unless an appeal is taken from the
decree making the appointment. But a *special* administrator may proceed notwithstanding an appeal is taken.[3]

---

[1] Gen. Sts. c. 95, § 7.   [2] Ibid. c. 101, § 13.
[3] Ibid. c. 94, § 6.

CHAPTER VI.

APPOINTMENT OF GUARDIANS.

THE probate court in each county, when it appears necessary or convenient, may appoint guardians to minors and others being inhabitants of, or residents in, the same county, and to such as reside out of this State and have any estate within the same.[1]

OF MINORS.

A father is the guardian by nature of his infant child; and on his death, the mother; the natural guardian has custody of the infant's person, but cannot act in matters relating to the infant's estate. If therefore an infant acquires property by inheritance or otherwise, the appointment of a guardian may be as necessary during the lifetime of the father as after his decease.

If the minor is under the age of fourteen years, the probate court may nominate and appoint his guardian. If he is above that age, he may nominate his own guardian, but his choice is not conclusive upon the court. If in the opinion of the court the person nominated is not suitable for the trust, the court will reject him; and if the infant will not choose a proper person, the court will nominate and appoint a guardian. If the minor resides without the State, or, after being cited, he

---

[1] Gen. Sts. c. 109, § 1.

neglects to nominate a suitable person, the court may appoint his guardian as if he were under the age of fourteen years.[1]

The minor, for whom a guardian has been appointed, may, on his arrival at the age of fourteen years, nominate a new guardian, but such nomination does not, as of right, vacate the appointment previously made. His choice will be sanctioned or not, as the discretion of the court shall direct.

The guardian of a minor has the custody and tuition of his ward, and the care and management of all his estate, and, unless sooner discharged according to law, continues in office until the minor arrives at the age of twenty-one years. But the father of the minor, if living, and in case of his death, the mother, they being respectively competent to transact their own business, and fit persons for the trust, are entitled to the custody of the person of the minor and the care of his education.[2]

Who are suitable for the Trust. — A guardian, having the control of the estate of his ward, should possess the qualifications necessary to its judicious management. The interests of the ward sometimes render necessary the sale of the estate, or portions of it, and a new investment of the proceeds; a proper discharge of the trust in such cases can be best promoted by the appointment of a guardian of business experience. In case of the death or unfitness of the minor's parents, the guardian has the custody and tuition of his ward, and he should therefore be a person not indifferent to the happiness of his ward, and competent to direct his education.

It is advisable, when practicable, that the guardian-

<hr/>

[1] Gen. Sts. c. 109, § 2.
[2] Ibid. § 4; Stat. 1871, c. 110; Stat. 1873, c. 307.

ship be given to some person whose natural affection for the ward will prompt him to the faithful discharge of his trust, for it often occurs that the minor's sole security is in the affection, or the personal integrity, of his guardian. The sureties on a guardian's bond, though entirely sufficient at the time they sign it, may prove, when the minor arrives at full age — perhaps at the end of ten or fifteen years — to be bankrupt as well as their principal; and in such case, if the guardian is dishonest, the minor is without remedy. The court can, of course, order the guardian to file a bond with new sureties at any time; but it is sometimes the fact that the only person living who can be expected to interest himself in the welfare of the ward, is the guardian who is wronging him, and thus the insufficiency of the bond may not be brought to the notice of the court until it is too late.

An administrator ought not, while he is engaged in the settlement of an estate, to be appointed guardian of a minor who is an heir to the same estate, unless there are decided personal reasons for the appointment. The two trusts are incompatible. It is the duty of the guardian to inspect the proceedings of the administrator, to examine his accounts, and to cause him to be cited if he is negligent in his administration. It is obvious that these essential duties might not be discharged when both the administration and guardianship were in the hands of the same person.

Testamentary Guardians. — A father by his last will in writing may appoint guardians for his children, whether born at the time of making the will or afterwards, to continue during the minority of the child or a less time. Such testamentary guardian has the same powers, and performs the same duties with regard to the person and estate of the ward, as a guardian appointed by the probate court. But a testator can appoint a guardian for his own children only. He cannot appoint guardians for other children, although he gives them his property.[1]

The Petition for the appointment of a minor under the age of fourteen years is usually made by the father or mother of the minor, if either of them are living ; if they are not living, by some relative or friend of the minor. If the petition is by any person other than a parent, the assent of the parents, or the survivor of them, to the appointment prayed for should be indorsed on the petition. If both parents are dead, such assent may be given by the next of kin ; or if there are no known next of kin, by the persons who have the care of the minor. When such assent is expressed, the appointment prayed for is usually made at once ; otherwise, a citation is issued to parties interested before any appointment is made. The petition should state the full name of the minor, the date of his birth, his residence, the full name and last place of residence of his father, and the ground upon which the petitioner claims the appointment.[2]

If the petition is for the appointment of some person other than a parent of the minor, and alleges the unfitness of the parents to have the custody of the child, the appointment prayed for cannot be made until after notice to the parents or surviving parent, and a hearing.[3]

If the minor is above the age of fourteen years, he may appear in court and nominate his guardian, or he may make his nomination before a justice of the peace, or the city or town clerk. In such cases, the petition may be made by the person nominated by the minor, and a certificate of the fact of the nomination should be

---

[1] Gilbert *v.* Hebard, 8 Met. 127 ; Wardwell *v.* Wardwell, 9 Allen, 518.
[2] See Appendix, forms Nos. 26–28.   [3] Stat. 1873, c. 367.

indorsed on the petition by the justice or clerk before whom it is made.[1] If the minor neglects to nominate a guardian, any person interested may petition.[2]

OF INSANE PERSONS AND SPENDTHRIFTS.

The probate court may appoint a guardian for an insane person, and for a person who so wastes his property by excessive drinking, gaming, idleness, or debauchery of any kind, as to expose himself or his family to want or suffering, or any place to charge or expense for the support of himself or his family.[3]

The application for the appointment of a guardian of an insane person may be made by the relations and friends of such person, or by the mayor and aldermen or selectmen of the city or town of which such person is an inhabitant or resident.

In the case of a spendthrift, the mayor and aldermen or selectmen of the city or town of which he is an inhabitant or resident, or upon which he is or may become chargeable, may complain to the probate court. The capacity in which the complainants act should be stated in the petition.[4]

In all cases, notice of not less than fourteen days is given to the supposed insane person or spendthrift of the time and place appointed for the hearing.[5] The notice

---

[1] See Appendix, form No. 29.   [2] Ibid. form No. 30.

[3] Gen. Sts. c. 109, §§ 8, 9.

[4] A copy of the complaint against a spendthrift, and of the order of notice thereon, may be filed in the registry of deeds for the county or district ; and if a guardian is appointed on such complaint, all contracts, except for necessaries, and all gifts, sales, and transfers of real or personal estate, made by the spendthrift after such filing of the complaint and order, and before the termination of the guardianship, will be void. Gen. Sts. c. 109, § 10; Chandler v. Simmons, 97 Mass. 508.

[5] Gen. Sts. c. 109, §§ 8, 9.

must be served in the manner directed by the court, and
no appointment can be made until after due service of
the notice.   If the insane person has previously been
under guardianship, and the office of guardian has in any
way become vacant, notice must be given to him before
a new guardian can be appointed ; and he is entitled to
be heard upon the subject of the complaint in like manner as if he had not been under guardianship.[1]

At the time and place named in the citation the complainants and the supposed insane person or spendthrift
will be heard.   Acts of the person complained of at or
near the time of making the complaint may be proved
for the purpose of showing the state of his mind and
his manner of life, but not his acts at a remote period.
If after a full hearing it appears that the person complained of is unable to take care of himself by reason
of insanity, or is so wasteful of his property that a guardian is needed to protect his family or the public, a suitable person will be appointed.

The guardian appointed should not only be a suitable
person in a general sense, but as far as is practicable
should be fitted to discharge the duties rendered necessary by the particular condition and necessities of the
ward.   It is not enough, in every case, that the guardian
is faithful and competent to manage the ward's estate to
advantage ; he should be a person capable of exercising
a proper influence and judicious control over his ward.
The permanent improvement and substantial welfare
of the ward are the main objects of the guardianship ; and
the guardian who has the care and custody of his person
should be personally fitted, by his relations to the ward
and otherwise, to promote these objects.   In many cases,
the determination of the question of suitability may be

---

[1] Allis v. Morton, 4 Gray, 63.

influenced by the wishes of the ward ; for a man may be so insane as to be a fit subject for guardianship, and yet have a sensible opinion and strong feeling as to the person to be placed over him ; and the reasonable wishes of such a person should be consulted by the court.

When a guardian is appointed for an insane person or spendthrift, the court makes an allowance, to be paid by the guardian, for all reasonable expenses incurred by the ward in defending himself against the complaint.[1] Such guardian has the care and custody of the person of his ward and the management of all his estate. He may be discharged by the probate court on the application of the ward or otherwise, when it appears that such guardianship is no longer necessary.[2]

OF PERSONS OUT OF THE STATE.

A guardian may be appointed for a minor insane person or spendthrift residing out of this State, and having estate here, upon the petition of any friend of such person, or any one interested in his estate, in expectancy or otherwise. The application may be made to the probate court of any county in which there is any estate of such absent person,[3] and after such notice to all persons interested as the court shall order, a guardian will be appointed. Such guardian has the same powers and duties with respect to any estate of the ward found within this State, and also with respect to the person of the ward, if he comes to reside therein, as are prescribed to other guardians.[4]

---

[1] Gen. Sts. c. 109, § 11. [2] Ibid. § 26.

[3] If the estate of the person liable to be put under guardianship consists in part of personal property held in trust for him, the probate court of the county where the trustee resides has jurisdiction to appoint the guardian. Clarke v. Cordis, 4 Allen, 466. See Appendix, form No. 81.

[4] Gen. Sts. c. 109, §§ 13, 14.

" In all cases where any guardian and his ward are residents of any other State or territory of the United States, and such ward is entitled to property of any description in this State, when such guardian produces to the probate court of the county in which such property or the principal part thereof is situated, a full and complete transcript from the records of a court of competent jurisdiction in the State or territory in which he and his ward reside, duly exemplified or authenticated, showing that he has been appointed guardian of such ward, and that he has given a bond and security in the State or territory in which he and his ward reside in double the value of the property of such ward, and also showing to such court in this Commonwealth that a removal of the property of such ward will not conflict with the terms or limitations attending the right by which the ward owns the same, then such transcript may be recorded in such court in this Commonwealth, and such guardian shall be entitled to receive letters of guardianship of the estate of such minor from such court in this Commonwealth which shall authorize him to demand, sue for, and recover, any such property, and remove the same to the place of residence of himself and his ward. And such court in this Commonwealth may order any resident guardian, executor, or administrator, having any of the estate of such ward, to deliver the same to such nonresident guardian." [1]

OF MARRIED WOMEN.

The recent statutes allowing married women to hold property to their own use free from the control of their husbands, rendered necessary some provisions for the

[1] Stat. 1875, c. 189.

care of the separate property of minor and insane married women. And it is now provided, that "when a married woman owns property, real or personal, a guardian may be appointed to her for the same causes, and in the same manner, and with the same powers and duties, as if she were sole, except as hereinafter provided. But no guardian shall be so appointed without such notice to her husband as the court may order.

Such guardian shall not have the care, custody, or education of his ward, except in case of the insanity of her husband, or of his abandoning his wife by absenting himself from the State, and making no sufficient provision for her.

Such guardian shall not apply the property of his ward to the maintenance of herself and family while she is married, unless authorized by the probate court on account of the inability of the husband suitably to maintain her or them, or for other cause which the court deems sufficient."[1]

And when a married woman is by reason of insanity incompetent to release her right of dower or right of homestead in her husband's lands, a guardian may be appointed for her in the same manner as if she were sole, with the powers and duties given to guardians of married women owning property, and the husband or any suitable person may be appointed.[2]

The petition for the appointment of a guardian of a married woman should be in the general form prescribed for petitions for guardians of minors and insane persons, as the case may be, and should particularly state the reasons for which the proposed guardianship is necessary.

---

[1] Gen. Sts. c. 108, §§ 16–18.   [2] Ibid. § 19.

GUARDIAN'S BONDS.

Every guardian of a minor appointed by the probate court is required to give bond, with surety or sureties to the judge of the probate court, in such sum as he shall order with condition :

" To make a true inventory of all the real estate, and all the goods, chattels, rights, and credits, of the ward, that shall come to his possession or knowledge, and to return the same into the probate court at such time as the court shall order ;

" To dispose of and manage all such estate and effects according to law and for the best interests of the ward, and faithfully to discharge his trust in relation thereto, and to the custody, education, and maintenance of the ward ;

" To render an account on oath of the property in his hands, including the proceeds of all real estate sold by him, and of the management and disposition of all such property, within one year after his appointment, and as often as once in three years thereafter, and at such other times as the probate court shall direct (but the guardian may be exempted by the probate court from giving bond for the proceeds of sales of real estate except when authorized to make such sales) ;

" And at the expiration of his trust to settle his accounts in the probate court, or with the ward or his legal representatives ; and to pay over and deliver all the estate and effects remaining in his hands or due from him on such settlement to the person or persons lawfully entitled thereto." [1]

A testamentary guardian gives bond with the same condition as if appointed by the court, except that when

[1] Gen. Sts. c. 109, § 16.

the testator has ordered or required in his will that a bond be not given, it is not required, unless from a change in the situation and circumstances of the guardian, or for other sufficient cause, the probate court deems it proper to require it.[1]

The condition of the bond given by the guardian of an insane person or spendthrift is the same as that given by the guardian of a minor, except that the provisions relating to the education of the ward are omitted.[2]

The condition of the bond given by the guardian of a person without the State is the same as is required when the ward lives within the State, except that the provisions respecting the inventory, the disposal of the estate and effects, and the account to be rendered, are confined to such estate and effects as come to his hands in this State; and the provisions respecting the custody of the ward are not applicable, unless he comes to reside within this State.[3]

Upon the approval of his bond by the judge of the probate court, the guardian receives his letter of guardianship, and has full authority to proceed in the discharge of his trust.

---

[1] Gen. Sts. c. 109, § 6.   [2] Ibid. § 12.   [3] Ibid. § 15.

CHAPTER VII.

APPOINTMENT OF TRUSTEES. — TRUSTS.

IN WHAT CASES TRUSTEES MAY BE APPOINTED.

IF in a will the testator has omitted to appoint a trustee in this Commonwealth, and if such appointment is necessary to carry into effect the provisions of the will, the probate court may, after notice to all persons interested, appoint a trustee who shall have the same powers, rights, and duties, and in whom the estate shall vest in like manner as if he had been originally appointed by the testator.[1]

And when a trustee under a written instrument declines, resigns, dies, or is removed before the objects thereof are accomplished, if no adequate provision is made therein for supplying the vacancy, the probate court, after notice to all persons interested, may appoint a new trustee to act alone or jointly with the others, as the case may be.[2] Such new trustee, upon giving the bonds and security required, has the same powers, rights, and duties, whether as a sole or joint trustee, as if he had been originally appointed; and the trust estate

[1] Gen. Sts. c. 100, § 7.

[2] H. devised property to H. and R., their heirs and assigns, and the survivor of them, upon certain trusts. R. died before the trusts were fully executed. Held, that it was the duty of the probate court, under Rev. Sts. c. 69, § 8 (Gen. Sts. c. 100, § 9), the will being silent on the subject, to appoint a co-trustee to act with the survivor. Dixon v. Homer, 12 Cush. 41.

vests in him in like manner as it had or would have
vested in the trustee in whose place he is substituted;
and the court may order such conveyances to be made
by the former trustee or his representatives, or by the
other remaining trustee, as may be proper or convenient
to vest in him, either alone or jointly with the others,
the trust estate.[1]

Trustees are appointed by the probate court to receive
and hold the amount paid for damages sustained by the
laying out, alteration, or discontinuance of a highway, in
cases in which an estate for life or for a term of years
in the property affected belongs to one person, and the
remainder or reversion in fee belongs to another, and a
party interested is incapacitated by legal disability from
choosing a trustee, or the parties in interest cannot
agree upon a choice. The appointment is made by the
court of the county in which the property is situated,
and the annual income of the amount allowed for
damages is paid to the person having the estate for life
or years, and the remainder to the person entitled to the
reversion in fee or his heirs or devisees.[2]

Whenever it appears that the real estate taken or
affected by the laying out, alteration, or discontinuance,
of a highway is incumbered by any contingent remainder, executory devise, or power of appointment, the
probate court of the county in which the land is
situated may appoint a trustee or trustees to hold the
money recovered as damages, and invest the same for the
benefit of the persons who would have been entitled to

[1] Gen. Sts. c. 100, §§ 9, 10. Parker v. Converse, 5 Gray, 336; Dixon
v. Homer, 12 Cush. 41; Nugent v. Cloon, 117 Mass. 219.

[2] Gen. Sts. c. 43, §§ 17, 18. This applies to cases only in which the
relation of tenant for life or years and remainder-man exists without modifi-
cation by contract between the parties or otherwise. Edmunds v. Boston,
108 Mass. 535.

said estate in the same manner as if such location, alteration, or discontinuance had not been made. The appointment may be made on the petition of the county commissioners, or of any person in possession or enjoyment of the land either as tenant of a freehold estate or of a term of years. If the commissioners and such tenant in possession neglect or refuse to petition, the appointment may be made on petition of any person in behalf of such person whether in being or not as may by any possibility be or become interested in the property.[1]

If a trustee holding funds, bequeathed to a city or town for any charitable, religious, or educational purpose, neglects to make an annual exhibit of the condition of such funds as required by law, or is incapable of discharging the trust, or unsuitable to manage the affairs of the same, the probate court may remove him and supply the vacancy.[2]

A widow who waives the provision made for her in the will of her husband, thereby becomes entitled to such portion of his estate as she would have been entitled to if he had died intestate ; provided, however, that if the share of the personal estate to which she thus becomes entitled exceeds the sum of ten thousand dollars, she receives that sum in her own right, and is entitled to the income only of the excess of said share above the sum of ten thousand dollars during her natural life. In such case, upon application by the widow or any one interested in the estate, the judge of probate may appoint one or more trustees to receive, hold, and manage such excess during her natural life.[3]

---

[1] Stat. 1875, c. 117.   [2] Gen. Sts. c. 31, §§ 9, 10.

[3] Stat. 1861, c. 164. Such trustees are subject to the provisions of chap. 100 of the Gen. Sts., so far as the same are applicable. Stat. 1870, c. 262.

" Whenever any real estate is incumbered by any contingent remainder, executory devise, or power of appointment, the supreme judicial court may, upon petition of any party who has an estate in possession in such real estate, appoint a trustee for such estate, and authorize said trustee to mortgage the estate for such amounts, on such terms and conditions, and for such purposes as may seem to such court judicious or expedient, and shall fix the form and amount of the bond to be given by such trustee.

Notice of the proceedings shall be given to all persons who are or may become interested in the real estate, and to all persons whose issue, not in being, may become interested therein, as the court may order. The court shall, in all such cases, appoint a suitable person to appear and act in such proceedings as the next friend of all minors, persons not ascertained or persons not in being, who may be or may become interested in such real estate, the cost of whose appearance and services, including compensation of counsel, to be determined by the court, shall be paid as the court may order, either out of the proceeds of the real estate or by the petitioners, in which latter case execution may issue in the name of such next friend. An order or decree made in any such proceedings, and a mortgage of real estate thereunder, shall be binding and conclusive."

The probate court for the county in which such incumbered estate is situated has concurrent jurisdiction with the supreme judicial court in cases arising under the foregoing provisions.[1]

" The probate court, when it appears that the wood and timber standing on land held in dower, or on land the use and improvement of which belongs, for life or

---

[1] Stat. 1871, c. 322.

otherwise, to any person other than the owner of the fee therein, has ceased to improve by growth, or for any cause ought to be cut, may appoint a trustee, and authorize and empower him to sell and convey said wood and timber, in the way and manner provided by law for the sale of real estate by guardians, to be cut and carried away within the time to be limited in the order of sale, and to hold and invest the proceeds thereof, after paying the expenses of such sale therefrom, and pay over the income, above the taxes and other expenses of the trust, to the person entitled to such dower, or right to the use and improvement, while the same continues; and at the expiration of such dower or right to the use and improvement, to pay the principal sum to the owner of such land." [1]

" When lands in this State are held in trust for persons resident here, by a trustee who derives his appointment or authority from a court having no jurisdiction within this Commonwealth, application may be made to the probate court in the county in which the lands are situated, and such trustee, after due notice of such application, shall be required to take out letters of trust from said court; and upon the neglect or refusal of the trustee to comply with the orders of the court therein, the court shall declare such trust vacant, and appoint a new trustee, in whom the estate held in trust shall vest in like manner as if he had been originally appointed or authorized by said probate court." The notice to the trustee may be given by serving on him a copy of the petition and the citation thereon fourteen days at least before the time fixed for the return of such citation, or by such other notice as the court may order.[2]

---

[1] Stat. 1869, c. 249.   [2] Stat. 1871, c. 327.

FORMAL PROCEEDINGS.

A trustee appointed by will should petition the probate court for a confirmation of his appointment. The petition should state in general terms the nature of the trust, the manner in which it was created, and the willingness of the petitioner to accept the trust and give the bond required.[1]

If the appointment is necessary in consequence of a vacancy in the office of trustee, the petition should set forth the fact, and state in what way the vacancy was occasioned, whether by the omission of the testator to make an appointment, or by the resignation or death of a former trustee, or otherwise.[2]

Any person interested in a trust estate may petition for the appointment of a trustee. A citation to parties interested will be ordered before an appointment is made, unless their written assent is given to the prayer of the petition.[3]

TRUSTEES' BONDS.

Every trustee under a will, unless exempted, is required, before entering upon the duties of his trust, to give bond with sufficient surety or sureties to the judge

---

[1] Trustees to whom real estate is devised with a power of sale, and who are exempt from giving bond, may legally execute the power without an appointment from the probate court. Parker v. Sears, 117 Mass. 513.

[2] See Appendix, forms Nos. 32, 34.

[3] A testator appointed three trustees, and provided that if a vacancy occurred in the number of trustees, the surviving or acting trustees should nominate a suitable person to be appointed by the judge of probate to fill the vacancy. A new trustee was so appointed without notice. Held, that the trustee was duly appointed, as in making the appointment the judge did not act officially, but under the will. Shaw v. Paine, 12 Allen, 293; Webster Bank v. Eldridge, 115 Mass. 424.

of the probate court for the county in which the will
was proved, with condition to make a true inventory of
all the estate belonging to him as trustee, and which
shall come to his possession or knowledge, and to return
the same into the probate court at such time as the
court directs; to dispose of and manage all such estate
and effects, and faithfully discharge his trust in relation
thereto, according to law and the will of the testator;
to render an account on oath of the property in his
hands, and of the management and disposition thereof,
within one year and at any other times when required
by the probate court; and at the expiration of his trust,
to settle his accounts with the probate court, and pay
over and deliver all the estate and effects remaining in
his hands or due from him on such settlement, to the
person or persons entitled thereto, according to law and
the will of the testator.[1]

"A trustee under a will shall be exempt from giving
a surety or sureties on his bond, when the testator has
ordered or requested such exemption;[2] or, that no bond
should be taken, or when all the persons interested in
the trust fund, being of full age and legal capacity,
request such exemption; but such trustee shall in all
cases give his own personal bond: *provided*, that the
judge of the probate court may at any time require a
bond, with sufficient surety or sureties, if he is of
opinion that the same is required by a change in the
situation or circumstances of such trustee, or for other
sufficient cause.

Every trustee under a will who neglects to give

---

[1] Gen. Sts. c. 100, § 1.

[2] The order or request of the testator need not be in express words.
If it can be gathered from the whole will, it is sufficient. Lowell, Appellant, 22 Pick. 215.

bond as required by this act, within such time as the probate court allows, shall be considered as having declined the trust: *provided*, that no trustee who has already undertaken a trust under laws heretofore existing shall be required by the provisions of this act to give bond, except when the judge of the probate court is of opinion that the same is required by a change in the situation or circumstances of such trustee or for other sufficient cause." [1]

A trustee appointed by the probate court to receive and hold money paid for damages sustained by the laying out, alteration, or discontinuance of a highway, is required to give a bond, with condition for the faithful performance of his duties.[2]

A trustee appointed under a deed is not required to give bond unless provision is made therefor in the instrument; and the bond, if one is required, must be framed and conditioned in conformity to the terms of the deed.

In all cases not otherwise provided for by law, trustees appointed by the probate court are required to give bond in the manner provided for trustees under a will or written instrument.[3] Any trustee appointed by the probate court, required by law to give a bond, is exempted from giving a surety or sureties on his bond when all persons interested in the trust fund, being of full age and legal capacity, request such exemption ; but the probate court may in all such cases, at any time, require a bond with sufficient surety or sureties.[4]

In any case not otherwise provided for by law where a trustee has been appointed by the probate court without having given a bond, the court, upon petition

---

[1] Stat. 1873, c. 122.   [2] Gen. Sts. c. 43, § 18 ; Stat. 1875, c. 117, § 2.
[3] Stat. 1869, c. 357.   [4] Stat. 1874, c. 352, § 2.

of any person interested therein, may order the trustee to give bond with sureties within a time fixed in the order; and if he fails to comply with the order he will be removed and a new trustee appointed in his stead.[1]

Sale and Investment of Trust Estates. The probate courts have original jurisdiction, concurrent with the supreme judicial court, over all matters relating to the sale of trust estates and the investment of the proceeds of such sale.[2] The sale will be ordered when it appears to the court to be necessary or expedient. If, upon application to the court, it shall appear that the trust estate " may be held in trust for, or that any remainder or contingent interest may be devised or limited over to, heirs at law, or other persons, whether in being or not in being, notice of such proceeding shall be given to such heirs at law or persons, and if such persons are not in being, to the parent or parents of such persons in such manner as the court shall order. The court in such case shall appoint a suitable and competent person to appear and act as the next friend of such persons in such proceedings, the cost of whose appearance and services, including compensation of counsel, to be determined by the court, shall be paid as the court may order, either out of the trust estate or by the persons commencing said proceedings, in which latter case execution may issue therefor in the name of the person appointed. Any order or decree made in any such proceedings, and any sale or transfer of property thereunder, shall be conclusive upon all persons for whom such property or any

---

[1] Stat. 1869, c. 357.
[2] Gen. Sts. c. 100, §§ 14–16; Stat. 1869, c. 331.

remainder or contingent interest therein is held in trust, or to whom the same is devised or limited over, in the same manner as if they had been in being and appeared and answered in the case or assented to the order or decree." [1]

Under these provisions of the statute, the trustee, in case of a difference of opinion between him and the persons interested in the estate in regard to the disposition to be made of the property in his hands, may protect himself by obtaining the direction of the court. And if the trustee should neglect to apply for the direction of the court, any person interested in the trust estate may make the application. It may happen that some particular disposition of the funds may be unsafe or improper, and such as the courts would not have sanctioned on a previous application, and yet it may not be such as to make the trustee liable as for misconduct in the discharge of his trust. In such a case, the loss or damage that would otherwise result may be prevented by an application to the court on the part of some person interested in the estate.

The application, whether made by the trustee or by a person interested in the estate, should state all the facts of the particular case, and pray for the direction of the court.

TERMINATION OF CERTAIN TRUSTS.

The statute provides that when it appears, upon petition or otherwise, to the probate court of the county where letters testamentary or of administration have been granted on the estate of a person deceased, that such person in his lifetime made a conveyance of his

---

[1] Stat. 1864, c. 168.

real estate in this State in trust for the benefit of his creditors, and the trustee certifies that all the debts secured thereby (due to other persons than himself) have been paid, or otherwise adjusted to the satisfaction of the creditors so far as known, and that he is desirous to settle his trust account and terminate the trust, the court shall appoint a time and place for hearing all persons interested therein; notice of which shall be given by advertisement in some newspaper printed in the county or otherwise as the court may order. Upon such hearing the court may terminate the trust, so far as the creditors and persons claiming under them are concerned, and discharge such real estate therefrom; and may settle the trust account, and make any further order as to the disposition, distribution, or partition of the remaining trust estate, not inconsistent with the provisions of the original instrument creating the trust. This provision does not apply to any case where the instrument creating the trust does not bear date more than six years previous to the time appointed for the hearing; nor can it affect the operation of the insolvent laws.[1]

GENERAL EQUITY JURISDICTION.

The probate courts in the several counties, concurrently with the supreme judicial court, have general equity powers in all matters relating to trusts created by will.[2]

All matters of trust of which probate courts have jurisdiction, except those arising under wills, are within the jurisdiction of the probate court for any county in which any of the parties interested in the trust reside,

---

[1] Gen. Sts. c. 100, § 17, 18.   [2] Ibid. § 22.

or in which any of the land held in trust is situated;
and such jurisdiction, when once assumed, excludes the
probate court for any other county from taking jurisdiction of any matter subsequently arising in relation to
the same trust.[1]

[1] Stat. 1874, c. 352, § 8.

CHAPTER VIII.

REMOVAL AND RESIGNATION OF EXECUTORS AND OTHERS.

IF an executor, administrator, guardian, or trustee, who may be required by the probate court to give a new bond, does not comply with the order within the time fixed by the court, he will be removed and some other person appointed in his stead ;[1] and if he become insane, or otherwise incapable of discharging his trust, or for any reason " evidently unsuitable " therefor, he may be removed, notice having first been given to him and to all parties interested.[2]

An executor or other officer appointed by the probate court may be incapacitated by physical debility, want of memory, or any infirmity which prevents the efficient performance of his trust ; and he may be evidently unsuitable because of his personal relations to the estate, either by reason of his being indebted to it, or of the interest he has under the will of his testator, or his situation as an heir at law, or because the prosecution of his individual claims against the estate would conflict with his official duties, or for other reasons. The statute does not enumerate any causes of unsuitability, but gives

---

[1] Gen. Sts. c. 101, § 17.   [2] Ibid. § 2; c. 100, § 8; c. 109, § 24.

8

the court a broad discretion to include the various cases that may arise.[1]

The relation existing between a guardian and his ward may require, for the proper discharge of its obligations, other than merely business qualifications; and the guardian may be unsuitable for the care and custody of the person of the ward, although no question be made of his integrity, disinterestedness, or general ability. The guardian of a person *non compos mentis* should be especially fitted for his trust, and in determining the question of personal suitableness, the peculiar condition, interests, and necessities of the ward must be considered. It is not enough, in every case, for the guardian to supply the material wants of his ward. It is his duty to make use of every available means to promote the ward's welfare, improvement, and happiness. With every disposition to discharge his obligations thoroughly and conscientiously, he may be, from various causes, incapable of exercising the beneficial influence over his ward that might be exerted by another. The continuance of the relation of guardian and ward under such circumstances might materially interfere with the permanent improvement and general welfare of the ward, and thus defeat the main object of the guardianship. Whenever, from any cause, the guardian becomes unable to perform any important and substantial part of the duties of his office, he is liable to be removed as " evidently unsuitable." [2]

When an executor or administrator residing out of this State, having been duly cited by the probate court, neglects to render his accounts and settle the estate, he

---

[1] Thayer *v.* Homer, 11 Met. 104; Winship *v.* Bass, 12 Mass. 200; Newcomb *v.* Williams, 9 Met. 538; Richards *v.* Sweetland, 6 Cush. 324; Andrews *v.* Tucker, 7 Pick. 250; Wildridge *v.* Patterson, 15 Mass. 148.

[2] See Perkins *v.* Finnegan, 105 Mass. 501.

may be removed.[1] If the executor or administrator neglects to settle his accounts within six months after the return of the insolvent commissioners, or the final liquidation of the demands of the creditors, or within such further time as the court shall allow, he may be forthwith removed.[2]

Any unfaithful administration which will sustain an action on the bond of an executor or other officer appointed by the probate court, is sufficient cause for his removal.[3]

A trustee may be removed on the application of the parties beneficially interested in the trust estate, if it appears that his removal is essential to their interests.[4]

A trustee who holds funds bequeathed to a city or town for any charitable, religious, or educational purpose, may be removed by the probate court for neglect to make the annual exhibit of the condition of such funds as required by law, or for incapacity or unsuitability.[5]

The person applying for the removal of an executor or other officer should set forth in his petition the particular fact of neglect or other maladministration which renders the removal proper;[6] and the burden of proof is upon him to sustain the allegations in his petition. In all cases, the person whose removal is asked for is entitled

---

[1] Gen. Sts. c. 101, § 2.   [2] Ibid. c. 99, § 26.

[3] It is no cause for the removal of an administrator that he declines to inventory, or commence proceedings to recover for the *benefit of the heirs*, certain real estate formerly belonging to the deceased, but which had been set off on an execution against him in his lifetime issued upon a judgment alleged by the heirs to have been recovered by the fraud of the plaintiff. Richards *v.* Sweetland, 6 Cush. 321. But otherwise, when creditors of an insolvent estate request the administrator to inventory real estate fraudulently conveyed by the intestate offering to indemnify him, and he refuses. Andrews *v.* Tucker, 7 Pick. 250.

[4] Gen. Sts. c. 100, § 8.   [5] Ibid. c. 31, § 10.

[6] See Appendix, form No. 35.

to notice, and to an opportunity to show cause why the removal should not be made. At the hearing, both the petitioner and the respondent may offer any evidence pertinent to the issue ; and either party may appeal from the decree of the court making, or refusing to make, the removal.

The removal of a trustee who holds funds bequeathed to a city or town for a charitable, religious, or educational purpose, must be on the petition of five persons.[1] In all other cases any person interested in the trust estate may petition.

When an executor or administrator is removed, or letters of administration are revoked, all previous sales, whether of real or personal estate, made lawfully by him, and with good faith on the part of the purchaser, and all other lawful acts done by such executor or administrator, remain valid and effectual.[2]

Upon the request of an executor, administrator, guardian, or trustee, the probate court may in its discretion allow him to resign his trust.[3] The executor or other officer applying for leave to resign, should present to the court with his petition a just and true account of his administration. Until his accounts are settled, after such notice to the parties interested as the circumstances of the case require, his request will not be allowed.[4]

If, after the granting of letters of administration as of an intestate estate, a will of the deceased is duly proved and allowed, the first administration will be revoked.[5]

The guardian of an insane person or spendthrift may be discharged by the probate court on the application of the ward or otherwise, when it appears that such guar-

---

[1] Gen. Sts. c. 81, § 10.   [2] Gen. Sts. c. 101, § 3.
[3] Ibid. § 5; c. 109, § 24; c. 100, § 5; Stat. 1874, c. 352.
[4] See Appendix, form No. 37.   [5] Gen. Sts. c. 94, § 5.

dianship is no longer necessary.[1]   Such application of
the ward may be resisted by the guardian; and all
reasonable expenses incurred by him in good faith for
the purpose of a proper inquiry into the condition of
the ward, will be allowed to him in the settlement of
his guardianship account.[2]

[1] Gen. Sts. c. 109, § 26.   See Appendix, form No. 89.
[2] Palmer v. Palmer, 1 Chandler (N. H.), 448.

CHAPTER IX.

INVENTORIES, AND THE COLLECTION OF THE EFFECTS OF DECEASED PERSONS AND WARDS.

THE bonds of executors, administrators, guardians, and trustees contain a condition that the party giving the bond shall return into the probate court a true inventory of all the estate that shall come to his possession or knowledge. Exceptions to this rule are made in favor of executors who are residuary legatees, who elect to give a bond for the payment of the debts and legacies, and run their own risk as to the sufficiency of assets;[1] and in favor of a trustee appointed in place of a former trustee who has deceased or has been removed, or has resigned, if the court deems an inventory unnecessary.[2] Every executor and administrator is required to return an inventory within three months after his appointment;[3] and every guardian and trustee within such time as the court may direct.[4]

The inventory is equally an advantage to the executor, or other trust officer, and to the heirs, creditors, or other persons interested in the estate. It is the basis upon which he is to make his accounts. It shows the amount for which he is chargeable, and limits his responsibility, unless there are assets not appraised that come to his hands. On the other part, the heirs or other persons

---

[1] Gen. Sts. c. 93, § 3; *ante*, p. 69. [2] Ibid. c. 100, § 11.
[3] Ibid. c. 96, § 1. [4] Ibid. c. 100, § 1; c. 109, § 17.

interested have, in the record of the inventory, the best
evidence that can be had under the circumstances, of
the value of the estate in the hands of the trustee ; and
it furnishes them with essential evidence in case it becomes necessary to institute proceedings against him, on
account of any misappropriation of the property or other
maladministration.

The inventory should include all the real estate,[1] and
all the goods, chattels, rights, and credits belonging to
the estate appraised.[2] All notes and accounts due to the
estate should be described in the inventory. The appraisers may find it difficult to appraise a note or account,
except as its face indicates its value, and for this reason
many administrators deem it unnecessary to include
either notes or accounts in their inventory, and consider
it sufficient to charge themselves with the proceeds of the
debts collected in their accounts of administration. This
course, if pursued in good faith, can work no wrong, but
it does not fulfil all the purposes of the law requiring an

---

[1] It is not the duty of an administrator, at the request and for the
benefit of the *heirs* of his intestate, to inventory, or institute proceedings
to recover certain real estate which once belonged to the intestate, but
which has been set off on an execution issued against him on a judgment
obtained by fraud. Richards *v.* Sweetland, 6 Cush. 824 ; otherwise, when
the proceeds of land fraudulently conveyed are needed for the payment of
debts due from the estate. Andrews *v.* Tucker, 7 Pick. 250. If there
was any specific personal property in the hands of the testator belonging
to others, which he held in trust or otherwise, it is not assets in the hands
of his executors, but is to be held by the executors as the testator himself held it. But if the testator has money or other property in his hands
belonging to others, whether in trust or otherwise, and it has no ear-mark,
and is not distinguishable from the mass of his own property, the party
owning it must come in as a general creditor, and it falls within the description of assets of the executor. Trecothick *v.* Austin, 4 Mason, 29.

[2] Corn or other product of the soil, raised annually by cultivation, and
in a proper state to be gathered, is personal estate, and goes to the executor on the death of the owner. Penhallow *v.* Dwight, 7 Mass. 34.

inventory to be made. The administrator, moreover, cannot be prejudiced by the mention of notes and accounts in the inventory, even if they prove to be worthless, for if they remain uncollected without his fault, a credit, corresponding in amount with the appraised value of the worthless debt, will be allowed him in his account.[1]

Orders for the Appraisal of Estates are issued by the probate court. The appraisers must be three suitable, disinterested persons.[2] No clerk or other person employed in the office of the probate court can be an appraiser in any case within the jurisdiction of the court unless his appointment is requested by all parties in interest.[3] The authority of appraisers appointed by the probate court extends to the appraisal of property situated in any part of the State. The order of appraisal is usually issued on the day when the executor or other officer is appointed and upon his verbal request.

Any disinterested justice of the peace may appoint appraisers of any part of the estate which may be in his county.[4]

Oath of Appraisers. Before proceeding to appraise the estate the appraisers must be sworn to the faithful discharge of their duties. The oath may be administered by any justice of the peace. and a certificate thereof must be indorsed on the order by the justice who administers the oath.

Return of the Inventory. The value of each parcel of real estate and of each article of personal property should be separately stated in the inventory. The blanks attached to the orders of appraisal indicate the form in which the return is to be made.

---

[1] Gen. Sts. c. 98, § 6.   [2] Ibid. c. 96, § 2.
[3] Ibid. c. 117, § 32.   [4] Ibid. c. 96, § 2. See Appendix, form No. 41.

If the deceased had been a member of a copartnership, and both partnership estate and separate estate have come to the possession of the executor, such partnership estate should be separately appraised and returned in a separate list.

The estates of two or more minors under guardianship of the same person should be returned in separate schedules, if the minors are interested in different property, or have unequal interests in the same property.

The inventory, when completed by the appraisers, is delivered to the executor or other person having charge of the estate appraised, who returns it to the probate office for record. He is required to make oath that it is a true and perfect inventory of all the estate that has come to his possession or knowledge. The oath may be administered by the judge or register of probate, in or out of court, or by any justice of the peace ; and a certificate of the oath must be made on the inventory by the officer who administers it, and recorded with the inventory.

An administrator is bound to return only one inventory. If additional property comes to his hands, he is bound to account for it, but not to inventory it.[1]

COLLECTION OF THE EFFECTS.

It is not only the duty of the executor or administrator to point out to the appraisers the estate that has come to his possession or knowledge, but to take such measures as may be necessary for the collection of debts due the deceased, and for the recovery of any money, goods, effects, or other estate in the fraudulent possession of other persons. The statute provides a process

[1] Hooker v. Bancroft, 4 Pick. 50.

for the discovery of facts, by an examination in the probate court, which may be advantageously used as a preliminary step to the institution of a suit for the recovery of property fraudulently withheld from the estate. The statute provides that,

" Upon complaint made to the probate court by an executor, administrator, heir, legatee, creditor, or other person interested in the estate of a person deceased, against any person suspected of having fraudulently received, concealed, embezzled, or conveyed away, any money, goods, effects, or other estate, real or personal, of the deceased, the court may cite such suspected person, though he is executor or administrator, to appear and be examined on oath, upon the matter of the complaint. If the person so cited refuses to appear and submit to examination, or to answer such interrogatories as are lawfully propounded to him, the court may commit him to the jail, there to remain in close custody until he submits to the order of the court.[1] The interrogatories and answers shall be in writing, signed by the party examined, and filed in the probate court."

Like proceedings may be had upon complaint of a guardian, ward, creditor, or other person interested in the estate of a ward, or having claims thereto in expectancy as heir or otherwise, against any one suspected of having fraudulently concealed, embezzled, or conveyed away any of the estate of the ward. The suspected person may be cited, though he is the guardian.[2]

The authority given to the probate court by the above provisions extends only to an examination for the purpose of discovery. No other power is given. The examination is not to be controlled by other evidence;

---

[1] Gen. Sts. c. 96, § 6. See Appendix, forms 42, 43.

[2] Ibid. c. 109, § 30; Sherman v. Brewer, 11 Gray, 210.

nor can relief be directly granted upon it by any decree of the probate court. The process can only result in a disclosure of facts to serve as the basis of other proceedings.[1]

[1] Selectmen of Boston v. Boylston, 4 Mass. 322. The lapse of thirty years since the transactions inquired into, is no bar to such examination. O'Dee v. McCrate, 7 Greenl. 467.

In a complaint to the judge of probate, for embezzlement of the estate of a person deceased, the complainant having described himself as "administrator and creditor," and it appearing that he was not entitled to act as administrator, it was held that the words "administrator and" were material, and could not be rejected as surplusage. Arnold v. Sabin, 4 Cush. 46; Milner v. Leishman, 12 Met. 320.

The court may permit the party cited to appear and be assisted by counsel in making answers to the interrogatories. Martin v. Clapp, 99 Mass. 470.

CHAPTER X.

ALLOWANCES TO WIDOWS, MINOR CHILDREN, AND OTHERS.

TO WIDOWS AND MINOR CHILDREN.

"THE articles of apparel and ornament of the widow and minor children of a deceased person shall belong to them respectively.

"Such parts of the personal estate of a person deceased as the probate court, having regard to all the circumstances of the case, may allow as necessaries to his widow, for herself and family under her care, or if there is no widow, to his minor children, not exceeding fifty dollars to any child; and also such provisions and other articles as are necessary for the reasonable sustenance of his family, and the use of his house and the furniture therein, for forty days after his death, shall not be taken as assets for the payment of debts, legacies, or charges of administration."[1]

"A widow may remain in the house of her husband forty days after his death without being chargeable with rent."[2]

The statute thus makes the apparel and ornaments of the widow and minor children of a deceased person their absolute property, and secures to them a home in his house for forty days after his death, with such provisions and other articles as are necessary for their reason-

---

[1] Gen. Sts. c. 96, §§ 4, 5.   [2] Ibid. c. 90, § 18.

able sustenance ; and in addition to this statute allowance for the forty days, the widow or minor children of the deceased, whether he was a housekeeper or not, are entitled to an allowance for necessaries, when their circumstances require it, from his personal estate.   The power of the probate court to make allowances is not limited to intestate estates.   It is given in all cases, provided there are personal assets from which the allowance can be made.   An allowance may be granted, although provision was made for the widow by her husband's will, in lieu of dower and accepted by her, and although the executor, being also residuary legatee, has given bond as such to pay the debts and legacies.[1]   And the widow may have a second allowance at any time before the personal estate is exhausted.[2]

The amount to be allowed the widow is determined by the court in its discretion.   There is no rule to regulate this discretion, and no rule could be framed to meet the great variety of circumstances upon which the allowance depends.   The amount is not ordinarily restricted to a sum merely sufficient for the necessaries of life, nor on the other hand is it to be increased to an extent inconsistent with the object of the allowance.   The allowance is intended to furnish the widow, when she is left in distress by the decease of her husband, with necessaries for her support for a reasonable time, within which she can make arrangements for her own support. It is not intended to furnish her with a capital for business purposes, or to establish a fund from which a permanent income may be derived.   Any and all facts bearing upon the question of her necessities are to be considered, such as the amount of her separate property and means ;[3]

---

[1] Williams v. Williams, 5 Gray, 24.   [2] Hale v. Hale, 1 Gray, 518.
[3] Hollenbeck v. Pixley, 3 Gray, 521.

the fact that she is accustomed to earn her own support, or the contrary; that she is disabled by age, or otherwise; the number of her children and the fact of their tender age, &c.

The value of the estate, as shown by the inventory and by additional evidence, is to be regarded. It may be that the personal estate has been materially diminished by gifts made by the deceased, shortly before his death, to his heirs and others, while the new duties and obligations imposed upon the widow are not lessened by such diminution. In such case, the fact that such gifts have been made may be important to show the actual condition of the estate and of the family. But facts as to the sum contributed by her on her marriage, to her husband's estate, or as to the value of the services rendered to him and his family, while they may show that she is equitably entitled to a considerable share of his estate, do not bear upon the question actually at issue, the allowance not being made to correct an injustice, but to provide for her necessities.[1]

The whole of the personal estate may be given to the widow as an allowance, when the amount is not so great as to be extravagant.[2] She is entitled to a reasonable allowance, even if the estate is insolvent; and she is entitled to the amount of her allowance in priority to the payment of her husband's debts, expenses of his last sickness and funeral, and the charges of settling his estate.[3]

Upon the petition of the widow or children, or either of them, the probate court may, after notice to all parties interested, make a reasonable allowance out of the in-

[1] Adams v. Adams, 10 Met. 170; Hollenbeck v. Pixley, 3 Gray, 525.
[2] Brazer v. Dean, 15 Mass. 183.
[3] Kingsbury v. Wilmarth, 2 Allen, 310.

come of the estate, real or personal, in the hands of a *special* administrator appointed on account of the pendency of a suit concerning the probate of a will, as an advancement for their support, not exceeding such portion of the income of the estate as they would be entitled to whether the will is finally proved or not. An appeal from the decree concerning such allowance will not prevent the payment of the sum decreed if the petitioner gives bond to the special administrator, with sureties approved by the judge, conditioned to repay the same if the decree is reversed.[1]

In all other cases the allowance is made from the personal property. It cannot be made from the proceeds of real estate sold for the payment of debts, for the surplus of such proceeds, if any, is required by statute to be treated as real estate, and disposed of among the same persons and in the same proportions as the real estate would have been if it had not been sold.[2]

The petition for an allowance to the widow or minor children sets forth the fact that there are personal assets belonging to the estate in question from which she or they are entitled to an allowance, and prays that an allowance may be decreed accordingly. When the next of kin of the deceased are other than his minor children, notice of the widow's petition is usually given to parties interested before a decree is made.[3]

The widow, or any person aggrieved by the decree of the court upon her petition, may appeal to the supreme

[1] Gen. Sts. c. 94, §§ 9, 10.

[2] Ibid. c. 102, § 44; Hale v. Hale, 1 Gray, 523; Haven v. Foster, 9 Pick. 130.

[3] If an allowance is made without notice to the parties interested, the supreme court of probate in its discretion will allow an appeal, after the expiration of thirty days upon a petition filed under Gen. Sts. c. 117, § 11. Wright v. Wright, 13 Allen, 207.

court of probate; and the appeal, except when the allowance is made from the income of the estate in the hands of a special administrator, stays all proceedings under the decree until the matter is determined by the supreme court of probate.

The allowance to the widow for necessaries is not to be confounded with her distributive share of her husband's estate. That is a vested right of property which she takes by a title as high as that of a child or other next of kin; and it goes to her personal representative.[1] But the provision for necessaries is temporary in its nature and personal in its character, and confers no absolute or contingent right of property which can survive her. If, therefore, an appeal is taken from a decree making an allowance, and she dies before the appeal is entered in the appellate court, all further proceedings are stayed; and the decree of the probate court, which was vacated by the appeal, cannot be revived.[2]

A widow's claim for an allowance made to her may be enforced, after demand and refusal, by an action brought by her against the executor.[3]

ALLOWANCES TO WIVES OF INSANE PERSONS UNDER GUARDIANSHIP.

The statute provides that the probate court for the county in which the guardian of an insane person was appointed, may make an allowance out of the estate of such insane person for the support of his wife, to be paid to her by the guardian during the continuance of

[1] Foster v. Fifield, 20 Pick. 67.
[2] Adams v. Adams, 10 Met. 170; Drew v. Gordon, 13 Allen, 120.
[3] Drew v. Gordon, 13 Allen, 120.

the guardianship in such manner as the court shall direct.[1]

Resort is not often had to proceedings under this provision of the statute. It is the duty of the guardian to provide for the support of the ward and his family, so far as the ward's estate is sufficient therefor, without any order of the court. The amount proper to be expended for their support can generally be determined by agreement between the parties interested. It is only when the guardian neglects his duty in this respect that the wife has occasion to apply to the court for an allowance.

The allowance under this provision is not limited merely to necessaries for the wife. It is intended for her support, and the amount of the allowance must be proportioned to the condition and circumstances of the husband. It should be sufficient for her support in a manner consistent with the prudent use and management of his estate.

The order of the court fixing the amount of the allowance may also direct the guardian as to the time and manner of its payment to the wife.[2]

[1] Stat. 1862, c. 116.   [2] See Appendix, form No. 44.

9

CHAPTER XI.

SALE OF PERSONAL ESTATE BY EXECUTORS AND
OTHERS. — INVESTMENTS BY GUARDIANS AND TRUS-
TEES. — COMPROMISE OF CLAIMS. — TEMPORARY IN-
VESTMENTS BY EXECUTORS, &c.

THE statute provides that "the probate court, on
application made by the executor, administrator, or any
person interested in the estate, after the return of the
inventory, may order any part or all of the personal
estate to be sold by public auction or private sale, as
shall be deemed most for the interest of all concerned ;
and the executor or administrator shall account therefor
at the price for which it sells." [1]

The personal property is generally sold by executors
and administrators without any previous order of the
court, and if they act in good faith and with sound discretion, the interests of no person concerned can be
injuriously affected by such proceeding. The subsequent
approval of the court is practically equivalent to a previous order. The executor or administrator, however,
makes a sale without first obtaining license at his own
risk, and when it is probable that the property cannot be
sold for its appraised value, he should apply to the court
for leave to make the sale, and thereby limit his responsibility to account.

---

[1] Gen. Sts. c. 98, § 3. Guardians account for and dispose of the personal estate of their wards in like manner as executors and administrators. Ibid. c. 109, § 17.

Mortgages of land and the debt secured thereby are personal estate in the hands of the administrator, and so are lands taken on execution for a debt due the testator or intestate; and real estate so held in mortgage or taken on execution, may be sold, subject to the right of redemption, at any time before the right of redemption is foreclosed, in the same manner as personal estate of a person deceased.[1]

The probate court upon petition of the executor or administrator, and after such notice thereof to the parties interested as the court may order, and a hearing thereon, may for the purpose of closing the settlement of an estate, license the executor or administrator to sell and assign any outstanding debts, claims, and assets which cannot be collected, received, or determined without inconvenient delay. The petition for leave to make such sale or assignment should set forth the nature of the debt, claim, or asset to be sold, and the reasons for the proposed sale.[2] The sale is required to be conducted in such manner as the court, having regard as far as it may be thought advisable or prudent to the law in relation to sales of real estate by executors and administrators, shall order. This provision for the sale of debts and claims does not deprive executors and administrators of the right to transfer at pleasure deeds of mortgage, and the real estate conveyed and the debts secured thereby.[3]

Probate courts may authorize executors, administrators, guardians, and trustees, to release and discharge, upon such terms and conditions as appear proper, any vested, contingent, or possible right or interest belonging to the persons or estates by them represented in or to any real or personal estate, whenever it appears to be

---

[1] Gen. Sts. c. 96, §§ 9, 12.   [2] See Appendix, form No. 40.

[3] Gen. Sts. c. 98, §§ 4, 5.

for the benefit of the persons or estates in trust.[1] Notice
of the application in such cases must be given as in cases
of sale of real estate.[2]

SALES AND INVESTMENTS BY GUARDIANS AND TRUSTEES.

The probate court, on the application of a guardian
or any person interested in the estate of a ward, after
notice to all other persons interested therein, may authorize or require the guardian to sell and transfer any stock
in the public funds, or in any corporation, or any other
personal estate or effects held by him as guardian, and
invest the proceeds thereof and all other moneys in his
hands in real estate, or in any other manner that shall
be most for the interest of all concerned. The court
may make such further order and give such directions
as the case may require, for managing, investing, and
disposing of the estate and effects in the hands of the
guardian.[3] And on the application of a trustee under
a will or of any person interested in the trust estate, the
court may authorize or require such trustee to sell any
personal estate or effects held by him in trust, and invest
the proceeds and any other trust money in his hands in
real estate, or in any other manner most for the interest
of all concerned therein. And the court may from time
to time give such further directions as the case may
require for managing, investing, and disposing of the
trust fund, subject to the provisions of the will.[4]

The guardian, trustee, or other person applying for an
order of the court for such investment should represent

---

[1] Gen. Sts. c. 101, § 11.   [2] Stat. 1863, c. 230.

[3] Gen. Sts. c. 109, § 22.   See May v. May, 109 Mass. 252.

[4] Ante, p. 109.

in his petition that the proposed investment will be for
the benefit of all parties interested, and should describe
the personal estate, if any, to be sold, and the property
in which it is proposed to invest the proceeds or the
money in the hands of the guardian or trustee.[1]

PURCHASE OF INTERESTS IN REAL ESTATE OF WARDS.

Probate courts, after notice to all persons interested,
may authorize guardians to purchase and obtain the
release and conveyance of any right of dower, homestead, life-estate, estate for years, or any interest, vested
or contingent, held, possessed, or owned by any person,
in or to any real estate of their wards, and to make any
contract for or concerning said rights or interests necessary to effect such purchase and provide for the payment
of the consideration thereof, or the performance of any
condition thereof; and also to bind the said estates of
their said wards by mortgage or otherwise, for the purpose aforesaid, when it shall appear to said court to be
for the interest of said wards.[2]

ADJUSTMENT OF DEMANDS BY ARBITRATION OR COMPROMISE.

Probate courts may authorize executors, administrators, guardians, and trustees, to adjust by arbitration or
compromise, any demands in favor of or against the
estates by them represented.[3] The executor or other
officer who is desirous of so adjusting a claim should
present a petition to the court setting forth the nature
of the demand, and representing that it can be adjusted

---

[1] See Appendix, form No. 48.   [2] Stat. 1869, c. 219.
[3] Gen. Sts. c. 101, § 10.

by arbitration or compromise, and that the interests of the estate represented by him will be promoted thereby.[1] Any adjustment by arbitration or compromise without leave of the court first obtained, would be at the risk of the executor or other person making it, and might give rise to questions upon the settlement of his accounts in the probate court.

Controversies between different claimants to the estate in the hands of executors, administrators, guardians, and trustees may be settled by arbitration or compromise upon application to the supreme judicial court.[2]

TEMPORARY INVESTMENTS BY EXECUTORS AND ADMINISTRATORS.

Any probate court may, upon application of a person interested in an estate in process of settlement in such court, direct the temporary investment of the money belonging to such estate in securities to be approved by the judge; or may authorize the same to be deposited in any bank or institution in this State, empowered to receive such deposits, upon such interest as said bank or institution may agree to pay.[3]

---

[1] See Appendix, form No. 50.
[2] Stat. 1861, c. 174, § 1. See Stat. 1864, c. 173; 1865, c. 186.
[3] Stat. 1873, c. 224.

CHAPTER XII.

THE statute provides that "every executor and administrator, within three months after giving bond for the discharge of his trust, shall cause notice of his appointment to be posted in two or more public places in the city or town in which the deceased last dwelt; or he may be required by the probate court to give notice by publishing in some newspaper, or in such other manner as the court, taking into consideration the business of the deceased and the circumstances of his estate, shall direct." [1] The letter testamentary or of administration, issued to the executor or administrator, directs the manner in which the notice is to be given in each case. A strict compliance with the terms of the order is necessary, in connection with the payment of debts, to protect the interests of the heirs or devisees as well as of the executor or administrator.[2] Unless the notice is given, the statute limiting the time within which suits may be brought against the executor or administrator will not apply.

The notice having been given, the statute provides a sure and convenient mode of perpetuating evidence of

---

[1] Gen. Sts. c. 97, § 1.

[2] An executor's notice is sufficient, though signed by him as "administrator," and he describes himself therein as "duly appointed administrator." Pinney v. Barnes, 97 Mass. 401.

the fact. An affidavit of the executor or administrator, or of the person employed by him to give such notice, being made before the judge or a justice of the peace, and filed and recorded with a copy of the notice in the probate office, within one year after giving bond, or at any time afterwards by permission of the court upon petition and satisfactory evidence furnished that the notice was given as ordered, is made evidence by statute, of the time, place, and manner in which the notice was given.[1] When it appears that such affidavit has not been made, any person, on petition to the probate court, may be permitted to make it.[2] The fact that notice was duly given may be proved whenever it becomes material by other evidence;[3] but questions as to the fact of notice may not be raised until after the lapse of several years, when it may be difficult and perhaps impossible for the executor or administrator to show his compliance with the order of the court by any of the ordinary means of proof. The affidavit should therefore be made and recorded in every case.

If by accident or mistake notice is not given, or the evidence is not so perpetuated, the probate court, on the petition of the executor or administrator, may order such notice to be given at any time afterwards ; in which case, the periods of time limited for the commencement of actions against executors and administrators and for other purposes, and which begin to run from the date of the administration bond, will run respectively from the time of passing such order. And no such order will exempt the executor or administrator from any liability for damages incurred by reason of his omission to give notice within the three months.[4]

[1] Gen. Sts. c. 97, § 2, Stat. 1876, c. 76.   [2] Stat. 1876, c. 71.
[3] Estes v. Wilkes, 16 Gray, 363.   [4] Gen. Sts. c. 97, §§ 3, 4.

PAYMENT OF DEBTS.

Limitation of Actions against Executors and Administrators. No executor or administrator, *after having given notice of his appointment*, as required by law, can be held to answer to the suit of any creditor of the deceased, unless it is commenced within two years from the time of his giving bond,[1] except when new assets come to his hand after the expiration of the two years, in which case he is liable to an action if brought within one year after the creditor has notice of the receipt of such new assets, and within two years after the same is actually received.[2] And if an action seasonably commenced fails of a sufficient service or return by unavoidable accident; or when the writ in such action is abated or defeated for a defect in its form, or by a mistake in the form of the proceeding, or when after verdict for the plaintiff judgment is arrested; or if a judgment for the plaintiff is reversed on a writ of error, the plaintiff may commence a new action for the same cause at any time within one year after the abatement or other determination of the original suit, or after the reversal of the judgment therein.[3]

---

[1] In computing the two years, the day on which the bond is given is to be excluded. Paul v. Stone, 112 Mass. 27.

[2] Gen. Sts. c. 97, §§ 5, 6. See Sturtevant v. Sturtevant, 4 Allen, 122; Veazie v. Marett, 6 Allen, 372; Cheney v. Webster, 8 Allen, 76; Alden v. Stebbins, 99 Mass. 616; Welsh v. Welsh, 105 Mass. 229; Robinson v. Hodge, 117 Mass. 222. The operation of this statute is not suspended by the statute provisions relating to the insolvent estates of deceased persons. Aiken v. Morse, 104 Mass. 277; Blanchard v. Allen, 116 Mass. 447.

[3] Gen. Sts. c. 97, §§ 5, 6, 7. Bigelow v. Bemis, 2 Allen, 496. An executor is not liable as such, after the expiration of two years from the time of his giving bond to an action on a covenant of warranty in a deed from his testator, although the covenant is not broken until after the expiration of the two years; and although the executor is also residuary

Special administrators are not liable to actions by any creditor of the deceased; and the time of limitation for all suits against the estate begins to run after the issue of letters testamentary or of administration in the usual form, in like manner as if such special administration had not been granted.[1]

In the case of a public administrator who has given a general bond covering all estates on which administration is granted to him, the limitation begins to run, as to each estate, from the date of letters of administration.[2]

A new administrator appointed on the death, resignation, or removal of an executor or administrator, is liable to the actions of creditors for two years after he gives bond, unless the same were barred under the previous administration. If he fails to give notice of his appointment in the manner prescribed for original administrators, he will have no benefit of the statute limitation. If new assets come to his hands after the expiration of the two years, he is liable on account of such new assets, in like manner as an original executor or administrator.[3]

devisee or legatee, and gives bond for the payment of the testator's debts and legacies, and takes the assets to himself without filing an inventory. Holden v. Fletcher, 6 Cush. 235.

An action on a decree of the probate court for the payment of a balance due from the estate of a deceased guardian to his ward is barred by statute 1852, c. 204 (Gen. Sts. c. 97, § 5), in two years from the appointment of the guardian's administrator, although the decree was not obtained until the two years had expired. Bemis v. Bemis, 13 Gray, 559. Creditors whose claims were not presented within the time limited by law may recover judgment by bill in equity. Stats. 1861, c. 174, § 2; 1863, c. 235; Garfield v. Bemis, 2 Allen, 445; Waltham Bank v. Wright, 8 Allen, 121; Bradford v. Forbes, 9 Allen, 245, 365; Wells v. Child, 12 Allen, 333; Richards v. Child, 98 Mass. 284; Allen v. Trustees of Ashley School Fund, 102 Mass. 262; Bigelow v. Morong, 103 Mass. 287.

[1] Gen. Sts. c. 94, § 13.   [2] Ibid. c. 95, § 9.
[3] Gen. Sts. c. 97, §§ 12, 13, 14.

Proceeding when the Creditor's Right of Action accrues after the two years. A further exception to the rule limiting actions against executors and administrators to two years after giving bond, is made by the statute in favor of a creditor whose right of action does not accrue within the two years. A creditor holding such a claim should present a full statement of it in writing to the probate court with a petition for such an order relative thereto as the law provides. And the court, if it appears on examination that the claim is justly due from the estate, will order the executor to retain in his hands sufficient to satisfy it; or, if a person interested in the estate offers to give bond to the alleged creditor with sufficient surety or sureties for the payment of the demand in case it is proved to be due, the court may order such bond to be taken instead of requiring assets to be retained.[1]

The decision of the probate court upon the claim of such creditor is not conclusive against the executor or administrator, or other person interested to oppose the allowance thereof; and they cannot be compelled to pay the same unless it is proved to be due in an action commenced by the claimant within one year after it becomes payable;[2] or, if an appeal is taken from the decision of the probate court, in an action commenced within one

---

[1] Gen. Sts. c. 97, § 8. See Appendix, forms Nos. 52–54.

[2] Gen. Sts. c. 97, § 9. "The action shall be brought against the executor or administrator, if he has been required to retain assets therefor; otherwise upon the bond given by the persons interested in the estate. If the action is brought on the bond, the plaintiff shall set forth his original cause of action against the deceased, in like manner as would be required in a declaration for the same demand against executors and administrators, and may allege the non-payment thereof as a breach of the condition of the bond; and the defendant may answer any matter of defence that would be available in law against the demand if prosecuted in the usual manner against the executor or administrator." Gen. Sts. c. 97, §§ 10, 11.

year after the final determination of the proceedings on
the appeal.[1] If the claim was not presented to the probate court, or, if presented, was not allowed, the creditor
may, by action commenced within one year after his
right of action accrues, recover the same against the
heirs and next of kin of the deceased, and the devisees
and legatees under his will, each one of whom is liable
to the creditor to an amount not exceeding the value of
the estate that he received from the deceased, unless
the will of the deceased makes other provision for the
payment of his debts.[2]

*When Executors, &c., may pay Debts without Personal
Liability.* No executor or administrator can be held to
answer to a suit of a creditor of the deceased, if commenced within one year after he gives bond, unless it is
on a demand that would not be affected by the insolvency of the estate, or is brought after the estate has
been represented insolvent for the purpose of ascertaining a contested claim.[3]   And if, within the year after
giving notice of his appointment, he does not have notice
of demands against the estate, which will authorize him
to represent it insolvent, he may proceed to pay the debts
due, without any personal liability on that account to
any creditor who shall not have given notice of his claim,
although the estate remaining should prove insufficient
to pay the whole.[4]

PAYMENT OF LEGACIES.

The probate court has no jurisdiction of the questions
to whom, or at what time, a legacy is to be paid.   The

[1] Stat. 1871, c. 238.   [2] Gen. Sts. c. 97, § 15, c. 101, § 32.

[3] This provision includes an executor who is also a residuary legatee,
and has given bond to pay debts and legacies. National Bank of Troy
v. Stanton, 116 Mass. 439.

[4] Gen. Sts. c. 97, §§ 16, 17. As to the payment of debts when the
estate is insolvent, see *post*, c. xiii.

executor pays the legacies under the authority given him by the will of the deceased.   The rule adopted by the courts, borrowed from the civil law, requires legacies to be paid, when the will prescribes no time for their payment, after the expiration of one year from the testator's death, it being presumed that the executor will be able to inform himself during the year of the sufficiency or insufficiency of the estate to meet the demands upon it.   As a general rule, interest is allowed to legatees after the expiration of the year; [1] but compound interest is not allowable if it does not appear that the failure to pay arose from the fault of the executor.[2] Demand of payment is not necessary to entitle the legatee to interest.[3]

If the executor has given the notice of his appointment required by law, he will be secure against the demands of creditors at the end of two years after the approval of his bond; and if an executor, or administrator with the will annexed, within the two years, is required by a legatee to pay the whole or part of his legacy, the probate court may protect him in making such payments, by requiring such legatee to first give bond to the executor or administrator with surety or sureties to be approved by the court, conditioned to refund the amount to be paid, or so much thereof as may be necessary to satisfy any demands that may be afterwards recovered against the estate of the deceased, and to indemnify the executor or administrator against all loss or damage on account of such payment.[4]

[1] Miller v. Congdon, 14 Gray, 114 ; Brooks v. Lynde, 7 Allen, 64.
[2] Kent v. Dunham, 106 Mass. 586.
[3] Ibid.
[4] Gen. Sts. c. 97, § 21.   See Appendix, form No. 66.

CHAPTER XIII.

INSOLVENT ESTATES OF DECEASED PERSONS.

" WHEN the estate of a person deceased is insolvent or insufficient to pay all his debts, it shall, after discharging the necessary expenses of his funeral, last sickness, and administration, be applied to the payment of his debts in the following order : —

" First. Debts entitled to a preference under the laws of the United States ;

" Second. Public rates, taxes, and excise duties ;

" Third. Debts due to all other persons.

" If there is not enough to pay all the debts of any class, the creditors of that class shall be paid ratably upon their respective debts ; and no payment shall be made to creditors of any class until all those of the preceding class or classes, of whose claims the executor or administrator has notice, are fully paid." [1]

THE REPRESENTATION OF INSOLVENCY.

If the estate is insolvent it is the duty of the executor or administrator to represent the fact to the probate court. His neglect to do so may make him personally liable to creditors of the deceased. He is allowed ample time to satisfy himself as to the condition of the estate. He is not held liable to answer to the suit of any cred-

[1] Gen. Sts. c. 90, § 1.

itor commenced within one year after he gives bond for the faithful discharge of his trust, unless the demand is one that would not be affected by the insolvency of the estate, or is brought after the estate has been represented insolvent for the purpose of ascertaining a contested claim.[1] If, within one year after giving notice of his appointment, he does not have notice of demands which will authorize him to represent the estate insolvent, he may proceed to pay the debts due from the estate ; and he will not be personally liable to any creditor in consequence of payments made before notice of his demand. If he so pays away the whole of the estate before notice of the demand of any other creditor, he is not required in consequence of such notice to represent the estate insolvent, but may plead that he has fully administered, and be discharged on proving such payments.[2] Or, if any effects remain, and such remainder is insufficient to satisfy a demand of which he afterwards has notice, he is liable to pay only so much as may then remain ; if there are two or more such demands, which together exceed the amount of assets remaining, he may then represent the estate insolvent and pay over the amount in his hands to such persons as the court shall order ;

[1] Gen. Sts. c. 97, § 16. But he is accountable for money paid on debts within the year, though without the knowledge that the estate was insolvent. Cobb v. Muzzey, 13 Gray, 57.

[2] Gen. Sts. c. 97, §§ 17, 18 ; Cushing v. Field, 9 Met. 180. It is no bar to an action against an administrator, on a debt of his intestate, that he gave due notice of his appointment, and had no notice within a year thereafter of demands against the estate which would authorize him to represent it insolvent, and applied in payment of the debts of the deceased all the personal and a sufficient portion of the real estate to pay the debts then ascertained ; and that the heirs at the same time sold all the residue of the real estate ; and the administrator rendered his final account which was allowed. The statute applies only when the whole of the estate has been exhausted. Hildreth v. Marshall, 7 Gray, 167.

but creditors who have been previously paid cannot be required to refund any part of the amount received by them.[1]

The executor or administrator is not to wait until the claims of creditors are proved at the law before he makes his representation of insolvency. He may believe that there is a good defence against a claim that is presented to him; but if its recovery would cause insolvency, he should represent the estate insolvent. If he suffers judgment to be recovered against him before he represents the estate insolvent, he must pay the full amount of the judgment, without regard to the amount of assets in his hands. And if, on demand made upon him to pay such judgment, or to show property of the deceased to be taken in execution, he neglects or refuses so to do, he and his sureties are liable on his administration bond to a suit by the judgment creditor, although the estate is in fact insolvent. Having had full opportunity to ascertain the condition of the estate, and having allowed the claim to be prosecuted to final judgment without interfering by a representation of insolvency, the law will presume that he has the means in his hands to satisfy it.[2]

---

[1] Gen. Sts. c. 97, § 19; Colgrove v. Robinson, 11 Met. 238. This provision of the statute applies to payments made *after* the expiration of the year. If the executor, *within* a year after giving notice of his appointment, pays a debt of his intestate, he may, if the estate afterwards proves insolvent, recover of the creditor the excess of the sum so paid over the amount awarded to the creditor by commissioners of insolvency. Heard v. Drake, 4 Gray, 514; Richards v. Nightingale, 9 Allen, 149. The administrator cannot recover unless he proves the insolvency of the estate by a commission of insolvency regularly issued, executed, and returned, and a dividend declared by the court. Bascom v. Butterfield, 1 Met. 536. See Austin v. Henshaw, 7 Pick. 46. The general statute of limitations will begin to run against the claim of the administrator from the date when the dividend is ordered. Richards v. Nightingale, 9 Allen, 149.

[2] Newcomb v. Goss, 1 Met. 333.

If it appears, upon the settlement of the administration account in the probate court, that the whole estate which has come to the hands of the executor has been exhausted in paying *debts preferred by law*, such settlement, the statute provides, shall be a sufficient bar to any action brought against the executor or administrator by a creditor who is not entitled to such preference, although the estate has not been represented insolvent.[1] But the executor or administrator who undertakes to pay the preferred claims without first making a representation of insolvency, must pay them strictly in the order prescribed by statute. The assets may not be sufficient to pay all the preferred debts, and in such case the several classes of creditors must be paid in their order. Taxes, for instance, cannot be paid until the two anterior classes of creditors have been fully satisfied; and if the assets are not sufficient to pay all the debts of any one class, the creditors of that class must be paid ratably. It seems that an executor who is residuary legatee, and who has given bond to pay the debts and legacies, cannot represent the estate insolvent, — the bond is a conclusive admission of sufficient assets.[2]

The representation of insolvency must be addressed to the probate court in the county in which the executor or administrator was appointed, and should set forth the amount of the indebtedness of the estate, so far as it can be ascertained (including the funeral expenses, charges of administration, and the allowance, if any, made to the widow or minor children), and the amount of the assets in the hands of the executor or administrator. There should also be filed a list of the claims against the estate, showing the name of each creditor and the sum

[1] Gen. Sts. c. 97, § 20.
[2] Alger v. Colwell, 2 Gray, 404; Jones v. Richardson, 5 Met. 247.

claimed by each. If the evidence of the fact of insolvency is satisfactory, the court will appoint two or more fit persons to be commissioners to receive and examine the claims of creditors.[1]

TIME ALLOWED FOR PROOF OF CLAIMS.

Six months are allowed after the appointment of the commissioners for the creditors to present and prove their claims: and the court will allow such further time for the proof of debts, not exceeding eighteen months from the date of the commission, as may be deemed necessary.[2] Such further time may be applied for in writing by any creditor who has not proved his claim. The application should fully set forth the reasons for which it is made.[3] The commission may be reopened at any time within the eighteen months, although the return of the commissioners may have been made to the probate court; and the party applying for such extension may appeal from a decree of the court denying the prayer of his petition.[4] And in case of an appeal from the commissioners, if it appears to the court that a just distribution of the estate requires a longer time for the proof of claims than eighteen months, further time may be allowed not extending more than one month beyond

---

[1] Or the court may proceed to receive and examine the claims, instead of appointing commissioners. Stat. 1873, c. 252.

Where a judge of probate had rejected a representation of insolvency made by an administrator, and upon a second application which the administrator offered to support by legal evidence, again refused to receive it, giving his former decision as a reason for the second denial, and an appeal was taken, he was directed to receive the evidence and thereupon to decree according to law and the justice of the case. Bucknam v. Phelps, 6 Mass. 448.

[2] Gen. Sts. c. 99, § 4.   [3] See Appendix, form No. 56.

[4] Walker v. Lyman's Administrators, 6 Pick. 458.

the final decision of the appeal.[1] And if a commissioner dies, resigns, fails to make the return required by law, or is removed, a new commissioner may be appointed, and in such case the time for making proof of claims is extended six months from the appointment of such new commissioner.[2]

Such extensions of time, however, do not relieve a creditor from the obligation to commence the prosecution of his claim, either at law or before commissioners within two years from the time when bond was given by the administrator. If proceedings are not commenced within that time his claim will be barred, unless it can be proved as a contingent claim, or unless new assets come to the hands of the administrator after the expiration of the two years.[3]

The commissioners cannot allow claims after the expiration of the time limited by statute or fixed by the court.[4]

PROOF OF CLAIMS.

The warrant issued to the commissioners contains instructions for their formal proceedings. They must first be sworn to faithfully discharge the duties of their office. The oath may be administered by any justice of the peace, and a certificate thereof should be made by him on the warrant, to be returned with their report. They are required to appoint convenient times and places for their meetings to receive and examine claims, and to give at least seven days' written notice of the time and place of each meeting, by mail or otherwise, to all known creditors of the deceased, and such other notice, by publishing in some newspaper or otherwise, as the court

---

[1] Stat. 1863, c. 217. [2] Stat. 1868, c. 327.
[3] Aiken v. Morse, 104 Mass. 277. [4] Bascom v. Butterfield, 1 Met. 536.

may order.[1] The executor or administrator is required to furnish them, fourteen days at least before their first meeting, the names and residences of all known creditors. The commissioners hold as many meetings, within the six months, as are necessary for the complete discharge of the trust committed to them.

The commissioners may require any claimant to make true answers, under oath, to all questions relating to his claim, and if he refuses to take such oath, or to answer fully all questions, they may disallow his claim. Either of the commissioners may administer such oath to the claimants and witnesses.[2]

The commissioners are to liquidate and balance all mutual demands subsisting between the deceased insolvent and his creditors. If the balance is found in favor of the creditor it should be allowed by the commissioners and included in their report; but if the balance is found to be against the creditor, it is not a subject of their report, which is to include claims against the estate only.[3]

Copartnership debts for which the deceased was liable may be proved against his estate.[4] A claim payable absolutely may be proved before its maturity.[5]

---

[1] See Appendix, form No. 58. [2] Gen. Sts. c. 99, §§ 15, 16.

[3] When the defendant in a suit brought by the administrator of an insolvent estate files in set-off a claim larger than that on which he is sued, he is entitled to judgment for the balance, and need not present his claim to the commissioners. The judgment is to be presented to the judge of probate, and by him added to the claims allowed by the commissioners. Bigelow v. Folger, 2 Met. 255. In such suit the defendant may set off a note which falls due pending the suit, though not due when the action was commenced. Ibid.

[4] A stipulation in partnership articles that in case of the decease of either partner the business may be carried on for one year by the survivor for the mutual benefit of both parties, does not, in case of the death

---

[5] Haverhill Loan & Fund Ass. v. Cronin, 4 Allen, 144.

A creditor whose claim is secured, or partly secured, by mortgage or otherwise, cannot prove his full claim before the commissioners unless he first surrenders his security for the benefit of the estate. But he may be allowed the balance of his claim remaining after deducting the value of the security. Such value may be determined by agreement between the creditor and executor, or by a sale of the security, or it may be estimated by the commissioners.[1]

Interest is to be allowed on all claims expressly bearing interest, and upon claims not expressly bearing interest where there is evidence establishing the creditor's right to receive interest. Upon claims not bearing interest and not matured a rebate of interest is to be made. The common practice is to compute this allowance and rebate of interest to the date of the death of the intestate. Except in very rare cases, it is immaterial whether the interest stops at the death of the debtor or

of one partner, justify the allowance against his insolvent estate of a debt contracted by the survivor within the year, with one who had notice of the death. Stanwood v. Owen, 14 Gray, 195. Payments made by the surviving partner while carrying on the partnership business pursuant to such stipulation, upon an account some items of which were contracted before, and some after, the death of the other partner, must be applied to the discharge of the first items. Ibid. A surviving partner may prove a claim against the estate of his deceased partner. Sparhawk v. Russell, 10 Met. 307.

[1] Farnum v. Boutelle, 13 Met. 159; Hooker v. Olmstead, 6 Pick. 481; Middlesex Bank v. Minot, 4 Met. 325; Haverhill Loan & Fund Ass. v. Cronin, 4 Allen, 144.

But this rule does not apply to a case where the collateral security was furnished by a third person not primarily responsible for the debt. A widow who has joined with her husband in a mortgage of her separate estate to secure his debt, which she has paid since his death for the purpose of exonerating her estate, may prove the amount before the commissioners. And a creditor may prove his debt without first surrendering a mortgage of the separate estate of the debtor's wife, which he holds as security. Savage v. Winchester, 15 Gray, 453.

at a later day in the settlement of the estate, inasmuch as the proportion in which the assets are distributed among the creditors will be the same by either mode of computation. The main object is to fix upon some date to which the affairs of the deceased shall be adjusted. But cases have occurred where the assets have proved more than sufficient to pay the debts as they existed at the time of the death of the insolvent, but not sufficient to pay them with interest computed to the time of the decree of distribution. In such cases, and whenever the equitable distribution of the assets requires it, the court will add interest on the claims allowed to the time of distribution.[1]

It is the duty of the executor or administrator to oppose the allowance of all claims improperly presented to the commissioners. If he is guilty of corrupt conduct in not opposing the allowance of illegal claims, he will be liable to an action on his bond.[2] He should be present at the meetings of the commissioners, and should take an appeal from their decision whenever an appeal is necessary to protect the rights of persons interested in the estate.

The claim of an executor or administrator against the estate which he administers should be presented for allowance to the probate court, not to the commissioners.

RETURN OF THE COMMISSIONERS.

At the expiration of the time limited for the proof of claims the commissioners are required by law to make their return to the probate court,[3] and performance of that

---

[1] Williams v. American Bank, 4 Met. 317.

[2] Parsons v. Mills, 2 Mass. 80.

[3] It is the duty of the commissioners to make their own return to the

duty may be compelled, on motion of any party interested, by the order of the court which appointed them.[1] Their return must give a list of all the claims presented to them, whether allowed or not, with the sum allowed on each, stated in separate classes, as follows: first, debts entitled to a preference under the laws of the United States; second, public rates, taxes, and excise duties; third, debts due to all other persons. Debts proved against the deceased as a member of a partnership firm must be stated in a separate list.

If the executor or administrator has settled his accounts in the probate court, the final distribution of the balance in his hands may be ordered after the expiration of thirty days from the return of the commissioners, and the settlement of the estate completed, unless there are contingent debts which could not be proved before the commissioners, or unless an appeal is taken from some decision of the commissioners.

PROVISIONS AS TO CONTINGENT CLAIMS.

The statute provides that "if at the return of the commission any person is liable as a surety for the deceased, or has any other contingent claim against his estate which could not be proved as a debt under the commission, the court upon proof thereof shall, in ordering a dividend, leave in the hands of the executor or administrator a sum sufficient to pay to such contingent

---

probate court. It is no part of the official duty of the administrator to receive the report of the commissioners and carry or send it to the judge of probate; if he receives the report and undertakes to return it, this is merely a personal engagement for the performance of which the sureties in his bond are not bound. Nelson v. Woodbury, 1 Greenl. 251.

[1] Blanchard v. Allen, 116 Mass. 447.

creditor a proportion equal to what shall then be paid to the other creditors. If such contingent debt becomes absolute within four years from the date of the administration bond, it may be allowed by the probate court if not disputed by the executor or administrator; and if disputed, it may be proved before the commissioners already appointed or others to be appointed by the judge, in like manner as if presented before the first return of the commissioners. Upon the allowance of such claim, the creditor shall be entitled to a dividend thereon equal to what has been paid to the other creditors, so far as the same can be paid without disturbing the former dividend; and if his claim is not finally established, or if the dividend due to him does not exhaust the assets in the hands of the executor or administrator, the residue of the assets shall be divided among all creditors who have proved their debts." [1]

These provisions of the statute apply only to cases where the claim is one that could not be proved as a debt under the commission. The surety on a promissory note made by the deceased which has been proved against the estate by the person holding it, cannot have such a contingent claim. His claim against the estate could have been proved by him. He could have paid the holder, made the note his own property, and proved it as his own claim. Moreover, the holder who proved the note will take the entire dividend allowed upon it, and the claim, so far as the insolvent estate is concerned, will be extinguished by the dividend paid to him. The surety cannot also take a dividend on the same debt. The statute refers to cases where the holder of the debt cannot, from some cause, prove his debt under the com-

[1] Gen. Sts. c. 90, §§ 5, 6, 7.

mission, or where the surety cannot make the debt his own by payment.[1]

APPEALS FROM DECISIONS OF THE COMMISSIONERS.

The determination of the commissioners is not necessarily conclusive in any case. Any person whose claim is disallowed in whole or in part, and any executor or administrator, and any heir, legatee, devisee, or creditor of the insolvent estate, who is dissatisfied with the allowance of a claim, may appeal from their decision, and the claim will thereupon be determined at common law in the county in which the probate or administration was granted.[2] The appeal is not taken from any order of the probate court, but from the decision of the commissioners. If the demand exceeds the sum of three thousand dollars in the county of Suffolk, or one thousand dollars in any other county, the appeal is taken to the supreme judicial court; otherwise to the superior court.[3] The appeal must be claimed and notice thereof given at the probate office within thirty days after the return of the commissioners.[4] If the appeal is by an executor or administrator he must give notice thereof to the creditor within said thirty days.[5] The appeal must be entered at the court appealed to held next after the expiration of the thirty days.

[1] Cummings v. Thompson, 7 Met. 132; French v. Hayward, 16 Gray, 512; Sears v. Willis, 7 Allen, 430.

[2] Gen. Sts. c. 99, § 8; Stat. 1865, c. 258.

[3] Gen. Sts. c. 99, § 8; Waters v. Randall, 8 Met. 132.

[4] Gen. Sts. c. 99, § 9. When the time for proof of claims is extended, an appeal from a decision of the commissioners disallowing the claim of a creditor may be filed within thirty days after their final return, though such claim was presented and disallowed before the first return of the warrant. Merriam v. Leonard, 6 Cush. 151.

[5] Gen. Sts. c. 99, § 9. See Appendix, forms Nos. 59, 60.

At the term of court at which the appeal is entered, the supposed creditor must file a statement in writing of his claim, setting forth briefly and distinctly all the material facts which would be necessary in a declaration for the same cause of action ; and like proceedings are thereupon had in the pleadings, trial, and determination of the cause, as in an action at law prosecuted in the usual manner, except that no execution is awarded against the executor for a debt found due to the claimant. The final judgment is conclusive, and the list of debts allowed by the commissioners will be altered if necessary to conform thereto.[1]

The party prevailing upon the appeal is entitled to costs, which, if recovered against the executor or administrator, may be allowed to him in his administration account.[2]

The statute provides that any person whose claim is disallowed by the commissioners, and who for other cause than his own neglect omits to claim or prosecute his appeal as above stated, may, by petitioning the supreme judicial court holden in any county, be allowed to claim and prosecute his appeal upon such terms as the court shall impose, if it appears that justice requires a further examination of his claim ; but such petition must be presented within two years after the date of the administration bond.[3] The petition in such case should set forth particularly the nature of the claim and the reason of the petitioner's omission to reasonably claim and prosecute his appeal.

The allowance of such appeal cannot disturb any distribution ordered before notice of the petition, or notice of the intention to present the same has been

[1] Gen. Sts. c. 99, § 10.   [2] Ibid. § 12.
[3] Ibid. § 13 ; Cross v. Cross, 7 Met. 211.

given in writing at the probate office, or to the executor
or administrator; but the debts thus proved and allowed
are paid only out of such assets as remain in or come
to the hands of the executor or administrator after
payment of the sums due on such prior decree of distribution.[1] The party who intends to petition for leave
to prosecute his appeal should therefore give immediate
notice at the probate office, or to the executor, of his
intention to present the same. The effect of such
notice, if distribution has not already been ordered, may
be to materially increase the amount of his dividend.

WAIVER OF APPEAL, AND ARBITRATION.

After the claiming of an appeal from a decision of
the commissioners, the parties may waive a trial at law
and submit the claim to the determination of arbitrators to be agreed on between them, and appointed accordingly by a rule of the probate court. The report
of such arbitrators, if accepted by the court, will be
conclusive in like manner as a judgment.[2]

The executor and the creditor, if they agree to submit the claim to arbitration, should join in a written
representation of the fact to the court, and state therein
the names of the arbitrators agreed upon.[3] The arbitrators must notify the parties of the time and place
fixed for the hearing, and after the hearing return to
the court their award, with the rule and any papers
issued therewith. They should also return a certificate
of the costs of the arbitration.

The arbitrators have no power to award that the
claimant is in fact indebted to the estate. They are to

[1] Gen. Sts. c. 99, § 14.   [2] Ibid. § 11.
[3] See Appendix, form Nos. 61–64.

find only what amount, if any, is due from the estate to the claimant.[1]

DISTRIBUTION OF INSOLVENT ESTATES.

After the expiration of thirty days from the return of the commissioners, the probate court decrees the distribution of the assets in the hands of the executor among the creditors whose claims have been allowed. If before making the decree the court has notice of an appeal from the commissioners, then claimed or pending, the decree may be suspended until the determination of the appeal, or a distribution may be ordered among the creditors whose debts are allowed, leaving in the executor's hands a sum sufficient to pay the claimant whose demand is disputed a portion equal to that of the other creditors.

Dividends may be ordered and paid to creditors whose claims have been allowed whenever the court may deem it proper, leaving in the hands of the executor or administrator a sum sufficient to pay claims that may probably be proved a proportion equal to what shall be then paid to the other creditors.[2]

If the whole assets are not distributed upon the first decree, or if further assets come to the hands of the executor or administrator, the probate court will make such further decrees for distribution as the case requires.[3]

No final distribution can be made until the accounts of the executor or administrator are settled in the probate court, and the sum to be distributed thereby ascertained. His accounts should be settled at the earliest day practicable after the return of the commissioners is made, and he may be liable on his bond for neglect in

---

[1] Gilmore v. Hubbard, 12 Cush. 220.   [2] Stat. 1868, c. 327.
[3] Gen. Sts. c. 99, § 19; White v. Swain, 3 Pick. 365.

this particular. The statute provides that if an executor or administrator neglects to render and settle his accounts in the probate court within six months after the return made by the commissioners, or the final liquidation of the demands of the creditors, or within such further time as the court shall allow, such neglect shall be deemed unfaithful administration, and he may be forthwith removed, and shall be liable in a suit on his bond, for all damages occasioned by his default.[1]

In making the distribution, the preferred creditors, if the assets are sufficient, are paid in full, in the order required by statute. If there is not enough to pay all the debts of any one class, the creditors of that class are paid ratably upon their respective debts. The balance remaining after the payment of the preferred claims is distributed ratably among the other creditors. If the deceased had been a member of a copartnership, and died in possession of both separate and partnership estate, and was indebted as a partner as well as on private account, his partnership debts are payable from the partnership estate and his separate debts from his separate estate. If there is a balance of the separate estate after the payment of his separate debts, it is added to the joint stock for the payment of the joint creditors. If there is a balance of the joint stock after the payment of the joint debts, it is divided among the separate estates of the partners according to their respective interests therein, as it would have been if the partnership had been dissolved without insolvency ; and the sum so appropriated to the separate estate of each partner is applied to the payment of his separate debts.[2]

---

[1] Gen. Sts. c. 99, § 26.

[2] Ibid. § 18 ; c. 118, § 109 ; Howe v. Lawrence, 9 Cush. 553 ; Fall River Whaling Co. v. Borden, 10 Cush. 458.

The order of distribution directs the executor or administrator to pay the balance in his hands to the persons named in the order, and specifies the sum to which each is entitled. He is also directed to give notice to each creditor of the amount of his dividend, and if any of the sums which he is ordered to pay remain for six months unclaimed, to deposit the same in a savings-bank (designated in the order) in the name of the judge of probate for the time being, to accumulate for the benefit of the person entitled thereto.[1]

When the executor or administrator has paid over or deposited the money in his hands as required by the decree of distribution, he may perpetuate the evidence thereof by presenting to the probate court, within one year after the decree was made, an account of such payments, which, being proved to the satisfaction of the court and verified by the oath of the party, is allowed as his final discharge. He may conveniently make such account by returning the original decree, with the receipts of the several creditors and the certificates of deposit annexed thereto, together with his own certificate that the several payments have been made as ordered.

After twenty years from the decree of distribution of an insolvent estate, the probate court, on application of any creditor whose claim was proved and allowed, and after notice of such application published for not less than two years on such days as the court shall direct, in one or more newspapers of the county, may order any unclaimed dividends with the interest received thereon, after deducting all expenses and charges of administra-

---

[1] When the person entitled to the money deposited satisfies the judge of his right to receive the same, the judge causes it to be paid over and transferred to him. Gen. Sts. c. 101, § 9. See Appendix, forms No. 73. 74.

tion since the decree of distribution, to be distributed anew among the creditors who have received their dividends.   If there is a surplus after satisfying the claims of such creditors with interest, it will be distributed to the heirs of the deceased.[1]

ACTIONS BY CREDITORS AFTER THE REPRESENTATION OF INSOLVENCY.

After the representation of insolvency and the appointment of commissioners, the law will not permit any of the assets of the estate to be taken from the executor or administrator by legal process, to satisfy the demand of any creditor, until the question of insolvency is determined.   No action can be maintained unless for a demand entitled to a preference, or unless the assets prove more than sufficient to pay all the debts allowed by the commissioners.   If the estate is represented insolvent while an action is pending for any demand not entitled to such preference, the action can be discontinued without payment of costs; or, if the demand is disputed, the action may be tried and determined, and judgment rendered thereon, in the same manner and with the same effect as in the case of an appeal from the award of commissioners; or the action may be continued without costs until it appears whether the estate is insolvent, and, if not insolvent, the plaintiff may prosecute the action as if no such representation had been made.[2]

[1] Gen. Sts. c. 99, § 27.
[2] Ibid. § 20; Cushing v. Field, 9 Met. 180; Johnson v. Ames, 6 Pick. 330; Hunt v. Whitney, 4 Mass. 624.

RECOVERY OF CLAIMS NOT PROVED BEFORE THE COMMISSIONERS.

Every creditor of an insolvent estate who does not present his claim for allowance will be barred from recovering it, unless further assets come to the hands of the executor or administrator after the decree of distribution ; in such case his claim may be proved and paid in the manner and with the limitations provided for contingent debts.[1] When such further assets come to the estate, the probate court, on application of such creditor, may open the commission. The creditor's petition must allege that further assets have come to the hands of the executor or administrator, and he must substantiate this allegation by proof. Without such proof the commission will not be opened. Either the creditor or executor may appeal from the decree of the probate court allowing or refusing the prayer of the petition.[2]

The claim of a creditor in whose favor the commission is reopened is not barred, in consequence of the lapse of time subsequent to the closing of the first commission, by any of the statutes of limitation. He may proceed by petition whenever there are new assets to be distributed. The executor or administrator is liable to account for all funds in his hands, though he may have received them more than twenty years after the decree of distribution was passed.[3]

If after the report of the commissioners the assets prove sufficient to pay all debts allowed, the executor or administrator pays them in full ; and if any other

---

[1] Gen. Sts. c. 99, § 21.

[2] The decree if not appealed from is conclusive, and cannot be inquired into in a subsequent appeal from the subsequent decision of the commissioners allowing or disallowing the claim. Ostrom v. Curtis, 1 Cush. 461.

[3] Ibid. ; White v. Swain, 3 Pick. 365.

debt is afterwards recovered against him, he is liable therefor only to the extent of the assets then remaining. If there are two or more such creditors, the assets, if insufficient to pay them in full, is divided between them in proportion to their debts. The executor or administrator, in an action brought against him on such demand, may prove the amount of assets in his hands, and thereupon judgment will be rendered in the usual form ; but execution will not issue for more than the amount of such assets ; and if there are two or more such judgments, the court will apportion the amount between them.[1]

If it is not ascertained, at the end of eighteen months after the granting of letters testamentary or of administration, whether an estate represented insolvent is or is not so in fact, any creditor whose claim has not been presented before the commissioners may commence an action therefor against the executor or administrator, which may be continued without costs for the defendant until it appears whether the estate is insolvent. If it appears solvent, the plaintiff may prosecute the action as if no such representation had been made.[2]   If it proves insolvent, he will have no remedy unless new assets come to the hands of the executor or administrator, in which case he may petition that the commission be opened ; and if the commission is opened, he can prove his claim.   All actions against an executor or administrator must be commenced within two years from the time he gives bond for the discharge of his trust except in the cases specified by statute.[3]

---

[1] Gen. Sts. c. 99, §§ 22–24.

[2] Ibid. § 25.   [3] Ibid. c. 97, §§ 6, 7; *ante*, p. 137.

PROVISIONS AS TO ESTATES OF DECEASED FOREIGNERS.

When an inhabitant of another State or country dies insolvent and leaves estate to be administered here, the estate found here is not to be transmitted to the foreign administrator until creditors who are citizens of this State have received their equitable dividends. If all the assets were transmitted to the foreign administrator, creditors in this State would be subjected to the expense of proving and collecting their demands abroad; and the pursuit of their claims in countries where the local law makes no provision for an equal distribution of the assets of a deceased insolvent, might be wholly fruitless. Under the provisions of our statute, citizens of this State cannot be put to the inconvenience of proving their claims abroad when there are assets here; nor, on the other hand, can the whole estate found here be expended in paying the claims of our citizens to the prejudice of foreign creditors; but the estate found here, as far as practicable, is to be so disposed of, that all creditors of the deceased, here and elsewhere, may receive each an equal share in proportion to their respective debts.[1]

To this end, the statute provides that the assets shall not be sent to the foreign administrator until all creditors who are citizens of this State have received the just proportion that would be due to them if the whole estate of the deceased wherever found, that is applicable to the payment of common creditors, were divided among all the creditors in proportion to their respective debts, without preferring any one species of debt to another,[2]

---

[1] Gen. Sts. c. 101, § 40; Dawes v. Head, 3 Pick. 128; Hooker v. Olmstead, 6 Pick. 481; Davis v. Esty, 8 Pick. 475.

[2] The local laws of some countries prefer debts on judgments, bonds,

in which case no creditor who is not a citizen of this State shall be paid out of the assets found here until all those who are citizens have received their just proportion.[1]

The statute further provides that if there is any residue remaining after such payment to the citizens of this State, it may be paid to any other creditors who have duly proved their debts here, in proportion to the amount due to each of them, but no one shall receive more than would be due to him if the whole estate were divided ratably among all the creditors. The balance may be transmitted to the foreign executor or administrator; or, if there is none, it shall, after the expiration of four years from the appointment of the administrator, be distributed ratably among all creditors, both citizens and others, who have proved their debts in this State.[2]

&c., to simple contract debts.   Such preferences are not to be regarded in the distribution here.

[1] Gen. Sts. c. 101, § 41.   [2] Ibid. § 42.

CHAPTER XIV.

SALES OF LAND BY EXECUTORS, ADMINISTRATORS, AND GUARDIANS.

SALES BY EXECUTORS AND ADMINISTRATORS.

WHEN the personal estate of a deceased person is insufficient to pay his debts with the charges of administration, his executor or administrator may sell his real estate for that purpose, having been first licensed therefor by the supreme judicial court or superior court in any county, or the probate court in which letters testamentary or of administration issued.[1] And when a tes-

---

[1] Gen. Sts. c. 102, §§ 1, 2.

An executor who is residuary legatee and gives bond for the payment of the debts and legacies, acquires an absolute title in the estate devised, and may convey it without license. Clark v. Tufts, 5 Pick. 337. And an executor duly authorized thereto by the terms of the will, may convey the lands of his testator without license. But when the executor, so empowered by the will, dies before making the conveyance, or renounces the office of executor, the power to sell does not devolve upon the administrator with the will annexed who succeeds him. Such administrator can sell only by license of court. Tainter v. Clark, 13 Met. 220; Greenough v. Wells, 10 Cush. 571; Larned v. Bridge, 17 Pick. 339; Conklin v. Egerton's administrator, 21 Wendell, 430. See Warden v. Richards, 11 Gray, 277. If the power to sell is given to two executors, one of whom resigns, the other may exercise it singly. Gould v. Mather, 104 Mass. 283.

If the executor is authorized to sell lands for trust purposes, he does not, by renouncing the office of executor, lose the power to convey as trustee under the will. His sales and conveyances, made after the renun-

tator has given a legacy, which with his debts and the charges of administration his personal estate is insufficient to pay, the executor or administrator with the will annexed may be licensed, in like manner, to sell real estate for that purpose.[1]

As the legal title to real estate vests in the heirs or devisees immediately upon the death of the owner, the administrator, as such, has nothing to do with the lands of his intestate, except to see that they are appraised, until he is licensed to sell them for the payment of debts and charges. Nor has the executor, unless under an authority given him by the will of his testator. When, therefore, lands are sold by executors and administrators, it is important for them to observe strictly the directions of the statute, from which alone they derive the power to make the conveyance.

Licenses to sell real estate are provided for by the statute only when the personal property is insufficient for the payment of debts, legacies, and charges of administration. The convenience of parties interested in the lands would be promoted, in some cases, by a sale of them by the administrator, although the proceeds are not needed for the payment of debts or legacies, but licenses cannot be granted under such circumstances (except to public administrators, whose sales under license are considered in a subsequent part of this chap-

---

ciation of his executorship and after his acceptance of the trust, are valid as against the devisees and their heirs. Clark *v.* Tainter, 7 Cush. 567.

Where, under the provisions of a will, the sale of devised real estate by a trustee or executor is dependent upon the consent of a person who shall have deceased, the judge of the probate court having jurisdiction of the proceedings in the settlement of the estate, may, in his discretion, authorize the sale of such real estate the same as though no such consent was required; provided all parties interested in the sale assent thereto. Stat. 1871, c. 329.

[2] Gen. Sts. c. 102, § 19.

ter'). The sale must be necessary for the payment of claims which can be enforced at law.[1]

The Real Estate liable to be sold includes all lands of the deceased, and all rights of entry and of action, and all other rights and interests in lands which by law would descend to his heirs, or which would have been liable to attachment or execution by a creditor of the deceased in his lifetime.[2] No claim to such lands by

---

[1] Lamson *v.* Schutt, 4 Allen, 359.

[2] All lands of the debtor in possession, remainder, or reversion, all his rights of entry into lands and of redeeming mortgaged lands, and all lands and rights above described fraudulently conveyed by him with intent to defeat, delay, or defraud his creditors, or purchased, or directly or indirectly paid for by him, the record title to which is retained in the vendor, or is conveyed to a third person with intent to defeat, delay, or defraud the creditors of the debtor or on a trust for him, express or implied, may (except homestead rights) be taken on execution for his debts. Gen. Sts. c. 103, § 1.

An executor or administrator licensed to sell lands fraudulently conveyed by the deceased, or fraudulently held by another person for him, or to which he had a right of entry or of action or a right to a conveyance, may first obtain possession thereof by entry or by action. Yeomans *v.* Brown, 8 Met. 51. He may make a formal entry on the premises and bring an action on his own seisin acquired by such entry, demanding the land as executor or administrator. Gen. Sts. c. 102, §§ 12, 13.

Real estate, conveyed by an intestate in his lifetime, without adequate consideration, and by way of gift, either in whole or in part, may be sold by his administrator to pay his debts, as estate conveyed by him with intent to defraud his creditors, if, at the time of the conveyance, he thereby rendered himself unable to pay his then existing creditors. Norton *v.* Norton, 5 Cush. 524.

The proceeds of a sale by an administrator of real estate conveyed by his intestate with a view to defraud creditors, though such conveyance was void at the time as against then existing creditors only, are applicable to the payment of all the creditors alike. Ibid.

If an administrator receives payment of a note given for the purchase-money of an estate, conveyed by his intestate to defraud creditors, he does not thereby ratify the conveyance; unless the payment is received with full knowledge of the facts, and the administrator is a party in interest, in which case it might be otherwise. Ibid.

The interest of a deceased partner in partnership real estate which is

entry or action can be made more than five years after the death of the grantor. When land is demised for the term of one hundred years or more, the term, so long as fifty years thereof remain unexpired, is regarded by the statute as an estate in fee-simple as to every thing concerning the sale thereof by executors, administrators, and guardians by license from any court.[1]

The executor or administrator may sell lands held in mortgage, or taken in execution for a debt due the deceased, at any time before the right to redeem them is foreclosed, in the same manner as personal estate. The legal title to such lands is in him. He holds it in trust for the persons who would be entitled to the money if the mortgage or other debt had been paid. But after the right of redemption is foreclosed, the executor should obtain license before making sale of the land, in the same manner as if the deceased had died seised of it. The license is not necessary to enable the executor to convey the legal title, which is already vested in him, but is intended solely to bind heirs and legatees, and make the title good against them as the owners of the beneficial interest.[2]

The Petition for License to sell Real Estate must be presented by the executor or administrator to the probate court of the county in which letters testamentary or of administration issued. If there are two or more execu-

---

not required for the settlement of the affairs of the firm, is to be treated as realty, and may be sold for the payment of legacies. Wilcox v. Wilcox, 13 Allen, 252.

[1] Gen. Sts. c. 90, § 20.

[2] Ibid. c. 96, § 9, et seq.

An executor, who, after foreclosing a mortgage held by his testator, sells and conveys the land, without license of court, is not liable to an action on the covenant of good right to convey in his deed, if the legatees have received the purchase-money ; nor, *it seems*, if they have not. Baldwin v. Timmins, 3 Gray, 302.

tors or administrators, all must join in the petition.[1] It may be presented as soon as the necessity of the proposed sale becomes apparent. It must be in writing, and the statute requires to be set forth therein the amount of the debts due from the deceased as nearly as they can be ascertained, the amount of charges of administration, and the value of the personal estate, exclusive of the amount allowed the widow or minor children, in the executor's hands. It is sufficient to state in the petition the gross amount of all the debts due, but the executor or administrator must file with his petition a list of the debts, so far as they can be ascertained, showing the name of each creditor and the sum due to each. Such list of claims should be signed by the petitioner and sworn to.[2]

If it is necessary to sell only part of the real estate, the petitioner may also set forth the value, description, and condition of the estate, or of such part as he proposes to sell, and the court may direct what specific part shall be sold. If the estate is so situated that by a partial sale the residue of the estate, or of some specific piece or part thereof, would be greatly injured, the facts should be stated in the petition.[3]

It is sometimes the case that the testator has made by will some disposition of his estate for the payment of his debts, or has given some directions which may vary the order in which the different parts of his estate shall be appropriated. Thus, though the personal property is first liable for payment of debts, the testator may expressly exempt it, or some portion of it, by making it

[1] Hannum v. Day, 105 Mass. 33.

[2] It is not necessary that the amount of the debts should have been previously ascertained by judgment against the executor, or by commission of insolvency. Tenny v. Poor, 14 Gray, 500.

[3] Gen. Sts. c. 102, §§ 3, 4; Yeomans v. Brown, 8 Met. 58.

the subject of a specific legacy, and may direct his debts
to be paid out of other funds, or may leave other funds
not exempted.   Such specific legacies are not to be
taken for the payment of debts, if there are other funds,
so first liable.   The law will respect the testator's directions so far as is consistent with the rights of creditors.
If the will contains any provision which may require or
induce the court to marshal the assets in any manner
different from that which the law would otherwise pre-
scribe, such devise or parts of the will must be set forth
in the petition, and a copy of the will must be exhibited
to the court.[1]   Undevised land is first chargeable with
the testator's debts in exoneration, as far as it will go,
of the real estate devised, unless a different arrangement is made by the will.[2]

Notice to Parties interested.   The license will not be
granted until notice of the petition, and of the time and
place appointed for hearing the same, has been served
either personally on all persons interested in the estate,[3]
at least fourteen days before the time appointed for the
hearing, or by publication three weeks successively in
some newspaper, as the court may order.   The petition

---

[1] Gen. Sts. c. 102, § 7.   [2] Ibid. c. 92, § 34.

[3] When the executor petitions for license to sell land of which his testator was disseised at the time of his death, for the purpose of paying
his debts, the disseisor in possession is not interested in the estate, within
the meaning of the statute, and is not entitled to notice of the petition in
order to render the license valid as against him.   Yeomans *v.* Brown, 8
Met. 51.

The practice in the probate court is to order notice in the manner prescribed by statute, and it is not made the duty of the executor to obtain
the appointment of guardians to all minors interested in the estate before
he can obtain a license.   Holmes *v.* Beal, 9 Cush. 226.

The wife of a devisee of real estate is not entitled to notice of a petition of the devisor's administrator for license to sell it for the payment
of debts, legacies, and charges of administration.   Harrington *v.* Harrington, 13 Gray, 513.

may be filed in the probate office on any day, and the order issued by the register of probate. But if all persons interested signify their assent in writing to the sale, notice may be dispensed with.[1] The assent should be indorsed on the petition.

The Necessity for the proposed Sale. The party applying for license to sell the real estate of his testator or intestate, must satisfy the court that a necessity exists for the sale he proposes to make. To do this, he must exhibit the condition of the estate at the time. If the inventory made of the estate was full and complete, the necessity of the sale may be apparent from a comparison of the list of debts with the inventory. But the inventory shows, in but very few cases, the full amount of the personal assets, and the better course, in all cases, is for the petitioner to render an account of his administration on or before the day when his application for a license is to be heard by the court.

The averment and admission of the executor that a certain debt is due from the estate, is not evidence to establish the fact. But any creditor of the deceased is a competent witness to prove his debt in support of the executor's petition.[2]

The adjudication of the probate court as to the existence of debts and charges is final, so far as it affects any title acquired by virtue of the license, but does not affect the right of the executor or administrator to contest the validity of such debts and charges.[3]

Any person interested may appear and object to the granting of the license, and if it appears to the court that either the petition or the objection thereto is un-

---

[1] Gen. Sts. c. 102, § 8.
[2] Chamberlain *v.* Chamberlain, 4 Allen, 184.
[3] Stat. 1874, c. 340.

reasonable, they may award costs to the prevailing party.[1]

It may be that the heirs or devisees prefer to keep the estate entire and in their own hands, or the value of the property may be temporarily depressed, so that it cannot be sold immediately without a considerable sacrifice. If for these reasons, or for any reasons, the persons interested wish to stay proceedings under the petition and prevent the sale, they can effect that result by paying to the executor or administrator the amount of money needed for the payment of claims against the estate, and the money so received will be assets of the estate to be administered and accounted for; and the executor or administrator will be liable on his bond for any failure to appropriate such assets to the payment of debts and legacies;[2] or any of the persons interested may give bond to the executor or administrator, in a sum and with sureties approved by the court, with condition to pay all debts mentioned in the petition that shall eventually be found due from the estate, and charges of administration, so far as the personal estate may prove insufficient therefor. If the money is so paid, or if such a bond is given, license to sell will not be granted.[3] The heirs may authorize the administrator to collect the rents and appropriate them to the payment of the debts, and thereby avoid the necessity for the sale.[4]

As to the License. If the facts set forth in the petition are proved, and no sufficient cause is shown to the contrary, the license to sell will be granted, and the

---

[1] Gen. Sts. c. 102, § 45. [2] Fay v. Taylor, 2 Gray, 154.

[3] Gen. Sts. c. 102, § 9. See Appendix, form No. 65.

[4] But the occupation of the real estate by one of two administrators, who is also one of the heirs, without paying or charging himself with any rent, is not of itself a bar to granting the license to sell. Palmer v. Palmer, 13 Gray, 326.

executor or administrator will thereupon be authorized to execute effectual conveyances of the estate.[1] The court may license in terms the sale of the whole of the estate of the deceased, when the executor represents in his petition, and it appears to the court, that a sale of the whole is necessary,[2] or may license the sale of such part thereof as is deemed necessary and most for the interest of all concerned, or may direct what specific part shall be sold.[3] The license is sufficient if it is in general terms, authorizing the sale of so much as will raise a certain sum ;[4] but the license must concur with and be based upon the petition.[5] If it is necessary, under the provisions of the will of the deceased, the court will marshal the assets, and the executor will appropriate the lands in the order specified by the court.[6]

License to sell is not usually granted after the expiration of the period (two years) limited for the commencement of actions against executors and administrators who have given due notice of their appointment. The object and general effect of the statute making this limitation,

[1] Gen. Sts. c. 102, § 10.

[2] Ibid. § 4; Sewall v. Raymond, 7 Met. 754. Under a license to sell the whole, the reversion of land assigned to the widow as dower may be sold. Bancroft v. Andrews, 6 Cush. 493.

[3] Gen. Sts. c. 102, §§ 3, 4, 7.   [4] Norton v. Norton, 5 Cush. 524.

[5] On the petition for license to sell a specific portion of the estate for the payment of debts and charges, and after publication of notice to show cause why license should not be granted to sell "the whole of the real estate of said deceased," a license to sell "the whole of the real estate of said deceased" is irregular and void; and will not support an action by the administrator, on the Gen. Sts. c. 102, § 12, to recover the specific portion, as having been fraudulently conveyed by the deceased. Verry v. McClellan, 6 Gray, 535.

The executor may be licensed to sell land sufficient to pay a larger sum than the amount of debts and charges named in the petition. Tenny v. Poor, 14 Gray, 500.

[6] Gen. Sts. c. 102, § 7; Hays v. Jackson, 6 Mass. 149.

is to discharge the lien of creditors on the land at the
expiration of the two years, thereby promoting the
speedy settlement of estates and establishing the titles
of the heirs.   If no claims exist but those against which
the statute of limitations furnishes complete protection,
the proceeds of the real estate are not needed for the
payment of debts, and a license to sell cannot be granted.
The question to be determined upon every application
for a license is, whether the proposed sale is necessary
for the payment of claims against the estate.[1]   A license
may be granted after the expiration of the two years,
provided there are claims against the estate upon which
the statute of limitations does not operate.[2]   But the
court will not grant a license after the two years have
elapsed, unless extraordinary circumstances render it
proper, especially when the effect will be to disturb
titles acquired under the presumption that all the debts
had been paid.[3]

In what Cases a Bond must be given.   The statute
requires an executor or administrator who is licensed
to sell more than is necessary for the payment of debts

---

[1] Lamson *v.* Schutt, 4 Allen, 359; Hudson *v.* Hurlburt, 15 Pick. 423;
Heath *v.* Wells, 5 Pick. 140; Tarbell *v.* Parker, 106 Mass. 347.

[2] Palmer *v.* Palmer, 13 Gray, 326; Richmond, Petitioner, 2 Pick. 567.

[3] Where an executor has paid debts of his testator, beyond the amount
of the personal assets, within the time limited by statute, he cannot afterwards be licensed to sell lands to reimburse himself, unless the estate
remains as it was at the death of the testator, and his application is made
in a reasonable time after his payment of the debts.   Allen, Petitioner,
15 Mass. 58.

But where the land had neither been sold nor divided among the heirs,
an administrator who had demands against his intestate and had made
advances to the estate out of his own funds, but had rendered no account
until after the time limiting the bringing of actions had expired, the
delay having been occasioned in part by an attempt to collect a debt
abroad, was licensed to sell.   Richmond, Petitioner, 2 Pick. 567; and see
Palmer *v.* Palmer, 13 Gray, 326.

to give bond with sufficient surety or sureties to the
judge of the probate court, conditioned to account for
and dispose of according to law all proceeds of the sale
remaining after payment of the debts and charges.[1] This
requirement of the statute does not apply to a case where
the sale may unexpectedly exceed the amount necessary
to be raised, but where it appears to the court at the
time that it will be more than is necessary.[2] When
license is granted to sell only so much as is necessary
for the payment of debts and charges, no separate bond
is necessary. [3]

As to the Time of Sale. No license to sell land continues in force more than one year after it is granted,
and sales must be made within the year, except when a
sale is made of land which was not in possession of the
deceased at the time of his death and is recovered by
the executor or administrator. Land so recovered may
be sold at any time within one year after possession is
obtained.[4] But it is not essential that the deed be delivered within the year, provided all the other proceedings are regular.

Notice of the Time and Place of Sale must be given
by notifications posted thirty days at least before the
sale, in some public place in the city or town where the
deceased last dwelt, and in two adjoining cities or towns,
if there are so many in the county, and also in the city
or town where the lands lie ; or by publishing the same
three weeks successively in a newspaper, as the court
may order.[5] Such notice is essential to the validity of
the sale. The form of the notifications is not material,

---

[1] Gen. Sts. c. 102, § 6.   [2] Sewell *v.* Raymond, 7 Met. 459.
[3] Fay *v.* Valentine, 8 Pick. 526 ; Tenny *v.* Poor, 14 Gray, 500.
[4] Gen. Sts. c. 102, §§ 12, 13, 43.
[5] Ibid. § 15. See Appendix, form No. 66.

but the time and place fixed for the sale should be distinctly stated. An error in this particular may invalidate the sale.[1] The conditions of the sale are not necessarily to be stated,[2] but the notifications should plainly identify the property [3] and convey to the public all such information in regard to it as, in the judgment of the executor, is best calculated to promote the interests of the estate. It is important to executors, for their own protection, to preserve evidence of the fact that the notice was given as required by the terms of the license, and the statute provides a mode of perpetuating such evidence. An affidavit of the executor, or of the person employed by him to give such notice, filed and recorded in the probate office within one year after the sale, or at any time afterwards by permission of the court, is made admissible evidence of the time, place, and manner of giving the notice.[4] When it appears that such affidavit has not been made, any person, on petition to the probate court, may be permitted to make it.[5] The fact may be proved by other evidence, but it may be difficult or impossible for the executor, after the lapse of years, in case a question is raised upon the covenants in his deed, to obtain such other evidence. In the absence of all evidence that such notice was given, there is no presumption within thirty years that it was given.[6] The affidavit, therefore, should be filed in all cases.

Adjournment of the Sale. If, at the time appointed

---

[1] Where the sale was advertised to be on Friday, the 17th, whereas Friday was in fact the 16th, and the sale was made on the 16th, it was held void, although in the last publication, which was on the day of sale, the error was corrected. Willman v. Lawrence, 15 Mass. 326.

[2] Paine v. Fox, 16 Mass. 129.

[3] N. E. Hospital v. Sohier, 115 Mass. 50.

[4] Gen. Sts. c. 102, §§ 15, 16 ; Stat. 1876, c. 76.

[5] Stat. 1876, c. 71.   [6] Thomas v. Le Baron, 8 Met. 355.

for the sale, the executor or administrator deems it for the interest of all persons concerned, that the sale be postponed, he may adjourn it for any time not exceeding fourteen days. Notice of such adjournment must be given by a public declaration at the time and place first appointed for making the sale ; and if the adjournment is for more than one day, further notice thereof must be given by posting or publishing as time and circumstances may admit.[1]

The Sale must be by public auction, and must be conducted with a view to insure an unrestrained and honest competition among bidders, and thus to procure the highest price for the land.[2] The executor or administrator making the sale cannot properly become the purchaser, directly or indirectly, though if it is purchased by him, under color of a sale to some other person, the sale is not absolutely void ; strangers to the property cannot call it in question, but it is voidable at the pleasure of the heirs of the deceased.[3] The heirs are not obliged to act jointly in avoiding the sale, but each one has an individual election.[4] If the land is subsequently sold to a *bona fide* purchaser, who had no notice that it had been bought at the administrator's sale for the administrator's benefit, such purchaser will hold it as against the heirs, though the sale might have been avoided by a suit against the first grantee, or one

[1] Gen. Stats. c. 102, §§ 17, 18.

[2] An agreement by an administrator or guardian, to offer the real estate of his intestate or ward for sale by auction, and to sell the same to a particular individual for an agreed price provided no higher sum should be bid, is valid. But such an agreement to sell the estate at a fixed price, without regard to the biddings, is void. Hunt *v.* Frost, 4 Cush. 54.

[3] Blood *v.* Hayman, 13 Met. 231 ; Jennison *v.* Hapgood, 7 Pick. 1 ; Harrington *v.* Brown, 5 Pick. 519 ; Wyman *v.* Hooper, 2 Gray, 141 ; Robbins *v.* Bates, 4 Cush. 104 ; Ives *v.* Ashley, 97 Mass. 198.

[4] Litchfield *v.* Cudworth, 15 Pick. 23.

claiming under him, who had notice of the irregularity.[1]
The same rules apply in cases of sales of land by guardians.

The essential particulars to which the purchaser ought
to look, in order to protect himself against suits by the
heirs, are specified in the statute.   He is not called upon
to inform himself as to every particular connected with
the administrator's or guardian's proceedings. He is not
expected, for instance, to inquire whether or not the
administrator obtained his license to sell by a false representation as to the condition of the estate.   That is a
matter in which the heirs are directly concerned, and
they have a remedy against an unfaithful administrator
on his bond.   It is enough for the purchaser to know,
so far as regards the license, that it was granted by a
court of competent jurisdiction.   The statute provides
that no sale of real estate by an executor, administrator,
guardian, or other person authorized thereto by license
of court, and no title under such sale, shall be avoided
on account of the deed not having been executed and
delivered within one year after the granting of the
license for such sale, nor on account of any irregularity
in the proceedings, if it appears that the license, bond,
and notice of time and place of sale, have been according to law, and that the premises were sold at public
auction and are held by one who purchased them in good
faith.[2]   If, however, in any particular, the purchaser is
guilty of any collusion with the administrator, or has
notice of any material defect in the proceedings, though
it be in something into which he was not bound to inquire, he will not be protected by this provision of the
statute.

[1] Blood v. Hayman, 13 Met. 231; Wyman v. Hooper, 2 Gray, 141.
[2] Stat. 1864, c. 137.

12

"If the validity of a sale is drawn in question by
a person claiming adversely to the title of the deceased
or the ward, or claiming under a title that is not derived from or through the deceased or ward, the sale
shall not be void on account of any irregularity in
the proceedings, if it appears that the executor, administrator, or guardian was licensed to make the sale
by a court of competent jurisdiction, and that he accordingly executed and acknowledged, in legal form, a
deed for the conveyance of the premises."[1] The question at issue in such a suit is not whether the claimant's
title is better than that of the administrator's ven-
dee, but whether it is better than that of the deceased
person or ward. If he shows a better title, he will
recover, notwithstanding the conveyance by the administrator; but if he has not a better title than that of the
deceased person or ward, it is no concern of his whether
the land goes to the heirs or to the person who holds
under the administrator. The particular proceedings of
the administrator or guardian are therefore not material
in such a suit.[2]

Every person licensed to sell lands is required, upon
application to the probate court by an heir, creditor,
ward, or other person interested in the estate, to make
answer upon oath to all matters touching his exercise

[1] Gen. Sts. c. 102, § 48.

[2] Actions for the recovery of lands sold by executors and administrators must be commenced within five years after the sale; and for lands
sold by guardians, within five years after the termination of the guardianship; except that persons out of the State, or under legal disability to
sue at the time when the right of action first accrues, may commence an
action within five years after the removal of the disability or their return
to the State. No entry, unless by judgment of law, can be made upon
the land sold, with a view to avoid the sale, unless within the time of limitation. Gen. Sts. c. 102, § 46.

and fulfilment of the license, including all proceedings from its first grant ; and if, in relation to the exercise of such license or the sale under it, there is any neglect or misconduct in his proceedings, by which a person interested in the estate suffers damage, he may recover compensation therefor on the probate bond or otherwise as the case may require.[1]

The Administrator's Deed. In his deed to the purchaser of the real estate, the executor, administrator, or guardian covenants with his grantee that, in making the sale, he was duly authorized by the court; that he has complied with the order of the court by giving the bond required by law, and by giving notice of the time and place of the sale ; and that he has in all things observed the rules and directions of law relative thereto. The date of the decree of the court granting the license should also be stated in the deed.[2]

The executor or other person selling land under license is not required by any duty of his office to enter into a personal covenant for the absolute perfection of the title which he undertakes to convey, or for the validity of the conveyance beyond his own acts. He is at liberty to do so, if he chooses thus to excite the confidence of purchasers and enlarge the proceeds of the sale ; and he may engage his own credit collaterally in the conveyance. But such covenant, although expressed to be made in his official capacity, is necessarily a per-

---

[1] Gen. Sts. c. 49.

[2] An administrator's deed is not rendered invalid by a misrecital of the time when the license was granted, if it also contains a recital of other facts which show that the sale was made under the true license. Thomas v. Le Baron, 8 Met. 355.

Nor is a deed in which the executrix making the sale describes herself as administratrix thereby rendered invalid. Cooper v. Robinson, 2 Cush. 184. See Appendix, form No. 67.

sonal covenant, for the breach of which he is personally liable.[1]

SALES BY FOREIGN EXECUTORS AND ADMINISTRATORS.

" An executor or administrator appointed in another State or in a foreign country on the estate of a person dying out of this State, upon whose estate there is no executor or administrator appointed in this State, may file an authenticated copy of his appointment in the probate court for any county in which there is real estate of the deceased ; after which he may be licensed by the same probate court, or the supreme judicial court, or superior court in any county, to sell real estate for the payment of debts, legacies, and charges of administration, in the same manner and upon the same terms and conditions as are prescribed in the case of an executor or administrator appointed in this State, except as hereinafter provided.

" When it appears to the court granting the license, that such foreign executor or administrator is bound with sufficient surety or sureties, in the State or country in which he was appointed, to account for the proceeds of such sale, and a copy of such bond duly authenticated is filed in the probate court where the copy of his appointment is filed, no further bond for that purpose shall be required of him here ; otherwise, before making such sale he shall give bond, with sufficient surety or sureties to the judge of the probate court for the same county, with condition to account for and dispose of said proceeds in the payment of debts, legacies, and charges of administration, according to the law of the State or country in which he was appointed.

" When such foreign executor or administrator is

---

[1] Sumner v. Williams, 8 Mass. 201.

licensed to sell more than is necessary for the payment of debts, legacies, and charges of administration, he shall before making the sale give bond with sufficient surety or sureties to the judge of the probate court, conditioned to account before the same court for all proceeds of the sale remaining after payment of said debts, legacies, and charges, and to dispose of the same according to law."

Every foreign executor or administrator licensed to sell real estate must give notice of the time and place of sale, and otherwise proceed as is prescribed for an administrator appointed here when making such sale; and the evidence of such notice may be perpetuated in the same manner.[1]

SALES BY GUARDIANS.

For the Payment of Debts.   When the goods, chattels, rights, and credits in the hands of a guardian are insufficient to pay all the debts of the ward, with the charges of managing the estate, the guardian may be licensed to sell the real estate for that purpose, by the probate court for the county in which he is appointed, or the supreme judicial court, or superior court in any county. The guardian must proceed by petition, and the petition may be substantially in the same form as that of an executor or administrator who applies for leave to sell real estate for the payment of debts. It must appear that a necessity exists for the sale proposed.[2]

If it is represented in the petition and appears necessary to sell some part of the real estate of the ward, and that by such partial sale the residue of the estate, or of some specific piece or part thereof would be greatly in-

---

[1] Gen. Sts. c. 102, §§ 20–23.   [2] Ibid. § 24.

jured, the court may license a sale of the whole of the
estate, or of such part thereof as it deems necessary and
most for the interest of all concerned, the guardian first
giving bond, if he is licensed to sell more than is necessary for the payment of debts, to account for and dispose of the surplus proceeds according to law. The
condition of such bond is the same as that of a bond
given by executors and administrators under like circumstances.[1]

For Maintenance and Investment. When the income
of a ward's estate is insufficient to maintain him and his
family, or when it appears that it would be for the benefit
of a ward that his real estate or any part thereof be sold,
and the proceeds put out at interest or invested in some
productive stock, his guardian may be licensed to sell
the same.[2]

A father is bound, to the extent of his ability, to support his minor child ; but if the minor's property is sufficient for his maintenance and education in a more
expensive manner than his father can reasonably afford,
regard being had to the situation of the father's family
and to all the circumstances of the case, the expenses of
the maintenance and education of such child may be defrayed out of his own property, in whole or in part, as
shall be deemed reasonable by the probate court ; and
when necessary his real estate may be sold for that purpose by the guardian under license.[3]

To obtain such license, the guardian must present to
the court a petition setting forth the condition of the
estate, and the facts and circumstances upon which his

---

[1] Gen. Sts. c. 102, § 25.

[2] Ibid. § 26. A guardian may be licensed to sell the homestead right
of his ward. Ibid. c. 104, § 14.

[3] Ibid. c. 109, § 21.

application is founded. If after a full examination, on the oath of the petitioner or otherwise, it appears either that it is necessary, or that it would be for the benefit of the ward, that the real estate or any part of it should be sold, the court may grant a license therefor, specifying therein whether the sale is to be made for the maintenance of the ward and his family, or that the proceeds may be put out and invested.[1]

Guardians licensed to sell real estate for maintenance of a ward or investment, are required, before the sale, to give bond, with sufficient surety or sureties, to the judge of the probate court for the county in which they are appointed, with condition to sell the same in the manner prescribed for sales of real estate by executors and administrators, and to account for and dispose of the proceeds in the manner provided by law.[2]

The estate of a minor may be sold for the purpose of investing the proceeds upon the petition and representation of any friend of the minor; and in such case the court may authorize the guardian or any other suitable person to convey the estate. When a sale for such purpose is ordered on the petition of the guardian of a minor, the court may authorize any suitable person other than the guardian to sell and convey the estate. The statute provisions in relation to the licenses and sales on the petitions of guardians apply to licenses and sales on the petition of a friend of the minor, except that upon a sale by a person other than the guardian, the proceeds are to be forthwith paid to the guardian upon his giving bond, with sufficient sureties, to the judge of the probate court for the county where the real estate is situate, conditioned to account therefor. If there is no guardian, the proceeds are required to be put out and

----

[1] Gen. Sts. c. 102, § 27.   [2] Ibid. § 28.

invested by the person authorized to sell the estate, in like manner as is required of a guardian.[1]

No license can be granted to a guardian until after notice, by public advertisement or otherwise, as the court shall order, for the next of kin of the ward, and all persons interested in the estate, to appear and show cause why the same should not be granted; but such notice may be dispensed with, if all persons interested signify in writing their assent to the sale. All who are next of kin, and heirs apparent or presumptive of the ward, are considered by the statute as interested in the estate, and may appear as such and answer to the petition of the guardian.

No guardian, except in the case of minors, can be licensed to sell his ward's real estate without seven days' previous notice of his petition therefor to the overseers of the poor of the place where the ward is an inhabitant or resides. The notice may be served upon any one of the overseers. This provision does not apply when the ward resides out of this State.[2]

Guardians appointed in this State or elsewhere, when licensed to sell real estate, are required to give notice of the time and place of sale, and otherwise proceed therein as prescribed in like cases for executors and administrators, except when licensed to sell fractional shares at private sale; and the evidence of giving notice may be perpetuated in the same manner.

SALE OF FRACTIONAL SHARES OF REAL ESTATE.

When it appears, by the petition of the guardian and upon the hearing thereon, that the ward's interest in the real estate is a fractional share thereof, or a right or

---

[1] Gen. Sts. c. 102, §§ 31, 32.   [2] Stat. 1874, c. 202.

interest in common with others, and that an advanta-
geous offer has been made to the guardian for the purchase
thereof, and that the interest of all parties concerned will
be best promoted by an acceptance of such offer, the court
may authorize the sale, in accordance with the offer, at
private sale, or upon such terms as may be adjudged
best, with or without public notice. The guardian so
licensed may sell at public auction, if he deems it best
so to do.[1]

SALES BY FOREIGN GUARDIANS.

" When a minor, insane person, or spendthrift, residing out of this State, is under guardianship in the State
or country in which he resides, and has no guardian appointed in this State, the foreign guardian may file an
authenticated copy of his appointment in the probate
court for any county in which there is real estate of the
ward; after which he may be licensed to sell the real
estate of the ward in any county, in the same manner
and upon the same terms and conditions as are prescribed
in this chapter (Gen. Sts. c. 102), in the case of a guardian appointed in this State, except as hereinafter provided.

" When it appears to the probate court, that a foreign
guardian, licensed to sell real estate for the payment of
the debts of his ward, is bound with sufficient surety or
sureties, in the State or country where he was appointed,
to account for the proceeds of such sale, and an authenticated copy of such bond is filed in said court, no further bond shall be required; otherwise he shall give
bond in like manner as is prescribed in this chapter in
case of sales by foreign executors or administrators.

" When such foreign guardian is licensed to sell more than is necessary to pay debts and charges, he shall, before making the sale, give bond with sufficient surety or sureties, to the judge of the probate court, conditioned to account before the same court for all proceeds of the sale remaining after payment of said debts and charges, and to dispose of the same according to law.[1]

" Every foreign guardian licensed to sell real estate for the maintenance of his ward or investment, shall before making the sale give bond with sufficient surety or sureties to the judge of the probate court, conditioned, in addition to the condition required in the bond of other guardians in such case, that he will account for and dispose of the proceeds, or so much thereof as may remain upon the final settlement of his accounts, to such persons, and in such proportions, as the real estate would have descended or been disposed of according to the laws of this State if it had not been sold." [2]

All proceedings in probate courts respecting sales by a foreign executor, administrator, or guardian must be had in the court for the county in which an authenticated copy of his appointment is first filed.[3]

SALES BY PUBLIC ADMINISTRATORS.

Public administrators may be licensed to sell real estate for the payment of debts. The petition for such sale and the proceedings thereon, and under the license, are the same as are prescribed for other administrators.[4]

Sales by public administrators are not limited to cases where the sales are necessary for the payment of debts. The statute provides that after three years from the date

---

[1] Gen. Sts. c. 102, §§ 33–35.   [2] Ibid. § 36.
[3] Ibid. § 42.   [4] Ibid. c. 95, § 10.

of letters of administration to a public administrator, he may sell the real estate, although not necessary for the payment of debts, upon obtaining a license from the probate court if it appears to the judge to be for the interest of all concerned. The petition, in such case, should be framed in accordance with the facts upon which it is founded, and the public administrator gives the bond, and otherwise proceeds as is required of administrators licensed to sell real estate more than is necessary for the payment of debts.[1]

CONVEYANCES OF LANDS BY EXECUTORS, ADMINISTRA-
TORS, AND GUARDIANS UNDER CONTRACTS — SPE-
CIFIC PERFORMANCE.

" When a person who has entered into a written agreement for the conveyance of real estate dies or is put under guardianship before making such conveyance, the probate court shall have jurisdiction concurrent with the supreme judicial court to enforce a specific performance, and, upon a petition therefor presented by any person interested in the conveyance, shall order the petitioner to give notice to all persons interested, that they may appear and show cause either for or against the prayer of the petition.

" If upon the hearing it appears that the deceased, if living, or the ward, if not under guardianship, would be required to make the conveyance, the court shall order the executor or administrator of the deceased or the guardian of the ward to make the same; and when so made it shall have like force and effect as if made by the person who entered into the agreement to convey."[2]

[1] Gen. Sts. c. 95, § 11.
[2] Ibid. c. 117, §§ 5, 6.   Reed v. Whitney, 7 Gray, 537; Miller v. Goodwin, 8 Gray, 542.   See Appendix, form Nos. 68, 69.

RELEASE OF INTERESTS IN LAND BY EXECUTORS AND OTHERS.

The statute provides that probate courts " may authorize executors, administrators, guardians, and trustees to release and discharge, upon such terms and conditions as appear proper, any vested, contingent, or possible right or interest belonging to the persons or estates by them represented, in or to any real or personal estate, whenever it appears to be for the benefit of the persons or estates in trust." [1]

This provision does not apply to sales of the land itself, and has not any reference to sales of land by executors and administrators for the payment of debts and legacies, nor to sales by guardians for maintenance or investment. Leave to release the remote interests mentioned in the statute may be granted, when it appears to be for the benefit of the parties interested, whether the proceeds are necessary for the payment of debts and legacies or not. The person applying for leave to release such an interest should state in his petition the names and residences of all persons interested, and fully describe the nature of the interest to be released. The same notice of the petition must be given as is required in cases of sale for the payment of debts.[2] When leave is granted, the court directs the manner in which the release shall be made.

MORTGAGE OF REAL ESTATE BY EXECUTORS AND ADMINISTRATORS.

Probate courts may authorize administrators to mortgage the real estate of their intestates for the purpose of

----

[1] Gen. Sts. c. 101, § 11.   [2] Stat. 1863, c. 230.

raising money to pay old debts, or to remove liens existing thereon. Such authority cannot be given except after a hearing, upon a petition from the executor or administrator, or some party interested therein. The petition must set forth a description of the lands to be mortgaged, the amount of money necessary to be raised, and the reasons therefor ; and the written assent of all the heirs or their guardians must be obtained, unless all join in the petition.[1]

The court having jurisdiction of the estate of any deceased person, when it shall appear to the court to be for the interest of the estate, may, on petition, notice, and hearing, authorize the executors and administrators with the will annexed to mortgage the real estate, or any part thereof, of the testator, for the purpose of paying debts, legacies, and charges of administration, or of paying any lien or mortgage on such estate, or any part thereof, or to make an agreement for the extension or renewal of any mortgage already subsisting thereon.

In such cases the court prescribes the maximum rate of interest, and may order the whole or any part of the principal of the mortgage to be paid, from time to time, out of the income of the estate mortgaged, and may further order the executor or administrator with the will annexed to give bonds, unless exempted therefrom by the laws relating to the giving of bonds in like cases.[2]

MORTGAGE OF REAL ESTATE BY GUARDIANS.

Guardians may be authorized to mortgage the real estate of their wards whenever, in the judgment of the court, it is necessary or expedient. The guardian so authorized is required to give a bond, with sufficient

[1] Stat. 1864, c. 212.   [2] Ibid. 1876, c. 79.

surety or sureties, for the faithful application of the
money received on such mortgage.[1]

MORTGAGE OF REAL ESTATE BY TRUSTEES.

" Probate courts having jurisdiction under the provisions of this act, after notice to all persons interested,
and hearing thereon, may authorize any trustee or trustees appointed under any will, trust, deed, or indenture,
and having the control or management of any real estate,
to mortgage the same for the purpose of paying the sums
assessed thereon for betterments, or the expense of repairs and improvements thereon made necessary by such
betterments, or by the lawful taking of such estate, or
any part thereof, by any city or town, or for the purpose
of paying the expense of erecting, altering, completing,
repairing, or improving any building on such estate,
when it shall appear to the court to be for the interest
of such estate ; and the interest on such mortgage, and
any portion of the principal which the court may order,
shall be paid out of the income derived from the estate
mortgaged as herein provided.

" The petition shall set forth a description of the estate
to be mortgaged, the amount necessary to be raised, and
the purposes for which the same is to be used, and shall
be made to the probate court for the county where the
will under which such trustee or trustees were appointed
was proved, in case the trust was created by will, or in
the county where the trust estate, or any part thereof
is located, in case such trust was created by deed or
indenture ; and the decree of the court thereon shall fix
the amount for which the mortgage may be given, and
the rate of interest which may be paid thereon.

[1] Stat. 1871, c. 282.

" The mortgage shall set forth that the same was executed by license of court, and the date of the license; but the court shall require such trustee or trustees to give bond with sufficient sureties for the faithful application of the money received on such mortgage; provided, however, that no bond shall be required, when all persons who are interested in the estate, other than creditors, being of full age and legal capacity, shall so request, or when the trustee or trustees are exempted from giving bond by the will, deed, or indenture creating the trust." [1]

" Whenever any real estate is incumbered by any contingent remainder, executory devise or power of appointment, the supreme judicial court (or the probate court for the county in which such real estate is situated), upon petition of any party who has an estate in possession in such real estate, may appoint a trustee for such estate, and authorize said trustee to mortgage the estate for such amounts, on such terms and conditions, and for such purposes, as may seem to such court judicious or expedient, and shall fix the form and amount of the bond to be given by such trustee.

" Notice of the proceedings shall be given to all persons who are or may become interested in the real estate, and to all persons whose issue, not in being, may become interested therein, as the court may order. The court shall, in all such cases, appoint a suitable person to appear and act in such proceedings as the next friend of all minors, persons not ascertained or persons not in being, who may be or may become interested in such real estate, the cost of whose appearance and services, including compensation of counsel, to be determined by the court, shall be paid as the court may order, either out

[1] Stat. 1872, c. 370.

of the proceeds of the real estate or by the petitioners, in which latter case execution may issue in the name of such next friend.   An order or decree made in any such proceedings, and a mortgage of real estate thereunder, shall be binding and conclusive." [1]

The court having jurisdiction of any trust created by will or other written instrument, when it shall appear to the court to be for the interest of the trust estate, may, on petition, notice and hearing, authorize the trustee or trustees to mortgage the real estate, or any part thereof, of which they are seised or possessed, for the purpose of paying any lien or mortgage on such estate or any part thereof, or to make an agreement for the extension or renewal of any mortgage already subsisting thereon.

In such case the court prescribes the maximum rate of interest, and may order the interest, and the whole or any part of the principal of the mortgage, to be paid from time to time out of the income of the estate mortgaged ; and may further order the trustee or trustees to give bonds, unless exempted therefrom by the laws relating to the giving of bonds in like cases.[2]

Every mortgage executed by an executor, administrator, or trustee, must set forth the fact that the same is executed by license of the court, and the date of such license.   Every such mortgage may contain a power of sale.[3]

SALE OF STANDING OR GROWING WOOD.

When the income of the estate of a ward is insufficient to maintain him or his family, or when it appears that it would be for the benefit of a ward that the standing or growing wood on his real estate, or any part

---

[1] Stat. 1871, c. 322.   [2] Ibid. 1876, c. 199.
[3] Ibid. 1873, c. 280.

thereof, should be sold, and the proceeds put out at interest, or invested in productive stock, his guardian may sell such wood, and grant the privilege of entering upon the land, and cutting and carrying away the same within such time as he may allow, upon obtaining a license therefor, and proceeding therein as provided by law for the sale of the real estate of wards by guardians.[1]

The probate court, when it appears that the wood and timber standing on land held in dower, or on land the use and improvement of which belongs, for life or otherwise, to any person other than the owner of the fee therein, has ceased to improve by growth, or for any cause ought to be cut, may appoint a trustee, and authorize and empower him to sell and convey said wood and timber, in the way and manner provided by law for the sale of real estate by guardians, to be cut and carried away within the time limited in the order of sale, and to hold and invest the proceeds thereof, after paying the expenses of such sale therefrom, and pay over the income, above the taxes and other expenses of the trust, to the person entitled to such dower, or right to the use and improvement, while the same continues; and, at the expiration of such dower or right to the use and improvement, to pay the principal sum to the owner of such land.   When said wood and timber has been cut off, as aforesaid, no more wood or timber shall be cut on such land by the person entitled to such dower, or use and improvement, without permission from said court." [2]

---

[1] Stat. 1867, c. 231.   [2] Ibid. 1869, c. 249.

CHAPTER XV.

ACCOUNTS OF EXECUTORS, ADMINISTRATORS, GUARDIANS, AND TRUSTEES.

EVERY executor and administrator is required by statute and by the condition of his bond to render to the probate court a true account of his administration within one year after giving bond, and such further accounts from time to time as may be necessary or convenient, or as the probate court may require.[1]

A public administrator, who gives a separate bond for each estate settled by him, is held to account like other administrators; if he gives a general bond covering all estates intrusted to him, he is held to render an account of each estate within one year after the date of his letters of administration thereon, and at least once in each year until the trust is fulfilled; and he is held further to render an account to the probate court first held in his county after the first day of January in each year, of all balances of estates then remaining in his hands.[2]

Special administrators are held to account whenever required by the probate court.[3]

Guardians are bound to render an account within one year after their appointment, and as often as once in three years thereafter, and at such other times as the probate court directs; and at the expiration of their

---

[1] Gen. Sts. c. 94, § 2; c. 98, § 9.
[3] Ibid. c. 94, § 7.   Stat. 1876, c. 200.

[2] Ibid. c. 95, §§ 6–8.

trust to settle their accounts in court or with their wards.[1]

Trustees are held to account within one year, and at any other times when required by the probate court.[2]

It is the practice, to some extent, of executors and other trust officers appointed by the probate court, to settle their accounts with the parties interested without rendering a final account to the court, and, in a majority of cases, no inconvenience results from that mode of proceeding. Such a settlement, however, between the administrator and the heirs, or between the guardian and his ward, is not a compliance with the condition of his bond; and he may be cited, on the petition of persons interested, to render his account in the probate court notwithstanding such settlement. He may be held to account, although he produces the receipts of all the heirs acknowledging the payment of their distributive shares in full.[3] Such receipts are evidence for the consideration of the probate court in determining whether a further settlement shall be ordered or not, but they do not estop the heirs, or the ward, from calling on the administrator, or the guardian, to settle his accounts in court.

When one of two or more joint executors or administrators dies, or is removed before the administration is completed, the account is rendered by the other or others.[4] When a sole executor or other trust officer dies, not having settled his account, it should be render-

---

[1] Gen. Sts. c. 109, § 16.   [2] Ibid. c. 100, § 1.

[3] Bard v. Wood, 3 Met. 74; Clark v. Clay, 11 Foster (N. H.), 393. Notwithstanding the settlement and receipt, the guardian is bound to answer on oath proper interrogatories respecting his account and the items thereof, and the ward may introduce evidence touching the execution and validity of the receipt. Wade v. Lobdell, 4 Cush. 511.

[4] Gen. Sts. c. 101, § 2.

ed by his executor or administrator,[1] and it has been held that it may be settled by the administrator of one of his sureties.[2]

CITATION TO RENDER ACCOUNT.

If the executor or other officer neglects or unreasonably delays the settlement of his account in the probate court, he may be cited for that purpose on the petition of any person interested in the estate concerning which the account is to be rendered. The petition should set forth the particulars in which the executor has been negligent, in accordance with the facts of the case.[3] Upon such petition, the court will issue a citation to the delinquent party, which must be served in the manner directed by its terms. If, after being cited, he neglects to appear or to render his account, leave will be granted to bring a suit on his bond; and he will be liable in like manner and to the same extent as an executor in his own wrong.[4]

FORM OF ADMINISTRATION ACCOUNT.

In his account, the executor or administrator charges himself with the amount of assets that have come to his hands, and asks to be allowed for the amount of all debts paid by him, and the expenses of the administration. With the account, stated in this form, must be filed a schedule, stating the names of all persons of whom he has received money, the sum received from each, and the time when each sum was received; and a second schedule, giving the several sums paid by him, the per-

---

[1] The guardian's administrator may be cited for that purpose on petition of the ward. Gregg v. Gregg, 15 N. H. 190.

[2] Curtis v. Bailey, 1 Pick. 199.

[3] See Appendix, form No. 70.   [4] Gen. Sts. c. 98, § 11.

son to whom, and the purpose for which, each sum was paid. The blanks, to be had on application at the probate offices, exhibit the form in which the account should be stated. If the estate has been represented *insolvent*, the executor or administrator does not ask in his first account to be allowed any sum for the payment of debts owed by the deceased, he having no authority to pay the debts except under a decree of distribution issued by the court. He credits himself with the charges of administration, the amount of loss, if any, necessarily sustained by the estate in his hands, and with the amount of the allowance, if any, made by the court to the widow or minor children of the deceased. The balance, thus exhibited, remains in his hands, until he is ordered by the court to distribute it among the creditors.

If the deceased insolvent had been a member of a copartnership and died in possession of both partnership estate and separate estate, and both partnership and separate claims are proved against his estate, the administrator should so state his account as to exhibit the amount of the partnership estate in his hands distinct from the separate estate. The expenses of administration in such case are to be deducted from the whole amount received by the executor, and the net proceeds of the joint stock are appropriated to pay the creditors of the firm, and the net proceeds of the separate estate to pay the separate creditors; the surplus, if any, of one fund being applied towards the liquidation of debts payable out of the other.

WITH WHAT THE EXECUTOR OR ADMINISTRATOR IS CHARGEABLE.

The first item with which the executor or administrator charges himself in the schedule annexed to his

first account is the value of the personal estate as shown
by the inventory. He should charge himself with the
full amount of the appraisal of the personal property,
whether he has disposed of it for more or less than that
amount.

If he has sold the personal estate for more than its appraised value, he next charges himself with the amount
of the gain.

After thus accounting for the personal property inventoried and for the gain, if any, on its sale, he charges
himself with all proceeds of real estate sold by him for
the payment of debts and legacies, with the proceeds of
any personal estate not included in the inventory, and
with all interest, profit, and income that may have come
to his hands from the personal estate of the deceased.[1]

[1] Manure taken from the barnyard of a homestead and piled on the
land, though not broken up nor rotten, nor in a fit state for incorporation
with the soil, is part of the realty, and is not chargeable to the administrator as personal estate. Fay v. Muzzey, 13 Gray, 53. But he is chargeable with the value of manure when it is personal property, although he
has spread it in the usual course of good husbandry on the land of the
deceased, and has sold the land for payment of debts. Ibid.

When the administrator of an insolvent estate sold real estate, under
license of probate court, and the land sold was mortgaged, and the mortgage recorded, but was unknown to him or the purchaser at the time of
the sale, it was held that he might apply the proceeds of the sale to the
payment in full of the mortgage debt, and that he was chargeable in his
account only for the balance of such proceeds. Church v. Savage, 7
Cush. 440.

Money received by an administrator from the government of the
United States, by means of a treaty with a foreign nation, as an indem-
nity for property taken from the intestate by such foreign nation, is
assets in the administrator's hands. Foster v. Fifield, 20 Pick. 67.

When personal property attached by the trustee process was assigned
by the owner subject to the attachment, and the attachment was dissolved
by the owner's death, it was held that the property passed by the assignment, and was not assets in the administrator's hands. Coverdale v.
Aldrich, 19 Pick. 391.

Where an executor sold lands of the testator and became himself a

He is chargeable with the value of personal property lost through his negligence, though it never came into his actual possession.[1] And if he has received money not belonging to the estate, and received it in his official capacity, he must charge himself with it, unless he can

purchaser with two others, under an agreement to share equally in the profits of resale, he was held to account for one third part of such profits. Jennison v. Hapgood, 10 Pick. 93.

If, to prevent a sale of the real estate, the heirs furnish the executor or administrator with money sufficient for the payment of all claims against the estate and the expense of administration, and thereby render any sale of the real estate unnecessary, the money so furnished by them is assets of the estate, to be accounted for by the administrator. Fay v. Taylor, 2 Gray, 159.

Money found, after the death of a testatrix, in a secret drawer of a chest belonging to her, does not pass by a specific bequest of the chest, but is a portion of the residuum of the personal estate, for which the executor is bound to account. Smith v. Jewett, 3 Chandler (N. H.), 513.

If an executor receive money for a deed of real estate made by the testator, but not delivered until after his death, he is bound to account for it. Loring v. Cunningham, 9 Cush. 87.

Salary voted to a person after his decease, and paid to his executor, is assets of the estate, to be accounted for by the executor. Ibid.

The amount of land damages paid for land taken for a railroad, after the death of the intestate, belongs to the heirs and not to the administrator; although the estate is insolvent, and the whole estate is afterwards sold by the administrator, under license, for the payment of debts. Boynton v. P. & S. Railroad, 4 Cush. 467; otherwise, if actually taken before the intestate's death. Moore v. Boston, 8 Cush. 274.

If the testator had money or other property in his hands belonging to others, whether in trust or otherwise, and it has no ear-mark, and is not distinguishable from the mass of his property, the party owning it must come in as a general creditor of the estate, and the property is assets, to be accounted for by the executor. Trecothic v. Austin, 4 Mason, 29; Johnson v. Ames, 11 Pick. 181.

[1] Two turkeys belonging to the intestate wandered away, after his death, to a neighbor's house, and there remained several months, when they were disposed of by the neighbor. They had never been in the administrator's possession, nor had he ever called for them. He was ordered to charge himself with their value. Tuttle v. Robinson, 33 N. H. 104.

show a liability to pay it over to one legally claiming it.[1]

When an executor is by the express terms of the will of his testator, or by necessary implication, made a trustee of any part of the estate, he will be required to account for the trust fund in his capacity of executor, unless for greater convenience and with the assent of the probate court he opens a new account as trustee; in which event he must give a new bond as trustee, and transfer to his account as trustee the property to be held and administered by him in that character, before his liability as executor will terminate.[2] If he continues to hold the trust fund as executor, it is his duty to separate it from the mass of the testator's property, and invest it in some secure and productive stock, or at interest on good security.   And if in this respect he acts with strict fidelity and due diligence, he will not be responsible should any loss happen, either of principal or interest.[3] But the mere mental determination of an executor to appropriate property to himself as trustee, is not such a setting apart as will cause a loss or depreciation of the trust fund to fall on the *cestui que trust;* the executor, in such case, must account for the entire trust fund, and the amount due from him must be stated by making annual rests, adding the interest each year to the principal.[4]

If an administrator appointed in this State collects funds in another State of debtors residing there, he must account for them here, unless he has taken out letters of ancillary administration in such other State; in that

---

[1] Jennison *v.* Hapgood, 10 Pick. 104.   [2] Prior *v.* Talbot, 10 Cush. 1.

[3] Dorr *v.* Wainwright, 13 Pick. 332; Brown *v.* Kelsey, 2 Cush. 248; Hubbard *v.* Lloyd, 6 Cush. 524.

[4] Miller *v.* Congdon, 14 Gray, 114.

case, he will be held to account here only for the surplus remaining in his hands upon the settlement of the ancillary administration.[1] But money collected there of debtors residing here must be accounted for here.[2]

An ancillary administrator appointed in this State must account to the court by which he was so appointed for all assets received by him under his ancillary appointment; but not for assets received by him as principal administrator in the place of the principal administration.[3]

When chargeable with Interest. An executor or administrator is not chargeable with interest on the money received by him in his official capacity unless he has made some profitable use of the money, or has been guilty of negligence in accounting for it.[4] An administrator is not expected to invest any part of the money belonging to the estate; nor is an executor, unless he is authorized to do so by the will of his testator. On the contrary, it is his duty to collect the assets and pay them over to the persons entitled to receive them as speedily as circumstances will allow. But if he has invested the money and received interest upon it, he must account for it; and the fact that he has received interest, or has made use of the money in his own business may be inferred from a long delay in settling his accounts, or his neglect to pay over balances after demand made upon him.[5] But if the delay was without negligence on his part, he will not be chargeable with interest unless he has made profit of the funds.[6] He is not to be charged with

---

[1] Hooker v. Olmstead, 6 Pick. 481; Jennison v. Hapgood, 10 Pick. 77.
[2] Ibid.   [3] Fay v. Taylor, 3 Met. 109.
[4] Wyman v. Hubbard, 13 Mass. 232; Stearns v. Brown, 1 Pick. 530; Boynton v. Dyer, 18 Pick. 1.
[5] Wyman v. Hubbard, 13 Mass. 232.
[6] Lamb v. Lamb, 11 Pick. 371.

interest in any case from the date of his appointment, or of his receipt of the money. He is to be allowed a reasonable time to settle the estate, and the time proper to be allowed for that purpose must depend upon the circumstances of each case. No general rule would do justice in all cases.[1] When the administrator employs the funds of the estate in his own business, he is liable to be charged with compound interest.[2]

Income of the Real Estate. The administrator has no official authority to collect the rents of real estate belonging to the estate of his intestate; nor has the executor, unless authorized by the will of his testator. The real estate vests in the heirs or devisees immediately upon the death of the owner, and all rents that become due subsequent to his death belong to them. Even if the estate is insolvent, they are entitled to the rents and profits until the land is sold, by license of court, for the payment of debts.[3] But rents collected by the executor or administrator to be applied, by agreement with the parties interested, to the payment of claims against the estate, thereby rendering unnecessary a sale of the land, are personal assets, to be charged against the administrator in his account.[4]

---

[1] See Clarkson *v.* De Peyster, 2 Wend. 77; Schiffelin *v.* Stewart, 1 Johns. Ch. 620; Jennison *v.* Hapgood, 10 Pick. 77.

[2] Boynton *v.* Dyer, 18 Pick. 1; Robbins *v.* Hayward, 1 Pick. 527; Schiffelin *v.* Stewart, 1 Johns. Ch. 620.

[3] Gibson *v.* Farley, 16 Mass. 280; Boynton *v.* P. & S. Railroad, 4 Cush. 469; Palmer *v.* Palmer, 13 Gray, 326; Kimball *v.* Sumner, 62 Maine, 305.

[4] Stearns *v.* Stearns, 1 Pick. 159. The statute provides (Gen. Sts. c. 98, § 8), that "if the real estate has been used or occupied by the executor or administrator, he shall account for the income thereof, as ordered by the probate court with the assent of the executor or administrator and of such other parties interested as are present at the rendering of the account. If the parties do not agree on the sum to be allowed, it shall be determined by three disinterested persons, to be appointed by the pro-

A *special* administrator, when authorized by the probate court to take charge of the real estate of his intestate, is chargeable with the rents and profits.

Debts due from the Executor or Administrator. If the administrator is himself a debtor to the estate, the debt owed by him is regarded as assets of the estate, to be accounted for by him. He must charge himself with the amount of the debt, as if he had received it of any other person ;[1] and he is bound to answer upon oath as to all facts tending to show that he was indebted to the deceased, even as to facts that take the claim out of the operation of the statute of limitations, though it may be apparently barred by that statute.[2]

The old rule, that a testator by making a debtor his executor thereby releases his debt, has never been in force in this State. The debt is assets in the executor's hands for which he and his sureties are liable.[3]

---

bate court, whose award being accepted by the court shall be final." This provision does not make executors and administrators officially liable for rents and profits that come to their hands, but was designed to facilitate the settlement between the executor and the devisees, or the administrator and the heirs, and prevent disputes among them. Newcomb *c.* Stebbins, 9 Met. 544 ; Almy *v.* Crapo, 100 Mass. 218; Choate *v.* Arrington, 116 Mass. 552.

[1] Ipswich Manufacturing Co. *v.* Story, 5 Met. 310; Winship *v.* Bass, 12 Mass. 199; Stevens *v.* Gaylord, 11 Mass. 256. Debts due to the estate of a testator from the executor named in his will, and from a firm of which he is a member, are to be accounted for as assets; although he and his firm were insolvent at the time when he accepted the trust, and although he has never charged them in his account, and an account has been allowed in which they were not included, but were mentioned as notes which it had been impossible to collect, and although he has resigned his trust, and an administrator *de bonis non* has been appointed in his place. Leland *v.* Felton, 1 Allen, 531.

[2] Sigourney *v.* Wetherell, 6 Met. 553.

[3] Ipswich Manuf. Co. *v.* Story, 5 Met. 313; Winship *v.* Bass, 12 Mass. 199; Stevens *v.* Gaylord, 11 Mass. 267.

WHAT IS ALLOWED TO THE EXECUTOR OR ADMINISTRATOR.

The executor or administrator of a solvent estate is allowed to credit himself in his account with all sums paid by him in satisfaction of debts due from the deceased at the time of his death.[1]

The estate is not liable for money paid in pursuance of a promise, the consideration of which arises after the death of the testator or intestate. Upon such a promise the executor or administrator is personally liable. Whether the amount is to be repaid to him from the estate is a question to be determined by the probate court, upon the settlement of his account.[2] It would be necessary for him to show, in support of his application for an allowance in such case, that the payment made by him was beneficial to the estate, or was made with the assent of the parties interested.

An administrator may pay assessments upon shares. in banks and other corporations which he holds as part of the assets of the estate, and will be allowed in his account for such payments, provided the assessments were legally laid and the payments were necessary to redeem the shares from a lien created by the assessment, and were beneficial to the estate. And if he acted in good faith he would undoubtedly be protected, even if the shares should have subsequently fallen in value in his hands.[3]

---

[1] An administrator is not allowed for personal property applied by him to repairs and improvements of the real estate, though so applied in executing an agreement of the intestate. Cobb v. Muzzey, 13 Gray, 57.

[2] Luscomb v. Ballard, 5 Gray, 403.

[3] Riply v. Sampson, 10 Pick. 373. Taxes paid by an executor on lands in another State where he had not taken out administration, were not allowed in his account. Jennison v. Hapgood, 10 Pick. 105.

The executor or administrator will not be allowed in his account for debts paid by him after they had become barred by the statute limiting the time (two years) within which suits can be brought against executors and administrators who have given legal notice of their appointment. The executor's promise to pay a claim so barred cannot affect the estate.[1]

It has been held in this State that an executor or administrator may revive by a new promise a claim barred by the *general* statute of limitation,[2] and that such new promise will bind the estate in his hands.[3] He cannot however revive a claim held by himself.[4] There seems to be no good reason for allowing an executor or administrator for payments made on debts barred by either statute of limitation.

If the estate has been represented insolvent, the executor is not allowed in his first account for the payment of debts, he having no authority to make such payments except under a decree of distribution issued by the court.[5] He credits himself only with the expenses of the last sickness and funeral of the deceased, charges of administration, the loss, if any, necessarily sustained by the estate in his hands, and with the amount of the allowances, if any, made by the court to the widow or minor children of the deceased. The balance thus exhibited remains in his hands until he is ordered by the court to distribute it among the creditors.

[1] Brown *v.* Anderson, 13 Mass. 201; Dawes *v.* Shed, 15 Mass. 6; Emerson *v.* Thompson, 16 Mass. 429.

[2] Foster *v.* Starkey, 12 Cush. 324.

[3] Manson *v.* Felton, 13 Pick. 206; Emerson *v.* Thompson, 16 Mass. 429.

[4] Richmond, petitioner, 2 Pick. 567.

[5] He is not allowed for sums paid on debts during the first year of his administration, though paid without knowledge that the estate was insolvent. Cobb *v.* Muzzey, 13 Gray, 57.

Funeral Charges and Expenses of the last Sickness.
The executor or administrator is allowed in his account
all reasonable sums paid for funeral expenses. The
amount to be allowed for such expenses must depend,
in some degree, upon the condition of the estate. If the
funeral was under the direction of the family of the
deceased, and the estate is solvent, the sum asked for
such charges is usually allowed; but no extravagant
expenses will be allowed as against the creditors of an
insolvent estate.[1] All expenses of the last sickness of
the deceased paid by the administrator are allowed in
his account.[2]

Charges of Administration. Executors and administrators are allowed their reasonable expenses incurred in
the execution of their respective trusts, and such compensation for their services as the court in which their
accounts are settled considers just and reasonable.[3]

Under the head of expenses of administration are included all sums which have been paid by the executor

---

[1] In McGlimsey's case (14 Serg. & Rawle, 64), the supreme court
allowed $358.75 for funeral expenses, including a vault and tombstone.
It was observed by the court: "The deceased had a good estate and no
children; and the widow, who was entitled to one half, wished to be lib-
eral in honor of his memory. A handsome tombstone was erected over
the vault in which the body was interred, and this was the principal article of expense. But there was one article which should be rejected. I
allude to a picture of the deceased, painted after his death. If the widow
desired a memorial of this kind she should pay for it herself."

A demand for mourning, furnished to the widow and family of the
deceased, is not a funeral expense. Johnson v. Baker, 2 Carr. & Payne,
207. But see Wood's estate (1 Ashmead), and Flintham's appeal (11
Serg. & R. 16).

[2] A testator at a distance from home during his last sickness, sent for
his wife and heirs, but died before they arrived. The executor was allowed to charge in his account their expenses which he had paid to them.
Jennison v. Hapgood, 10 Pick. 88.

[3] Gen. Sts. c. 98, § 10. Edwards v. Ela, 5 Allen, 87.

in the course of a faithful and prudent administration; such as the expense of appraising the estate, of collecting the effects and paying the debts, of attending the probate and other courts upon business of the estate, of advertising as required by law or any order of the court, and sums paid for legal and other necessary assistance.[1] The expenses of assigning dower, or making partition of land among the heirs or devisees, are not charges of administration, and are not allowed in the administration account.

As a general rule, the executor or administrator is not allowed interest on money advanced by him for the payment of debts due from the estate. It is no part of his duty to advance his own funds for that purpose;[2] but if, not having assets of the estate in his hands, he advances his own money to redeem land of the deceased, mortgaged for less than its value, he is entitled to interest on the money advanced.[3]

If judgment is rendered against an executor or administrator for costs in a suit commenced or prosecuted by him in that capacity, the estate in his hands cannot be taken in execution therefor, but execution is awarded against him as for his own debt; and the amount paid by him thereupon is allowed in his administration ac-

---

[1] Administrator's charges for attending probate court at hearings in relation to estates connected with that of his intestate, for inquiring and ascertaining the existence of property in another jurisdiction supposed to belong to the estate, and for taking legal advice in respect to such property, although it could be administered only in the other jurisdiction, allowed. Wendell *v*. French, 19 N. H. 205.

The acts of the administrator done in good faith and at the request of all the parties interested, will be protected in the settlement of his accounts, even if he has not administered strictly according to law. Poole *v.* Munday, 103 Mass. 174.

[2] Storer *v*. Storer, 9 Mass. 37.

[3] Jennison *v.* Hapgood, 10 Pick. 102.

count, unless it appears to the probate court that the
suit was commenced or prosecuted unnecessarily or without reasonable cause.[1]   But such costs are not allowed
in the administration account, until they have been
actually paid by him.   Their payment is a condition
precedent to their allowance.[2]

Since the repeal of the statute allowing to executors
and administrators a commission on the sums accounted
for by them, there has been no rule common to all the
probate courts in this State in regard to their compensation.   The executor or administrator usually credits
himself in his account with such a sum as he considers
himself entitled to receive, and the court, in its discretion, allows the sum asked for, or a less sum, regard
being had to the character of the services rendered
necessary by the condition of the estate, and actually
performed.

An executor is sometimes entitled to credits in his
account that he could not claim as administrator of an
intestate estate.   It being his duty to administer according to law and the will of his testator, he may be called
upon, in order to carry out the provisions of the will,
to perform services and incur expenses that would be
irregular and unnecessary in a case of ordinary administration.   For all such services faithfully performed
and expenses properly incurred he is entitled to be
allowed.[3]

[1] Gen. Sts. c. 98, § 13; Hardy v. Call, 16 Mass. 530.

[2] Thacher v. Dunham, 5 Gray, 26.

[3] Unfaithful administration will not deprive an executor of his right
to compensation for his services so far as they have been beneficial to
the estate.   Jennison v. Hapgood, 10 Pick. 112.

When services not obviously alien to the administration have been
rendered at the special request and advice of a party interested in the
estate, he is estopped from objecting to the allowance of a just compensa-

Loss on Sale of the Personal Estate. The executor or administrator is not required to sustain any personal loss in consequence of the decrease or destruction, without his fault, of any part of the estate. If he has sold it for less than the appraised value, he will be allowed in his account for the loss, if it appears that the sale was expedient and for the interest of all concerned in the estate;[1] and he is entitled to be allowed for the amount of any debts inventoried as due to the deceased, if it appears to the court that they remain uncollected without his fault.[2]

Allowances to the Widow and Minor Children. The executor or administrator is allowed in his account for all sums paid by him, under order of the probate court, as allowances to the widow or minor children of the deceased; but, if he pays money for their support without being first authorized by the court, he makes the payment at his own risk.[3]

Debts due the Executor or Administrator from the deceased. If the executor or administrator is himself a creditor of the estate, he should procure the assent of the heirs, or other parties interested in the estate, to the

tion for them in the settlement of the administrator's account. Wendell *v.* French, 19 N. H. 205.

Upon a controversy between the administrator and the heirs, charges by him of time and money expended while endeavoring to effect a private settlement with them, are not proper items of charge against the estate as expenses of administration. Clark *v.* Clay, 11 Foster (N. H.), 393.

Where an executor, to whom real estate is devised in trust, is authorized by the will to take down any part of the testator's buildings, and to rebuild, to erect additional buildings, and to hire money for the purpose of bettering the trust estate, he may advance his own money for the like purposes, and charge it in his general administration account. Watts *v.* Howard, 7 Met. 478. And see Wiggin *v.* Sweet, 6 Met. 194.

[1] Gen. Sts. c. 98, § 2.   [2] Ibid. § 6.

[3] Washburn *v.* Hale, 10 Pick. 429; Brewster *v.* Brewster, 8 Mass. 131.

allowance of his claim, before he presents his account to the probate court. If his claim is disputed by any person interested in the estate, he must file in the probate court a separate statement, setting forth distinctly and fully the nature and grounds of his claim ; and it may then be submitted under an order of the court to one or more arbitrators, to be agreed on by the claimant and the party objecting. The court has like power to discharge the rule by which the claim is referred, and to reject and disallow the award, or to recommit it to the arbitrators, as may be exercised by the common-law courts with regard to cases referred by a rule of those courts. The award of the arbitrators, if accepted by the probate court, is final and conclusive.

If the parties do not agree in the appointment of arbitrators, or if the award is not confirmed by the probate court. the judge will decide on the claim ; and if either party appeals from his decision to the supreme court of probate, either party or the court may have the claim submitted to a jury.[1]

If the claim of the executor or administrator results from a course of dealing, or involves mutual debts and credits, the balance only is the actual debt, and the whole account on both sides must be examined, in order to ascertain that balance ; and, of course, all the items on both sides are put in issue.[2]

The executor or administrator is entitled to interest on his claim only for such a length of time, after taking administration, as is reasonably needed for the settlement of the estate.[3]

Distributive payments by an executor to residuary legatees are not allowed in his account rendered to the

---

[1] Gen. Sts. c. 97, §§ 26, 27. [2] Willey v. Thompson, 9 Met. 329.
[3] Richmond, petitioner, 2 Pick. 567.

probate court. The settlement of the account determines the amount of residue subject to distribution, but not the rights or shares of those who are entitled.[1]

It may be necessary for the executor or administrator to render more than one account of his administration of the estate committed to him. He is required to render an account within one year after giving bond, and from time to time, as the condition of the estate may demand or the probate court may order, until the estate is fully settled. If he receives assets, though they come to his hands more than twenty years after the supposed final settlement and distribution of the estate, he is bound to account for them.[2] In stating any account after the first, he brings forward the balance of his last preceding account, and charges himself with the amount of all sums received by him not previously accounted for; and asks to be allowed for the amount of any additional payments made by him and expenses of administration. And he must annex schedules giving full details of such receipts and expenditures.

FORM OF GUARDIAN'S AND TRUSTEE'S ACCOUNTS.

The guardian or trustee presents his account in substantially the same form as that of an executor or administrator. He charges himself with the amount of the assets received by him, and asks to be allowed for the payments made by him and the charges of the trust. With the account must be filed a schedule stating the several sums received by him, the person of whom, and the time when, each sum was received; a second schedule containing a full statement of the payments and

---

[1] Granger v. Bassett, 98 Mass. 462.

[2] White v. Swain, 3 Pick. 365.

charges ; and a third stating particularly the manner in which any balance remaining in his hands is invested.

WITH WHAT THE GUARDIAN OR TRUSTEE IS CHARGEABLE.

The guardian or trustee is required to charge himself with the value of the personal estate in his hands, according to the inventory ; with the gain, if any, realized from its sale ; with the rents and profits of the real estate belonging to the ward, or *cestui que trust ;* and with all sums received by him in his official capacity, from whatever source.

He is held strictly to account for the interest arising from the trust fund. The general rule is that he is bound to take the same care of the trust fund as a discreet and prudent man would take of his own property ; to manage it for the exclusive benefit of the ward or *cestui que trust,* and to make no profit or advantage out of it for himself ; to keep it at all times, when practicable, profitably invested, and punctually to account for the income as well as the principal. If any of these duties are neglected, the loss resulting from the neglect must fall upon him, and not on the ward, or *cestui que trust.* Hence, if through gross carelessness or ignorance he makes a bad investment, and thereby loses the whole or part of the trust fund, he will be held to replace it, and must charge himself with it in his account.[1] But he is not liable for losses occasioned by bad investments, provided he acts in good faith, and with sound discretion.[2]

[1] Harding *v.* Larned, 4 Allen, 426; Clark *v.* Garfield, 8 Allen, 427; Richardson *v.* Boynton, 12 Allen, 138.

[2] A loan by a guardian, upon the promissory note of the borrower, payable in one year with interest, secured by a pledge of shares in a man-

If he wholly neglects to invest the trust funds, he is chargeable with the income that would have been derived from a proper investment; and in cases of gross neglect, or if he employs the money in his own business, he is liable to be charged with compound interest.[1] He may not be chargeable with interest from the date of his appointment, or of his receipt of the money. He is entitled to a reasonable time in which to make the investment, and the length of time that will be deemed reasonable for that purpose must depend upon the condition of the property at the time he received it, his opportunity of making investments, or other circumstances controlling his proceedings.[2]

ufacturing corporation, the amount of the loan being about three quarters of the par value of the shares, and less than three quarters of their market-value, was held to be an investment made with sound discretion ; and although the borrower failed before the note became due, and the shares fell in value below the amount of the note, the guardian was held not to be responsible for the loss.

And the guardian having sold the shares and taken the purchaser's note for the price, with two indorsers, and the notes of another person secured by a mortgage on land, he was held to have exercised a sound discretion, and not to be responsible for a loss occasioned by the failure of all the parties to the notes, and a fall in the value of the mortgaged premises. Lovell v. Minot, 20 Pick. 116. And see Harvard College v. Amory, 9 Pick. 459 ; Thompson v. Brown, 4 Johns. Ch. 628.

[1] Boynton v. Dyer, 18 Pick. 1. Where the guardian had received rents and income from stocks, and had rendered no account for many years, it was ordered that an account should be settled with a rest for every year. and the balance thus struck carried forward, to be again on interest whenever the sum should be so large that a trustee acting faithfully and discreetly would have put it in a productive state ; and $500 was held to be such a sum. Robbins v. Hayward, 1 Pick. 528, note.

Simple interest only was allowed on a note due on demand from the guardian to the ward, the note being so small that it was not a sufficient object to make a new investment with the interest. Fay v. Howe, 1 Pick. 527.

[2] In Boynton v. Dyer (18 Pick. 1), one year was deemed a reasonable time. In Clarkson v. Depeyster (2 Wend. 77), six months was held sufficient ; and in Schieffelin v. Stewart (1 Johns. Ch. 620), two years were allowed.

If the guardian is also executor of the will in which a legacy is given to his ward, he cannot charge himself in his guardianship account with the amount of the legacy until, by the terms of the will, it becomes payable; until that time he must account for it as executor. This distinction, while it does not affect his personal liability, may be of importance to his sureties.[1]

WHAT IS ALLOWED TO THE GUARDIAN OR TRUSTEE.

The guardian is allowed to credit himself with all sums properly paid by him for the support and education of his ward. He may expend a part or the whole of the income of the ward's estate for these purposes, as occasion requires, and if the income is not sufficient, the principal; but such expenses must be consistent with a prudent management of the estate. If the ward is a minor, and has a father living, the expense of his maintenance and education is to be paid by the father, unless the ward's property is sufficient to support him in a manner more expensive than his father can reasonably afford; in which case the expense of the maintenance and education of the minor may be defrayed out of his own property, in whole or in part, as the probate court deems reasonable.[2] If the ward is a married woman,

[1] Livermore v. Bemis, 2 Allen, 394.

[2] Gen. Sts. c. 109, § 21. Strong v. Moe, 8 Allen, 125. A husband who receives into his family the children of his wife by a former marriage stands to them *in loco parentis*, and, in the absence of express contract or of circumstances showing a different arrangement, has a right to their services, and is liable for their support and education. And where, for seven years, he has lived in a house belonging to his wife and her three children by a former marriage, has been appointed guardian of the children, and kept them in the house with himself and their mother, has no property of his own, has only earned enough during the time to support the united family, and has sold the real estate of his wards by leave of

the guardian cannot expend her estate for her support, unless authorized by the court, on account of the inability of the husband suitably to maintain her and her family, or for other cause which the court deems reasonable.[1]

In all cases, the amounts to be allowed to the guardian in his account for his ward's expenses will be determined with reference to the condition and circumstances of the ward.[2]

If the guardian has advanced his own money for the payment of debts and expenses of his ward, under circumstances that render that course of proceeding proper, he is entitled to interest on the money so advanced.[3]

Guardians and trustees are allowed for all necessary expenses incurred in the execution of their respective trusts, and such compensation for their services as the court may consider just and reasonable.[4]

court, is not to be charged in his account with any previous rent thereof, or credited with taxes paid thereon, or for the board and clothing of his wards, but may be allowed a reasonable amount paid for the expense of one of his wards at a boarding-school. Mulhern v. McDavitt, 16 Gray, 404. See Wilkes v. Rogers, 6 Johns. 566.

[1] Gen. Sts. c. 108, § 18.

[2] The guardian (of an insane person) is appointed for the welfare, comfort, and security of the ward; and not for the increase of the estate in his hands by accumulations from the income, in order to enlarge the wealth of remote or collateral relatives who may ultimately succeed to the inheritance. It is no part of his duty to diminish the reasonable comforts of his ward, or to prevent him from enjoying such luxuries, or indulging such tastes, as would be allowable and proper in the case of a man similarly situated in other respects, but in the full possession of his faculties. Ames, J., in May v. May, 109 Mass. 256.

[3] Hayward v. Ellis, 13 Pick. 272.

[4] Reasonable expenses incurred by the guardian of an insane person, in resisting the application for a revocation of the guardianship on the ground of his restoration to sanity, when it admits of any reasonable doubt, and the guardian appears to have incurred the expenses in good faith, for the purpose of a proper inquiry into the ward's condition, are

If the same person is guardian of two or more wards, although they may be equally interested in the property in his hands, he should render a separate account of his guardianship of each, and is bound to account whenever either of them arrives at full age.

ALLOWANCE OF PROBATE ACCOUNTS.

The administrator or other party accounting will avoid some delay and expense if, before presenting his account to the probate court, he submits it to the heirs, or other parties interested, and obtains their assent in writing to its allowance. Such assent may be conveniently indorsed on the account. If they do not so express their assent, the court, before proceeding to pass upon the account, will order such notice to be given to them as the circumstances of the case require. Guardianship accounts, rendered before the ward becomes of age, are not allowed, unless the next of kin assent thereto, or are cited, and a guardian *ad litem* is also appointed, who examines the account and the vouchers; nor after the ward becomes of age, unless he assents thereto or is cited.

Any person interested in the estate may appear and object to the allowance of the account, either that the

to be allowed the guardian in his account. Palmer *v.* Palmer, 1 Chandler (N. H.), 418.

A trustee or guardian is not allowed in his account for the expenses of a controversy occasioned in a great measure by his own fault. A guardian who is also trustee is not allowed full compensation in each capacity for the same service. Blake *v.* Pegram, 101 Mass. 592. A guardian is not allowed compensation for changing investments of his ward's property in the form of commissions on the amounts invested. May *v.* May, 109 Mass. 252. He is not allowed compensation for taking care of a trust fund while he himself is the borrower of it. Farwell *v.* Steen, 46 Vt. 678.

administrator or other trustee has not charged himself
with all the assets that have come to his hands, or that he
has credited himself with sums that ought not to have
been paid from the estate, or that he claims a larger
sum for compensation than he is justly entitled to receive, or because of any overcharge or omission in his
account. The executor or guardian is not only required
to make oath to the correctness of his account, but to
answer specifically all questions concerning it.[1] And
the party at whose instance interrogatories have been
proposed to him touching his account, has a right to
offer evidence to disprove his answers.[2]

The court, upon the hearing, may order the account-
ant to charge himself with sums not included in his
account, if it appears that he has received them in his
official capacity, and may disallow any of the items with
which he credits himself ; and the decree of the court
allowing the account, as it may be finally adjusted, is
conclusive, unless appealed from. The supreme court
will not, as a court of chancery, resettle an administration account alleged to have been fraudulently settled
in the probate court ;[3] nor can the decree of the probate
court, duly allowing the final account of an administrator, be impeached in an action at law against him upon
a claim against the deceased.[4] The person aggrieved
by the decree can take his objections to the supreme
court of probate only by appeal. If the proceedings in
the probate court were such that they may be treated as
a nullity on account of fraud, the administrator may be
cited to account anew.

---

[1] Gen. Sts. c. 98, § 9; Sigourney v. Wetherell, 6 Met. 553; Wade v.
Lobdell, 4 Cush. 510.

[2] Higbee v. Bacon, 8 Pick. 484.

[3] Jennison v. Hapgood, 7 Pick. 1 ; Sever v. Russell, 4 Cush. 513.

[4] Parcher v. Bussell, 11 Cush. 107.

The accounts of two or more joint executors, administrators, guardians, or trustees, may be allowed by the probate court upon the oath of one of them.[1]   The oath may be administered by the judge or register in or out of court, or by a justice of the peace; but the judge may require the oath to be taken before him in open court.[2]

WHEN SETTLED ACCOUNTS MAY BE OPENED.

" When an account is settled in the absence of any person adversely interested, and without notice to him, the account may be opened, on his application at any time within six months thereafter; and upon the settlement of any account by an executor or administrator (or trustee), all his former accounts may be so far opened as to correct any mistake or error therein;[3] except that any matter in dispute between two parties, which had been previously heard and determined by the court, shall not again be brought in question by either of the same parties without leave of the court."[4]

To avail himself of the exception provided by the above section, the administrator should take care that any matter heard and determined should be so stated as to appear in the decree of the court allowing his account. If his account is disputed, he should call upon the party objecting to specify in writing the items to which he objects.   His account being then settled, the entire proceedings will appear upon the records of the court, and

---

[1] Gen. Sts. c. 101, § 6.   [2] Stat. 1871, c. 122.

[3] Wiggin v. Sweet, 6 Met. 194.

[4] Gen. Sts. c. 98, § 12; Stat. 1870, c. 366; Granger v. Bassett, 98 Mass. 462; Blake v. Pegram, 101 Mass. 592.   Upon the settlement of an account by a trustee or guardian, a former account may be opened, although an appeal was taken from its allowance in the probate court, and determined in the supreme court of probate.   Blake v. Pegram, 109 Mass. 541.

no doubt can afterwards arise as to the particular items disputed and determined. Even then, by leave of the court, the account may be opened, though undoubtedly the court would be cautious in exercising such a power in regard to a subject once controverted and once judicially settled.[1]

Where an account has been settled for many years, the heirs or other parties concerned acquiescing in the settlement, it will not be opened on their application unless good cause is shown for the delay, but the administrator or other trust officer may be cited at any time to account for assets not included in his settled accounts.[2]

[1] Field v. Hitchcock, 14 Pick. 405 ; Smith v. Dutton, 4 Shepley, 308.

[2] An administrator settled his first account in 1818, and a second account in 1822; but in 1825, on the petition of the residuary legatee, a rehearing was had in the probate court, and the administrator was ordered to credit the estate with an additional sum. From this decree the legatee appealed, on the ground that a larger sum should be credited, but failed to prosecute the appeal, and it was dismissed. The legatee thereupon demanded payment of the administrator of the sum so ordered to be credited, and upon his refusal to pay brought an action against him, in which judgment was rendered, in 1835, in favor of the administrator, on the ground that the decree had been vacated by the appeal. In 1836, the legatee filed a petition in the probate court for a second rehearing, on the ground that the account had been settled fraudulently, but the petition was dismissed by that court in 1837 ; on appeal, it was ordered that unless the respondent should pay to the legatee the amount he had been ordered to credit the estate in 1825, with interest from the time of the demand and costs, the prayer of the petition should be granted. Davis v. Cowden, 20 Pick. 510. See Sever v. Russell, 4 Cush. 518.

CHAPTER XVI.

DESCENT, or hereditary succession, is the title whereby a person, on the death of his ancestor, acquires his estate by right of representation, as his heir.

DESCENT OF REAL ESTATE.

Chapter two hundred and twenty of the acts of 1876, which prescribes the rules regulating the descent of intestate estates, provides: —

"SECT. 1. When a person dies seised of land, tenements, or hereditaments, or of any right thereto, or entitled to any interest therein, in fee-simple or for the life of another,[1] not having lawfully devised the same,

---

[1] This description of the real estate is so framed as to include not only lands of which the ancestor was actually seised, but also remainders and reversions, and the right to lands of which he had been disseised, or in any other way ousted. Com. Rep. 1854, note to c. 61.

Contingent interests, both in real and personal estate, are transmissible like vested interests. Winslow v. Goodwin, 7 Met. 363; Dalton v. Savage, 9 Met. 28.

By a devise of land in trust to the separate use of a married woman, her heirs and assigns, to be managed and invested under her direction, and the income, or, if she require it, the principal, to be paid to her; and upon the death of her husband, the whole property to be conveyed to her in fee-simple; and upon her death, to be conveyed to such persons as she may appoint, or, on failure of such appointment, to her children; the children, on the death of their mother, without having made such

they shall descend, subject to his or her debts, in manner following : —

" First.   In equal shares to his or her children, and the issue [1] of any deceased child by right of representation ; and if there is no surviving child of the intestate, then to all his or her other lineal descendants.   If all the descendants are in the same degree of kindred to the intestate, they shall share the estate equally ; otherwise, they shall take according to the right of representation.

" Second.   If the intestate leaves no issue, then in equal shares to his or her father and mother.

" Third.   If the intestate leaves no issue nor mother, then to his or her father.

" Fourth.   If the intestate leaves no issue nor father, then to his or her mother.

" Fifth.   If the intestate leaves no issue and no father nor mother, then to his or her brothers and sisters, and to the issue of any deceased brother or sister, by right of representation.

" Sixth.   If he leaves no issue, and no father, mother, brother, nor sister, then to his next of kin in equal degree ; except that when there are two or more collateral kindred in equal degree, but claiming through different ancestors, those who claim through the nearest ancestor shall be preferred to those claiming through an ancestor who is more remote.

appointment, take as purchasers under the will and not by descent from her. Hubbard v. Rawson, 4 Gray, 242.

Real estate held by an executor or administrator in mortgage, or on execution for a debt due the deceased, is considered personal assets in his hands, and if not sold by him or redeemed does not descend to the heirs as real estate, but is assigned and distributed to the same persons and in the same proportions as if it had been part of the personal estate of the deceased. Gen. Sts. c. 96, § 14.

[1] The word " issue," as applied to the descent of estates, includes all the lawful lineal descendants of the ancestor. Gen. Sts. c. 3, § 7, cl. 9.

" Seventh. If the intestate leaves a widow and no kindred, his estate shall descend to his widow; and if the intestate is a married woman, and leaves no kindred, her estate shall descend to her husband.

" Eighth. If the intestate leaves no kindred, and no widow or husband, his or her estate shall escheat to the Commonwealth.

" Sect. 2. Section one of chapter ninety-one of the General Statutes is hereby repealed.

" Sect. 3. The descent prescribed by section one of this act shall be subject to and controlled by the provisions of law respecting dower, curtesy, and homestead estates.

" Sect. 5. This act shall take effect on the first day of October next, but shall not affect the descent or distribution of the estate of any person deceased prior to that date." [1]

---

[1] Section one of chapter ninety-one of the General Statutes, under which the estates of persons deceased prior to October 1, 1876 descend, provides that : —

" When a person dies seised of land, tenements, or hereditaments, or, of any right thereto, or entitled to any interest therein, in fee-simple or for the life of another, not having lawfully devised the same, they shall descend, subject to his debts, except as provided in chapter one hundred and four (relating to homestead rights) in manner following : —

" First. In equal shares to his children and the issue of any deceased child, by right of representation ; and if there is no child of the intestate living at his death, then to all his other lineal descendants; if all the descendants are in the same degree of kindred to the intestate, they shall share the estate equally ; otherwise, they shall take according to the right of representation ;

" Second. If he leaves no issue, then to his father ;

" Third. If he leaves no issue nor father, then in equal shares to his mother, brothers, and sisters, and to the children of any deceased brother or sister by right of representation ;

[This provision does not include the children of a deceased child of a deceased brother or sister. Bigelow v. Morong, 103 Mass. 287.]

" Fourth. If he leaves no issue, nor father, and no brother nor sister,

AS TO ILLEGITIMATE CHILDREN.

"An illegitimate child shall be heir of his mother and any maternal ancestor, and the lawful issue of an ille-

living at his death, then to his mother, to the exclusion of the issue, if any, of deceased brothers or sisters ;

" Fifth. If he leaves no issue, and no father, mother, brother, nor sister, then to his next of kin in equal degree ; except that when there are two or more collateral kindred in equal degree, but claiming through different ancestors, those who claim through the nearest ancestor shall be preferred to those claiming through an ancestor who is more remote : *provided ;*

" Sixth. If a person dies leaving several children, or leaving one child and the issue of one or more others, and any such surviving child dies under age and not having been married, all the estate that came to the deceased child by inheritance from such deceased parent, shall descend in equal shares to the other children of the same parent, and to the issue of any such other children who have died, by right of representation ;

" Seventh. If at the death of such child who shall have died under age and not having been married, all the other children of his said parent are also dead, and any of them have left issue, the estate that came to such child by inheritance from his said parent shall descend to all the issue of the other children of the same parent ; and if all the issue are in the same degree of kindred to the child, they shall share the estate equally ; otherwise they shall take according to the right of representation ;

[The sixth and seventh clauses modify the antecedent rule under certain circumstances. The share of the child who dies under age and unmarried, goes exclusively to the surviving issue of the deceased parent. The distribution first made of the parent's estate is ineffectual as to the share of the child who has not lived to dispose of it, and that share is considered as having reverted to the parent's estate. It is considered, not as the estate of the child, but as estate of the parent remaining to be distributed ; and it descends to the children or grandchildren of the parent in like manner as if he had not died until after the death of the child. This provision applies only to estate inherited from the parent. Estate *devised* to the child by the parent descends to the heirs of the child under the general rule regulating the descent of intestate estates.]

" Eighth. If the intestate leaves a widow and no kindred, his estate shall descend to his widow ; and if the intestate is a married woman and leaves no kindred, her estate shall descend to her husband ;

" Ninth. If the intestate leaves no kindred, and no widow or husband, his or her estate shall escheat to the Commonwealth."

gitimate person shall represent such person and take by
descent any estate which the parent would have taken
if living.[1]

"If an illegitimate child dies intestate, without lawful
issue, his estate shall descend to his mother.

"An illegitimate child whose parents have intermar-
ried and whose father has acknowleged him as his child,
shall be considered legitimate."

RIGHT OF REPRESENTATION.

Inheritance or succession, "by right of representation,"
takes place when the descendants of a deceased heir take
the same share or right in the estate of another person
that their parent would have taken if living.[2] If the
ancestor leaves children, and there is no living issue of
any deceased child, they will share his estate equally;
if he leaves grandchildren only, they will take it in
equal shares; and if he has no children or grandchildren
living at the time of his death, his great-grandchildren,
if any, being his lineal descendants, and all of an equal
degree of consanguinity to him, will take the inheritance equally.*

But when the lineal descendants of the ancestor,
living at the time of his death, are not of an equal degree of consanguinity to him, — as, for instance, when
he leaves one son and two or more grandchildren who
are the children of a deceased son, — the rule of representation applies. The son, in such case, takes half the
estate, and the children of the deceased son represent

[1] A bastard and his issue cannot inherit from his mother's collateral
kindred. Pratt v. Atwood, 108 Mass. 40; Haraden v. Larrabee, 113 Mass.
430.

[2] Gen. Sts. c. 91, § 12.

their father, and, together, take the other half, which
is the same share that their father would have taken if
living. Or suppose the ancestor leaves B., his only surviving son, and D. and E., grandsons by his deceased
son C., and F. and G., great-grandsons by H., a daughter of C., H. being also dead. Here would be lineal
descendants living in three different degrees of consanguinity; namely, a son, two grandsons, and two great-
grandsons: B., the son, would take the half estate; D.
and E., two of the three children of C., would take
two thirds of the other half; and F. and G. would take
the remaining third of the second half; and all would
hold as tenants in common.

AS TO THE NEXT OF KIN.

The " next of kin," to whom the estate descends when
the intestate leaves no issue, and no father, mother,
brother, or sister, are to be ascertained by reference to
the rules of the civil law, according to which the degrees of kindred are computed.[1] According to those
rules, the father of the intestate stands in the first degree, his grandfather in the second, his great-grandfather
in the third, etc. The child of the intestate is also in
the first degree, his grandchild in the second, his great-
grandchild in the third ; the rule of computation being
the same, both in the ascending and descending lines.
The degree of kindred in which a collateral kinsman
stands is calculated by counting upwards from the intestate to the common ancestor of both, and then downwards to such collateral relative, reckoning one degree
for each person. Thus, the intestate and his cousin are
related in the fourth degree : the intestate's father being

[1] Gen. Sts. c. 91, § 5.

in the first degree; his grandfather, their common ancestor, in the second; his uncle, counting downwards from the common ancestor, in the third; his uncle's son (his cousin) in the fourth. The intestate's brother stands in the second degree, his nieces and nephews in the third.

The statute makes no distinction between ascendants and descendants, and none between kindred on the father's and on the mother's side;[1] but when there are two or more collateral kindred, in equal degree, those claiming through the nearest ancestor are preferred to those claiming through an ancestor more remote. The intestate's nephew, for instance, is preferred to the intestate's uncle, though both are in the same degree of kindred. The common ancestor of the intestate and his uncle is the intestate's grandfather, while the nephew claims through the intestate's father, the nearer ancestor.

Kindred of the half-blood inherit equally with those of the whole blood in the same degree.[2]

POSTHUMOUS CHILDREN.

A posthumous child is one born after the death of the parent. Posthumous children inherit, in all cases, in like manner as if they were born in the lifetime of the parent and had survived him.[3]

WHEN THE STATUTE APPLIES TO TESTATE ESTATES.

The statute of descents may apply to a certain extent to testate estates. "When a testator omits to provide

---

[1] The next of kin of a deceased intestate, being her paternal grandmother and her maternal grandfather and grandmother, are each entitled to a third part of the intestate's estate. Knapp v. Windsor, 6 Cush. 156.

[2] Gen. Sts. c. 91, § 5; Larrabee v. Tucker, 116 Mass. 562.

[3] Gen. Sts. c. 91, § 12.

in his will for any of his children, or for the issue of a deceased child, they shall take the same share of his estate, both real and personal, that they would have been entitled to if he had died intestate; unless they shall have been provided for by the testator in his lifetime, or unless it appears that the omission was intentional, and not occasioned by accident or mistake." [1]

That the omission was intentional, and not occasioned by accident or mistake, may be manifest from the will itself. It has been held that the fact that the child was named in the will, though no legacy was given to him, was sufficient to show that he was not forgotten by the testator, and that the omission to provide for him was intentional. And where the testator devised estate to the children of his daughter, describing them as such, but giving her no legacy, the same rule was applied.[2] The fact that the omission was designed may also be shown by parol evidence. Evidence of the statement of the testatrix to the attesting witnesses, when the will was executed, that she intended to exclude a child, has been admitted to show that the omission was intentional.[3] The burden of proof is upon the party opposing the claim of the child to show that the omission was intentional.[4] The statute applies to children born after the making of the will, and before the death of the father;[5] but it has

---

[1] Gen. Sts. c. 92, § 25. A child of a testator, born after his death, cannot, in any proper sense of the term, be deemed provided for in his will by a general devise of a reversion to the heirs of the testator. Waterman v. Hawkins, 63 Maine, 156.

[2] Terry v. Foster, 1 Mass. 146; Church v. Crocker, 3 Mass. 17; Wild v. Brewer, 2 Mass. 570; Wilder v. Goss, 14 Mass. 357.

[3] Wilson v. Fasket, 6 Met. 400; Converse v. Wales, 4 Allen, 512; Ramsdill v. Wentworth, 101 Mass. 125.

[4] Ramsdill v. Wentworth, 106 Mass. 320.

[5] A testator gave a small legacy to each of his children, living at the date of his will, by name (all of whom died before him without issue),

been held not to apply to cases where the testator omits to provide for an illegitimate child.[1] Nor does it apply to cases where the testator has a power of appointment over the estate to dispose of the inheritance, but only to cases where it is the testator's own estate in fee.[2]

A child for whom the testator has unintentionally omitted to provide may cause his share of the personal estate to be ascertained, by applying to the probate court for a decree of distribution.[3] His share or proportion of the real estate, if certain and not disputed by parties interested, may also be assigned to him by the probate court ;[4] if his share is disputed and uncertain, he must apply to the common-law courts for an assignment of his share of the real estate.

And " when a child of the testator, born after his father's death, has no provision made for him by his father, in his will or otherwise, he shall take the same share of his father's estate, both real and personal, that he would have been entitled to if his father had died intestate." Devisees and legatees are required to contribute equally, in proportion to the value of what they respectively receive under the will, to the share of a posthumous child, or a child omitted in the will of his parent ; unless there is some provision in the will requiring a different apportionment in order to give effect to the intention of

and the residue of his property to his wife ; and afterwards had other children born to him. *Held*, that evidence of his having said to his wife, since the birth of his younger children, " you will have all there is," was not sufficient to show an intent to omit to provide for them in his will ; and that they were entitled to the same share of his estate as if he had died intestate. Bancroft *v.* Ives, 3 Gray, 367.

[1] Kent *v.* Barker, 2 Gray, 535.

[2] Blagge *v.* Miles, 1 Story, 426. And see Wilder *v.* Thayer, 97 Mass. 439 ; Bowdlear *v.* Bowdlear, 112 Mass. 184.

[3] See Appendix, form No. 71.

[4] See *post*, Chap. XVII. on Partition.

the testator as to that part of his estate which passes by his will.[1]

DISTRIBUTION OF PERSONAL ESTATE.

The statute[2] provides that when a person dies possessed of personal estate,[3] or any right or interest therein,[4] not lawfully disposed of by will, it shall be applied and distributed (the allowances, if any, made to the widow and minor children, and the debts of the deceased, with the charges of his funeral and of the administration having first been paid) among the same persons who would be entitled to his real estate, and in the same proportions, except that:

" If the intestate was a married woman, her husband shall be entitled to the whole of the residue ;

" If the intestate leaves a widow and issue, the widow shall be entitled to one-third of the residue ;[5]

---

[1] Gen. Sts. c. 92, §§ 26, 27.　　　　[2] Ibid. c. 94, § 16.

[3] The surplus of proceeds of land sold by an executor or administrator, remaining on the settlement of his accounts, is considered *real* estate, and is disposed of to the same persons and in the same proportions as the land would descend if not sold. Gen. Sts. c. 102, § 44.

[4] The statute extends to contingent as well as vested interests. Dalton *v.* Savage, 9 Met. 37.

[5] A widow who waives the provision made for her in the will of her husband thereby becomes entitled to such portion of his estate as she would have taken if he had died intestate ; provided, however, that if the share of the personal estate to which she would thus become entitled exceeds the sum of ten thousand dollars, she is entitled, in such case, to receive in her own right the ten thousand dollars, and the income only of the excess of said share above said sum of ten thousand dollars, during her natural life. Stat. 1861, c. 164 ; Firth *v.* Denny, 2 Allen, 468. The $10,000 does not bear interest until an effectual order for its payment to the widow has been made. And the court in its discretion may make such order without waiting for the final distribution of the estate. Atherton *v.* Corliss, 101 Mass. 40 ; Scullings *v.* Richmond, 13 Allen, 277. But the income of the excess of her share is to be computed from the time of the husband's death. Pollock *v.* Learned, 102 Mass. 49.

A widow filed her waiver and died before the probate of her husband's

"If there is no issue, the widow shall be entitled to the residue to the amount of five thousand dollars, and to one-half the excess of such residue above ten thousand dollars; and

"If there is no husband, widow, or kindred of the intestate, the whole shall escheat to the Commonwealth." [1]

The distribution of intestate estates is within the peculiar and exclusive jurisdiction of the probate courts. The administrator, or either of the distributees, on application to the probate court, can obtain a decree of distribution specifying the names of persons who are entitled to share in the estate and the amount to which each is entitled. In the great majority of cases of persons dying intestate, the heirs and distributees will be the children, parents, brothers, and sisters, or other near connections, all of whom may be known to the administrator; and in such cases the administrator is practically safe in paying to each distributee the amount to which he is entitled and taking his receipt therefor, without first obtaining a decree of distribution. But when the heirs or any of them are residing out of the State, or when the administrator has doubts as to who is entitled to share in the estate, or as to the proportions of the several heirs, he should apply to the court for a decree of distribution. And a decree, made after such notice as the court may order, settles the facts as to who are entitled, and what

will. *Held*, that the waiver was sufficient, and that her share of the estate passed to her representatives. Atherton *v.* Corliss, 101 Mass. 40.

The mere right to make the waiver does not pass to her representatives. Sherman *v.* Newton, 6 Gray, 307.

If the widow is insane or a minor, her guardian may make the waiver. Stat. 1871, c. 97.

The rents and profits of real estate received by the administrator are not personal estate, and therefore the widow is not entitled to a distributive share thereof. Stearns *v.* Stearns, 1 Pick. 157.

[1] As to distribution of insolvent estates, see Chap. XIII.

kin are living, and will protect an administrator, acting
in good faith, in conforming to it;[1] and he is held by
his bond to distribute the estate as the court may order.

A decree of distribution may also be necessary to enable the next of kin to bring a suit on the bond of an
unfaithful administrator for the recovery of his distributive share of the estate.

THE PETITION FOR DISTRIBUTION.

The petition for a decree of distribution should state
the names and residences of each of the supposed distributees, the degree of kindred in which each of them
stands to the intestate, the balance in the hands of the
administrator for distribution, the amount of any advancement made by the intestate in his lifetime to
either of the heirs, and whether such advancement was
made from the real or personal estate, or both. The
petition may be made by the administrator, or any party
interested in the distribution.

Upon such petition, such notice must be given as will
be most likely to reach the parties interested. The supreme court of probate, in the case of an English subject
dying in this State, has ordered notice to be published
in a London paper. The order, whatever may be its
terms, must be complied with by the petitioner, before a
decree of distribution can issue.

THE DISTRIBUTION.

A decree of distribution expressed in the general terms
used by the statute to designate the heirs at law is not
sufficient. It is for the court to ascertain who are the
existing individuals entitled, under the statute, to share
in the estate, to decree distribution to them by name,

---

[1] Loring v. Steineman, 1 Met. 204. See Stat. 1866, c. 122.

and determine the amount due to each.[1] If all the parties appear upon notice, or are known to be living, these questions are easily determined. A more difficult question sometimes arises when a descendant or next of kin of the intestate is absent from the State and cannot be found. Whether such person shall be included in the distribution, as he is entitled to be if living, must be determined by the rules of evidence and presumptions of facts from circumstances, which are resorted to by all tribunals in determining questions of fact. The possibility of mistake cannot prevent the distribution, and the distribution when made must be of the entire estate. If such absent heir left his usual home for temporary purposes of business or pleasure, and has not been heard from or known to be living for the term of seven years, the presumption of life ceases and that of his death arises. It must appear that he has not been heard of by those persons who would be likely to hear of him, or that search has been ineffectually made for such a person.[2] This presumption of death may be rebutted by counter evidence. Where other circumstances concurred, the fact of death has been found, without direct evidence, from the lapse of a shorter period than seven years; as, when the party sailed in a vessel which had not been heard from for a much longer time than was necessary for the accomplishment of the voyage;[3] but

---

[1] Loring v. Steineman, 1 Met. 204. The court will not order a distributive share to be paid to a person to whom the heir has assigned it; the investigation of such an assignment is not within the jurisdiction of the probate court. Knowlton v. Johnson, 46 Maine, 489; Wood v. Stone, 2 Chandler (N. H.), 572. Nor will the court order the share of an heir to be paid to the other heirs on the ground that he is indebted to them. Hancock v. Hubbard, 19 Pick. 167.

[2] France v. Andrews, 15 Adol. & E. 756.

[3] Watson v. King, 1 Stark. 97.

the presumption of law does not attach to the mere lapse of time short of seven years.

If such person was unmarried at the time he went abroad, there is no presumption of his subsequent marriage ; and if the fact of his marriage is proved, there is no presumption that he left issue. These are facts to be proved, and the burden of proof of the affirmative is on the party who avers it.[1]

Under some circumstances, it is impossible to ascertain with certainty what persons are entitled to inherit an estate, as when several near relatives perish by shipwreck, or other common disaster. In the absence of all evidence of the particular circumstances of the calamity, it is presumed that all perished together, and that therefore neither could transmit rights to the other. Thus, where a father and his only child perished at sea, there being no evidence showing which survived, it was decided that his estate should go to his nephews and nieces, his heirs-at-law, and not to her uncles and aunts, who would have taken it, if she had survived her father and the estate had vested in her.[2] It would be reasonable and proper to hold that one of middle age and in the full vigor of life would ordinarily survive a mere infant or a person well stricken in years. And evidence of circumstances, however slight, attending the disaster, are important, as from slight circumstances inferences of fact materially affecting the question may be drawn.

The time when distribution can be properly made must depend upon the circumstances of each case. If all the persons entitled to shares are known, the distribution may be made at any time after the debts are paid.

[1] Loring *v.* Steineman, 1 Met. 211; Doe *v.* Griffin, 15 East, 293; In the Goods of Main, 1 Swabey & Tris. 11.

[2] Coye *v.* Leach, 8 Met. 371.

But as the administrator is liable to the actions of creditors for two years after he gives bond, the payment of any distributive share during the continuance of such liability, may be attended with risk, unless the distributee first gives bond, as the court may require him to do, for the protection of the administrator.[1]

The court, after notice to all persons interested, may order a partial distribution, when it can be made without detriment to the estate.[2]

ADVANCEMENTS.

The subject of advancements is necessarily to be considered in connection with the descent and distribution of intestate estates. Advancements may be made of real or personal estate, and to any child or other lineal descendant. They are usually made with a view of establishing a son in business, or on the event of marriage. If the advancement is equal to, or exceeds, the amount in value of the share which the child would have taken in the estate, if no advancement had been made, such child will be excluded from any share in the distribution ; if it is less in amount, such child will be entitled to sufficient in the distribution to make up his full share, and no more. If he dies before the intestate, leaving issue, the amount of his advancement is regarded as so much received by his representatives towards their share of the estate, in like manner as if the advancement had been directly to them.[3] He is not required to refund any part of the advancement, although it exceeds his share ;[4] and interest is not to be computed on it.

If the advancement is made in real estate, its value is

[1] Gen. Sts. c. 97, § 21.   See Appendix, form No. 72.

[2] Stat. 1873, c. 221.   [3] Gen. Sts. c. 91, § 10.

[4] Ibid. § 6; Stearns v. Stearns, 1 Pick. 161.

considered as part of the real estate to be divided ; if in personal estate, as part of the personal estate ; and if in either case it exceeds the share of real or personal estate, respectively, that would have come to the heirs so advanced, he does not refund any part of it, but receives so much less out of the other part of the estate as will make his whole share equal to those of the other heirs who are in the same degree with him.[1]

Questions concerning advancements are determined by the probate court, and the judgment of the court is conclusive unless appealed from.   Questions as to advancements of personal property are settled by the decree of distribution, and of real estate by the decree of partition.

EVIDENCE OF ADVANCEMENTS.

The advancement must be proved to have been intended as such, chargeable on the child's share of the estate ; otherwise, it will be deemed an absolute gift, or a loan, as the case may be.   The statute prescribes what shall be the requisite evidence of an advancement.   "All gifts and grants shall be deemed to have been made in advancement, if they are expressed in the gift or grant to be so made, or if charged in writing by the intestate as an advancement, or acknowledged in writing as such by the child or other descendant."[2]   It is not expressly provided that an advancement shall not be proved in any other manner, but that is undoubtedly the meaning of the statute.   It has accordingly been held that where a note was given by a son for money received by him of his father, oral testimony was inadmissible to prove that the money so received was an advancement.[3]   Various

[1] Gen. Sts. c. 91, § 7 ; Bemis v. Stearns, 16 Mass. 200.
[2] Gen. Sts. c. 91, § 8.   [3] Barton v. Rice, 22 Pick. 508.

sums of money, charged by the parent in the usual way of keeping accounts, have been held not to be an advancement.[1] And where land was conveyed by the father to the son, there being nothing in the deed to show the fact, it was held not to be an advancement.[2] The execution of a will merges all prior advancements, it being deemed that the testator graduated the amount of his legacies with reference to them ; but the execution of a will which is afterwards revoked cannot operate as a merger.[3]

VALUE OF ADVANCEMENTS.

The statute prescribes the manner in which the value of advancements shall be ascertained. "If the value of the estate so advanced is expressed in the conveyance, or in the charge thereof made by the intestate, or in the acknowledgment by the party receiving it, it shall be considered as of that value in the division and distribution of the estate ; otherwise, it shall be estimated according to its value when given."[4]

---

[1] Ashley, appellant, 4 Pick. 21.

[2] Bullard v. Bullard, 5 Pick. 527. A written acknowledgment, signed by husband and wife, in these words, " Received of J. S. $500, it being a part of my wife's portion," and found among the notes of J. S. after his decease, is sufficient proof of an advancement to the wife. So of an acknowledgment in writing by a husband, whose wife is insane, of a gift from her father for her support, " as a part of her portion out of her father's estate," preserved by the father in a bundle of letters relating to her support at an insane asylum. A book of accounts, kept by the deceased, with three leaves cut out, together with evidence of his declarations that he had made charges in his book, as advancements to his children, are not competent evidence of such advancements. Hartwell v. Rice, 1 Gray, 587. And see Fitts v. Morse, 103 Mass. 164 ; Bigelow v. Poole, 10 Gray, 104 ; Loring v. Blake, 106 Mass. 592.

[3] Hartwell v. Rice, 1 Gray, 587.   [4] Gen. Sts. c. 91, § 9.

THE WIDOW'S SHARE WHEN ADVANCEMENTS HAVE BEEN MADE.

If the intestate leaves a widow and issue, and any of the issue received an advancement from the intestate, the value of such advancement is not taken into consideration in computing the widow's one-third. She is entitled only to the third part of the residue of the personal estate, after deducting the value of the advancement.[1]

DISTRIBUTION WHEN ADVANCEMENTS HAVE BEEN MADE.

To ascertain the share to which each heir is entitled, in a case where advancements have been made: first, if there is a widow, deduct from the sum to be distributed one-third for her share; to the remainder add the advancement of each heir who has received *less than a full share*,[2] and divide the sum by the number of such heirs. The quotient will be the amount of a full share of the estate. Each heir who has had no advancement will be entitled to a full share, and each of the others to a full share less the amount of his advancement. Thus, suppose the administrator's final account shows a balance in his hands of $9,000 ; that the intestate left a widow, four children, A, B, C, and D, and two grandchildren, sons of E, a deceased son of the intestate, and that A has been advanced $2,000, C $1,000, D $800, and E $400 : —

[1] Gen. Sts. c. 94, § 17.

[2] To find whether either of the heirs has received more than a full share, add *all* the advancements to the remainder, and divide the amount by the number of *all* the heirs; if the quotient be less than the advancement made to any heir, such heir and the amount of his advancement must be altogether omitted in the computation.

Amount to be distributed $9,000
Deduct widow's share, one-third 3,000

$6,000
Add A's advancement 2,000
   ,,   C's   ,, ... 1,000
   ,,   D's   ,, ... 800
   ,,   E's   ,, ... 400

There being five shares . . . . . . 5)10,200

Amount of a full share $2,040
A will take 40
B, having had no advancement, will take a
   full share 2,040
C will take 1,040
D ,,   ,, ... 1.240
The two grandsons together will take . . 1.640

$6,000

PERPETUATION OF EVIDENCE OF PAYMENTS UNDER THE DECREE OF DISTRIBUTION — DISCHARGE OF EXECUTOR, &c.

The decree of distribution contains the names of all the persons entitled to share in the personal estate of the deceased, and specifies the amount to which each is entitled. The administrator is directed to give written notice, by mail or otherwise, to each of the persons named in the decree of the amount due him or her, and if any of the sums remain for six months unclaimed, to deposit the same in a savings-bank (designated in the order), in the name of the judge of the probate court for the time being, to accumulate for the benefit of the persons entitled thereto. The statute provides that when the money has been paid or deposited by an executor, administrator, guardian, or trustee in accordance with the terms of the decree, he may perpetuate the evidence thereof by presenting to the probate court, within one year after the decree is made, an account of such payments; which being proved to the satisfaction of the court, and verified by the oath of the party, shall be allowed as his final discharge.[1]

Papers or instruments discharging any claim, or purporting to acknowledge the performance of any duty or the payments of money for which an executor, administrator, guardian, or trustee is chargeable or accountable in probate court, may be recorded in the registry of probate upon the request of a party interested.[2]

The administrator may conveniently render his account of payments and deposits made under a decree of distribution by returning to the court the original decree, with the receipts of the several distributees and certificates of deposit, and his own certificate of the fact that the terms of the order have been complied with. In a majority of cases, the administrator is practically safe in taking receipts from the persons to whom he makes payments, without rendering a further account; but it is only by rendering such an account that he can obtain a formal discharge from liability under the decree.

When the person entitled to a sum of money deposited in a savings-bank by the administrator under a decree of distribution satisfies the judge of his right to receive the same, the judge will cause it to be paid over to him. The person so entitled to the money should make a representation in writing to the court showing the grounds of his claim, and, if the money is ordered to be paid to

---

[1] Gen. Sts. c. 101, §§ 7, 8.

[2] Stat. 1864, c. 93.

him, should procure an attested copy of the order for presentation at the bank.[1]

The guardian of a ward who removes or resides out of this State may pay the proceeds of the sale of the ward's real estate, and transfer all his personal estate, to any guardian, trustee, or committee duly appointed in the State or county where the ward resides, upon such terms and in such manner as the probate court for the county in which such estate is found may decree, upon a petition filed and after notice to parties interested.[2]

BALANCES IN THE HANDS OF PUBLIC ADMINIS-TRATORS.

" When an estate has been fully administered by a public administrator, and the debts paid according to law, he shall deposit the balance of such estate remaining in his hands with the treasurer of the Commonwealth, who shall receive and hold it for the benefit of those who may have lawful claims thereon.

" If at any time within six years after such deposit is made with the treasurer, any person applies to the probate court which granted said letters of administration, and makes it appear that he is legally entitled by the will of the deceased or otherwise to the administration of said estate, the court shall grant administration thereof, or, upon probate of such will, shall grant letters testamentary to such applicant, or at his request to some other suitable person ; provided that, before granting such administration, the court shall order personal notice of the application to be served at least fourteen

---

[1] Gen. Sts. c. 101, § 9.   See Appendix, forms Nos. 73, 74.
[2] Stat. 1866, c. 122.

days before the hearing, upon a public administrator of the county, who shall appear in behalf of the Commonwealth ; and either party may appeal from any decree therein.

" After the expiration of thirty days from the appointment of an executor or administrator, as provided in the preceding section, if no appeal is claimed by any person interested, the treasurer shall pay over to such executor or administrator all money deposited in the State treasury to the credit of such estate, to be administered in like manner as the estates of other deceased persons."

" Upon the death, resignation, or removal of a public administrator, the probate court shall issue a warrant to some other public administrator in the same county on his application therefor, requiring him to examine the accounts of such late public administrator, touching the estates on which he has taken out letters of administration, and to return into the probate court a statement of all such estates, not fully administered, and of the balance of each estate remaining in his hands at the time of his death, resignation, or removal.   And thereupon the court shall issue to the public administrator making the return, upon his giving the requisite bond, letters of administration upon such of said estates as are not already administered, although the personal estate remaining may not amount to twenty dollars.

" When a public administrator neglects to return an inventory, settle an account, or perform any other duty incumbent on him, in relation to any estate, and there appears to be no heir entitled thereto, the district-attorney for the district within which the administrator received his letters, shall, in behalf of the Commonwealth, prosecute all suits and do all acts necessary and proper to insure a prompt and faithful administration of the estate, and the payment of the proceeds thereof into the treasury."[1] In all suits and legal proceedings under this section, if no heir has appeared and made claim in the probate court for his interest in any estate under administration by a public administrator within two years after granting letters of administration, it will be presumed that there is no such heir, and the burden of proving the existence of such heir is upon the public administrator.[2]

" It shall be the duty of every public administrator, whenever money or personal property of a value less than twenty dollars is delivered to him by a coroner according to law, and in every other case, where the total property of an intestate which has come into his possession or control is of a value less than twenty dollars (unless the same is the balance of an estate received from a prior public administrator, according to the statute), forthwith to reduce all such property into money, not taking administration thereon, and to deposit such money, first deducting his reasonable expenses and charges, with the treasurer of the Commonwealth, who shall receive and hold it for the benefit of those who shall have legal claims thereon.

" Every public administrator, upon making such deposit, shall file with the treasurer a true and particular account, under oath, of all his dealings, receipts, payments, and charges, on account of the property from which the money so deposited proceeds, including the name of the intestate, if known to him, and the treasurer shall thereupon deliver to him a receipt for such money.

---

[1] Gen. Sts. c. 95, §§ 12–17.
[2] Stat. 1874, c. 105.

And such deposit with the Commonwealth shall exempt the public administrator making it from all responsibility to any party or person whomsoever, by reason of his having received and disposed of the property of the intestate, as herein provided." [1]

[1] Stat. 1874, c. 254.

CHAPTER XVII.

PARTITION OF LANDS IN THE PROBATE COURT.

THE probate court in which the estate of any deceased person is settled, or in a course of settlement, may make partition of all his real estate lying within the State among his heirs or devisees, and all persons holding under them by conveyance or otherwise; [1] and the probate court in each county has concurrent jurisdiction with the supreme judicial and superior courts of petitions for partition of lands within the county held by joint tenants, coparceners, or tenants in common.[2]

The proceedings for partition among heirs and devisees must be in the probate court of the same county in which letters testamentary or of administration were regularly granted. No other probate court can have jurisdiction; and, if the grant of administration was void for want of jurisdiction, the court in which such void administration was granted has no power to order partition.[3]

No partition can be made by the probate court when the shares or proportions of the respective parties are in dispute between them, or appear to the judge to be uncertain, depending upon the construction or effect of any devise or other conveyance, or upon other questions that he deems proper for the consideration of a jury and a court of common law.[4]

---

[1] Gen. Sts. c. 136, § 48.   [2] Stat. 1874, c. 266.

[3] Sigourney v. Sibley, 21 Pick. 101.

[4] Gen. Sts. c. 136, § 60. It is the duty of the probate court to make

Partitions may be made, notwithstanding the existence of any lease of the whole or a part of the estate to be divided; but the partition cannot prejudice the right of a lessee. Partitions may be made, notwithstanding any of the tenants in common may be, alone or jointly with others, trustee, attorney, or guardian of any other tenant.[1]

When an estate or right of homestead exists in property in which other parties have an interest, the party entitled to the homestead, or any other party interested, may upon petition have partition thereof like tenants in common.[2]

The court will not order a partition when all the owners of the real estate in question join in the petition. If all the owners desire partition, they can make it among themselves by deed.[3]

The statute requires the partition, when made on the application of an heir, shall be made of all the estate that descended from the ancestor, and which any party interested, whether the applicant or others, requires to

the partition if there is no real uncertainty as to the shares or proportions of the parties, although one of the parties may insist that there is a dispute or controversy concerning them. Dearborn v. Preston, 7 Allen, 192.

If the probate court has properly assumed jurisdiction and issued a warrant to commissioners, the court may retain its jurisdiction, although it subsequently appears that the shares or proportions of the parties are uncertain. Potter v. Hazard, 11 Allen, 187.

If it appears, upon petition for partition among joint tenants, co-parceners or tenants in common," that the shares are in dispute or uncertain, the court may order the case removed to the superior court, and the case shall be so removed at the request of any party in interest." — Stat. 1874, c. 266.

[1] Gen. Sts. c. 136, §§ 67, 68.

[2] Ibid. c. 104, § 9; Parks v. Reilly, 5 Allen, 77; Woodward v. Lincoln, 9 Allen, 241.

[3] Winthrop v. Minot, 9 Cush. 405; Swett v. Bussey, 7 Mass. 503.

have included in the partition; and when made on the application of a devisee, it shall be made of all the estate held by the applicant jointly or in common with others holding under the testator, which he or any other devisee requires to have included. The same rule applies when the application is made by any person holding under an heir or devisee.[1]

Upon every such partition the court not only assigns to the applicant his share in the premises, but causes the residue to be divided among the parties interested, and the share of each one to be assigned to him, unless two or more of the parties consent to hold their shares together and undivided.[2]

A widow's right to dower is no bar to a partition among tenants in common.[3]

PRELIMINARY PROCEEDINGS IN PROBATE COURT.

Proceedings for partition in the probate court are commenced by petition signed by one or more of the parties interested in the real estate. The petitioner should state the proportion which his share bears to the whole estate, and whether he claims as heir or devisee. The names and residences of all the other parties interested should be stated, and if any of them are married women, the names of their husbands; if any are minors, the fact should appear, and the names and residences of the guardians, if any, should be stated. If any part of the land of the deceased lies in common with that of another person, a description of such land should be annexed to the petition, and the share of the deceased therein, and the names of the cotenants should

---

[1] Gen. Sts. c. 136, § 54.   [2] Ibid. § 55.

[3] Ward v. Gardner, 112 Mass. 42.

be stated. If there are any advancements made by the deceased to be considered in making the partition, the several sums advanced and the names of the persons who received them should be fully stated.

A guardian may petition for the partition of his ward's real estate.[1]

Notice of the petition is required to be given to all the parties interested to appear and show cause against it. The citation may be issued by the register of probate on any day when the petition is filed in the probate office. The notice must be served fourteen days before the time appointed for the hearing on the parties personally if they can be found within the State, and, if not, it must be published once a week for three weeks at least, before such hearing, in such newspapers as the court shall order.[2] A cotenant must be served by delivering to him an attested copy of the citation, or by leaving such copy at his place of abode in this State.[3]

All persons who would be bound by the partition are entitled to notice, whether they have an estate of inheritance, for life or years, in possession, remainder, or reversion, and whether vested or contingent; and if the petitioner holds an estate for life or years, the person entitled to the remainder or reversion is entitled to notice as one of the parties interested. In cases in which remainders or estates are devised or limited to, or in trust for, persons not in being at the time of the application for partition, notice must be given to the persons who may be parents of such persons, setting forth the origin and nature of the remainder or interest so devised or limited.[4]

At the time named in the order of notice, any person interested may appear and be heard upon the petition.

---

[1] Gen. Sts. c. 109, § 20.   [2] Ibid. c. 136, § 51.

[3] Ibid. § 62.   [4] Ibid. c. 136, §§ 6, 69.

If it appears that any infant or insane person is interested in the premises, and has no guardian within the State, the court assigns him a guardian for the suit, to appear for him and defend his interests therein.[1] And in cases in which remainders or estates are devised or limited to, or in trust for, persons not in being at the time of the application for partition, the court appoints a suitable person to act as the next friend of such persons in all proceedings touching the partition, the cost of whose services, including compensation of counsel, is determined by the court and paid by the petitioner; and execution may be issued therefor in the name of the person appointed.[2]

If, upon the hearing, it appears that the partition prayed for should be made, the court appoints three or five disinterested persons as commissioners to make the division.[3] No clerk or other person employed in the office of the probate court can act as commissioner, unless his appointment is requested by all the parties in interest.[4] If the estate to be divided lies in different counties, the judge may, if he thinks fit, issue a separate warrant and appoint different commissioners for each county; and the partition in such case is made in each county in like manner as if there were no other estate, or the entire estate may be divided by the same commissioners. The warrant states the name of each heir or devisee, and the share of the estate to which each is entitled. If there are any advancements made by the deceased to be considered in making the partition, the names of the persons who received the advancements and the sum received by each should also be stated in the warrant or in a paper appended thereto.

---

[1] Gen. Sts. c. 136, § 53. [2] Ibid. § 69.
[3] Ibid. § 49. [4] Ibid. c. 117, § 32.

After the appointment of the commissioners, some disinterested person is appointed agent by the court for any heir at law or devisee absent from the State, to act for such absent heir or devisee in all things relating to the partition.[1]

PROCEEDINGS OF THE COMMISSIONERS.

Before proceeding to make the partition, the commissioners must make oath that they will faithfully and impartially execute their duties, and a certificate of their oath should be made on the warrant by the justice who administers it.

The commissioners are required to give sufficient notice of the time and place appointed by them for making the partition to all persons interested who are known and are within the State, and to the agent of any absent heir or devisee appointed by the court. The notice should be in writing and signed by the commissioners,[2] and served upon each of the persons interested, by giving him a copy thereof, or leaving a copy at his place of abode ; and a return, stating the manner in which the service was made, should be indorsed by the officer or other person making it, upon the original notice. If the service was made by a person other than an officer qualified to serve civil process, the return should be accompanied by his affidavit.

All the commissioners are required to meet for the performance of any of their duties, but the acts of a majority of them are valid.[3]

At the time and place appointed for making the partition, the commissioners proceed to appraise all the estate to be divided, and, after hearing the parties who

---

[1] Gen. Sts. c. 136, § 50. [2] See Appendix, form No. 75.
[3] Gen. Sts. c. 136, § 24.

may be present, to make the partition among the persons entitled thereto, regard being had to the value of the advancements, if any, made by the deceased in his lifetime.[1]   The petitioner's share is not alone to be set off, but the share of each person interested is to be assigned to him, unless two or more of the parties consent to hold their shares together and undivided.   And the partition must embrace the entire estate when either of the parties interested requires it.   If there are several parcels of land, the commissioners are not obliged to set off to each heir a portion of every parcel, but they may assign to one, or more, or all, an entire parcel each, as the situation of the land may make it advisable.

When a messuage, piece of land, or other part of the premises is of greater value than either party's share, and cannot be divided without great inconvenience to the owners, it may be set off to any one of the parties who will accept it, he paying to any one or more of the others such sums of money as the commissioners award to make the partition just and equal.   In such an assignment, males are preferred to females, and, among children of the deceased, elder to younger sons.[2]

When such real estate cannot be divided without damage to the owners, the whole or any part thereof may be set off to one or more of the parties among whom partition is ordered to be made, he or they paying to the other parties such sums of money as the commissioners award.[3]

If a party dies during the pendency of the petition, the share or proportion belonging to him may be assigned in the name of such deceased person to his estate, to be

---

[1] As to distribution when advancements have been made, see *ante*, page 234.

[2] Gen. Sts. c. 136, § 57.   [3] Ibid. § 58.

held and disposed of in the same manner as if the partition had been made prior to his decease.[1]

" In making partition of lands held by joint-tenants, coparceners, or tenants in common, at the time of appointing commissioners or subsequently, by agreement of parties or after such notice to all persons interested as shall have been ordered, the court may order the commissioners to make sale and conveyance of the whole or any part of such lands as cannot be advantageously divided, upon such terms and conditions, and with such securities for the proceeds thereof as the court may direct in such order, and to distribute and pay over the proceeds of the sale in such manner as to make the partition just and equal. Such sale shall be at public auction, after like notice required for the sale of lands by administrators, and the evidence thereof may be perpetuated in like manner, by returns filed with the clerk, register, or recording officer of the court where the proceedings are had. The conveyance shall be made by the commissioners, and shall be conclusive against all parties to the proceedings of partition, and those claiming by, through, or under them.

" When any distributive share of the money arising from such sale remains unpaid at the time of confirming the proceedings or establishing the partition by the courts, the commissioners shall deposit the same in such saving bank or banks, or other like institutions as the court may direct, in the name of the judge of the probate court for the county, to accumulate for the person entitled thereto," subject to the statute provisions relating to unclaimed money in the hands of administrators.[2]

---

[1] Stat. 1874, c. 266.
[2] Stat. 1871, c. 111, *ante*, page 239.

RETURN OF THE COMMISSIONERS AND PROCEEDINGS THEREON.

The return of the commissioners should fully set forth their proceedings under the warrant. The fact that they gave notice to parties interested of the time and place of making the partition should appear in their report, and the fact that the persons notified were present, or not, should be stated. The original notice to parties, with the return of the person who made the service, should be annexed to the report. Their appraisal of the several parcels of real estate should be stated in words at length, and the share assigned to each heir or devisee should be described by metes and bounds. When a piece of land of more value than one equal share of the estate is given to one of the heirs, the fact that it could not be divided without great inconvenience to the owners should be stated, in terms, in the return, and the sums of money to be paid by such heir to the other owners should be stated. The commissioners should also present with their report a statement of the expenses, including their own compensation, of making the partition. The warrant under which they acted must be returned with their report.

If the report of the commissioners is satisfactory to all the persons interested, they should certify their approval thereof in writing before it is presented to the court; and if either of the parties is entitled to a sum of money, to be paid by one or more of the other parties, under an award of the commissioners, some delay and expense may be avoided if his certificate of the fact that the money has been paid or secured to his satisfaction, is returned with the report; unless the parties interested express their assent to the establishment of the partition as made by the commissioners, notice to them will be ordered before any decree is made upon the report.

Any party interested may appear and object to the report of the commissioners. In all cases, the court may, for any sufficient reason, set aside the return and commit the case anew to the same or other commissioners.[1] Any mistake, neglect, or misconduct on the part of the commissioners, by which an injustice is done to either party interested, would, of course, be sufficient reason for setting aside the return. And it is a valid objection that the division made by them is unequal or inconvenient.[2] The partition cannot be confirmed by a decree of the court, until all sums of money awarded by the commissioners to make the partition equal are paid to the persons entitled thereto, or secured to their satisfaction or that of the court. A decree without such payment or security is erroneous, and will not establish the partition.[3]

The partition is made complete by a decree of the court accepting the report of the commissioners and as-

---

[1] Gen. Sts. c. 136, § 74.

[2] But as the committee is appointed by the court, and persons selected on whose integrity and judgment the court thinks it can safely rely, and against whom neither party can raise any objection, great confidence is placed by the court in the report of the committee; and it will not be held to be any objection to a report, that witnesses can be found who will testify that the division is, in their opinion, unjust or inconvenient. To induce the court to set aside the report, the inequality or inconvenience must be clearly and distinctly pointed out, and shown to the court by clear and direct evidence. It is much more safe to rely upon the judgment of an impartial committee than upon the opinion of witnesses selected by the parties. Richardson, C. J., in Morrill v. Morrill, 5 N. H. 329. See Peck v. Metcalf, 8 R. I. 386; Field v. Hanscomb, 15 Maine, 865; Wilbor v. Dyer, 39 Maine, 109.

[3] Gen. Sts. c. 136, § 71; Jenks v. Howland, 3 Gray, 536.

signing to each of the parties interested a share of the
land in severalty.[1]

Expenses of the Partition. The expenses and charges
incurred in making the partition are ascertained and
allowed by the court, and paid by all the parties interested in proportion to their respective shares or interests
in the premises. If any one neglects to pay his part,
an execution therefor may be issued against him.[2]

Record of the Partition. The return of the commissioners, when accepted by the court, remains in the registry of probate; but the statute requires that a copy
thereof, certified by the register, shall be recorded in the
registry of deeds for the county or district where the
land lies.[3]

PROCEEDINGS WHEN THE LAND OF THE DECEASED LIES IN COMMON.

When any part of the real estate of the deceased lies
in common and undivided with that of another person,
the probate court may cause it to be divided and set off
from the part held by such cotenant, before making partition among the heirs or others claiming under the
deceased.

In such case notice is given to the cotenant, containing a description of the premises to be divided, with a

---

[1] Thayer *v.* Thayer, 7 Pick. 209.

[2] Gen. Sts. c. 136, § 59. The commissioners are entitled to compensation for their services and their reasonable expenses, although their
return is not accepted, or their charges allowed, by the probate court, and
may maintain an action therefor against the petitioners for partition. A
party to the proceedings who has paid the expenses of making the partition is entitled to contribution from all the other parties in interest, and
may have the execution provided for by statute. Potter *v.* Hazard, 11
Allen, 187.

[3] Gen. Sts. c. 136, § 75.

statement of the share or proportion claimed as belonging to the estate of the deceased, and of the time and place appointed for hearing the case. The notice is served by delivering to the cotenant an attested copy, or by leaving such copy at his place of abode in this State, fourteen days at least before the time appointed for the hearing.

If it appears in any stage of the proceedings that any person interested in the premises, other than the heirs and devisees of the deceased and those claiming under them, was absent from the State when the notice was served, and has not returned, the probate court either dismisses the application for partition, or stays further proceedings until such absent party appears and answers, or signifies in writing his assent to the proposed partition.[1]

UPON WHOM THE PARTITION IS BINDING.

The partition, when finally confirmed and established, is conclusive on all the heirs and devisees of the deceased, and all persons claiming under them ; on all other persons interested in the premises who appeared and answered in the case, or assented to the proposed partition as above mentioned ; and on every person so interested on whom notice was served by delivering him a copy thereof, or by leaving it at the place of his abode at a time when he was within the State. And on persons not in being at the time of the petition, if notice was duly given to their parents and they were represented in the proceedings for partition.[2]

---

[1] Gen. Sts. c. 136, §§ 61–63.   [2] Ibid. §§ 64, 69.

PARTITION OF LANDS HELD BY THE EXECUTOR, &c., IN MORTGAGE AND ON EXECUTION.

Partition may also be made in the probate court of land held by an executor or administrator in mortgage, or on execution, if it is not redeemed, or sold by him for the payment of debts.[1] Land so held is always treated in the settlement of estates as personal property, the title to which is vested in the administrator and not in the heirs, and is distributed to the same persons and in the same proportions as if it had been part of the personal estate of the deceased. The widow of an intestate is entitled to one-third, not as dower, but absolutely; and other persons interested take under the statute of distributions,[2] not according to the rules of descent of real estate. The form of proceeding in the probate court is the same as in cases of partition of land held by the deceased in his lifetime. The petition for the partition should set forth the fact that the land is held by the administrator in mortgage, or on execution, as the case may be; and the names of the persons entitled to share in the distribution, and their relationship to the deceased, should also be stated. It is only by a decree of the probate court that the title of the administrator is determined, and such decree for the assignment and distribution of the estate is necessary to determine in whom and in what proportions the estate shall vest.[3]

---

[1] Gen. Sts. c. 96, § 14.   [2] Ibid.

[3] Taft v. Stevens, 3 Gray, 504; Richardson v. Hildreth, 8 Cush. 225.

CHAPTER XVIII

ASSIGNMENT OF DOWER AND OTHER LIFE-ESTATES.

WHEN THE PROBATE COURT MAY ASSIGN DOWER.

THE statute provides that "every woman shall be entitled to her dower at common law in the lands of her husband, to be assigned to her after his decease, unless she is lawfully barred thereof;" and that "when a widow is entitled to dower in lands of which her husband *died seised*, and her right *is not disputed by the heirs or devisees*, it may be assigned to her, in whatever counties the lands lie, by the probate court for the county in which the estate of the husband is settled."[1]

The assignment of dower is not incident to the administration of estates of deceased persons, nor is it analogous to any proceeding of the probate court as a court of ecclesiastical jurisdiction. The probate court, therefore, assigns dower only in the cases in which jurisdiction is expressly given by statute. If the husband did not die seised of the land, or if the widow's right is disputed by the heirs or devisees,[2] the probate court cannot

---

[1] Gen. Sts. c. 90, §§ 1, 3.

[2] Lazell *v.* Lazell, 8 Allen, 575; Woodward *v.* Lincoln, 9 Allen, 241; Mercier *v.* Chace, Ibid. 242; French *v.* Crosby, 23 Me. 276.

Dower may be assigned by the heirs, without any order of court and without a deed, it not being a conveyance of title. The widow holds her estate by law and not by contract, and requires nothing but to have her part distinguished from the rest of the land. Conant *v.* Little, 1 Pick.

17

make the assignment, and she must pursue her remedy in the common-law courts. Interesting questions as to the sufficiency of the husband's seisin, and as to the effect of the wife's acts in release of her dower, are raised in cases where the land in which dower is claimed was conveyed by the husband during his lifetime, but cases involving such questions are not within the jurisdiction of the probate court.

THE ESTATE OF DOWER.

Dower at common law exists where a man is seised of an estate of inheritance and dies in the lifetime of his wife. In that case, she is entitled to be endowed for her natural life of all the lands of which her husband was seised, either in deed or in law, at any time during the coverture, and of which any issue that she might have had might by possibility have been heir.[1] Her right is so protected by law that no act of the husband can deprive her of it. And she is entitled to her dower, though her husband dies insolvent.

To establish a claim to dower at common law, it must be shown that there was a marriage, and a seisin by the husband at some time during the coverture, and that the husband is dead. Without the concurrence of these three circumstances, no title to dower can be consummated. To enable the probate court to assign dower, it must further appear that the husband was seised at the time of his death.

189; Shattuck v. Gregg, 23 Pick. 88. A guardian may assign dower in his ward's estate to any widow entitled thereto. Gen. Sts. c. 109, § 20.

The widow may occupy the land jointly with the heirs, or may receive one third of the rents and profits, so long as the heirs do not object, without having her dower assigned. Gen. Sts. c. 90, § 7.

[1] 4 Kent, Com. 35.

Dower attaches to all marriages not absolutely void and existing at the death of the husband. Though the marriage was voidable, if it was not annulled by decree during the husband's lifetime, the widow will take her dower. Dower belongs to a marriage within the age of consent, though the husband dies within that age.[1] A divorce from bed and board does not bar the wife's right of dower, but her right is barred by a divorce from the bond of matrimony in all cases, except when the divorce was decreed on account of the adultery or imprisonment of the husband.[2]

OF WHAT LANDS THE WIDOW IS DOWABLE.

As to Wild Lands. A widow is not entitled under the statute to dower in wild lands of which her husband dies seised, but she is entitled to dower in any wood-lot, or other land used with the farm ˙ or dwelling-house, although such wood-lot or other land has never been cleared.[3] Her right in such land is limited to wood and timber used and consumed on the estate, and for purposes connected with its proper use, occupation, and enjoyment.[4]

Mines and Quarries. A widow is entitled to dower

---

[1] 4 Kent. Com. 37. But if the parties separate during such nonage, and do not afterwards cohabit, the marriage will be void without a decree of divorce or other legal process. Gen. Sts. c. 107, § 3.

[2] Ibid. § 38. In this State a woman is not barred of her right to dower merely by leaving her husband and living with an adulterer. Lakin *v.* Lakin, 2 Allen, 45.

[3] Gen. Sts. c. 90, § 12.

[4] White *v.* Cutler, 17 Pick. 248 ; White *v.* Willis, 7 Pick. 143. When it appears that the wood and timber have ceased to improve by growth, or for any cause ought to be cut, the probate court may appoint a trustee and authorize him to sell it, invest the proceeds, and pay to the widow the income thereof during her life, and at her death to pay the principal sum to the owner of the land. Stat. 1869, c. 249.

in such mines and quarries as were actually opened and used during the lifetime of the husband, whether he continued to work them to the period of his death or not.[1] A bed of iron ore of considerable extent is regarded as opened, although the openings which had been wrought by the husband had been partially filled up and abandoned, and other openings into the same bed had been made by the heirs.[2] The tenant in dower may work an open mine or quarry for her own benefit, but it is waste for her to open and work it.

Lands of Tenants in Common. A widow is entitled to dower in lands owned by her husband as tenant in common with other persons. But land purchased by partners, with partnership funds, for partnership purposes, is considered in equity as partnership stock. Though conveyed to them as tenants in common, it vests in them and their respective heirs in trust for the purposes of the partnership, and is to be applied, if necessary, towards payment of the partnership debts. If so required for the payment of debts, the widows of partners are not entitled to dower in such land.[3]

If the land, though purchased with partnership funds, was purchased in such a manner as to preclude such implied trust, the widow will be entitled to her dower

---

[1] Stoughton v. Leigh, 1 Taunt. 402.

[2] Coates v. Cheever, 1 Cowen, 460. A husband died seised of four acres of land consisting of a slate quarry, mostly below the surface of the ground, but partially above ground. One quarter of an acre of the quarry had been dug over, and the practice was to take a section of ten or twelve feet square on the surface, and go down to a certain depth, and then begin on the surface again. *Held,* that not only that portion of the quarry which had been actually dug, but the whole extent owned by the husband, must be considered as opened, and so the widow was entitled to dower in the same. Billings v. Taylor, 10 Pick. 460.

[3] Dyer v. Clark, 5 Met. 562; Howard v. Priest, Ibid. 582; Burnside v. Merrick, 4 Met. 537.

therein. This may be the case when there is an express agreement at the time of the purchase that the property is to be held by the partners separately for their separate use, or a similar provision in the articles of copartnership, or where the price of the purchase is charged to the partners respectively, in their several accounts with the firm.[1]

Lands incumbered by Mortgage. A widow is not entitled to dower at common law in estates of which her husband is only equitably seised. But our statute extends her right of dower to equities of redemption of mortgaged estates. If she has released her right of dower upon a mortgage made by her husband, or if he is seised of land subject to a mortgage which is valid and effectual as against her, she is nevertheless entitled to dower in the mortgaged premises as against every person except the mortgagee and those claiming under him. If the heir or other person claiming under the husband redeems the mortgage, the widow can either repay such part of the money paid by him as is equal to the proportion which her interest in the mortgaged premises bears to the whole value thereof, or she can at her election take dower only according to the value of the estate after deducting the money paid for redemption.[2]

Applications for dower in mortgaged lands are not usually made to the probate court, although that court may assign dower in such lands when all the parties interested consent. The legal estate is in the mortgagee; but as the mortgage is intended only as security for a debt, it is considered as between the mortgagor and all the world except the mortgagee and his assigns only as a pledge and an incumbrance, the mortgagor still re-

---

[1] Dyer *v.* Clark, 5 Met. 579.   [2] Gen. Sts. c. 90, § 2.

maining the owner of the estate. If, therefore, the heirs or devisees do not dispute the widow's claim, and *the mortgagee consents*, the probate court may assign dower in the whole estate mortgaged, and the assignment will be valid, although the widow joined her husband in the mortgage-deed for the purpose of relinquishing her dower.[1] But if the mortgagee does not consent, an assignment by the probate court will be invalid *as against him*, although the widow has never released her dower.[2]

Leased Lands. When land is demised for the term of one hundred years or more, the term, so long as fifty years thereof remain unexpired, is regarded by the statute as an estate in fee-simple, as to every thing concerning the right of dower therein, and the estate in lieu of dower.[3] When dower, or an estate in lieu of dower, is assigned out of such land, the widow and her assignee is held to pay to the owner of the unexpired residue of the term, in case of dower, one-third, and in case of an estate in lieu of dower, one-half, of the rent reserved in the lease.[4]

DOWER, WHEN THE WIDOW WAIVES THE PROVISION MADE FOR HER BY WILL.

A widow may have dower in her husband's lands, although they may have been disposed of by his will. The statute provides, that " when a man dies having lawfully disposed of his estate by will, and leaving a widow, she may at any time within six months after the probate of the will, file in the probate office in writing her waiver of the provisions made for her in the will;

---

[1] Henry's case, 4 Cush. 257 ; Draper *v.* Baker, 12 Cush. 288.
[2] Raynham *v.* Wilmarth, 13 Met. 414.
[3] Gen. Sts. c. 90, § 20.   [4] Ibid. § 22.

and shall in such case be entitled to such portion of his
real and personal estate as she would have been entitled
to if her husband had died intestate. . . . If she makes
no such waiver, she shall not be endowed of his lands,
unless it plainly appears by the will to have been the
intention of the testator that she should have such provisions in addition to her dower."[1] And if no provision
is made for her, she may waive the provisions of the will
with like effect.[2]

At common law, a devise or bequest to the wife of
a testator was presumed to be in addition to her dower,
unless it was clearly the testator's intention that it
should be in lieu of dower; but our statute reverses
this presumption, and the provision made for the widow
by the will is deemed to be *in lieu* of dower, unless it
plainly appears that the testator intended such provision
to be *in addition* to her dower. It is, therefore, for the
demandant, if she claims both, to make it plainly appear
by the will that, in addition to the provision therein
made for her, she is entitled to dower ; and if the testator's intention is left in doubt, she cannot take dower
unless she first waives the provision made for her in the
will.[3] The inadequacy of the provision merely will not
justify the inference that it was intended to be in addi-

---

[1] Stat. 1861, c. 164. The right given to the widow to waive the provisions of her husband's will is a personal right, and does not pass to her
representatives though she die before probate of her husband's will.
Sherman *v.* Newton, 6 Gray, 307.

[2] Stat. 1871, c. 200.

[3] Adams *v.* Adams, 5 Met. 278.   Where a testator devised specific
parts of his real estate to his wife in fee, and bequeathed to her all his
personal property, and ordered that the other part of his real estate
should be disposed of as the law directs, and the wife accepted the devise
and bequest made to her ; it was held that she was not entitled to dower
in such other part of the real estate.   Ibid. ; and see Reed *v.* Dickerman,
12 Pick. 146.

tion to dower. The question must be determined by the language of the will.

The widow may make her election to take her dower effectual by filing in the probate office, in writing, at any time within six months after the probate of the will, her waiver of the provisions made for her.[1] When any legal proceeding is instituted, wherein the validity or effect of the will is drawn in question, the probate court may, within six months after probate of the will, on petition of the widow and after notice, authorize her to file her waiver within six months after the final determination of such proceeding.[2] If she is insane or a minor, her guardian may make the waiver.[3] If she makes no such waiver, she cannot take dower, unless it plainly appears from the will that the testator intended that she should have such provisions in addition to her dower.

DOWER BARRED BY JOINTURE OR PECUNIARY PROVISION.

A woman may be barred of her dower by a jointure settled on her, with her assent, before her marriage ; provided, such jointure consist of a freehold estate in lands for the life of the wife at least, to take effect in possession or profit immediately on the death of the husband ; her assent to such jointure being expressed, if she is of full age, by her becoming a party to the conveyance by which it is settled, and, if she is under age, by her joining with her father or guardian in such conveyance. Any pecuniary provision made for the benefit of an intended wife, and in lieu of dower, if so assented to, will bar her right of dower in her husband's lands.

---

[1] See Appendix, form No. 76.   [2] Stat. 1873, c. 58.
[3] Stat. 1871, c. 97.

If such jointure or pecuniary provision is made before the marriage, and without the assent of the intended wife, or if it is made after marriage, it will bar her dower, unless within six months after the death of her husband she makes her election to waive such provision and be endowed of his lands. If the husband dies while absent from his wife, she may make her election within six months after notice of his death, and in all cases she has six months for that purpose, after she has notice of the existence of such jointure or provision.[1]

No provision is made by statute as to the manner in which the widow may signify her election in such cases, but she can make her election effectual by commencing proceedings for the recovery of her dower, by petition or otherwise, within the six months.

WITHIN WHAT TIME DOWER MUST BE CLAIMED.

The statute provides that after the eighteenth day of March, in the year 1863, widows shall not be entitled to make claim or commence any proceeding for the recovery of dower, unless the same is made or commenced within twenty years from the decease of the husband; except that if at the time of the husband's death the widow is absent from the State, under twenty-one years of age, insane, or imprisoned, she may commence proceedings at any time within twenty years after such disability ceases.[2]

PROCEEDINGS IN PROBATE COURT.

The petition for the assignment of dower must be presented to the probate court in which the estate of

---

[1] Gen. Sts. c. 90, §§ 9–11; Vincent v. Spooner, 2 Cush. 467.

[2] Ibid. § 6.

the husband is settled, and should set forth the facts
that the husband died seised of certain lands in this
Commonwealth, that the petitioner is entitled to dower
in such land, and that her right is not disputed by the
heirs or devisees. The names and residences of all persons interested in the lands must be stated in the petition. If any of the persons interested are married
women, the names of their husbands should be given ;
and if any are minors the names and residences of their
guardians.

If the widow omits to petition or demand her dower
within one year·from the death of her husband, the petition may be made by the heirs or devisees of her husband, or any of them, or by any person having any
estate in the lands subject to dower, or by the guardian of
any such heirs, devisees, or persons having said estate." [1]

The petition may be filed in the probate office on any
day, and a citation thereon issued by the register.

If any part of the land in which dower is claimed was
owned by the husband in common with any other person, a description of such land should be annexed to the
petition, and the proportion owned by the husband, and
the names of the cotenants, must be stated. The petition may be made by the widow or by any person entitled to petition for assignment of dower.[2] The citation
issued in such cases must be served on each of the cotenants, together with a copy of the description of the
land annexed to the petition.

If upon the hearing it appears that the husband died
seised of the land in which dower is claimed, and that
the right of the widow is not disputed by the heirs or
devisees, the court issues a warrant to three discreet
and disinterested persons, authorizing them to set off

[1] Stat. 1876, c. 89.   [2] Ibid.

the dower, and empowering them, if the circumstances of the case require it, first to make partition of any land owned by the husband as tenant in common.

PROCEEDINGS OF THE COMMISSIONERS.

Before proceeding to set off the dower, or to make partition, the commissioners must be sworn to perform their duty faithfully and impartially according to their best skill and judgment. The oath may be administered by any justice of the peace, and a certificate thereof should be made upon the warrant.

If partition is to be made before the dower can be assigned, the commissioners must give notice, as in other cases of partition,[1] of the time and place appointed for that purpose to all persons interested who are known and are within the State, that they may be present if they see fit.

If the commissioners are to assign dower only, and there is no partition to be made, they are not required by statute to give notice to parties interested, but it is advisable to give such notice in all cases of assignments of interests in real estate.[2]

In making the assignment, all the lands of which the husband died seised are first to be appraised by the commissioners at their present value. The authority of the commissioners extends to all lands of which the husband died seised within the Commonwealth. The lands should be appraised with reference to the amount of annual income they produce; it not being the object of the law to assign the widow one-third of the land in quantity, but to give her such a part as will yield her one-third of its entire income.[3]

---

[1] See Appendix, form No. 75.   [2] See Appendix, form No. 77.

[3] Conner v. Shepherd, 15 Mass. 167; Leonard v. Leonard, 4 Mass. 533.

The third assigned to the widow must be set off by metes and bounds, where it can be done without damage to the whole estate. But where the estate consists of a mill or other tenement which cannot be divided without damage to the whole, the dower may be assigned of the rents, issues, or profits thereof, to be had and received by the widow as a tenant in common with the other owners of the estate.[1] The widow in such case may have her dower in an alternate occupancy of the whole estate, or a third of the rents and profits. The ancient rule gave her every third toll-dish for her dower in a mill, or the use of the whole mill every third month or year. It is not material in what way the result is reached, provided the rights of the parties are plainly defined and established. Assignments of this kind are usually made by agreement between the parties; a proper spirit of accommodation will enable them to reach an adjustment more satisfactory to themselves than any action of the commissioners is likely to prove.

If the entire estate in which dower is claimed consists of a dwelling-house, certain rooms in the house, with the right of using the stairways, halls, &c., may be set off to the widow. But the part of the premises so assigned to her must be sufficient for her substantial enjoyment of the third part of the estate.[2] It seems that at common law the widow is not compelled to take dower so assigned, but may claim a rent issuing out of the estate.[3] But the practice has the sanction of long usage in this State.

[1] Gen. Sts. c. 90, § 5.

[2] In Howard v. Candish (Palmer, 264), the sheriff assigned to the widow a third part of each chamber, and chalked out her part; this was held to be an idle and malicious assignment, and the sheriff was committed to prison.

[3] White v. Story, 2 Hill (N. Y.), 543; Park on Dower, 254.

The return of the commissioners to the probate court should give a detailed report of their proceedings under the warrant directed to them. The fact that notice was given to persons interested, and the manner in which it was given, should be stated. If the parties notified were present at the time and place appointed for making the partition or assignment, the fact should appear in the return. The sums at which the several parcels of land belonging to the estate were appraised should be expressed in words at length; and if the dower is set off by metes and bounds, the boundaries should be so described as to leave no uncertainty as to the portion assigned.

The assent of all parties in interest to the assignment as made by the commissioners should be indorsed on the return; otherwise a citation will issue to them before final action is had. The assignment of dower is made complete by the confirmation by the court [1] of the return of the commissioners, and its record in the probate office. In cases where the husband was a cotenant, and partition was made previous to the assignment of dower, the return should also be recorded in the registry of deeds for the county in which the land lies.

WHEN WIDOWS MAY BE ENDOWED ANEW.

" If a woman is lawfully evicted of lands assigned to her as dower or settled upon her as jointure, or is deprived of the provision made for her by will or otherwise in lieu of dower, she may be endowed anew in like manner as if such assignment, jointure, or other provi-

---

1 The confirmation relates back to the time of the assignment. Parker v. Parker, 17 Pick. 236 ; Mansfield v. Pembroke, 5 Pick. 449.

sion, had not been made;"[1] as, when she has been endowed of lands mortgaged by her husband before his
marriage, and has been evicted by the mortgagee.[2]

A widow is "deprived of the provision made for her
by will," within the meaning of the statute, when all
her husband's estate is taken for the payment of his
debts; as, where the husband gave his wife by will the
whole of his estate, on condition that she should pay his
debts and legacies, and the estate proved to be insolvent.
She is entitled, in such case, to her dower, although she
may not have formally waived the provision made for
her by will, the provision made for her having wholly
failed. But before dower can be assigned to her, it
must be ascertained that the whole estate, estimating
its value without the incumbrance of the widow's
dower, is not sufficient to discharge the liabilities.[3]
And it is no objection, in such case, to an application
for an assignment of dower, that a previous application
had been made and refused before there was sufficient
evidence that the widow would be deprived of the provision made by the will, and that she did not appeal
from the decree of refusal.[4]

PRESENT VALUE OF DOWER ESTATES.

The following table affords a ready means of determining the present value of dower estates. The table
is deduced from the Wigglesworth and "Combined
Experience" tables of mortality. The Wigglesworth
tables were adopted many years ago by the supreme
judicial court, but the more recently prepared tables,

[1] Gen. Sts. c. 90, § 13.   [2] Scott v. Hancock, 13 Mass. 168.
[3] Thompson v. McGaw, 1 Met. 66.   [4] Ibid.

founded on the combined experience of various life-insurance companies, exhibit the results of a more extended observation, and are practically safer in determining the value of life-estates.

To determine the present value of a dower estate, find in the column of age, in the following table, the age of the person to whom the dower estate belongs. The sums named opposite the number representing the age will show the present value of every $100 of the dower estate, according to the Wigglesworth and " Combined Experience " tables respectively. Multiply that present value by the number of hundreds in the entire estate, and the product will be the present value of the dower estate.   For example : —

Suppose a widow whose age is 30, is entitled to dower in an estate worth $6,000: opposite the number 30, representing the age, is the sum $23.59; multiply that sum by 60 (the number of hundreds in 6,000), and the product is $1415.40, which is the present value of her dower according to the Wigglesworth tables.   According to the " Combined Experience " tables it is $1581.00.

TABLE

Showing the present value of a widow's dower in an estate worth $100, at any age from 15 to 98 inclusive, computed at six per cent, according to the Wigglesworth and " Combined Experience" Tables of Mortality.

Age.	Wiggles-worth.	Combined Experience.	Age.	Wiggles-worth.	Combined Experience.	Age.	Wiggles-worth.	Combined Experience.
15	$24.71	$28.30	43	$22.30	$23.22	71	$12.45	$10.87
16	24.63	28.20	44	22.21	22.90	72	11.98	10.40
17	24.56	28.11	45	22.10	22.56	73	11.50	9.92
18	24.49	28.00	46	21.88	22.21	74	11.04	9.46
19	24.42	27.90	47	21.65	21.85	75	10.57	9.00
20	24.36	27.79	48	21.41	21.47	76	10.08	8.55
21	24.30	27.67	49	21.17	21.09	77	9.59	8.10
22	24.23	27.55	50	20.91	20.70	78	9.10	7.66
23	24.16	27.42	51	20.63	20.30	79	8.63	7.24
24	24.10	27.29	52	20.35	19.88	80	8.19	6.82
25	24.05	27.15	53	20.05	19.46	81	7.72	6.41
26	23.97	27.00	54	19.74	19.03	82	7.27	6.00
27	23.88	26.85	55	19.42	18.59	83	6.88	5.61
28	23.78	26.69	56	19.08	18.14	84	6.60	5.21
29	23.69	26.53	57	18.72	17.69	85	6.53	4.82
30	23.59	26.35	58	18.34	17.22	86	6.01	4.42
31	23.50	26.17	59	17.94	16.75	87	5.55	4.03
32	23.42	25.98	60	17.53	16.27	88	5.23	3.63
33	23.33	25.79	61	17.08	15.79	89	5.08	3.24
34	23.25	25.58	62	16.61	15.30	90	5.46	2.86
35	23.17	25.36	63	16.12	14.81	91	4.84	2.48
36	23.09	25.14	64	15.59	14.31	92	4.10	2 11
37	22.94	24.90	65	15.03	13.82	93	3.37	1.76
38	22.83	24.65	66	14.63	13.32	94	2.65	1.43
39	22.72	24.39	67	14.22	12.83	95	2.04	1.14
40	22.61	24.12	68	13.80	12.33	96	1.46	.90
41	22.51	23.84	69	13.36	11.84	97	1.11	.72
42	22.40	23.54	70	12.91	11.36	98	.94	.47

ESTATE IN LIEU OF DOWER, &c.

In a certain class of cases the statute gives to the widow a life-estate in one-half the lands of her husband. " When a man dies seised of lands, tenements, or hereditaments, or of any right or interest therein in fee-simple, not having lawfully devised the same, and leaving a widow, *but no issue,* the widow in lieu of dower shall be entitled to one-half of said estate during her natural life ; and if any part thereof taken by the widow is wild or woodland, she may use, clear, and improve the same." If the widow chooses to take dower instead of this larger provision, she must file in the probate office her election to take dower within six months after the date of letters of administration.[1]

When a widow is entitled to any undivided part, or the use and improvement of any undivided part, of the real estate of her husband, for the term of her life or widowhood, by the provisions of the will of her husband, in lieu of dower, or by any provisions of law, the probate court in the county where the estate of the husband is settled may cause her interest in said estate to be set off and assigned to her in like manner as dower.[2]

ESTATES OF HOMESTEAD.

Every householder having a family[3] may have an estate of homestead, to the extent in value of eight

---

[1] Gen. Sts. c. 90, §§ 15, 16.   [2] Ibid. § 17.

[3] The householder's estate of homestead, once acquired, is not defeated by the death or removal of his wife and children from the premises, or by her obtaining a divorce from bed and board and a decree giving her the custody of the children, if he continues to reside thereon. She cannot by her act deprive him of such estate. Doyle *v.* Coburn, 6 Allen, 71 ; Silloway *v.* Brown, 12 Allen, 30.

hundred dollars in the farm or lot of land and buildings thereon owned, or rightly possessed by lease or otherwise,[1] and occupied by him as a residence.[2] To constitute such estate of homestead and to entitle it to be exempt from attachment or levy on execution, it must be set forth in the deed by which the property is acquired, that it is designed to be held as a homestead; or, after the title has been acquired, such design must be declared by writing duly signed, sealed, acknowledged, and recorded in the registry of deeds.

The right of homestead may be released by a deed in which the wife of the householder joins for the purpose of releasing it, but if it exists at the time of his death, it "shall continue for the benefit of his widow and minor children, and be held and enjoyed by them, if some one of them occupies the premises[3] until the youngest child is twenty-one years of age, and until the marriage or death of the widow." And the estate may be set off to the parties entitled thereto in the same manner that dower may be set off to a widow.[4]

---

[1] This does not apply to land for which a party has only a bond for a deed. Thurston v. Maddocks, 6 Allen, 427.

[2] The estate is not necessarily limited to that part of a dwelling-house occupied by the family, but may exist in the whole of a house, some rooms of which are let to tenants. Mercier v. Chace, 11 Allen, 194. It may exist in a country hotel. Lazell v. Lazell, 8 Allen, 575

[3] Gen. Sts. c. 104, §§ 1, 2 The right of possession and enjoyment will be in such only of the parties who have title as remain in occupation of the premises. Abbott v. Abbott, 97 Mass. 136. The use of a room in the house by the widow, for the purpose of storing furniture, is a sufficient occupation. Brettun v. Fox, 100 Mass. 234.

[4] An assignment of dower to the widow in part of a dwelling-house will not prevent her from claiming an estate of homestead in the residue of it. Mercier v. Chace, 11 Allen, 194. There is nothing inconsistent in the right to both dower and homestead in the same estate. Monk v. Capen, 5 Allen, 146.

If a widow whose homestead estate has not been assigned to her, but

The probate court has no jurisdiction to set out an estate of homestead, if the right to it is disputed by the heirs or devisees.[1]

The widow, and the guardian of the minor children, when he has obtained a license therefor from the probate court, as in the case of sales of real estate of minors, may join in a sale of such estate of homestead ; or, if there is no widow entitled to such rights therein, the guardian upon such license may make sale thereof; and the widow may make such sale if there are no minor children. The purchaser shall have the right to enjoy and possess the premises for the full time that the widow and children or either of them might have continued to hold and enjoy the same if no sale had been made. The probate court may apportion the proceeds of the sale among the parties entitled thereto.[2]

RELEASE OF DOWER AND HOMESTEAD RIGHTS BY GUARDIANS OF INSANE MARRIED WOMEN.

When a married woman is, by reason of insanity, incompetent to release her right of dower, or right of homestead, in her husband's real estate, a guardian may be appointed for her,[3] and the probate court may authorize her guardian to release her right of dower or of home-

---

who has had one-third of the rents and profits set off as her dower, and has conveyed the interest so assigned to her, she waives and relinquishes her right of homestead. Bates v. Bates, 97 Mass. 392.

It seems that homestead cannot be assigned out of the rents and profits of the land and buildings, and cannot be held in common with other owners. Thurston r. Maddocks, 6 Allen, 427 ; Silloway r. Brown, 12 Allen, 30 ; Bates v. Bates, 97 Mass. 302 ; Bemis r. Driscoll, 101 Mass. 418.

[1] Woodward v. Lincoln, 9 Allen, 239 ; Mercier v. Chace, Ibid. 242 ; Lazell v. Lazell, 8 Allen, 575.

[2] Gen. Sts. c. 104, § 14.   [3] *Ante*, page 97.

stead.   The proceedings in the probate court in such cases are detailed by the statute. (Gen. Sts. c. 108, § 20, *et seq.*)

Sect. 20.   When the husband of an insane woman is desirous of conveying any of his real estate, whether absolutely or by way of mortgage, he may by petition, describing the same, ask leave of the probate court that the dower of his wife, or any estate of homestead therein, may be released, setting forth the facts and reasons why his prayer should be granted.[1] After notice in some newspaper to all persons interested, and a hearing thereon, the court, if satisfied that such dower or estate of homestead ought to be released, shall authorize her guardian to make such release, by joining in any deed of conveyance, to be made within five years thereafter, either by the husband or any trustee for him, and whether such deed pass the whole or only separate parcels or lots of said real estate.

Sect. 21.   If the guardian is so authorized to release the dower of his ward, and the probate court deems it proper that some portion of the proceeds of such real estate, or of any sum loaned on mortgage thereof, should be reserved for the use of such married woman, the court may order that a certain sum, not exceeding thirty-three and one third per cent of the net amount of such proceeds or sum actually to be realized from such sale or mortgage, exclusive of any incumbrance then existing on the estate, shall be set aside and paid over to such guardian, to be invested and held by him for her benefit, if she survives her husband ; the income of such sum to be received and enjoyed by the husband during the life of his wife, or until otherwise ordered by the court, upon

---

[1] See Appendix, form Nos. 89, 90.

good cause shown ; and the principal to be his, and to be paid over to him, if he survives her.

SECT. 22.   If the guardian is so authorized to release the estate of homestead, and the probate court deems it proper that some portion of the proceeds of such real estate, or of any sum loaned on mortgage thereof, should be reserved for the use of such married woman, the court may order that a certain sum, not exceeding eight hundred dollars, be set aside and paid over to such guardian, to be invested in a homestead, and held by him for the benefit of such married woman, if she survives her husband ; the rent or use thereof to be received and enjoyed by the husband during the life of his wife, or until otherwise ordered by the court, upon good cause shown ; and the homestead to be his, and to be conveyed to him by said guardian, if he survives her.

SECT. 23.   When the husband of an insane woman has conveyed any real estate in trust, without the power of revocation, and in such conveyance provision is made for his wife, which, in the opinion of the probate court, to be certified on petition, notice, and hearing, is sufficient in lieu of dower therein, the trustee in such conveyance shall be authorized to pass title to such real estate free from all right of dower.

SECT. 24.   If, in the opinion of the probate court, certified as aforesaid, such provision is sufficient in lieu of dower of such insane woman in all the real estate owned by her husband at the date of the petition, or in any particular portions thereof, her guardian shall be authorized to release her dower in all such real estate, or such particular portions, by joining in a deed of conveyance of the same.

SECT. 25.   All proceedings in the probate court, under the five preceding sections, shall be had in the county where the husband of the insane woman resides, if an inhabitant of this State, and if not, then in some county where any of his real estate is situated; and a certified copy of all final orders or decrees therein shall be recorded in the registry of deeds in every county or district in which such real estate is situate."

CHAPTER XIX.

PROBATE BONDS.

AS TO BONDS GENERALLY.[1]

THE sureties in every bond given to the judge of the probate court must be inhabitants of this State, and such as the judge approves; and no bond required to be given to the judge, or filed in the probate office, is sufficient, unless examined and approved by the judge, and his approval thereof under his official signature is written thereon.[2]

Whenever bonds are required to be given to the judge of a probate court by two or more persons acting jointly as executors, administrators, trustees, or otherwise, such persons may give either separate or joint bonds.[3]

---

[1] As to the conditions of bonds given to the judge of probate, in the course of proceedings in the probate court, see the chapters referring to the several proceedings in which bonds are required.

[2] Gen. Sts. c. 101, § 12.

[3] Stat. 1874, c. 366. An executor's bond, approved by the judge, in which the sureties are each bound in half the sum in which the principal is bound, is not for that cause void, but is binding on the obligors, and sufficient to give effect to the executor's appointment, and to render his acts as such valid; but it seems that the supreme court, on an appeal from the decree of the judge of probate approving a bond in that form, would not countenance such a departure from the usual course of proceeding. Baldwin v. Standish, 7 Cush. 207.

On a joint and several bond given by two executors both are liable for a default of either during the joint executorship; but, if one of them dies, his heirs and legal representatives are not liable for the subsequent misconduct of the survivor. Brazer v. Clark, 5 Pick. 96; Ames v. Armstrong, 106 Mass. 15.

All bonds given to the probate court must be in such sum as the judge shall order, and made payable to the judge and his successors in office; in cases when the office is vacant, to the acting judge and his successors.[1]

In practice, particularly when the sureties reside at a distance from the place of holding the probate court, bonds are executed in anticipation of the probate of the will, or other decree requiring a bond to be given, and are held in readiness to be offered for approval whenever the decree is passed. When this course is followed, care should be taken by the party offering the bond that the instrument be unexceptionable, both as to the penal sum and the sufficiency of the sureties. The amount of the penalty of the bond should be proportioned to the extent of the interest to be protected, regard being had to the situation of the estate and to all the circumstances of the case.[2] In a majority of cases, the sum named in the bond should be double the value of the property which the bond is intended to secure; and as the judge may not have, at the time when the bond is offered for approval, any knowledge either of the value of the estate or of the responsibility of the sureties, the party offering the bond should be prepared to show the written opinion, on both points, of the persons interested in the estate, or, if they cannot be reached, of some persons known to the judge. This precaution may enable ex-

---

[1] Gen. Sts. c. 119, § 5.

[2] In an application by a foreigner for ancillary letters of administration, for the purpose of collecting a debt, a bond was taken by the supreme court of probate in $5,000, which amount was less than that of the debt to be collected, it appearing that the heirs and foreign creditors were secured under the laws of the intestate's domicile, and that there were probably no creditors in the United States. Piquet, appellant, 5 Pick. 65.

ecutors and others living at a distance from the place of holding the court to avoid expense and delay.

WHEN NEW BONDS MAY BE REQUIRED.

When the sureties or the penal sum in any bond given to the probate court are insufficient, the supreme judicial court, or the probate court, on the petition of any person interested, and after notice to the principal in the bond, may require a new bond with such surety or sureties, and in such penal sum, as the court shall direct.[1]

In case of the marriage of a woman who is executrix, administratrix, guardian, or trustee, her bondsmen, on petition to the probate court, may be released from liability on their bond, beyond accounting for and paying over the money and property already in her hands.[2]

Any surety may, upon his petition to the supreme judicial court, or the probate court, be discharged from all further responsibility, if the court, after due notice to all persons interested, deems it reasonable and proper; and the principal will thereupon be required to give a new bond.[3]

---

[1] Gen. Sts. c. 101, § 15. The guardian of a minor, who had given bond in the form required by law, having represented to the judge of probate, that, since his appointment, his ward had received a legacy exceeding in amount the penalty of the bond; and having suggested that the judge should make such order in the premises as to law and justice might appertain; the judge ordered him to file a new bond in a larger sum; and the guardian filed a new bond accordingly, with a new surety. Held, that both bonds were valid; that the sureties were to be deemed co-sureties; and that, being sureties in different sums, they were, as between themselves, compellable to contribute in proportion to the different penalties of their respective bonds. Loring v. Bacon, 3 Cush. 465. See Appendix, form Nos. 78, 79.

[2] Stat. 1854, c. 420.

[3] Gen. Sts. c. 101, § 16. See Appendix, form Nos. 80, 81.

If the principal fails to give a new bond within such time as is ordered by the court, he will be removed, and some other person appointed in his stead.[1]

When a new bond is so required, the sureties in the prior bond are liable for all breaches of the condition committed before the new bond is approved by the judge.[2]

SUITS ON BONDS OF EXECUTORS AND ADMINISTRATORS.

Suits on probate bonds are brought in the name of the judge of the probate court,[3] and, except in certain classes of cases specified by the statute,[4] are brought only on leave granted by the court. There are three cases, and only three, in which a person can sue the bond of an executor or administrator for his own benefit, without first obtaining authority from the probate court: 1st. When the claim is by a creditor who has recovered judgment against the executor or administrator;[5] 2d. When the estate is insolvent, and the amount due the creditor has been ascertained by a decree of distribution; 3d. By a person next of kin whose distributive share of

---

[1] Gen. Sts. c. 101, § 17.   [2] Ibid. § 18.

[3] When the judge is obligor as principal or surety in a bond given to a former judge of the court, suit may be brought upon the bond in the name of the judge mentioned therein, his executors or administrators. Gen. Sts. c. 101, § 23.

[4] Ibid. §§ 19, 20, 21.

[5] If an administrator suffers judgment to be recovered against him before he represents the estate insolvent, he must pay the full amount of the judgment, even if the estate is insolvent, and he and his sureties are liable to a suit by the judgment creditor on the bond. Newcomb v. Goss, 1 Met. 333.

In an action on a bond against an administrator and his sureties for a refusal to pay a judgment recorded against him, such judgment, if not obtained by fraud or collusion, is conclusive on the sureties, in regard to all matters of defence affecting the merits of the claim as between the parties to the judgment. Heard v. Lodge, 20 Pick. 53.

the personal estate has been ascertained by a decree of the probate court. In each case, the person bringing the action must first have made an ineffectual demand upon the executor or administrator. These, it will be seen, are cases in which the right of the claimant has been liquidated and ascertained by matter of record, amounting to a conclusive judgment between the parties, and nothing remains but payment.[1]

In all other cases, the party aggrieved by the failure of the executor or administrator to perform his duty, must obtain leave of the probate court before bringing an action on the bond. This is the course to be pursued by a legatee when the executor neglects to pay his legacy;[2] and by a creditor, or one next of kin (whose claim or share has not been ascertained by a judgment or decree), or other person aggrieved by any maladministration.[3] These are cases in which the maladministra-

---

[1] Loring v. Kendall, 1 Gray, 316; Newcomb v. Williams, 9 Met. 536; Barton v. White, 21 Pick. 60.

[2] Newcomb v. Williams, 9 Met. 525; Fay v. Taylor, 2 Gray, 158; Conant v. Stratton, 107 Mass. 474.

[3] For the failure of the administrator to account within one year, no action lies on the probate bond, after the allowance by the judge of probate, at the request of the parties in interest, of an account subsequently rendered by him. Loring v. Kendall, 1 Gray, 305.

Where a creditor gives up his securities against an estate, on a personal promise by the executor to pay his debt, it seems that he thereby loses his remedy on the executor's bond, given to pay debts and legacies. Stebbins v. Smith, 4 Pick. 97.

If an executor be also appointed trustee in the will, but give bond only as executor, he is chargeable in that capacity for the property in his hands, until he has given bond as trustee, and charged himself with the property as trustee. Prior v. Talbot, 10 Cush. 1.

Where a general legacy is given to one for life with remainder over, and no special trustee is appointed to manage the same, the executor is liable on his bond, if he does not renounce the trust, for any default in reference to such legacy. Dorr v. Wainwright, 13 Pick. 328.

An administrator's bond given here, does not cover proceedings under

tion may have been alike injurious to all the creditors, next of kin, or legatees. No one of them is exclusively entitled to prosecute an action, and the statute therefore authorizes the probate court to designate some one of

letters of ancillary administration taken out in another State. Hooker v. Olmstead, 6 Pick. 481.

A bond given by an administrator, on being licensed to sell so much only of his intestate's real estate as is sufficient for the payment of debts and charges, is not a probate bond, and an action upon it cannot be commenced originally in the supreme judicial court. Fay v. Valentine, 8 Pick. 526.

A probate bond is not provable in bankruptcy against one of the sureties before a breach of condition of the bond; nor, it seems, before judgment in an action brought for such breach. Loring v. Kendall, 1 Gray, 305.

Where a testator devised an annuity to his widow, and authorized his executor to sell lands sufficient to raise a fund, the interest of which should be equal to the annuity, the executor's neglect to raise said fund was held to be a breach of his bond. Prescott v. Pitts, 9 Mass. 376.

When the same person is executor of a will and guardian of a minor to whom a legacy is given by the will, he holds the amount of the legacy in his capacity of executor, and not as guardian, until he settles an account of his administration in the probate court, crediting himself as executor with the legacy, and charging himself therewith as guardian. Until such account is allowed by the probate court, an action cannot be maintained against him and his sureties on his guardianship bond, for neglect to pay the legacy; but an action may be maintained against him and his sureties on the bond given by him as executor. Conkey v. Dickinson, 13 Met. 51.

A suit on the administrator's bond can be maintained for the benefit of the heirs, for waste in suffering property to be sold at a disadvantage and loss, on execution. Brazer v. Clark, 5 Pick. 96; Dawes v. Winship, Ibid. 97.

Where an executor sold real estate under a license obtained by his misrepresentations as to the condition of the estate in his hands, it was held that such sale was a breach of his bond. Chapin v. Waters, 110 Mass. 195.

A devisee of real estate, having only a contingent interest therein, or a present interest defeasible upon a condition subsequent, is not entitled to bring an action on the administration bond. Stevens v. Cole, 7 Cush. 467. Whether a devisee of real estate is a person interested in the estate

the persons interested to bring an action for the benefit
of all.[1]

An action may be brought on a probate bond at any
time within twenty years after the breach of the condition relied on as a cause of action.[2]

Any person interested in the estate may petition for
leave to sue the bond.[3] The petition should state clearly
all the facts necessary for the consideration of the court,
or proper to be notified to the adverse party. Upon the
petition, a citation usually issues to the administrator
and his sureties, and the petitioner must see that the
citation is served in the manner required by its terms.[4]

The petitioner must be prepared, at the time fixed for
the hearing, to show that the administrator has so failed
to perform his duty as to render proper a suit on his

---

of a testator and entitled as such to bring an action on the administration
bond, *quære*. Ibid.

A refusal by an administrator to comply with a decree of the probate
court in itself void, is not a breach of his bond. Hancock *v.* Hubbard,
19 Pick. 167 ; Dawes *v.* Head, 3 Pick. 128. His refusal to pay a judgment recovered against him by default in an action commenced more
than two years after the filing of his administration bond does not render his sureties liable to the judgment creditor. Robinson *v.* Hodge, 117
Mass. 222.

[1] Gen. Sts. c. 101, § 22.   [2] Prescott *v.* Reed, 8 Cush. 365.

[3] The father of an infant interested in the estate having himself no
adverse interest therein, may petition, as next friend of the infant, for
leave to sue the bond. Stevens *v.* Cole, 7 Cush. 467. See Appendix,
form Nos. 82, 83.

[4] Leave may be granted to a legatee to bring an action on a probate
bond, without notice to the obligors of the application for such leave, or
previously summoning the principal obligor to render an account, and
ordering distribution thereon. Richardson *v.* Oakman, 15 Gray, 57.
Upon a special bond given by an administrator licensed to sell more
real estate than is necessary for the payment of debts, to account for the
surplus proceeds, an action will lie after neglect for an unreasonable time
to render such an account in the probate court, although he has not been
cited to do so. Bennett *v.* Overing, 16 Gray, 267.

bond. The leave to bring the action can only be granted by a decree in writing.[1] An appeal lies from a decree of the probate court refusing leave to sue the bond; but the signers of the bond cannot appeal from a decree allowing a suit;[2] nor contest the validity of the decree in the action.[3]

When the judge is obligor, as principal or surety, in a bond given to a former judge of the court, the register of the probate court for the county in which such bond was given may authorize a suit thereon, in like manner and upon the same conditions as the court may in other cases.[4]

Every suit on an administration bond must be brought in the supreme judicial court, held for the county in which the bond was taken. The writ must be indorsed by the persons for whose benefit or at whose request the action is brought, or by their attorney, and the indorsers are liable for the costs of suit. If the action is brought by a judgment creditor, or by a creditor or distributee, the amount of whose claim or share has been established by a decree of distribution, there must be a further indorsement specifying that it is brought for the use or benefit of such creditor or next of kin;[5] and execution, if he obtains judgment, will be awarded for his own use. In every other case the recovery is of all damages occasioned by the default of the delinquent administrator, not the especial damage sustained by any one person. The suit is for the benefit of all persons interested. One judgment is rendered for the entire penalty, and execution is awarded in the name

---

1 Fay v. Rogers, 2 Gray, 175.   2 Ibid.
3 Bennett v. Woodman, 116 Mass. 518.
4 Gen. Sts. c. 101, §§ 23, 24.
5 Ibid. § 25; Bennett v. Russell, 2 Allen, 537.

of the judge of probate as the rights of the parties interested require.[1]

The money received on such execution is assets of the estate to be administered, and goes into the hands of the rightful executor or administrator for that purpose. Generally, maladministration which constitutes a breach of his bond will disqualify an administrator and cause his removal. But if there were two or more executors, and separate bonds were given, there may be a coexecutor not implicated, in which case the money is paid to him. And it may be that the breach of the bond was of such a nature as not to implicate the integrity of the executor, as when the suit was brought to settle some question of right, in which case he may charge himself with the amount of the judgment recovered, and settle the estate. But when the breach of the bond is followed, as is generally the case, by the removal of the executor or administrator, and there is no coexecutor not implicated, the money recovered on the execution is paid to the administrator appointed in his stead, to be administered according to law.[2] In case the awards of execution do not exhaust the whole penalty, the judgment for the residue stands for any other breach, which may at any time afterwards occur, to be sued for by *scire facias*, either for the benefit of a party entitled to claim in his own right, or by the judge of the probate court as trustee for others.[3]

---

[1] See Gen. Sts. c. 101, § 28; Chapin *v.* Waters, 110 Mass. 195; Choate *v.* Arrington, 116 Mass. 552.

[2] Gen. Sts. c. 101, § 29. Newcomb *v.* Williams, 9 Met. 538; Wiggin *v.* Sweet, 6 Met. 198. The entry of judgment may be suspended until opportunity has been afforded for an application to the probate court for the removal of the administrator. Bennett *v.* Russell, 2 Allen, 537.

[3] Gen. Sts. c. 101, § 30.

SUITS UPON BONDS OF TRUSTEES AND GUARDIANS.

Bonds given by trustees may be put in suit by order of the probate court for the use and benefit of any person interested in the trust estate;[1] and bonds given by guardians, for the use and benefit of the ward or any person interested in the estate.[2] The proceedings in either case are conducted in like manner as suits on the bonds of executors and administrators, but no suit can be maintained unless it is brought by leave of the probate court.

Actions against sureties in a guardian's bond are limited to four years from the time the guardian is discharged, except that if, at the time of the discharge, the person entitled to bring the action is out of the State, it may be commenced at any time within four years after his return.[3] By the term "discharged" in the statute is intended any mode by which the guardianship is effectually determined, either by the removal, resignation, or death of the guardian, the arrival of a minor ward at full age, or otherwise.[4] The limitation applies as well to bonds given by guardians on obtaining license to sell real estate, as to the general guardianship bond.[5]

---

[1] Gen. Sts. c. 100, § 12.   [2] Ibid. c. 109, § 28.   [3] Ibid. § 29.

[4] Loring v. Alline, 9 Cush. 68.

[5] Ibid. 70. If the bond originally given by the guardian binds him to account for the proceeds of real estate sold by him, it covers his liability as to accounting for such proceeds at the expiration of his trust; and the special bond given upon his being licensed to sell real estate for the purpose of investing the proceeds applies only to a proper compliance with the prerequisites to such sale, and a faithful discharge of his duties in conducting it. The sureties in such special bond are not liable for the failure of the guardian, at the expiration of the trust, to pay over the proceeds of the sale or the securities therefor to the person legally entitled thereto. Fay v. Taylor, 11 Met. 539. See Brooks v. Brooks, 11 Cush. 22.

A guardian, licensed to sell real estate for the purpose of investment, did not duly invest the proceeds, but charged himself with such proceeds, and with interest thereon from year to year, in his general guardianship account, which was allowed by the court, and expended sums equal to such interest for the support of his ward *Held*, that he was responsible for such proceeds upon the special bond given by him on obtaining the license; but for the interest thereon upon his general bond. Mattoon *v.* Cowing, 13 Gray, 387.

A guardian is responsible on his general bond, for money due from him to his ward at the time of his appointment, and for the rent of real estate occupied by the guardian before that time.   Ibid.

The sureties on a guardian's bond are not discharged from liability by the fact that the guardian's account is not settled until more than two years after his death, and after the right of action against his administrator is barred by the statute of limitations. Chapin *v.* Livermore, 13 Gray, 561.

A bill in equity for the recovery of a debt due from the ward cannot be sustained against the guardian; the remedy is by action on the bond. Conant *v.* Kendall, 21 Pick. 36.   The guardian is not liable, in an action of assumpsit, to one who has furnished necessaries for the ward, but only in an action on his bond.   Cole *v.* Eaton, 8 Cush. 587.   And see Brooks *v.* Brooks, 11 Cush. 18.

19

CHAPTER XX.

APPEALS FROM THE PROBATE COURT.

THE supreme judicial court is also the supreme court of probate, and has appellate jurisdiction of all matters determinable by the probate courts. The statute provides that "any person aggrieved by an order, sentence, decree, or denial of the court or judge, except in cases otherwise provided for, may appeal therefrom to the supreme judicial court."[1] This provision of the statute applies to all decrees or orders of the probate court. The "cases otherwise provided for" are proceedings before the judge, but not in probate court, such as commitments to the Industrial and State Reform schools; in which cases the statute provides for appeals to the superior court.[2]

WHO ARE ENTITLED TO APPEAL.

The right to appeal depends upon the relations of the appellant to the subject-matter of the decree or other order. It is not limited to the parties directly connected with the proceeding in question, but is given to "any *person* aggrieved."[3] Mere dissatisfaction with the decree gives no right to an appeal from it. But a person

---

[1] Gen. Sts. c. 117, §§ 7, 8.   [2] Ibid. c. 75, § 12; c. 76, § 24.

[3] The surety in a guardian's bond may appeal from a decree allowing the account of his principal. Livermore v. Bemis, 2 Allen, 394. And see Farrar v. Parker, 3 Allen, 556.

is aggrieved within the meaning of the statute whenever his rights are concluded or in any way affected by it.[1] He may be aggrieved when the rights and interests to be affected are those which he has in a representative capacity; an administrator *de bonis non* may appeal from the decree allowing the administration account of the original executor or administrator;[2] and an administrator appointed in another State, on the estate of a person there deceased, may appeal from the decree of a probate court in this State, appointing an administrator here.[3] One who has purchased lands of the heirs or devisees may be so interested as to appeal from a decree respecting the estate of the testator or intestate;[4] and so may

[1] One claiming property of a deceased person under a gift *causa mortis*, is not affected by decrees of the probate court charging the administrator with the property and ordering it to be distributed to the next of kin; and cannot appeal from such decrees, though he appeared and produced witnesses in that court. Lewis v. Bolitho, 6 Gray, 137.

A testator bequeathed money to trustees to be managed as an accumulating fund for sixty years, and then to be paid to the town of N. or its agents, for the purpose of purchasing land within the town for a model farm. *Held*, that the town could appeal from a decree respecting the testator's will. Northampton v. Smith, 11 Met. 390.

From a decree of the probate court appointing a guardian to a minor child, the trustees of a fund bequeathed for the benefit of such child have no authority to appeal. Deering v. Adams, 34 Maine, 41.

A creditor of the estate of a deceased person cannot appeal from a decree refusing the petition of the administrator for leave to sell real estate of the deceased for the payment of debts. Henry v. Esty, 13 Gray, 336.

[2] Wiggin v. Swett, 6 Met. 194.

[3] Smith v. Sherman, 4 Cush. 408.

[4] A purchaser of the reversionary interest in land of a deceased insolvent assigned to his widow as dower, may appeal from the decree of the probate court appointing an administrator *de bonis non*. Bancroft v. Andrews, 6 Cush. 493.

M. died seised of land, one-half of which descended to his daughter S.; she married B., who survived her, and became tenant by the curtesy of said half of the land. B. conveyed his interest to C. *Held*, that C. could appeal from a decree allowing an account which showed a balance

a creditor of the heir or devisee under some circumstances.[1]

MANNER OF CLAIMING AND ENTERING THE APPEAL.

The appeal must be claimed and notice thereof given
at the probate office within thirty days after the date of
the act appealed from, and must be entered in the supreme judicial court at the rule day appointed by said
court for the same county, next after the expiration of
fifty days from the date of the act so appealed from.
The notice given at the probate office must be in writing.[2]

The appellant must also file in the probate office his
reasons of appeal, and cause an attested copy thereof to
be served on the adverse party fourteen days at least
before the time when the appeal is to be entered.[3] All
the reasons of appeal upon which the appellant relies
should be stated, as he is restricted at the trial in the
appellate court to the points specified in his reasons,
though he is not restricted to the evidence or arguments
presented as to the same points in the probate court. The
copy should be served on the adverse party by an officer
authorized to serve civil process, and his return should
be filed with the papers in the case.

due to M.'s administrator, the land being liable to be sold to satisfy such
balance. Bryant v. Allen, 6 N. H. 116.

Where a guardian was licensed to sell real estate of his ward, and the
next of kin of the ward appealed on the ground that he, and not the
ward, was the owner of the land, it was held that the question of title
could not be settled in a probate court, and that the appeal could not be
entertained. Ayer v. Breed, 110 Mass. 518.

[1] When a will, by which the testator's land was devised, was allowed
by the probate court, it was held, that a creditor of one of the heirs at
law of the testator was not entitled, merely as such, to appeal from the
decree. Otherwise, if the creditor has attached such land at the time of
the decree and appeal claimed, in an action against the heir. Smith v.
Bradstreet, 16 Pick. 264.

[2] See Appendix, form No. 84.

[3] Gen. Sts. c. 117, §§ 9, 10. See Appendix, form No. 85.

The party appealing is not required by statute to recognize or give any bond for the prosecution of his appeal.

Proceedings when Appeal is omitted to be taken in Season. The statute provides that if a person aggrieved omits to claim or prosecute his appeal, without default on his part, the supreme court of probate, if it appears that justice requires a revision of the case, may, on the petition of the party aggrieved, and upon such terms as it deems reasonable, allow an appeal to be entered and prosecuted with the same effect as if it had been done seasonably. Such petition may be entered in the clerk's office at any time, and the order of notice thereon may be made returnable at a rule day.[1] A copy of the record, attested by the register of probate should be filed with the petition. Such appeal cannot be allowed without due notice to the party adversely interested, nor unless the petition therefor is filed within one year after passing the decree or order complained of, except that if the petitioner was without the United States at the time of passing the decree or order, he may file his petition at any time within three months after his return, and within two years after the act complained of.[2] The appeal should be entered at the term at which leave is granted.[3]

---

[1] As to petition, see Appendix, form No. 86.

[2] Gen. Sts. c. 117, §§ 11–13. This provision does not authorize the entry of an appeal when the decree of the court below has been executed. After a widow has received the amount of an allowance, no appeal can be taken by her, nor allowed on her petition, from the decree making the allowance. Hale v. Hale, 1 Gray, 522.

An heir at law, who has notice of an appeal taken by another heir at law from the probate of a will, and takes no steps towards prosecuting

---

[3] Robinson v. Durfee, 7 Allen, 242.

EFFECT OF THE APPEAL.

After an appeal is claimed and notice given at the probate office, all proceedings in pursuance of the order, sentence, decree, or denial appealed from cease until the determination of the supreme court of probate is had.[1] But if the appellant, in writing, waives his appeal before the entry thereof, proceedings may be had in the probate court as if no appeal had been taken.[2]

THE PROCEEDINGS IN THE APPELLATE COURT.

Appeals and petitions for appeal are entered on a docket in the appellate court with cases in equity, and have the same rights as to hearing and determination as such cases.

The supreme court of probate may reverse or affirm, in whole or in part, the sentence or act appealed from, and may pass such decree thereon as the probate court

that appeal, cannot, after the expiration of thirty days, though within a year, from the decree, and after it has been affirmed by the supreme court, by consent of the first appellee, obtain leave to make a new appeal, under this statute, or to have the decree of affirmance set aside. Such heir might have petitioned to become a party to the appeal, or to enter an appeal in his own behalf, and then have prosecuted it to a final result, although the first appellant had withdrawn his appeal. Kent v. Dunham, 14 Gray, 279. See Livermore v. Bemis, 2 Allen, 394.

[1] Arnold v. Sabin, 4 Cush. 46. But in case of an appeal from a decree appointing a special administrator, he nevertheless proceeds in the execution of his duties until it is otherwise ordered by the supreme court of probate. And an appeal from a decree making an allowance to the widow or children of the deceased, from the income of the estate in the hands of a special administrator, will not prevent the payment of the allowance, if the petitioner gives bond to the special administrator, with sureties approved by the judge conditioned to repay the same, if the decree is reversed. Gen. Sts. c. 94, §§ 6, 10.

[2] See Appendix, form No. 87.

or judge ought to have passed, and remit the case for further proceedings, or take any other order therein as law and justice may require.

If, upon the hearing, any question of fact occurs proper for trial by jury, the court may cause it to be so tried upon an issue formed for that purpose under the direction of the court.[1]

The appeal gives no jurisdiction to the appellate court to proceed in the settlement of an estate, but only to reconsider the order appealed from; and its judgment is carried into effect by the probate court, whose jurisdiction over the cause and the parties is not taken away by the appeal.[2]

An appeal lies from the decision of a single judge of the supreme court of probate to the full court in matter of fact, as well as of law.[3]

COMPLAINT FOR AFFIRMATION OF DECREE.

If the appellant fails to enter and prosecute his appeal, the supreme court of probate may, upon the complaint of any person interested, affirm the former sentence, or take such other order as law and justice require. Such complaint must be in writing, and should set forth the fact that the appeal was taken, and that the appellant has failed to enter and prosecute it, and pray for an affirmation of the decree and for an allowance of costs. With the complaint must also be filed a copy of the decree appealed from, and of the papers in the case, attested by the register of probate.[4]

---

[1] Gen. Sts. c. 117, §§ 14, 16, 18.
[2] Dunham v. Dunham, 16 Gray, 578.
[3] Wright v. Wright, 13 Allen, 207.
[4] Gen. Sts. c. 117, § 17. See Appendix, form No. 88.

CHAPTER XXI.

ADOPTION OF CHILDREN AND CHANGE OF NAME.

ADOPTION.

[Stat. 1876, c. 213.]

SECT. 1. Any person of the age of twenty-one years or upwards, may petition the probate court in the county of his residence, for leave to adopt as his child any other person, younger than himself, except as hereinafter provided. If the petitioner have a husband or wife living, who is competent to join in such petition, the prayer of the petition shall not be granted unless the husband or wife joins therein, and upon adoption the child shall be deemed the child and heir of both.

SECT. 2. No decree for such adoption shall be made, except as hereinafter provided, without the written consent of the child, if above the age of fourteen years; and also, of the lawful parents, or surviving parent, — of the parent having the lawful custody of the child, if the parents be divorced, or are living separate, — of the guardian of the child, if any, — of the mother only of the child if illegitimate, — or of the person or persons who shall be substituted for either of the above named, by the provisions of this act. No person whose consent is hereby made requisite shall be debarred from being the adopting parent in said proceedings. In case of a subsequent adoption, the consent of the previous adopting parent shall also be required : *provided, however*, that the consent of the persons hereinbefore named shall not be required in the cases hereinafter excepted.

SECT. 3. The consent of the persons other than the child named in the preceding section, shall not be requisite, if the person to be adopted be of adult age.

SECT. 4. The consent of any person other than the child named in sections one and two, shall not be necessary, if such person be adjudged by the court hearing the petition to be hopelessly insane, or is imprisoned in the state prison or a house of correction in this State, under sentence for a term of which more than three years remain unexpired at the date of the petition, nor if he has wilfully deserted and neglected to provide proper care and maintenance for such child for two years next preceding the date of the petition; nor if he has suffered such child to be supported by any charitable institution incorporated by law, or as a pauper by any city or town, or by the State, for more than two years continuously, prior to the petition, nor if he has been convicted of being a common drunkard and neglects to provide proper care and maintenance for such child ; nor if such person has been convicted of being a common night-walker, or of being a lewd, wanton, and lascivious person, and neglects to provide proper care and maintenance for such child : *provided, however*, that a giving up in writing of the child, for the purpose of adoption to any charitable institution incorporated by law, shall operate as a consent to any adoption subsequently approved by such institution. Notice of said petition shall be given to the visiting agent of the board of state charities, in case the child is supported as a pauper by any city or town, or by the State.

SECT. 5. Whenever the written consent required by the preceding sections is not submitted to the court with the petition, the court shall order notice, by personal service on the parties, of a copy of the petition and order thereon, or, if they be not found within the State, by publication thereof once a week, for three successive weeks, in such newspaper or newspapers as the court shall order, the last publication to be seven days at least before the time appointed for the hearing. And in any case the court may require such additional notice and consent as may be deemed proper.

SECT. 6. Any person not appearing at the appointed time and place, and then objecting to such adoption, shall be held to have consented thereto, except as provided in section twelve of this act; but if no one consents or appears, the court may, if it see fit, appoint a guardian *ad litem*, with power to give or withhold consent.

SECT. 7. If satisfied of the identity and relations of the parties, and that the petitioner is of sufficient ability to bring up the child, and furnish suitable nurture and education, and that it is proper such adoption should take place, the court shall make a decree, by which, except as regards succession to property, all rights, duties, responsibilities and other legal consequences, including settlement, of the natural relation of child and parent, shall thenceforward exist between the child and the petitioner and his kindred, and shall, except as regards marriage, incest, or cohabitation, terminate between the person so adopted and his natural parents and kindred, or any previous adopting parent; and the court may also decree such change of name as the petitioner may request: *provided, however*, that if the person so adopted be of adult age, he shall not thereby be freed from the obligations of section four of chapter seventy of the General Statutes.[1]

SECT. 8.   As to the inheritance of property, any person adopted in accordance with the provisions of this act, shall take the same share which he would have taken if born to said adopting parent in lawful wedlock, of any property which such parent could have devised by will. In respect to inheritance also, he shall stand in regard to the legal descendants, but to no other of the kindred, of his adopting parent in the same position as if born to him in lawful wedlock.   In case the person adopted dies intestate, his property, acquired by himself, or by gift or inheritance from his adopting parent, or the kindred of such parent, shall be distributed according to the provisions of chapters ninety-one and ninety-four of the General Statutes, among the persons who would have been his kindred if he had been born to his adopting parent in lawful wedlock; and any property received by gift or inheritance from his natural parents or kindred, shall be distributed in the same manner as if no act of adoption had taken place; such distribution to be ascertained in such manner as the court may decree.   No person shall, by being adopted, lose his right to inherit from his natural parents or kindred.

SECT. 9.   The term "child," or its equivalent, in any grant, trust-settlement, entail, devise, or bequest, shall be held to include any child adopted by the settler, grantor, or testator, unless the contrary plainly appears by the terms thereof; but in no other case shall a child by adoption have, under such an instrument, the rights of a child born in lawful wedlock to the adopting parent, unless it plainly appears to have been the intention of

[1] Providing for the support of poor and indigent persons by their kindred.

the settler, grantor, or testator to include an adopted child : *provided, however,* that nothing in this act shall be construed to restrict any right to the succession to property which may have vested in any person already adopted in accordance with the laws of this Common-wealth.

SECT. 10.   No person shall adopt as a child, his or her wife or husband, brother, sister, uncle, or aunt, either of the whole or half blood ; nor any married woman without the written consent of her husband.   No act of adoption, however, shall be held to place the adopting parent or adopted child in any relation to any person except such parent or child different from that before existing, as regards marriage, or as respects rape, incest, cohabitation, or other sexual crime committed by either or both : *provided,* that no marriage shall be contracted between any person and his or her adopted child.

SECT. 11.   Any inhabitant of any other State, adopted as a child in accordance with the laws thereof, shall, upon proof of such fact, be entitled in this Commonwealth to the same rights, as regards succession to property, as he would have enjoyed in the State where such act of adoption was executed, except in so far as they conflict with the provisions of this act.   Any child adopted in this Commonwealth in accordance with the laws thereof, shall retain the rights thereby conferred upon him, so far as the jurisdiction of this Commonwealth extends. In case a person not an inhabitant of this State desires to adopt a child residing here, the petition may be made to the probate court in the county where the child resides.

SECT. 12.   Any person aggrieved by an order, denial, or decree of the probate court under the provisions of this act, may appeal therefrom to the supreme judicial court, in like manner as appeals may be taken from other decrees of the probate court; and the supreme judicial court, in its discretion, may allow any parent who had no personal notice of the proceedings before the decree, to appeal at any time within one year after actual notice thereof: *provided, however*, that such parent, so appealing, shall first make oath that he was not, at the time of the petition for adoption, undergoing imprisonment as specified in section four, or that, if so imprisoned, he has since been pardoned on the ground of innocence, or has had his sentence reversed.

SECT. 13. In case of a second adoption, all the legal consequences of the first decree shall terminate, except so far as any interest in property shall have vested in the child, and a decree to that effect shall be entered on the records of the court.

CHANGE OF NAMES.

[General Statutes, Chap. 110.]

SECT. 11. Applications for change of names of persons may be heard and determined by the probate courts in the several counties. No lawful change of the name of a person, except a woman upon her marriage or divorce, shall be made in this State, unless for sufficient reason consistent with the public interest and satisfactory to said court in the county where the party resides.

SECT. 12. Before decreeing a change of name, except as is provided in the following section, the court shall require public notice of the application therefor to be given, that all persons may appear and show cause, if any they have, why the same should not be granted. The court shall also require public notice to be given of the change decreed, and on return of proof thereof may grant a certificate, under the seal of the court, of the name the party is to bear, and which shall thereafter be his legal name.

SECT. 13. If, in a petition for the adoption of a child, a change of the child's name is requested, the court, upon decreeing the adoption, may also decree such change of name, and grant a certificate thereof, without the notices required by the preceding section.

SECT. 14. Each judge shall annually, in the month of December, make a return to the office of the Secretary of the Commonwealth of all changes of names made in his court under this chapter; and the same shall be published in a tabular form with the statutes of the following year.

APPENDIX.

PRINTED forms of petitions, &c., adapted to most of the proceedings in the probate courts, are furnished at the probate offices to persons having occasion to use them. The forms contained in this Appendix generally relate to proceedings for which blanks are not so furnished. Some of the printed blanks, however, such as petitions for the probate of wills, and for the appointment of administrators and guardians, are necessarily very general in form, and are to be variously filled, as may be required by the facts of each case. Forms of these petitions are introduced here, adapted to supposed cases, showing the manner in which they are to be filled under the different circumstances that may exist so far as they can be anticipated. The printed forms now in use were prepared by a committee of the judges of the probate courts, and have been recognized by an order of the Supreme Judicial Court as standard forms, to be adopted and used in all the probate courts of this State. They should, therefore, be used in all the proceedings to which they apply.

FORMS OF PETITIONS, &c.

[No. 1.]

Petition for Probate of Will presented by the Executor.

To the Honorable the Judge of the Probate Court in and for the county of M.

Respectfully represents A. B., of L., in the county of M., that C. D., who last dwelt in S., in said county of M., died on the —— day of ——, in the year of our Lord one thousand eight hundred and——, possessed of goods and estate remaining to be administered, leaving a widow whose name is H. D., and as his only heirs at law and next of kin, the persons whose names, residence, and relationship to the deceased are as follows, viz.

J. D. and S. D., children of said deceased.

That said deceased left a will (and codicil, *if such is the fact*), herewith presented, wherein your petitioner is named executor.

Wherefore your petitioner prays that said will may be proved and allowed, and letters testamentary granted to him.

Dated this —— day of ——, A. D. 18 —.

A. B.

[No. 2.]

Assent of Persons interested to be annexed to the foregoing Petition.

The undersigned, being all the heirs at law and next of kin, and the only parties interested in the foregoing petition, desire the same may be granted, without further notice.

J. D.
S. D.
H. D.

[No. 3.]

Petition for Probate of a Will presented by a Person other than the Executor.

To the Honorable the Judge of the Probate Court in and for the county of M.

Respectfully represents H. D., of G., in the county of B., that C. D., who last dwelt in S., in said county of M., died on the —— day of ——, in the year of our Lord one thousand eight hundred and ——, possessed of goods and estate remaining to be administered, leaving no widow, and as his only heirs at law and next of kin the persons whose names, residence, and relationship to the deceased are as follows, viz.

J. D., of ——, in the State of New York, C. D., of said C., and H. D., your petitioner, all of them brothers of said deceased.

That said deceased left a will (and codicil) herewith presented, wherein no person is named executor (*or*, A. B., of ——, is named executor but that said A. B. has deceased; *or*, refuses to accept said trust, as by his renunciation in writing hereto annexed fully appears; *or*, is a minor, and therefore incompetent to administer, &c.).

Wherefore your petitioner prays that said will may be proved and allowed, and letters of administration with the will annexed granted to him.

Dated this —— day of ——, A. D. 18 —.

H. D.

Assent of Persons interested to be annexed to the foregoing Petition.

The undersigned, being all the heirs at law and next of kin, and the only parties interested in the foregoing petition, desire the same may be granted, without further notice.

J. D.

C. D.

H. D.

Refusal of Executor to accept the Trust.

To the Honorable the Judge of the Probate Court in and for the county of H.

The undersigned, who is named in the last will and testament of C. D., late of S., in the county of H., deceased, to be the executor thereof, respectfully represents that he declines to accept said trust, and prays that administration with the will annexed of the estate of the said C. D. may be granted to the person or persons by law entitled to the same (*or*, to E. F., of ——, &c.).

Dated this —— day of ——, A. D. 18 —.

A. B.

Summons for Attesting Witnesses.

Commonwealth of Massachusetts.

——, ss.

To A. B., S. R., and G. F., all of S., in said county, Greeting : —

You are hereby required, in the name of the Commonwealth of Massachusetts, to make your appearance at the probate court to be holden at ——, in said county, on the —— day of ——, then and there to give evidence of what you know relating to the execution of a certain instrument purporting to be the last will and testament of C. D., late of S., in the county of ——, aforesaid, deceased. Hereof fail not, as you will answer your default under the pains and penalty of the law in that behalf provided.

Dated at ——, in said county of ——, this —— day of ——, in the year of our Lord one thousand eight hundred and ——.

J. S., *Justice of the Peace.*

[No. 6.]

Petition for Probate of a Will accidentally destroyed.

To the Honorable the Judge of the Probate Court in and for the county of ——.

Respectfully represents A. B., of S., in said county of ——, that C. D., who last dwelt in said S., died on the —— day of ——, in the year of our Lord one thousand eight hundred and ——, possessed of goods and estate remaining to be administered, leaving a widow whose name is H. D., and as his only heirs at law and next of kin the persons whose names, residence, and relationship to the deceased are as follows, viz.

L. D. and J. D., both of said S., children of said deceased.

That said deceased left a will, wherein your petitioner was named executor; that said will was not revoked by said C. D., and was in his possession at the time of his death, but that since the death of said C. D., to wit, on the —— day of —— last past, the said will was accidentally burnt and destroyed.

Wherefore your petitioner herewith presents a true and exact copy of said will destroyed as aforesaid, being the written paper hereto annexed marked A, and prays that said last will of said C. D., as written and expressed in the said paper marked A, may be proved and allowed, and letters testamentary granted to him.

Dated this —— day of ——, A. D. 18—.

A. B.

Assent of Persons interested to be annexed to the foregoing Petition.

The undersigned, being all the heirs at law and next of kin, and the only parties interested in the foregoing petition, desire the same may be granted, without further notice.

J. D.
L. D.
H. D.

[No. 7.]

Decree admitting to Probate a Will accidentally destroyed.

——, ss.   At a probate court holden, &c.

On the petition of A. B., of S., in the county of ——, representing that C. D., late of said S., deceased, left a will executed in due form of law, and that said will was accidentally destroyed after the death of said C. D., and that the paper writing annexed to said petition marked A, is a true copy of said will, and praying that the will of said C. D., as written and expressed in said paper marked A, may be proved and allowed, and letters testamentary issued to him, the executor therein named; and the heirs at law, next of kin, and all other persons interested having been duly notified according to the order of court to appear and show cause, if any they have, against the same. And it appearing that said C. D. did legally execute a will, of which the said paper marked A is a true copy, and that said testator was, at the time of making the same, of full age and sound mind, and that said will was accidentally destroyed after the death of said C. D., and that said petitioner is a competent person to be appointed to said trust.

It is therefore decreed, that the will of said deceased, as written and expressed in said paper marked A, be approved and allowed as his last will and testament, and letters testamentary be issued to said petitioner, he first giving bond with sufficient sureties for the due performance of said trust.

M. S., *Judge of Probate Court.*

[No. 8.]

Petition for Probate of a Nuncupative Will.

To the Honorable the Judge of the Probate Court in and for the county of ——.

Respectfully represents A. D., of, &c., that C. D., who last dwelt in ——, in said county of ——, died at ——, on the —— day of ——, in the year of our Lord one thousand eight hundred and ——, possessed of goods and estate remaining to be administered, leaving a widow, and as his only heirs at law and next of kin the persons whose names, residence, and relationship to the deceased are as follows, viz. &c., &c.; that said C. D., at the time of his death, was a mariner at sea, on board the ship ——, in the course of a voyage from —— to —— (or, was a soldier in actual service in the —— regiment, &c.); that while on such voyage (or, in such actual service), said deceased made a nuncupative will, in the presence and hearing of E. F. and G. H., of, &c., whereby he disposed of his wages and other personal estate in the manner following (or, as is fully set forth in the paper hereto annexed).

Wherefore your petitioner prays that said nuncupative will may be proved and allowed, and letters testamentary issued to him, the executor therein named.

Dated, &c.

A. D.

[No. 9.]

Decree admitting Nuncupative Will to Probate.

——, ss.   At a probate court holden, &c.

On the petition of A. D., of, &c., praying that the nuncupative will of C. D., late of ——, in said county of ——, deceased, may be proved and allowed, and letters testamentary issued to him the executor therein named, and the heirs at law, next of kin, and all other persons interested, having been duly notified according to the order of court, to appear and show cause, if any they have, against the same; and it appearing by the testimony in court of E. F. and G. H., of, &c., that said C. D., at ——, on the —— day of ——, A. D. 18—, in their presence and hearing, did declare and pronounce the following words, to wit, &c., &c.; and it further appearing that said C. D., at the time of declaring and pronouncing the same, was a mariner at sea, and on a voyage from —— to ——, and was of sound mind, and that, by the words so declared and pronounced, the said

C. D. intended to make a testamentary disposition of the personal estate therein described, and that said petitioner is a competent person to be appointed to said trust.

It is therefore decreed, that said testamentary words be approved and allowed as the nuncupative will of said deceased, and letters testamentary be issued to said petitioner, &c.   J. S., *Judge of Probate Court.*

[No. 10.]

Petition that one having Custody of a Will may be cited to deliver it into the Probate Court.

To the Honorable the Judge of the Probate Court for the county of ——.

Respectfully represents A. B., of S., in said county, that C. D., late an inhabitant of said S., has lately, to wit, on the —— day of —— last past, deceased; that the said C. D., at some time previous to his death, made and executed in due form of law his last will and testament, and gave the same to the custody of one T. T., of said S.; that said will is now in the custody of said T. T., and that said T. T. has had notice for more than thirty days of the death of said C. D., but has neglected and still neglects to deliver the same into the probate court, or to the executors named in said will, as by law he is required to do; that your petitioner has reason to believe, and does believe, that he is made a legatee in and by said will. He therefore prays that said T. T. may be cited to deliver said will into the probate court, and that such further proceedings may be had in the premises as law and justice may require.

Dated this —— day of ——, A. D. 1861.

A. B.

[No. 11.]

Complaint against one suspected of retaining or concealing a Will.

To the Honorable the Judge of the Probate Court for the county of ——.

A. B., of S., in said county, on oath complains that she has cause to believe, and does believe, that T. T., of said S., has retained and concealed, and is now retaining and concealing, with intent to hinder and prevent the probate thereof, a certain instrument made and executed in due form of law by C. B., late of said S., deceased, as and for his last will and testament (*or*, that T. T., J. T., and D. T., all of said S., have combined and conspired among themselves, and are now so combined and conspired, to retain and conceal, with intent, &c.); that your complainant is the widow of said C. B., and is interested in the estate of said deceased. Wherefore she prays that said T. T. may be cited to appear and answer to this complaint, and that such further proceedings may be had relative thereto as the law requires.

A. B.

——, ss. Subscribed and sworn to this —— day of ——, A. D. 18—, before me,

L. N., *Justice of the Peace.*

[No. 12.]

Citation on the foregoing Complaint.

Commonwealth of Massachusetts.

——, ss. Probate Court.

To T. T., of S., in said county.

Whereas, complaint on oath has been made to said court by A. B., of said S., who claims to be interested in the estate of C. B., late of said S., deceased, that she has reason to believe, and does believe, that you have retained and concealed, and are now retaining and concealing, with intent to hinder and prevent the probate thereof, a certain instrument made and executed by said C. D. in due form of law as and for his last will and testament.

You are hereby cited to appear at a probate court to be holden at ——, in and for said county of ——, on the —— day of —— next, at —— o'clock in the forenoon, to be then and there examined on oath upon the matter of said complaint.

And said A. B. is hereby directed to cause said T. T. to be notified of the time and place appointed for said examination, by serving him with a copy of this order —— days at least before said court.

Witness, J. S., Esquire, judge of said court, this —— day of ——, A. D. 18—.

S. W., Register.

(The above general form may be adapted to all cases in which citations are required.)

[No. 13.]

Return to be made on Citations.

I have served the foregoing citation as therein ordered.

A. B.

——, ss. —— ——, A. D. 18—. Then personally appeared the above-named A. B., and made oath that the above return by him subscribed is true. Before me,

L. N., Justice of the Peace.

[No. 14.]

Warrant to commit a Person complained of for retaining and concealing a Will.

Commonwealth of Massachusetts.

——, ss. To the sheriff of the county of ——, his deputies, or either of the constables of the town of ——, in said county, and to the keeper of the jail in said county,

Greeting.

Whereas, complaint was made to the probate court holden, &c., by A. B., of S., in said county, who claims to be interested in the estate of C. D., late of said S., deceased, that T. T., of said S., had retained and concealed, and was then retaining and concealing, a certain instrument made and executed in due form of law by said C. D., as and for his last will and testament, with intent to hinder and prevent the probate thereof, whereupon said T. T. was duly cited to appear and answer thereto; and whereas, said T. T. refuses so to appear and submit to examination (*or*, to answer interrogatories lawfully propounded to him) touching the matter of said complaint, and is thereupon ordered to be committed to the jail in said county, there to remain in close custody until he submits to the order of the court.

You and each of you are therefore required, in the name of the Commonwealth of Massachusetts, to take the body of the said T. T., and convey him to the jail in said county, and deliver him to the keeper thereof, and make return of this precept with your doings thereon.

And you, the said keeper, in the name of the Commonwealth aforesaid, are hereby required to receive said T. T. into your custody in said jail, and him there safely keep until he shall consent to be examined and answer interrogatories upon oath as aforesaid, or until he be otherwise discharged in due course of law. Hereof fail not at your peril.

Given under my hand and the seal of said court this ——— day of ———, A. D. 18—.

J. S., *Judge of Probate Court.*

[No. 15.]

Petition for Administration by Widow, the next of Kin being incompetent.

To the Honorable the Judge of the Probate Court in and for the county of B.

Respectfully represents A. D., of S., in the county of B., that C. D., who last dwelt in said S., died on the ——— day of ———, in the year of our Lord eighteen hundred and ———, intestate, possessed of goods and estate remaining to be administered, leaving as his only next of kin the persons whose names, residence, and relationship to the deceased are as follows, viz.

L. D., C. A. D., and J. D., children of said deceased, and each of them a minor under the age of twenty-one years.

That your petitioner is the widow of said deceased, and is entitled to take such administration.

Wherefore she prays that she may be appointed administratrix of the estate of said deceased.

Dated this —— day of ——, A. D. 18—.

A. D.

[No. 16.]

Petition for Administration by next of Kin, the Widow assenting.

To the Honorable the Judge of the Probate Court in and for the county of S.

Respectfully represents L. D., of D., in the county of B., that C. D., who last dwelt in C., in said county of S., died on the —— day of ——, in the year of our Lord eighteen hundred and ——, intestate, possessed of goods and estate remaining to be administered, leaving a widow whose name is E. D., and as his only next of kin the persons whose names, residence, and relationship to the deceased are as follows, viz.

S. A., wife of P. A., of L., in said county, a daughter of said deceased.

J. D. and L. D., of said C., sons of said deceased.

That your petitioner is entitled, as next of kin of said deceased, to take such administration.

Wherefore he prays that he may be appointed administrator of the estate of said deceased.

Dated this —— day of ——, A. D. 18—.

L. D.

The undersigned, being all the parties interested in the foregoing petition, desire the same may be granted without further notice.

E. D. (Widow.)

J. D.

S. A.

[No. 17.]

Petition by One requested by the Parties interested to administer.

To the Honorable the Judge of the Probate Court in and for the county of H.

Respectfully represents A. B., of L., in the county of W., that C. D., who last dwelt in H., in said county of H., died on the —— day of ——, in the year of our Lord eighteen hundred and ——, intestate, possessed of goods and estate remaining to be administered, leaving no widow, and as his only next of kin the persons whose names, residence, and relationship to the deceased are as follows, viz.

J. D., of said H., a son of said deceased.

S. D., of said H., a daughter of said deceased.

That there are no creditors of the said C. D. known to your petitioner, and that he is requested by the next of kin of said deceased to take such administration.

Wherefore your petitioner prays that he may be appointed administrator of the estate of said deceased.

Dated this —— day of ——, A. D. 18—.

A. B.

The undersigned, being all the parties interested in the foregoing petition, desire the same may be granted without further notice.

J. D.
S. D.

————————

[No. 18.]

Petition for Administration by a Creditor.

To the Honorable the Judge of the Probate Court in and for the county of M.

Respectfully represents A. B., of C., in the county of ——, that C. D., who last dwelt in L., in said county of M., died on the —— day of ——, in the year of our Lord eighteen hundred and ——, intestate, possessed of goods and estate remaining to be administered, leaving a widow whose name is H. D., and as his only next of kin the persons, whose names, residence, and relationship to the deceased are as follows, viz.

B. D., of said L., and J. D., of Albany, in the State of New York, both of whom are sons of said deceased.

That the widow and next of kin of said C. D. have neglected for thirty days since his death, and still neglect, to take administration of his estate; and that your petitioner is one of the principal creditors of said deceased.

Wherefore your petitioner prays that he may be appointed administrator of the estate of said deceased.

Dated this —— day of ——, A. D. 18—.

A. B.

[No. 19.]

Petition for Administration by Husband.

To the Honorable the Judge of the Probate Court in and for the county of B.

Respectfully represents A. C., of D., in said county of B., that L. C., who last dwelt in said D., died on the —— day of ——, A. D. 18—, intestate, possessed of goods and estate remaining to be administered, leaving as her only next of kin the persons whose names, residence, and relationship to the deceased are as follows, viz.

S. A. and B. A., both of H., in the county of N., brothers of said deceased.

That your petitioner was the husband of said deceased at the time of her death, and is entitled to administer her estate.

Wherefore your petitioner prays that he may be appointed administrator of the estate of said deceased.

Dated this —— day of ——, A. D. 18—.

A. B.

[No. 20.]

Petition for Administration when Intestate was an Inhabitant of another State.

To the Honorable the Judge of the Probate Court in and for the county of M.

Respectfully represents A. D., of L., in the county of M., that C. D., who last dwelt in Albany, in the State of New York, died on the —— day of ——, A. D. 18—, intestate, possessed of goods and estate in said county of M., remaining to be administered, leaving a widow whose name is S. D., and as his only next of kin the persons whose names, residence, and relationship to the deceased are as follows, viz.

J. D. and H. D., both of said Albany, and A. D., of said L., all of them children of said C. D.

That your petitioner is entitled, as next of kin of said C. D., to administer his estate.

Wherefore your petitioner prays that he may be appointed administrator of the estate of said deceased.

Dated this —— day of ——, A. D. 18—.

A. D.

[No. 21.]

Petition for Administration by a Public Administrator.

To the Honorable the Judge of the Probate Court in and for the county of S.

Respectfully represents A. B., of B., in said county of S., that C. D., who last dwelt in said B., died on the —— day of ——, in the year of our Lord eighteen hundred and ——, intestate, possessed of goods and estate in said County of S. remaining to be administered, and not leaving a widow nor any next of kin in this Commonwealth.

That your petitioner is a public administrator in and for said county of S., and is entitled to administer the estate of said deceased.

Wherefore your petitioner prays that administration of the estate of said deceased may be granted to him.

Dated this —— day of ——, A. D. 18—.

A. B.

[No. 22.]

Petition for Administration with the Will annexed.

To the Honorable the Judge of the Probate Court in and for the county of H.

Respectfully represents H. D., of S., in said county of H., that C. D., who last dwelt in said S., died on the —— day of ——, in the year of our Lord eighteen hundred and ——, testate, possessed of goods and estate remaining to be administered, leaving as his only next of kin the persons whose names, residence, and relationship to the deceased are as follows, viz.

L. D. and S. D., both of said S., children of said deceased, both of whom are minors under the age of twenty-one years.

That the last will and testament of said deceased was duly approved and allowed at a probate court holden at W., in said county, on the —— day of —— last past, and that no person is named in said will as the executor thereof; (*or*, that the sole executor named in said will has refused to accept said trust; *or*, having been duly cited to appear and accept said trust, has neglected so to do; *or*, has neglected for more than twenty days since said will was proved as aforesaid, and still neglects, to give bond for the faithful discharge of his trust; *or*, has deceased; *or*, is a minor under the age of twenty-one years).

That your petitioner is widow of said C. D., and is entitled to administer his estate.

Wherefore your petitioner prays that she may be appointed administratrix with the will annexed of the estate of said deceased.

Dated this —— day of ——, A. D. 18—.

H. D.

———

[No. 23.]

Petition for Administration de bonis non.

To the Honorable the Judge of the Probate Court in and for the county of F.

Respectfully represents A. B., of N., in the county of H.,

that C. D., who last dwelt in G., in said county of F., died on the —— day of ——, in the year of our Lord eighteen hundred and ——, intestate, possessed of goods and estate remaining to be administered; that at a probate court holden at C., in said county of F., on the —— day of ——, A. D. 18—, E. F., of said G., was duly appointed administrator of the estate of said deceased; that said E. F. accepted said trust, but has recently deceased (*or*, that by a decree of a probate court holden at ——, in said county of F., on the —— day of ——, A. D. 18—, said E. F. was removed from his said office of administrator; *or*, was allowed to resign his said office, &c.), and that there is personal estate of said deceased remaining to be administered to the amount of twenty dollars (*or*, that there are debts to the amount of twenty dollars remaining due from the estate of said deceased).

That your petitioner is heir at law (*or*, is a creditor, &c.) of said C. D., and is interested in said estate.

Wherefore your petitioner prays that he may be appointed administrator of the estate of said deceased not already administered.

Dated this —— day of ——, A. D. 18—.

A. B.

[No. 24.]

Petition for Administration de bonis non with the Will annexed.

To the Honorable the Judge of the Probate Court in and for the county of F.

Respectfully represents H. D., of L., in the county of E., that the will of C. D., late of S., in said county of P., was duly proved and allowed in said court on the —— day of ——, A. D. 18—, and L. D., of said S., appointed executor thereof; that said executor entered upon the discharge of his trust, but has lately, to wit, on the —— day of ——, A. D., died (*or state other cause of the vacancy according to the facts*), without having fully executed said will, there being (*here state wherein the will has not been fully executed*) ; (*or*, there being debts to the amount of twenty dollars remaining due from the estate of said C. D.) ; (*or*, there being personal estate of said C. D. not administered to the amount of twenty dollars).

That your petitioner is one of the legatees named in said will (*or*, is a creditor, &c., &c.), and is interested in the estate of said C. D.

Wherefore your petitioner prays that he may be appointed administrator with the will annexed of the estate of said deceased not already administered.

· Dated, &c.
H. D.

Assent of Persons interested to be annexed to the foregoing Petition.

The undersigned, being all the legatees and parties interested in the foregoing petition, request that the prayer thereof be granted, without further notice.

J. D.
S. D.
H. D.

[No. 25.]

Petition for Special Administration.

To the Honorable the Judge of the Probate Court in and for the county of H.

Respectfully represents A. D., of S., in the county of H., that C. D., who last dwelt in C., in said county of H., died on the —— day of ——, in the year of our Lord one thousand eight hundred and ——, possessed of goods and estate remaining to be administered, and that there is delay in granting letters testamentary (*or*, of administration) on his estate by reason of a suit concerning the proof of the last will and testament of said C. D. (*or state any other reason for the appointment in accordance with the facts*).

That your petitioner (*here state the relation of the petitioner to the estate, whether as heir, creditor, &c.*).

Wherefore your petitioner prays that he may be appointed special administrator of the estate of said deceased; and may be authorized to take charge of all the real estate of said deceased, and to collect the rents and make necessary repairs.   Dated this, &c.

A. D.

Assent of Persons interested to be annexed to the foregoing Petition.

The undersigned, being all the parties interested in the foregoing petition, request that the same may be granted, without further notice.

J. D.
S. D.
H. D.

[No. 26.]

Petition by Widow to be appointed Guardian of her Children.

To the Honorable the Judge of the Probate Court in and for the county of H.

Respectfully represents A. B., of ——, in the county of ——, that there is occasion for the appointment of a guardian of J. B., who was born on the —— day of ——, A. D. 18—, and S. B., born on the —— day of ——, A. D. 18—, both of W., in the county of H., minors, and children of C. B., late of said W., deceased, and your petitioner, and she prays that she may be appointed to that trust.

Dated this —— day of ——, A. D. 18—.

A. B.

[No. 27.]

Petition of a Person not a Relative of the Minor to be appointed his Guardian, the surviving Parent assenting.

To the Honorable the Judge of the Probate Court in and for the county of ——.

Respectfully represents H. J., of ——, in the county of ——, that there is occasion for the appointment of a guar-

21

dian of N. D., who was born on the —— day of ——, A. D.
18—, now of ——, in the county of ——, a minor, and child
of C. D., late of ——, in the county of ——, deceased, and
E. D., his widow; that your petitioner is requested by said
E. D. to take such guardianship, and prays that he may be
appointed to that trust.

Dated this —— day of ——, A. D. 18—.

H. J.

I, the surviving parent of said minor, hereby assent to the
granting of the foregoing petition.   E. D.

[No. 28.]

*Petition of a Person not a Relative of the Minor to be ap-
pointed his Guardian, the next of Kin, &c., assenting.*

To the Honorable the Judge of the Probate Court in and
for the county of ——.

Respectfully represents H. J., of ——, in the county of
——, that there is occasion for the appointment of a guardian of N. D., who was born on the —— day of ——, A. D.
18—, now of ——, in the county of ——, a minor, and child
of C. D., late of ——, in the county of ——, deceased, and
E. D., who is also deceased. That the only next of kin of
said minor known to your petitioner are J. D. and R. D.,
brothers of said minor, both of ——, &c. (*or*, that there are
no next of kin of said minor known to your petitioner, and
that said minor has lately been in the care of P. R., of ——,
&c.).

That your petitioner has been requested by said J. D. and
R. D. to take such guardianship, and prays that he may be
appointed to that trust.

Dated this —— day of ——, A. D. 18—.

H. J.

We, the next of kin of said minor (*or*, having the care of
said minor), hereby assent to the granting of the foregoing
petition.

J. D.
R. D.

[No. 29.]

Petition of Person nominated by a Minor over the age of fourteen.

To the Honorable the Judge of the Probate Court in and for the county of ——.

Respectfully represents H. J., of ——, in the county of ——, that there is occasion for the appointment of a guardian of N. D., who was born on the —— day of ——, A. D. 18—, now of ——, in the county of ——, a minor, and child of C. D., late of ——, in the county of ——, deceased, and E. D., his widow. That said minor has nominated your petitioner to be his guardian, and your petitioner prays that he may be appointed to that trust.

Dated this —— day of ——, A. D. 18—.

H. J.

——, ss.   —— ——, A. D. 18—.

Personally appeared the above-named N. D., a minor, above the age of fourteen years, and nominated said H. J. to be his guardian.

Before me,

J. S., *Justice of the Peace.*

[No. 30.]

Petition for Guardianship of Minor, over fourteen, who neglects to nominate.

To the Honorable the Judge of the Probate Court in and for the county of B.

Respectfully represents A. D., of ——, &c., that there is occasion for the appointment of a guardian of J. D., who was born on the —— day of —— , A. D. 18—, now of ——, in the county of B., a minor, and child of C. D., late of ——, in the county of B., deceased, and E. D., who is also deceased ; that said minor is above the age of fourteen years, but has neglected and still neglects to nominate any person to be his guardian ; that your petitioner is a brother of said minor and his only next of kin, and your petitioner prays that he may be appointed to that trust.

Dated this —— day of ——, A. D. 18—.

A. D.

[No 31.]

Petition for Guardianship of a Minor residing out of the State.

To the Honorable the Judge of the Probate Court in and for the county of M.

Respectfully represents A. B., of, &c., that there is occasion for the appointment of a guardian of J. D., who was born on the —— day of ——, A. D. 18—, now of New York, in the State of New York, minor, and child of C. D., late of said New York, deceased, and E. D., his widow; that said minor has certain estate situate in said county of M., and that your petitioner is (*here state the relations of the petitioner to the minor, or to his estate, in accordance with the facts of the case*); and your petitioner prays that he may be appointed to that trust.

Dated this —— day of ——, A. D. 18—.

A. B.

[No. 32.]

Petition for Appointment of Trustee to fill Vacancy.

To the Honorable the Judge of the Probate Court in and for the county of B.

Respectfully represents A. B., of ——, in the county of ——, that C. D., late of ——, in said county of B., deceased, testate, by his last will and testament, duly proved and allowed on the —— day of ——, in said court, did therein give certain estate in trust for the use and benefit of E. F., of ——, &c. (*here state any material facts in regard to the objects of the trust*), and appointed G. H., of, &c., trustee under said will; that said G. H. declines to accept said trust (*or state the fact of the removal or death of the former trus-*

tee, as the case may be). He therefore prays that he may be appointed (*or*, that K. L., of, &c., may be appointed) trustee, in the place of said G. H., according to the provisions of the law in such case made and provided.

Dated this —— day of ——, A. D. 18—.

A. B.

Assent of Persons interested to be annexed to the foregoing Petition.

The undersigned, being the only parties interested in the foregoing petition, desire the same may be granted, without further notice.

J. D.
S. D.
H. D.

[No. 33.]

Petition for appointment of Trustee, under Statute "concerning Provisions for Widows in certain Cases." (Stat. 1861, c. 164.)

To the Honorable the Judge of the Probate Court in and for the county of ——.

Respectfully represents A. B., of, &c., that in the will of C. D., late of S., in said county of ——, deceased, which has been duly proved and allowed in said court, certain provision was made for H. D., widow of said C. D.; that said H. D. has filed in the probate office, in writing, her waiver of the provision made for her in said will, and has thereby become entitled to receive the sum of ten thousand dollars of the personal estate of said C. D. in her own right, and the income during her natural life of the further sum of —— dollars, as fully appears by the final account of L. M., executor of the will of said C. D., allowed and recorded in the probate office; that there is occasion for the appointment of a trustee to receive, hold, and manage said sum of —— dollars during the life of said H. D., and that your petitioner is named a legatee in the will of said C. D., and is interested in said estate.

Wherefore your petitioner prays that he may be appointed trustee as aforesaid, according to the provisions of the law in such case made and provided.

Dated this —— day of ——, A. D. ——.

A. B.

Assent of Persons interested to be annexed to the foregoing Petition.

The undersigned, being all the legatees, and the only parties interested in the foregoing petition, desire the same may be granted, without further notice.

T. D.
S. D.
H. B.

[No. 34.]

Decree on the foregoing Petition.

At a probate court holden, &c.

On the petition of A. B., of, &c., praying to be appointed trustee to receive, hold, and manage a certain portion of the personal estate of C. D., late of S., in said county of ——, deceased, during the natural life of H. D., widow of said C. D., being that portion of said personal estate to the income of which said H. D. is entitled by reason of her waiver of the provision made for her in the will of said C. D.

It appearing by the waiver of said H. D., on file in the probate office, and by the final account of L. M., executor of the will of said C. D., which has been duly allowed and recorded, that said H. D. is entitled to the sum of ten thousand dollars of the personal estate of said deceased in her own right, and to the income of the further sum of —— dollars during her natural life, and that notice of the pendency of said petition has been given to parties interested therein as ordered, and no party objecting thereto; it is decreed that said petitioner be appointed trustee, to receive, hold, and manage said sum of —— dollars, and to pay the income thereof to said H. D. during her natural life, and at the death of said H. D. to pay said sum to the persons entitled by law and the will of said deceased to receive the same.

J. S., *Judge of Probate Court.*

[No. 35.]

Petition for the Removal of an Administrator.

To the Honorable the Judge of the Probate Court for the county of ——.

Respectfully represents A. B., of S., in said county, that he is heir at law of C. D., late of said S., deceased, and is interested in the estate of said C. D.; that at a probate court holden at E., in said county, on the —— day of ——, A. D. ——, one F. G. was duly appointed administrator of said estate, and accepted said trust; that the said F. G. (*here state the grounds upon which the removal is asked, whether it be personal unfitness, or neglect of duty, or other maladministration*), and is not now suitable for the discharge of said trust.

Wherefore he prays that the said F. G. may be removed from his said office of administrator.

Dated this —— day of ——, A. D. 18—.

A. B.

(Petitions for the removal of unsuitable or unfaithful executors, guardians, and trustees may be made substantially in the same form.)

[No. 36.]

Decree on the foregoing Petition.

At a probate court holden at, &c.

On the petition of A. B., of, &c., representing that he is heir at law of C. D., late of S., in said county of ——, deceased, and is interested in his estate, and praying that F. G., administrator of the estate of said C. D., may be removed from his said trust for the reason that, &c.

It appearing that notice thereof has been given to said
F. G., and that the allegations set forth in said petition are
true, and that said F. G. is therefore evidently unsuitable for
the faithful discharge of said trust.

It is decreed that said F. G. be, and he is this day, removed from his said office of administrator of the estate of
said C. D.

J. S., Judge of the Probate Court.

[No. 37.]

Resignation of Administrator.

To the Honorable the Judge of the Probate Court for the
county of ——.

Respectfully represents A. B., of W., in said county, that
at a probate court holden at said W., on the —— day of
——, A. D. 18—, he was duly appointed administrator of the
estate of C. D., late of S., in said county, deceased, intestate, and gave bond for the discharge of said trust as required by law ; that said estate is not fully administered,
but that he is unable, by reason of ill health (*or other cause*),
to give such personal attention to the duties of said trust as
the interests of said estate require.

Wherefore, he herewith files a just and true account of his
administration of said estate, and prays that he may be allowed to resign his said trust.

Dated this —— day of ——, A. D. 18—.

A. B.

[No. 38.]

Decree on the foregoing.

At a probate court holden, &c.

On the petition of A. B., of, &c., administrator of the
estate of C. D., late of S., in said county of ——, deceased,
praying that he may be allowed to resign his said office of
administrator for the reason that, &c.

It appearing that notice thereof has been given to all parties interested, as ordered, and that it is proper that the prayer of said petition be granted, it is decreed that said A. B. be allowed to resign his said trust, and he is thereby discharged therefrom.

J. S., Judge of Probate Court.

[No. 39.]

Petition of Ward to be discharged from Guardianship.

To the Honorable the Judge of the Probate Court for the county of ——.

Respectfully represents A. B., of ——, in said county of ——, that by a decree of the probate court holden at ——, in and for said county, on the —— day of ——, A. D. 18—, he was adjudged to be an insane person (or, a spendthrift), and C. D., of ——, in said county, was duly appointed his guardian, and accepted the trust; that said appointment has never been revoked, and that said C. D. still continues to have custody of the person of your petitioner and the management of his estate.

Your petitioner further represents that he believes that he is now capable of managing his own estate, and that the necessity for such guardianship no longer exists.

Wherefore he prays that he may be discharged from said guardianship.

Dated this —— day of ——, A. D. 18—.

A. B.

[No. 40.]

Decree on the foregoing Petition.

On the petition of A. B., of, &c., a person adjudged insane, (or, a spendthrift,) and under guardianship, representing that such guardianship is no longer necessary, and praying that C. D., his guardian, may be discharged from his said trust.

It appearing that notice thereof has been given to all persons interested therein, and that said A. B. has become restored to his right mind (*or*, has become correct in his habits), and is competent to manage his estate, and that such guardianship is no longer necessary; it is decreed that the prayer of said petition be granted, and said C. D. be and he is hereby discharged from his said trust of guardian of said A. B.

·J. S., *Judge of Probate Court.*

[No. 41.]

Justice's Order to Appraisers.

—— ss.

To A. B., F. G., and N. O., all of S., in said county.

You are hereby appointed to appraise, on oath, the estate and effects of C. D., late of said S., deceased (*or*, of B. A. and G. F., of said S., minors), which may be in said county. When you have performed that service, you will deliver this order and your doings in pursuance thereof to J. S., administrator of the estate of said deceased (*or*, executor of the last will and testament of said deceased, *or*, guardian of said minors, as the case may be), that he may return the same to the probate court for the county of ——.

Given under my hand this —— day of ——, A. D. 18—.

L. N., *Justice of the Peace.*

—— ss.   A. D. 18—.   Then the above-named A. B., F. G., and N. O., personally appeared and made oath that they would faithfully and impartially discharge the trust reposed in them by the above order.   Before me,

L. N., *Justice of the Peace.*

[No. 42.]

Complaint for Embezzlement.

To the Honorable the Judge of the Probate Court for the county of ——.

A. B., of L., in said county, on oath complains that he has good cause to suspect, and does suspect, that T. T., of said L., has fraudulently received, concealed, embezzled, and conveyed away certain articles of personal property belonging to the estate of C. D., late of said L., deceased (*or*, of G. F. and H. F., both of P., in said county, minors), to wit (*here describe the articles*) : that your complainant is administrator of the estate of said C. D. (*or*, is legatee, creditor, heir at law, &c. ; *or*, guardian of said minors, *as the case may be*), and is interested in said estate.

Wherefore he prays that said T. T. may be cited to appear before said court, to be examined upon oath upon the matter of this complaint, and that such further proceedings may be had in the premises as the law requires.

A. B.

—— ss. Subscribed and sworn to this —— day of ——, A. D. 18—, before me,

L. N., *Justice of the Peace.*

[No. 43.]

Warrant to commit a Person complained of for Embezzlement.

Commonwealth of Massachusetts.

—— ss. To the Sheriff of the county of ——, his deputies, &c., and to the keeper of the jail in said county.

Greeting.

Whereas, complaint was made to the probate court holden, &c., by A. B., of L., in said county, administrator of the estate of C. D., late of said L., deceased, that he has good cause to suspect, and does suspect, that T. T., of said L., has fraudulently received, concealed, embezzled, and conveyed away certain articles of personal property therein described, whereupon said T. T. was duly cited to appear and be examined on oath, upon the matter of said complaint ; and whereas, said T. T. refuses so to appear and submit to examination (*or*, to answer interrogatories lawfully propounded to him), touching the matter of said complaint, and is thereupon ordered to be committed to the jail in said county, there to remain in close custody until he submits to the order of the court.

You and each of you are therefore required, in the name of the Commonwealth of Massachusetts, to take the body of the said T. T. and convey him to the jail in said county, and deliver him to the keeper thereof, and make return of this precept with your doings thereon.

And you, the said keeper, in the name of the Commonwealth aforesaid, are hereby required to receive said T. T. into your custody in said jail, and him there safely keep, until he shall consent to be examined and answer interrogatories upon oath as aforesaid, or until he be otherwise discharged in due course of law.

Given under my hand and the seal of said court this —— day of ——, A. D. 18—.

J. S., *Judge of Probate Court.*

[No. 44.]

Petition of Wife of a Person under Guardianship for Insanity for an Allowance.

To the Honorable the Judge of the Probate Court for the county of ——.

Respectfully represents C. D., that she is the wife of A. D., of S., in the county of ——, an insane person; that at a probate court holden at ——, in said county, on the —— day of ——, A. D. 18—, E. F., of said S., was duly appointed guardian of said A. D.; that said appointment has not been revoked or determined, and that there is certain estate of said A. D. in the hands of said E. F., out of which she is entitled to an allowance for her support, to be paid to her by said E. F., during the continuance of said guardianship.

Wherefore she prays that an allowance may be decreed to her accordingly.

Dated the ——, day of ——, A. D. 18—.

C. D.

[No. 45.]

Decree on the foregoing Petition.

At a probate court held, &c.

On the petition of C. D., representing that she is the wife of A. D., of S., in said county, an insane person and under guardianship, and that there is certain estate of said A. D. in the hands of E. F., of said S., guardian of said A. D., out of which she is entitled to an allowance for her support, during the continuance of said guardianship.

It appearing that the petitioner is the wife of said A. D., and is entitled to an allowance as aforesaid, it is decreed that the sum of —— dollars be allowed to her annually for her support, to be paid to her by said E. F., in equal quarterly payments (*or otherwise*), during the continuance of said guardianship, or until otherwise ordered by the court.

J. S., *Judge of Probate Court.*

[No. 46.]

Petition of Administrator for License to sell Debts due the Estate of his Intestate.

To the honorable the Judge of the Probate Court in and for the county of ——.

Respectfully represents A. B., of, &c., administrator of the estate of C. D., late of S., in said county, deceased, that there are certain claims due to the estate of said C. D., to wit (*here describe the claims or assets to be sold*) : which claims cannot be collected by your petitioner without inconveniently delaying the settlement of said estate, for the reason that (*here state the particular reason for the proposed sale*).

Wherefore your petitioner prays that he may be licensed to sell and assign said claims, for the purpose of closing the settlement of said estate agreeably to the law in such case made and provided.

Dated this —— day of ——, A. D. 18—.

A. B.

[No. 47.]

Decree on the foregoing Petition.

——, ss.

At a probate court holden, &c.

On the petition of A. B., administrator of the estate of
C. D., late of S., in said county of ——, deceased, representing that there are certain claims in favor of said estate, to
wit (*specify the claims*) : which claims cannot be collected
without inconvenient delay, and praying that he may be
licensed to sell and assign the same, for the purpose of closing the settlement of said estate.

All parties interested having been duly notified, and it
appearing, after a hearing thereon, that the prayer of said
petition ought to be granted, — it is decreed, that said administrator be licensed to sell and assign said claims, for the
purpose aforesaid (*if the sale is to be public, add*), by public
auction, first giving notice of the time and place thereof
by, &c.

J. S., *Judge of Probate Court.*

[No. 48.]

Petition for Leave to sell Personal Estate in the Hands of a Guardian or Trustee, and invest the Proceeds in Real Estate.

To the Honorable the Judge of the Probate Court in and
for the county of ——.

Respectfully represents A. B., of, &c., that he holds, in
his capacity of guardian of E. F., of, &c. (*or*, trustee under
the will of C. D., late of S., in said county, deceased), twenty
shares of the capital stock of the (*here describe the property*) ; that it would be for the interest of said E. F., and of
all concerned therein (*or*, of all concerned in said trust
estate), that the same be sold, and the proceeds thereof invested in certain real estate situate in, &c. (*here describe the
land*).

Wherefore your petitioner prays that he may be authorized to sell the said stock (*or other property*), and invest the proceeds thereof in the purchase of the real estate herein described.

Dated, &c.

A. B.

[When this petition is made by some person other than the guardian or trustee, he should set forth his relations to the estate to be sold, and pray that the guardian or trustee may be " required " to sell, &c. If the guardian or trustee has money to be invested, and there is no personal estate to be sold, the petition must be varied to meet the facts of the case, and the amount to be invested should be stated.]

[No. 49.]

Order on the foregoing Petition.

At a probate court holden, &c.

On the petition of A. B., representing that he holds, as guardian of E. F., of, &c., twenty shares in the capital stock of the ——, and that it would be for the interest of said E. F., and of all concerned therein, that the same be sold and the proceeds thereof be invested in certain real estate therein described.

It appearing that notice thereof has been given to all persons interested, as ordered, and that it would be most for the interest of said E. F., and of all persons concerned therein, that the prayer of said petition be granted; it is decreed, that said A. B. be, and he is hereby, authorized to sell said stock at public auction, first giving notice of the time and place of said sale by, &c. (*or*, at private sale), and to invest the proceeds of said sale in the purchase of the real estate described in said petition.

J. S., *Judge of Probate Court.*

[No. 50.]

Petition of Administrator for Authority to compromise a Demand.

To the Honorable the Judge of the Probate Court in and for the county of A.

Respectfully represents A. B., administrator of the estate of C. D., late of S., in said county of A., deceased, that he has, as such administrator, a demand against E. F., of, &c., said demand being (*describe the claim*); (*or*, that E. F., of, &c., has brought an action in the —— court to recover of said estate the sum of $——, for —— (*describe the demand*), —— that in the judgment of your petitioner it will be for the benefit of all persons interested in said estate that said demand be adjusted by a compromise (*or*, by submitting the same to arbitration), and that he has reason to believe that it can be so adjusted.

He therefore prays that he may be accordingly authorized to adjust said demand by compromise (*or*, by arbitration).

Dated, &c.

A. B.

Assent of Persons interested to be annexed to the foregoing Petition.

The undersigned, being the only parties interested in the foregoing petition, desire the same may be granted, without further notice.

J. D.
S. D.
H. D.

The same general form may be used by executors, guardians, and trustees.

———

[No. 51.]

Decree on the foregoing Petition.

——, ss.   At a probate court held, &c.

On the petition of A. B., administrator of the estate of

C. D., late of S., in said county of E., deceased, to be authorized to adjust by compromise a demand made against said estate by E. F., of, &c., said demand being, &c., &c.; it appearing that notice thereof has been given as ordered, and that the prayer of said petition ought to be granted, it is decreed that said A. B. be authorized to adjust said demand by a compromise upon such terms, to be agreed upon by the petitioner and said E. F., as will be for the benefit of all persons interested in said estate.

J. S., *Judge of Probate Court.*

[No. 52.]

Petition of Creditor whose Right of Action does not accrue within the Time limited for bringing Suits against Administrators.

To the Honorable the Judge of the Probate Court for the county of ——.

Respectfully represents A. B., of E., in said county, that at a probate court holden at said E., on the —— day of ——, A. D. 18—, H. J., of S., in said county, was duly appointed executor of the last will and testament of C. D., late of said S., deceased, and that on the same day the bond given by the said H. J., for the faithful discharge of said trust, was approved by the judge of said court; that said executor has given due notice of his said appointment; that your petitioner has a just claim against the estate of the said C. D., a full statement of which is hereto annexed, but that no right of action on said claim will accrue to your petitioner until after the expiration of two years from the giving of said bond by the said H. J. Wherefore your petitioner prays that said executor may be ordered to retain in his hands, of the estate of the said C. D., a sum sufficient to satisfy said claim, or that such other order may be made in the premises as justice requires.

Dated this —— day of ——, A. D. 18—.

A. B.

(Annex to this petition a full statement of the claim.)

[No. 53.]

Decree on the foregoing Petition.

At a probate court holden, &c.

On the petition of A. B., of, &c., representing that he has a claim against the estate of C. D., late of S., in said county, deceased, on which claim no right of action will accrue within two years after the giving of the bond of H. J., executor of the will of said C. D., and praying that said executor may be ordered to retain in his hands a sum sufficient to satisfy said claim when the same shall become payable

It appearing that notice thereof has been given to all persons concerned therein, and that said claim is justly due from the estate of said C. D., and no one interested in said estate appearing to give bond to said petitioner for the payment of the same, in case it is proved to be due; it is decreed, that said executor retain in his hands a sum sufficient to satisfy said claim, to wit, the sum of —— dollars, until the expiration of one year from the time when the same becomes payable, or until the rendering of final judgment in any suit for the recovery of the same commenced within one year after the same becomes payable, unless said claim shall have been sooner adjusted and settled, saving to said executor all right of defence against said claim which by law he may have.

J. S., *Judge of Probate Court.*

[No. 54.]

Bond to pay Creditor whose Right of Action does not accrue within the Time limited for bringing Suits.

KNOW ALL MEN BY THESE PRESENTS, that we, N. A., of B., in the county of M., as principal, and S. A. and N. O., both of said B., as sureties, and all within the Commonwealth of Massachusetts, are holden and stand firmly bound and obliged unto A. B., of E., in said county, in the full and just sum of —— dollars, to be paid to the said A. B., his executors and administrators; to the true payment whereof we do bind ourselves and each of us, our and each of our heirs, executors, and administrators, jointly and severally, by these presents. Sealed with our seals. Dated the —— day of ——, A. D. 18—.

THE CONDITION OF THIS OBLIGATION is such, that, whereas the said A. B. has presented to the probate court of said county a claim against the estate of C. D., late of S., in said county, deceased, a statement of which claim is annexed to the petition of said A. B. on file in said court ; and whereas the said A. B. alleges in his said petition that no right of action will accrue on said claim within two years after the giving of the bond of H. J., executor of the last will and testament of said deceased, and prays that said H. J. may be ordered to retain in his hands, of the estate of the said C. D., a sum sufficient to satisfy said claim ; and whereas the said N. A. is interested in the estate of said C. D., and is desirous that said estate shall be distributed and settled without delay. Now, therefore, if the said N. A. shall pay to the said A. B. the full amount of said claim, in case the same shall be proved to be due, or such part thereof as shall be proved to be due, then this obligation to be void, otherwise to remain in full force and virtue.

In presence of

    B. O.

    S. T.

                    N. A. (seal.)

                    S. A. (seal.)

                    N. O. (seal.)

[No. 55.]

Bond of Legatee to indemnify Executor.

KNOW ALL MEN BY THESE PRESENTS, that we, D. D., of S., in the county of ——, as principal, and H. L. and R. O., both of said S., as sureties, and all in the Commonwealth of Massachusetts, are holden and firmly bound unto A. B., of H., in the county of ——. in the full and just sum of —— dollars, to be paid to the said A. B., his executors, administrators, and assigns, to which payment well and truly to be made we bind ourselves and each of us, our and each of our heirs, executors, and administrators, jointly and severally, firmly by these presents. Sealed with our seals. Dated this —— day of ——, in the year of our Lord one thousand eight hundred and ——.

THE CONDITION OF THIS OBLIGATION is such, that, whereas the said A. B., in his capacity of executor of the last will and testament of C. D., late of said H., deceased (*or*, administrator with the will annexed, &c.), has this day, and within two years after having given bond for the discharge of his said trust, paid to said D. D. the sum of —— dollars, said sum being the amount of a legacy given to said D. D. by said will of said C. D.; now, therefore, if the said D. D. shall refund to said A. B. the said sum of —— dollars, or so much thereof as may be necessary to satisfy any demands that may be hereafter recovered against said estate, and shall indemnify the said A. B. against all loss and damage on account of such payment, then this obligation to be void, otherwise to remain in full force.

Signed, sealed, and delivered
     in presence of   D. D. (seal.)
        J. D.   H. L. (seal.)
        N. A.   R. O. (seal.)

ss. —— ——, A. D. 18—.   Examined and approved.
           J. S., *Judge of Probate Court.*

[No. 56.]

Petition for Allowance of further Time to prove Claims against an Insolvent Estate.

To the Honorable the Judge of the Probate Court in and for the county of ——.

Respectfully represents A. B., of, &c., that he is a creditor of the estate of C. D., late of ——, in the county of ——, deceased; that at a probate court holden in and for said county of ——, on the —— day of ——, A. D. 18—, said estate was represented insolvent, whereupon commissioners were appointed to receive and examine the claims of creditors against the same, and the term of six months was allowed to creditors to present and prove their claims; that the claim of your petitioner consists of (*here describe the claim*) ; that your petitioner has been absent from the State during the whole of said term of six months, and had no notice of said proceedings until said term had expired (*or*, state other cause of the omission in accordance with the facts), and has thereby been prevented from presenting his claim to said commissioners.

Wherefore your petitioner prays that further time may be allowed to creditors to present and prove their claims against said estate.

Dated this —— day of ——, A. D. 18—.

A. B.

[No. 57.]

Decree on the foregoing Petition.

—— ss. At a probate court holden, &c.

On the petition of A. B., of, &c., representing that he has a claim against the estate of C. D., late of S., in said county of ——, deceased, represented insolvent, and that by reason of, &c., &c., he was unable to present the same to the commissioners appointed to receive and examine the claims of creditors against said estate within the time allowed by an order of this court for that purpose, and has not presented his said claim, and praying that the time allowed to creditors to present and prove their claims against said estate may be extended.

It appearing that the prayer of said petition ought to be granted, it is decreed, that the further time of —— months from the —— day of ——, A. D. 18—, be allowed to creditors to present and prove their claims against said estate, and that the commission issued in the matter of said estate be reopened accordingly.

J. S., *Judge of Probate Court.*

[No. 58.]

Commissioners' Notice of Time and Place of Meeting to examine Claims.

COMMISSIONERS' NOTICE. Estate of C. D., late of B., in the county of S., deceased, represented insolvent.

The subscribers, having been appointed by the probate court for said county commissioners to receive and examine all claims of creditors against the estate of said C. D., hereby give notice that six months from the —— day of ——, A. D. 18—, are allowed to creditors to present and prove their claims against said estate, and that they will meet to examine the claims of creditors at ——, on the —— day of —— next, at —— o'clock in the forenoon.

B——, January 1, 18—.   F. G. }
                             H. D. } *Commissioners.*

[No. 59.]

Creditor's Notice of Appeal from Decision of the Commissioners to be filed in Probate Office.

To the Honorable the Judge of the Probate Court for the county of ——, and H. G., administrator of the estate of C. D., late of S., in said county, deceased.

A. B., of S., in said county, gives notice that his claim against the estate of said C. D. having been disallowed by the commissioners appointed to receive and examine the claims of creditors against said estate, he claims an appeal from the decision of said commissioners to the supreme judicial court (*or*, superior court), next to be holden at ——, in and for said county, on the —— day of —— next.

Dated the —— day of ——, A. D. 18—.

A. B.

[No. 60.]

Executor's Notice of Appeal from Decision of the Commissioners to be filed in the Probate Office, and served on the Creditor.

To the Honorable the Judge of the Probate Court for the county of ——, and B. N. (*the adverse party*), of ——, &c.

H. J., administrator of the estate of (or executor of the last will and testament of) C. D., late of said S., deceased, represents that he is dissatisfied with the decision of the commissioners appointed to receive and examine the claims of creditors against the estate of the said C. D., allowing the claim of one B. N., of said S., and hereby gives notice that he claims an appeal from said decision of said commissioners to the supreme judicial court (*or*, superior court), next to be holden at ——, in and for said county, on the —— of —— next.

Dated this —— day of ——, A. D. 18—.

H. J.

[No. 61.]

Agreement to submit Claim against an Insolvent Estate to Arbitration.

To the Honorable the Judge of the Probate Court in and for the county of A.

Respectfully represent A. B., administrator of the estate of C. D., late of S., in said county of A., deceased, and E. F., of, &c., that said E. F. presented a claim, a statement of which is hereto annexed, to the commissioners appointed to receive and examine the claims of creditors against said estate, which claim was disallowed by said commissioners, as by their report filed in said court appears, from which disallowance said E. F. gave notice of an appeal to the —— court, to be held in and for said county on, &c., &c.; that said A. B. and E. F. have agreed to waive a trial at law, and to submit said claim to the determination of G. H., N. O., and A. H., of, &c., arbitrators, whose award thereon, if accepted by the court, shall be final. They therefore pray that said G. H., N. O., and A. H. may be accordingly appointed by a rule of the probate court, agreeably to the statute in such case provided.

Dated this —— day of ——, A. D. 18—.   A. B.
E. F.

(Annex a statement of the claim to be submitted.)

[No. 62.]

Decree on the foregoing.

At a probate court holden, &c.

On the petition of A. B., administrator of the estate of C. D., late of S., in said county of ——, deceased, and E. F., of, &c., praying that the claim of said E. F. against the estate of said C. D. may be submitted to the determination of ——, ——, and ——, arbitrators.

It is ordered that said ——, ——, and —— be appointed arbitrators accordingly.

         J. S., *Judge of Probate Court.*

[No. 63.]

Rule issued to Arbitrators.

To ——, ——, and ——, of, &c.

You are hereby appointed arbitrators to liquidate and adjust the claim of E. F., of, &c., against the estate of C. D., late of S., in the county of ——, deceased.

You will appoint a convenient time and place to hear the parties interested in said claim, and give sufficient notice thereof to the said A. B. and E. F. In case either the said A. B. or E. F. shall neglect to attend, after having been duly notified, you will proceed *ex parte.*

And you will return this rule, with your doings thereon, to the probate court, as soon as may be.

In witness whereof, I have hereunto set my hand, &c., &c.

         J. S., *Judge of Probate Court.*

[No. 64.]

Award of Arbitrators.

To the Honorable the Judge of the Probate Court in and for the county of A.

The subscribers, arbitrators appointed by the probate court to liquidate and adjust the claim of E. F., of, &c., against the estate of C. D., late of, &c., after having duly notified the parties interested therein, met them at, &c., on the —— day of, &c., and after having heard their several pleas, proofs, and allegations, and maturely considered the same, do award and determine, and this is our final award and determination in the premises, to wit: that there is due to the said E. F. from the estate of the said C. D. the sum of —— dollars, and no more. And we further award that the sum of —— dollars, being the amount of the costs of arbitration, be paid as follows, to wit: ——, all which is duly submitted.   Dated at, &c.
&c., &c.

$$\left.\begin{array}{l}\text{——,}\\ \text{——,}\\ \text{——,}\end{array}\right\}Arbitrators.$$

[No. 65.]

Bond of Heirs to pay Debts, given to prevent Sale of Real Estate.

Know all men by these Presents, that we, A. B. and G. B., both of S., in the county of W., as principals, and H. O. and B. A., both of said S., as sureties, and all within the Commonwealth of Massachusetts, are holden and stand firmly bound and obliged unto H. J., of said S., in the full and just sum of —— dollars, to be paid to the said H. J., his executors, administrators, and assigns, to the true payment whereof we do bind ourselves and each of us, our and each of our heirs, executors, and administrators, jointly and severally, by these presents. Sealed with our seals. Dated the —— day of ——, A. D. 18—.

The condition of this obligation is such, that, whereas the said H. J., in his capacity of administrator of the estate of C. D., late of said S., deceased, has presented to the probate court in said county his petition for license to sell the real estate of the said C. D. for the payment of the debts due from said estate, and the charges of administration; and whereas the said A. B. and G. B. are heirs at law of said deceased, and are desirous that said real estate should not be sold; now, therefore, if the said A. B. and G. B. shall pay all the debts mentioned in the said petition of said H. J. that shall eventually be found due from said estate, with the charges of administering the same, so far as the goods, chattels, rights, and credits of said deceased shall be insufficient therefor, then the above-written obligation shall be void, or else shall abide and remain in full force.

Executed in presence of   A. B. (seal.)
 W. H.   G. B. (seal.)
 J. P.   H. O. (seal.)
              B. A. (seal.)

——ss. —— ——, A. D. 18—. Examined and approved.
      J. S., *Judge of the Probate Court.*

[No. 66.]

Notice of Sale of Land under License.

By license of the probate court for the county of ——, the subscriber, administrator of the estate of C. D., late of S., in said county, deceased (*or*, executor of the last will and testament of, &c.; *or*, guardian of E. F.), will sell at public auction on the premises (*or*, at the house of ——), on the —— day of —— next, at —— o'clock in the ——noon, the house and lot on —— Street, in said S., belonging to the estate of said C. D. (*or*, belonging to said E. F.), said property is (*here state any facts which the interests of the estate require to be brought to the notice of bidders*).

S——, ——, A. D. 18—.   A. B., *Administrator*
           (*or, Executor or Guardian*).

[No. 67.]

Administrator's Deed of Lands.

KNOW ALL MEN BY THESE PRESENTS, that I, A. B., of S., —— county, Massachusetts, administrator of the estate of C. D., late of said S., deceased, by authority of the probate court holden at ——, in and for said county, on the —— day of ——, A. D. 18—, and in consideration of —— dollars paid by F. G., of H., in said county, the receipt whereof is hereby acknowledged, do hereby give, grant, sell, and convey unto the said F. G., his heirs and assigns, a certain tract of land situate in said H., bounded and described as follows, to wit (*here describe the land*).

To have and to hold the above-granted premises to the said F. G., his heirs and assigns, to his and their use and behoof for ever; and I do for myself, my heirs, executors, and administrators covenant with the said F. G., his heirs and assigns, that in making sale of the real estate above described, I am duly authorized by the court aforesaid; that I have complied with the order of said court, by giving bond and taking the oath by law required, and by giving public notice of the intended sale as therein directed; and that I have in all things observed the rules and directions of law relative thereto.

In witness whereof, I, the said A. B., have hereunto set my hand and seal this —— day of ——, A. D. 18—.

Executed and delivered   A. B (seal.)
    in presence of
        B. J.
        J. C.

[The above form may be used by guardians; the only change necessary being the substitution of the words, "Guardian of A. D., a minor, and heir of C. D., late of said S., deceased," for the words, "administrator," &c.]

[No. 68.]

Petition for the Conveyance of Land of a deceased Person, or Ward, according to Agreement.

To the Honorable the Judge of the Probate Court in and for the county of ——.

Respectfully represents A. B., of H., in said county, that C. D., late of said H., deceased, during his lifetime, to wit (*or*, that G. H., of H., in said county, an insane person, and now under guardianship, at a time previous to such guardianship, to wit), on the —— day of ——, A. D. 18—, entered into an agreement in writing with your petitioner, a copy of which agreement is hereto annexed, whereby said C. D. (*or*, G. H.) agreed with your petitioner to convey to him, upon the terms and conditions set forth in said agreement, certain real estate situate in B., in said county, and fully described in said agreement; that said C. D. died without making such conveyance (*or*, that said G. H. has not made such conveyance, and is not now competent to make the same by reason of such guardianship); and that your petitioner is ready to perform all the conditions of said agreement on his part.

Wherefore your petitioner prays that a specific performance of said agreement may be decreed, and that E. F., administrator of the estate of said C. D. (*or*, guardian of said G. H.), may be ordered to convey said real estate to him agreeably to the terms thereof.

Dated, &c.   A. B.

[No. 69.]

Decree on the foregoing Petition.

At a probate court holden, &c.

On the petition of A. B., of H., in said county, representing that during the lifetime of C. D., late of said H., deceased, he and the said C. D. made an agreement in writing whereby the said C. D. agreed to convey to said A. B. certain real estate situate in B., in said county, and described as follows, to wit, &c., upon the terms and conditions therein set forth;

that said C. D. died without making such conveyance; and praying that E. F., administrator of the estate of said C. D., may be ordered to make such conveyance, according to the terms of said agreement.

It appearing that notice thereof has been given to all parties interested, and upon a hearing thereon that said C. D., if living, would be by law required to make a conveyance of said real estate to said A. B., it is decreed that E. F., administrator as aforesaid, make conveyance of said real estate to said A. B., payment being first made to said administrator by said A. B., of the sum named in said agreement, said conveyance when made to have the like force and effect as if made to said A. B. by said C. D. during the lifetime of said C. D.

J. S., *Judge of Probate Court.*

[No. 70.]

Petition that an Administrator may be cited to settle his Account in Probate Court.

To the Honorable the Judge of the Probate Court for the county of ——.

Respectfully represents B. D., of S., in said county, that he is heir at law of C. D., late of said S., deceased, and is interested in the estate of the said C. D.; that at a probate court holden at C., in said county, on the —— day of ——, A. D. 18—, one A. B., of said S., was duly appointed administrator of the estate of said C. D., and gave bond for the faithful discharge of said trust; that more than one year has elapsed since the said appointment of the said A. B., but that the said A. B. has neglected, and still neglects, to render his account of administration. Wherefore your petitioner prays that said administrator may be cited to settle his accounts in the probate court, and that your petitioner may be authorized to bring an action in the supreme judicial court upon the bond of said administrator, in the name of the judge of the probate court, for the recovery of all damages sustained by such neglect of said A. B.

Dated this —— day of ——, A. D. 18—.

B. D.

[No. 71.]

Petition of Child omitted in the Will of his Parent for distributive Share.

To the Honorable the Judge of the Probate Court for the county of ——.

Respectfully represents A. B., of ——, in said county of ——, that he is guardian of E. D., a minor child of C. D., late of ——, in said county, deceased, testate ; that the said C. D. made no provision for the said E. D., either in his lifetime or in his last will and testament ; and that the omission of the said C. D. to provide for the said E. D. in his will was not intentional, but was occasioned by accident and mistake.

Wherefore your petitioner prays that the same share of the personal estate of said deceased that said E. D. would have been entitled to if said C. D. had died intestate may be assigned to the said E. D., agreeably to the statute in such case provided.

Dated this —— day of ——, A. D. 18—.

A. B.

———

[No. 72.]

Bond of Distributee, to indemnify Administrator.

KNOW ALL MEN BY THESE PRESENTS, that we, D. D., of S. county, Massachusetts, as principal, and H. L. and R. O., both of said S., as sureties, are held and firmly bound unto A. B., of H., in said county, in the sum of —— dollars, to be paid to the said A. B., his executors, administrators, and assigns, to which payment well and truly to be made we bind ourselves and each of us, our and each of our heirs, executors, and administrators, jointly and severally, firmly by these presents. Sealed with our seals. Dated this —— day of ——, A. D. 18—.

The condition of this obligation is such, that, whereas the said A. B., in his capacity of administrator of the estate of C. D., late of said S., deceased, has this day, and within two years after having given bond for the discharge of said trust, paid to the said D. D. the sum of —— dollars, said sum being his distributive share of the estate of the said C. D.; now, therefore, if the said D. D. shall refund to the said A. B. the said sum of —— dollars, or so much thereof as may be necessary to satisfy any demands that may be hereafter recovered against said estate, and shall indemnify the said A. B. against all loss and damage on account of such payment, then this obligation to be void, otherwise to remain in full force.

Executed in presence of   D. D. (seal.)
     L. H.   H. L. (seal.)
     O. R.   R. O. (seal.)

——, ss. ——, A. D. 18—. Examined and approved.

        J. S., *Judge of Probate Court.*

[No. 73.]

Petition of Person entitled to Money deposited by an Executor, &c., under a Decree of Distribution.

To the Honorable the Judge of the Probate Court for the county of ——.

Respectfully represents A. D., of, &c., that he is heir at law of C. D., late of S., in said county of ——, deceased; that a probate court holden at W., in and for said county, on the —— day of ——, A. D. 18—, H. J., administrator of the estate of said deceased, was ordered to distribute and pay the balance of said estate in his hands to the persons named in said order, and in the amounts therein specified; that, according to said order, your petitioner was entitled to receive the sum of $——, as his share of said balance; and that on the —— day of ——, A. D. 18—, said administrator deposited said sum of $—— in the —— savings bank, in the name of the judge of the probate court, to accumulate for the benefit of your petitioner; all of which appears by the decrees of said court, and the accounts of said administrator recorded in the probate office; and that your petitioner is entitled to the said sum of $——, deposited as aforesaid, and to the interest accrued thereon.

Wherefore your petitioner prays that said sum of $——, and the interest thereon, may be paid over and transferred to him.

Dated the —— day of ——, A. D. 18—.

A. D.

[No. 74.]

Order on the foregoing Petition.

—— ss.

At a probate court holden at ——, in and for said county of ——, on the, &c.

On the petition of A. D., praying that the sum of —— dollars, deposited in the name of the judge of the probate court of the county of ——, in the —— bank, on the —— day of ——, A. D. 18—, by H. J., administrator of the estate of C. D., late of S., in said county, deceased, with the interest accrued thereon, may be paid over and transferred to him; it appearing that said A. D. is the person entitled by law to receive the same, it is therefore ordered, that the treasurer of said —— bank pay over and transfer to the said A. D. the sum of —— dollars, deposited as aforesaid, with any and all sums of interest that may have accrued thereon since the time when said deposit was made.

J. S., *Judge of Probate Court.*

[No. 75.]

Notice to Heirs or Devisees of the Time and Place for making Partition.

To A. B., of, &c., and J. H. and A. N., both of, &c., and P. S., guardian (*or* agent) of said A. N.

You are hereby notified that the undersigned have been appointed by the probate court of the county of ——, to make partition of all the real estate of C. D., late of S., in said county, deceased, lying within this State, which any party interested requires to have included in the partition among the heirs (*or* devisees) of said deceased. And that the —— day of ——, in the year 18—, and the house of E. F., in said S., are the time and place appointed for making said partition, at which time and place you may be present.

Dated this —— day of ——, A. D. 18—.

$$\left. \begin{array}{l} \text{H. M.} \\ \text{O. H.} \\ \text{W. S.} \end{array} \right\} \text{Commissioners.}$$

[No. 76.]

Widow's Waiver of the Provision made for her in her Husband's Will.

To the Honorable the Judge of the Probate Court in and for the county of H.

Respectfully represents A. D., of, &c., that she is widow of C. D., late of S., in said county, deceased; that said deceased made certain provision for her in his last will, which will has been duly proved and allowed in said court within six months last past, and that she hereby waives the provision so made for her in said will, and gives notice that she will claim her dower in the lands of said deceased, and her distributive share of his personal estate.

Dated this —— day of ——, A. D. 18—.

A. D.

[No. 77.]

Notice to Parties interested of the Time and Place appointed to set off Dower.

To A. B., E. D., and J. H., all of, &c.

You are hereby notified that the undersigned have been appointed by the probate court of the county of —— commissioners to set off the dower of S. D., widow of C. D., late of S., in said county, deceased, in the lands of which he died seised in this Commonwealth. And that the —— day of ——, in the year 18—, and the house of ——, in said S., are

23

the time and place appointed for setting off said dower, at which time and place you may be heard in relation thereto.

Dated this —— day of ——, A. D. 18—.

A. M.
O. H. } Commissioners.
W. S.

[No. 78.]

Petition that the Administrator may be required to furnish a new Bond.

To the Honorable the Judge of the Probate Court for the county of ——.

Respectfully represents D. D., of S., in said county, that he is heir at law of C. D., late of said S., deceased, and is interested in the estate of the said C. D.; that at a probate court holden at B., in and for said county, on the —— day of —— last past, H. J., of W., in said county, was duly appointed administrator of said estate, and gave bond in the sum of —— dollars, with E. F. and G. H., both of said W., as sureties, for the faithful discharge of his trust; that said estate is not fully administered, and that said sureties are not sufficient to ensure the faithful discharge of said trust, the said G. H. having removed from the Commonwealth (*or* become insolvent, &c.). Wherefore he prays that said H. J. may be required to give a new bond, with such sureties and in such sum as the court may direct.

Dated this —— day of ——, A. D. 18—.

D. D.

[No. 79.]

Decree on the foregoing Petition.

—— ss.   At a probate court holden at, &c.

On the petition of D. D., representing that he is heir at law of C. D., late of S., in said county of ——, deceased, and that the sureties in the bond of II. J., administrator of the estate of said C. D., are not sufficient to ensure the faithful discharge of his said trust, for the reason, &c., and praying that said II. J. may be required to furnish a new bond with sufficient sureties :

It appearing that notice thereof has been duly given to said II. J., and that the allegations contained in said petition are true ; it is decreed that said II. J. file in the probate office, on or before the —— day of —— next, a new bond, with further and sufficient sureties, in the sum of —— dollars, for the faithful discharge of his said trust.

J. S., Judge of Probate Court.

[No. 80.]

Petition of Surety in a Probate Bond to be discharged.

To the Honorable the Judge of the Probate Court in and for the county of ——.

Respectfully represents E. F., of W., in said county, that at a probate court holden at said W., on the —— day of ——, A. D. 18—, II. J., of said W., was duly appointed executor of the last will and testament of C. D., late of S., in said county, deceased, and gave bond for the faithful discharge of said trust ; that your petitioner is one of the sureties in said bond ; that the estate of the said C. D. is not yet fully administered, and that your petitioner is unwilling to remain longer liable as surety in said bond, for the reason that (here state the reason for which the application is made).

Wherefore your petitioner prays that he may be discharged from all further responsibility as such surety, and that said II. J. may be ordered to furnish a new bond.

Dated this —— day of ——, A. D. 18—.

E. F.

[No. 81.]

Decree on the foregoing Petition.

—— ss. At a probate court holden, &c.

On the petition of E. F., of W., in said county of ——, one of the sureties in the bond of H. J., executor of the last will and testament of C. D., late of S., in said county, deceased, praying that he may be discharged from all further responsibility as such surety, for the reason that, &c., and that said H. J. may be ordered to furnish a new bond.

All persons interested having had due notice thereof, and it appearing reasonable and proper that the prayer of said petition be granted; it is decreed, that said H. J. file in the probate office, on or before the —— day of —— next, a new bond, with further and sufficient sureties, in the sum of —— dollars, for the faithful discharge of his said trust, and that said E. F. be discharged from all further responsibility as such surety, whenever such new bond shall have been filed and approved.

J. S., *Judge of Probate Court.*

[No. 82.]

Petition for Leave to sue an Administration Bond.

To the Honorable the Judge of the Probate Court for the county of ——.

Respectfully represents D. H., of S., in said county, that he is a creditor of the estate of C. D., late of said S., deceased; that at a probate court holden at ——, in and for said county, on the —— day of ——, A. D. 18—, A. B., of W., in said county, was duly appointed administrator of said estate, and gave bond, with E. F. and G. H., both of said W., as sureties, for the faithful discharge of said trust; that afterwards, to wit, on the —— day of ——, 18—, the said A. B. represented said estate to be insolvent, and that upon such representation commissioners were duly appointed to receive and examine the claims of creditors against said estate; that said commissioners made their return to the probate

· court on the —— day of —— last past, and reported the claim of your petitioner against said estate to have been allowed by them; that more than six months have elapsed since said return was made by said commissioners, but that said A. B. has neglected and still neglects to render any account of his administration of said estate, and is thereby delaying the distribution of the assets in his hands among the persons entitled thereto (*or state any other maladministration, as the facts of the case require*). Wherefore your petitioner prays that he may be authorized to bring an action in the supreme judicial court upon the bond of said administrator in the name of the judge of the probate court, for the recovery of the damage sustained by such neglect of the said A. B.

Dated this —— day of ——, A. D. 18—.

D. H.

[No. 83.]

Decree on the foregoing Petition.

At a probate court holden, &c.

On the petition of D. H., of S., in said county, representing that he is a creditor of the estate of C. D., late of said S., deceased, and that A. B., administrator of said estate, has neglected to render his account of administration, and has thereby delayed the distribution of said estate among the persons entitled thereto, and praying that he may be authorized to bring an action, in the name of the judge of the probate court, upon the bond of said A. B.:

It appearing that notice thereof has been given as ordered, and that more than six months have elapsed since the return of the commissioners appointed to receive and examine the claims of creditors against said estate was made to this court, and that said A. B. has neglected and still neglects to render and settle his accounts, and is thereby delaying the distribution of said estate, and that said D. H. is aggrieved by such neglect of said A. B.; it is decreed, that said D. H. be and he is hereby authorized to bring an action in the su-

preme judicial court on the bond of the said A. B., in the
name of the judge of the probate court, for the recovery of
any and all damages sustained by such maladministration
of said A. B.

J. S., *Judge of Probate Court.*

[No. 84.]

Notice of Appeal to be filed in the Probate Office.

To the Honorable the Judge of the Probate Court for the
county of ——.

A. B., of S., in said county, represents that he is heir at
law of C. D., late of said S., deceased, and is interested
in the estate of said deceased ; that he is aggrieved by a
decree of the probate court, holden at B., in said county, on
the —— day of —— last past, admitting to probate a certain
instrument purporting to be the last will and testament of
the said C. D. (*or, otherwise designate the decree, as the facts
require*). And he hereby gives notice that he claims an
appeal from said decree to the supreme judicial court.

Dated this —— day of ——, A. D. 18—.

A. B.

[No. 85.]

*Reasons of Appeal to be filed in Probate Court and served
on the adverse Party.*

To the Honorable the Judge of the Probate Court for the
county of ——, and F. G. (*the adverse party*), of H., in said
county.

A. B., of S., in said county, heir at law of C. D., late of
said S., deceased, having given due notice at the probate
office that he claimed an appeal from the decree of the probate court holden at B., in the county aforesaid, on the ——
day of —— last past, admitting to probate a certain instrument purporting to be the last will and testament of said
C. D., now files in the probate office his reasons of appeal, as
follows, to wit :

1st. Because the said C. D., at the time when he executed said instrument, was not of sound mind.

2d. Because the persons who subscribed said instrument as witnesses did not attest and subscribe the same in the presence of the said C. D., &c., &c.

Dated this —— day of ——, A. D. 18—.

A. B.

[No. 86.]

Petition for leave to enter an Appeal not seasonably claimed.

To the Honorable the Justices of the Supreme Judicial Court, next to be holden at ——, in and for the county of ——, on the —— Tuesday of ——, A. D. 18—.

Respectfully represents A. B., of S., in said county, that he is heir at law of C. D., late of said S., deceased, and is interested in the estate of said deceased; that he is aggrieved by a decree of the probate court holden at B., in said county, within two years last past, to wit, on the —— day of ——, A. D. 18—, admitting to probate a certain instrument purporting to be the last will and testament of the said C. D., copies of which instrument and of said decree are hereto annexed; that at the time of passing said decree your petitioner was without the United States, and has been without the United States until within the three months last past; that his omission to claim an appeal from said decree, and to give notice thereof at the probate office, was without default on his part. Your petitioner further represents that the said C. D., at the time when he executed said instrument, was not of sound mind (*or state other reasons of appeal in accordance with the facts*), and that justice requires a revision of the case. He therefore prays that he may be allowed to enter and prosecute an appeal from said decree of the probate court.

Dated this —— day of ——, A. D. 18—.

A. B.

[No. 87.]

Waiver of Appeal.

To the Honorable the Judge of the Probate Court in and for the county of B.

Respectfully represents A. B., of S., in said county of B., that he is heir at law of C. D., late of said S., deceased; that on the —— day of ——, &c., he gave notice at the probate office of his appeal from a decree of the probate court, holden, &c., admitting to probate a certain instrument, purporting to be the last will and testament of said C. D.; that he hereby waives his said appeal, and consents that further proceedings may be had in the probate court, in the matter of said will, as if said appeal had not been taken.

Dated at, &c.

A. B.

[No. 88.]

Complaint for Affirmation of Decree, where Appellant fails to enter his Appeal.

To the Honorable the Justices of the Supreme Judicial Court holden at ——, in and for the county of ——, on the —— Tuesday of ——, A. D. 18—.

D. D., of S., in said county, complains that at a probate court holden at B., in and for said county, on the —— day of ——, A. D. 18—, the last will and testament of C. D., late of said S., deceased, was duly admitted to probate by a decree of said court, as fully appears from the copy of the record filed herewith, from which decree one A. B., of said S., appealed to this court; that said A. B. has failed to enter and prosecute his said appeal; that your petitioner is the executor named in said will (or, is made a legatee in and by said will, &c.), and is interested in the probate thereof. Wherefore your complainant prays that said decree of the probate court may be affirmed, with costs.

Dated this —— day of ——, A. D. 18—.

D. D.

[No. 89.]

Petition of Husband of an Insane Woman that her right of Dower in his Lands may be released.

To the Honorable the Judge of the Probate Court for the county of ——.

Respectfully represents A. B., of S., in said county, that he is seised of a certain parcel of real estate situate in said S., bounded and described as follows (*here insert a description of the land*); that he is desirous of conveying said real estate in fee (*or*, in mortgage), but that A. B., his wife, is incompetent, by reason of insanity, to release her right of dower (*or*, homestead) in the same; that the interests of your petitioner require that such conveyance should be made, and that the right of his said wife in said real estate should be released; that (*here state any particular facts or reasons why the petition should be granted*). He therefore prays that C. D., guardian of said H. B., may be authorized and empowered to join him in a conveyance of said real estate, for the purpose of releasing her right of dower (*or*, right of homestead) therein.

Dated this —— day of ——, A. D. 18—.

A. B.

[No. 90.]

Decree on the foregoing Petition.

——, ss.   At a probate court holden, &c.

On the petition of A. B., of, &c., representing that he is the owner of certain real estate situate in S., in said county of ——, bounded (*here describe the land*), and that he is desirous of conveying the same, and that H. B., his wife, is an insane person, and is therefore incompetent to release her right of dower (*or*, right of homestead) in said real estate, and praying that C. D., guardian of said H. B., may be authorized to release her said rights in said land; and the said H. B. having been notified according to law to appear and show cause why the prayer of said A. B. should not be granted, does not appear to object thereto ; and after a hearing thereon, the court being satisfied that said right of dower (*or*, right of homestead) ought to be released ; it is decreed that said C. D., guardian of said H. B., be, and he is hereby, authorized to make said release by joining in any deed of conveyance made by said A. B., or any trustee for him, within five years next after the passing of this decree, whether such deed pass the whole or only separate parcels or lots of said real estate (*if the court deems it proper that a portion of the proceeds of the land should be reserved for the use of the wife, add*), the said A. B. first paying over to said C. D. the sum of —— dollars, to be invested and held by said guardian for the benefit of the said H. B., if she survives said A. B., the income of said sum to be received and enjoyed by said A. B., during the life of said H. B., or until otherwise ordered by the court, and the principal to be paid over to said A. B., if he survives the said H. B.

J. S., *Judge of Probate Court.*

[No. 91.]

Petition for sale of Standing Wood on Land held in Dower.

To the Honorable the Judge of the Probate Court in and for the county of ——.

Respectfully represents A.B., widow of C. D., late of W., in said county, deceased, that dower has been duly assigned to her out of the real estate of said deceased, situate in ——, in the county of ——; that said assignment of dower includes —— acres of woodland, more or less, bounded and described as follows : (*here describe the land assigned in dower*) ; and said A. B. further represents that the wood and timber standing on said land so held by her in dower has ceased to improve by growth (*or state other reasons as the facts require*), and ought to be cut ; wherefore she prays that E. F., of ——, in the county of ——, or some other suitable person, may be appointed a trustee, and that he be authorized and empowered to sell and convey said wood and timber, in the way and manner provided by law for the sale of real estate by guardians, to be cut and carried away within the time limited in the order of sale, and to hold and invest the proceeds thereof, after paying the expenses of such sale therefrom, and pay over the income, above the taxes and other expenses of said trust, to the person entitled to such dower or right to the use and improvement thereof, while the same continues, and at the expiration of such dower pay the principal sum to the owner of such land.

Dated this —— day of ——, A. D. 18—.

A. B.

[No. 92.]

Decree on the foregoing Petition.

At a probate court holden, &c.

On the petition of A. B., widow of C. D., late of W., in said county, deceased, praying that a trustee may be appointed, and that he be authorized and empowered to sell and convey certain wood and timber standing on land held by her in dower and described in said petition, in the way and manner prescribed by law for the sale of real estate by guardians; all persons interested having been duly notified, and no person objecting thereto, and it appearing that said wood and timber has ceased to improve by growth and ought to be cut.

It is ordered that E. F., of ——, in the county of ——, be appointed trustee, he first giving bond with sufficient sureties for the due performance of the trust herein set forth; and that he be authorized and empowered to sell and convey said wood and timber, in the way and manner provided by law for the sale of real estate by guardians, to be cut and carried away within —— months from the date of sale.

And said trustee is to hold and to invest the proceeds thereof, after paying the expenses of such sale therefrom, in ——, ——, and not otherwise, and pay over the income, above the taxes and other expenses of said trust, to the person entitled to such dower or right to the use and improvement thereof, while the same continues, and at the expiration of such dower pay the principal sum to the owner of said land.

And said trustee is to report his doings in the premises and an account of such sale to this court within —— from the date of the sale.

J. S., Judge of Probate Court.

[No. 93.]

Condition of the Trustees' Bond.

The condition of this obligation is such, that if the above-bounden E. F., trustee duly appointed by the probate court upon the petition of A. B., widow of C. D., late of ——, in said county of ——, deceased, to sell and convey certain wood and timber standing on land held in dower by said A. B., shall,

1st. Sell and convey said wood and timber in accordance with the license therefor;

2d. Dispose of and manage the proceeds of the sale, and faithfully discharge his trust in relation thereto, according to law and the decree of said court;

3d. Render an account, on oath, of the property in his hands, and of the management and disposition thereof, within one year from the date of the sale, and at any other time when required by said court; and

4th. At the expiration of his trust, settle his accounts with said court, and pay over and deliver all the estate and effects remaining in his hands, or due from him on such settlement, to the person or persons entitled thereto, according to law and the decree of said court, then this obligation to be void, otherwise to remain in full force and virtue.

E. F. (seal.)
G. H. (seal.)
I. J. (seal.)

Signed, sealed and delivered in presence of

S. T.
M. R.

INDEX.

(See separate Index to Forms of Petitions, &c., *post.*)

A.

374

INDEX.

D.

G.

J.

K.

L.

N.

R.

S.

INDEX TO FORMS.

H.

I.

L.

N.

P.

Cambridge: Press of John Wilson & Son.

www.ingramcontent.com/pod-product-compliance
Lightning Source LLC
Chambersburg PA
CBHW021335110726
47900CB00005B/1476